Rock a Bye Baby

Mia Dolan

EBURY
PRESS

1 3 5 7 9 10 8 6 4 2

Published in 2009 by Ebury Press, an imprint of Ebury Publishing
A Random House Group Company

The Random House Group Limited Reg. No. 954009

Addresses for companies within The Random House Group Limited
can be found at: www.randomhouse.co.uk/offices.htm

A CIP catalogue record for this book is available from the British Library

The Random House Group Limited supports The Forest Stewardship
Council (FSC®), the leading international forest certification organisation.
Our books carrying the FSC label are printed on FSC® certified paper.
FSC is the only forest certification scheme endorsed by the leading
environmental organisations, including Greenpeace. Our
paper procurement policy can be found at
www.randomhouse.co.uk/environment

Typeset in Goudy by Palimpsest Book Production Limited,
Grangemouth, Stirlingshire

Printed and bound in Great Britain by Clays Ltd, St Ives PLC

ISBN 9780091953508

To buy books by your favourite authors and register for offers visit
www.randomhouse.co.uk

Mia Dolan is the star of ITV's *Haunted Homes* and the bestselling author of *The Gift*, *Mia's World*, and *Haunted Homes*. Her work spans from live shows in front of hundreds of people to helping the police. She also runs a psychic school which helps others develop their own gifts. In 2007, Mia also won the paranormal celebrity edition of *The Weakest Link*.

Rock a Bye Baby is her first novel and is set largely on the Isle of Sheppey where Mia grew up and still lives.

Acknowledgements

I would like to thank the following for being as excited and motivated as myself in the creation and launch of my first novel:

To all the team at Ebury especially Alex Young, Di Riley and Zeb Dare from marketing, Hannah Telfer and Mel Yarker from sales; Sarah Bennie, Hannah Robinson and Ed Griffiths from publicity. I am also grateful to Publishing Director Hannah MacDonald for believing in me from the start and to my editor, Gillian Green, for always smiling, and never losing her patience.

To Hannah and Matthew Parrett who have never given up on me.

I'm also forever thankful for my family for never putting boundaries on me, especially my daughter, Tanya, who never expected a normal mum.

And my biggest thanks go to Jeannie Johnson, without whom this book would never have been finished.

For my mum, Pat Dolan.
My hero, my rock, my best friend.

Chapter One

1965

The woman in the cockle booth sniffed a pinch of snuff from the back of her hand. Once the small tin was tucked away, she turned back to face the promenade. 'Get yer cockles 'ere,' she bellowed. Pulling up a corner of the sack she wore as an apron, she swiped dismissively at a few stray specks beneath her nostril.

Marcie sat with her legs bunched beneath her, her back against the warmth of the old stone wall. She was staring at the cockle woman and wondering, but not about buying cockles – that was the last thing she'd want to do. She was wondering about how the woman had got to being what she was – fat, old, not caring too much about standards. So how had she come to be like that? A deeper thought hovered behind that one: would she herself end up like this woman? She shivered at the harrowing vision. No one wanted to end up like that.

The pungent aroma of malt vinegar and hot food wafted up Marcie's nostrils.

'Chips!' Rita was back. 'Yum, yum.'

Marcie made her self comfortable against the stone wall separating the beach from the promenade and opened up her packet of sandwiches.

Rita slumped down beside her.

Rita licked the Rimmel Pan Stick from her lips and popped a chip in her mouth. She pulled a face. 'Hmm. Needs a little something extra. Think I'll get myself some cockles.' She got to her feet. 'Coming?'

Marcie made a face. 'I can't stand cockles. They look like fishes' eyes.'

'Aw, come on. Keep me company. You don't have to buy any yourself.'

Rita didn't like doing anything by herself. Bloody nuisance at times. But they were best mates, so Marcie did as requested. Holding on to the hem of her skirt, she got up as elegantly as she could. Her mini skirt was mid thigh and if she wasn't careful everyone would be treated to a glimpse of white knickers. As it was, she only flashed her stocking tops and a glimpse of suspenders. Just as well. One of her suspenders was missing a button and a farthing was doing the honours.

Rita was trying to cadge a few more cockles.

'Come on, Gran. Be generous.'

The woman screwed up her eyes and placed hands as speckled as hens' eggs on the counter.

'Cheeky bugger. You'll 'ave what you get. An' don't call me Gran. I'm not your bloody Gran.'

'Don't be like that,' said Rita with a cheeky grin.

'You're Rita Taylor,' said the old girl.

'Yeah, that's me.' Rita giggled, giving Marcie a nudge. 'I'm famous. What do you think of that then?'

'I knew your mother. Used to go up town a lot during the war. Famous for doing war work she was.'

Rita ignored the toothless grin and didn't catch on to what the old girl was saying – really saying.

'What about me? Know my name as well?' said Marcie, determined not to be outdone and nudging Rita as hard as she'd been nudged.

The woman's toothless smile faltered. 'Oh, aye. That I do. I know yer grandmother. Who don't know Rosa Brooks? Famous she is. Knew your mother too, though she's famous for a different reason.'

Marcie swallowed. The woman's comment made her feel uncomfortable. Her mother had disappeared somewhere around Marcie's fifth birthday. She hadn't heard from her since, and her grandmother had made it clear that her mother's name was never to be mentioned. Not questioning why and not saying had become a habit. Her grandmother's words, still flavoured with her Maltese origins, echoed in her brain.

'Gone away with a man. Left me and your father to look after you. Not a good mother to go away and leave her child. Wrong! Very wrong!'

Oh yes, her grandmother was famous alright.

Thank God for friends, Marcie thought to herself.

Rita bubbled like a hot stew on a gas ring. At this moment in time her best and oldest friend had got the old girl to pour the cockles over her chips and added generous splashes of vinegar.

Marcie pretended to vomit. 'Christ, Rita. Don't know how you could.'

'Cockles are lovely.'

'Well, I don't like them. I think they're disgusting!'

'Fab,' said Rita between salty mouthfuls. 'Here,' she said, lowering her voice while her eyes slid sidelong to the cockle seller. 'What was that she was on about? Her reckoning she knew your mother. Must have been a while ago. Your mother's been gone for a long time, ain't she?'

'Yeah. A long time.'

'So you don't remember what she was like?'

Marcie shook her head and turned her face to the breeze sweeping in from the Thames Estuary. She didn't want Rita to see her face just in case she guessed she was lying. Anyway, it wasn't exactly a lie. She'd never heard from her mother in ten years or more. She might be dead. On the other hand she might be alive and living the life of Riley.

Rita glanced at her watch.

'Bloody hell! Late again.'

Marcie finished her sandwich, screwed up the brown paper bag her lunch had been wrapped in and tossed it into a bin. Determined to eat every chip and every cockle, Rita re-wrapped hers. 'I'll eat it this afternoon. Not wasting good food for nobody.'

Not long out of school, both girls had been taken on selling rock and candy floss in adjoining booths on the edge of the beach at Leysdown. Out of sight in their clapperboard booths, they chatted all afternoon or sang snatches of the latest pop songs.

Marcie had acquired a transistor radio – a present from her father sent via a friend of a friend. At first she'd tuned into Radio Luxembourg, but that didn't come on air until after six. It was only since the arrival last year of the pirate radio station Radio Caroline that they'd had daytime pop songs.

Since the advent of a radio channel that understood the tastes of the younger generation, Marcie had got into the habit of bringing the transistor into work. All in all work wasn't turning out so bad. On a warm day it was pleasant. On a bad day – depending on wind direction – she got soaked through.

They finished at six.

Rita burst into song. 'Hi ho, hi ho . . .' She always sang the tune from *Snow White* at this time of the day.

Marcie interrupted her. 'Coming for a coffee later?'

The off-key singing came to a halt. Rita winked. 'Now which café would we be going to?'

Marcie was good at hiding a guilty expression –

she'd had years of practice living with her grand-mother.

'I fancy the Lucky Seven.'

Rita chortled. 'I know what you fancy, and coffee and a bottle of coke got nothing to do with it! Leather jacket and tight denim jeans that shows all a bloke's got – that's what you got in mind. Your gran going to let you out?'

Marcie grinned in a meaningful fashion that Rita knew well. 'If she says no, I'm going to bed early.'

'Out the window and down the drainpipe, you mean.' They both laughed.

A girl they knew from school waved to them from the pavement. She was pushing a pram.

Marcie waved back. 'Hello, Nancy.'

Rita mutely waved. 'Crikey. Look at her. Dropped a kid the minute she got out of school.'

'She's married now, though,' said Marcie who liked Nancy and felt sorry for her. 'She married Gary Champion. Her dad gave him a hiding to make sure he did the right thing. Couldn't have a bastard in the family, he said.'

'Gary Champion? I don't know him,' said Rita. She frowned as she said it. Rita liked to think that she knew everybody.

'You wouldn't want to know him. I saw Nancy close up the other day. She had a massive bruise on her arm, all purple in the middle and yellow around the edges. According to Nancy he drinks a lot more since they got married. He works on the docks. Mind you, she reckoned she was used to it. Her dad used to hit her about anyway. Half the time he mistook her for her mother. Swine!'

'Glad he's not my dad,' said Rita.

'Glad he's not mine,' Marcie echoed.

Hearing what Nancy's dad was like made her feel grateful that hers was away in London. Every once in a while he sent her a present. Therefore he must care about her, though he'd never actually gone out of his way to show affection. Things would have been really great if he hadn't married Barbara.

If it hadn't been for Barbara with her peroxide hair and her Bridget Bardot lips, she would have been an only child. Barbara had presented Tony Brooks with two sons, two brothers that Marcie would have preferred not to have, and a baby daughter, Annie. All the same, her dad was still a gent compared with Fred Tucker, Nancy's old man.

'My dad's not like that,' said Rita with a tinge of pride in her voice. 'He's a diamond, my dad.'

It was nothing but the truth. Alan Taylor was well off, let her do anything she liked and bought her anything she wanted. Rita probably didn't need to work but for some reason her dad had thought it would be good for her. Though he would have liked her to have a better job than she did and to have done better at school, but as long as she was happy that was alright by him. Rita's dad owned businesses, and they lived in a nice bungalow with a garage and a gravel drive. He was also a mate of Marcie's dad. But Marcie couldn't let her dad be outdone.

'My dad's great too. I can't fault him.'

'That's because he's never home. You'd find a difference then,' Rita pointed out.

Marcie felt her face turning hot. 'Well, he can't help having to work in London. That's where the money is. He does a lot of work up there. That's how come he's able to send me nice things.' Using just one finger, she swung the transistor radio on its pink leather carrying strap. 'I mean, wouldn't send me presents like this if he was anything else, would he?'

Rita gave a quick nod that could be interpreted as acquiescence. If that was what Marcie believed, it was fine by her. But Sheerness was a small place. The Isle of Sheppey itself was a small place. Word got round, and the word Rita had heard was that her best mate's old man was in Wandsworth, London – the prison. But she wouldn't voice what she'd heard was the truth and upset her best pal. Best friends don't do that. Not unless they fell out, then she'd probably tell all and sundry. If they didn't know already.

Back in the booth and halfway through the afternoon, Rita spread out her newspaper-wrapped chips and swiftly ate the lot.

'All gone,' she said, licking her lips and wiping her greasy fingers down her generous thighs.

The chips were wrapped in two sheets from an upmarket daily. Rita threw the crumpled up top piece into the bin. Marcie began reading the sheet that was left.

'Shame Nancy Tucker didn't read this,' said Marcie.

Rita glanced over her shoulder. 'What's that then?'

Marcie pointed at the headline. 'Government Votes on Abortion'. Rita not being much for reading anything, Marcie contracted the subject matter for her benefit.

'They'd already voted but were asked to think again. If it passes it'll mean if you get knocked up and don't want to marry the bloke, you can get rid of it legally.'

'That's handy,' said Rita blithely.

Marcie frowned. 'That depends.'

Rita shrugged. 'On what?'

Sometimes Rita was great fun to be with. At other times her shallow attitude to serious matters made Marcie wonder whether they should be friends at all.

'It's a baby, Rita. A human being. It can't be that easy.'

'Well, I would if I had to. And so would you.'

The sheet of newspaper was suddenly taken off by a breeze and sent tumbling and fluttering along the beach.

A young couple with four small children came to the booth to buy penny shrimps made from sickly pink rock. Four excited faces turned upwards to choose their wares and hand over their pennies.

'Looks as though you've got your hands full,' Marcie said to their parents, who looked to be still in their twenties. It was obvious from their appearance that they didn't have much money.

Mum and Dad smiled. Mum shook her head. 'At times it's hard to make ends meet, but there, I wouldn't be without them. Not for all the world.'

Chapter Two

Marcie pushed open the front door of the small terraced cottage she shared with the rest of her family. The Brooks family consisted of Gran, her stepmother Barbara, called Babs, half-brothers Archie and Arnold, and baby half-sister Annie. Dad didn't really count because he was seldom there, 'working' in London for a stretch at a time.

The door bounced back against the mass of coats hanging from hooks in the tiny hallway. The smell of her grandmother's version of shepherd's pie wafted out from the kitchen. Gran's shepherd's pie was a little spicier than the English version thanks to the addition of tomato sauce and chopped herbs that she grew in a pot outside the kitchen door.

Her gran's voice sounded from the kitchen. 'That you, Marcie?'

Of course it bloody well was. Who else was it likely to be? But she answered yes anyway, and certainly didn't swear. Most people minded their language in front of Gran. They wouldn't dare otherwise.

'Get our Archie from out the back yard, would you, love?' Babs's voice, throaty with smoking, wheedled with just the right hint of menace. Marcie gritted her teeth.

Her dad had taken up with Barbara – Babs – only a few months after her mother had gone off. Babs had presented him with three kids – Archie was the eldest, nine years old and a right chip off the old block; Arnold was a year younger.

There was a larger gap between the birth of the boys and that of baby Annie. Tony Brooks had been away for quite a while and had been absent again between Annie's conception and her birth. He'd only seen her once since she was born when Babs had gone on a prison visit.

Marcie went out into the kitchen. An old black range squatted like a fat spider in the fireplace. Two armchairs were placed either side of the fireplace and a dark-green dresser ran the length of one wall. The middle of the room was occupied by a scrubbed pine table and six mismatched chairs.

Gran was smothered in richly smelling steam rising from cabbage, carrots and the giant dish of pie she'd just fetched out of the oven. She looked over her shoulder.

'Wash your hands, Marcie. Your supper's nearly ready.'

Babs was sitting at the table smoking a cigarette and reading a magazine – *True Romance*. She had bleached blonde hair lacquered into a French pleat at the back of her head. Two kiss curls, stiff with hair lacquer, appeared glued to her cheeks. Her fringe was a series of equally stiff curls hanging like dead caterpillars on her forehead. She seldom offered to help her mother-in-law with getting any meal ready.

'Pass me a drop of water would you, love? I got a bit of a frog in me throat.' Babs had sneaky ways of getting her own way.

Lazy cow!

Marcie was intentionally slow, turning on the tap and pouring herself a cup of water before she did anything. Babs would hate the fact that she didn't jump to it. She could feel her stepmother's eyes boring into the back of her head. Babs liked to boss her around. She never even tried to mother her but had treated her as little more than a skivvy since she'd moved in years before. 'She's a right cow,' Marcie had said to Rita. 'She's not my real mother, so why should I do as she says?'

'Did you hear what I said, our Marcie?'

At the sound of her stepmother's voice, Marcie's fingers tightened around the cup.

'What did your last servant die of?' she muttered, loud enough to be overheard.

Babs looked up from her reading. Her hard look – thick eye make-up, clotted pores above thick pink lips – hardened further. She pointed a threatening finger. 'Less of your bleeding cheek, young lady!'

'Barbara! I do not tolerate swearing in my house.'

Rosa Brooks had black button eyes that glittered when they fixed on you. Babs wilted under her mother-in-law's gaze.

'Sorry, Mum, but I've been at work all day, I have, and I am her stepmother. I do have a right to tell her what to do until she's of an age. Isn't that right, Mum?'

Despite her appearance, Babs was no fool. There was an art to buttering up and Babs was skilled at it. Her problem was that using bad language came naturally. She'd been brought up that way.

Eyes glowing with triumph she turned back to Marcie. 'Now get yer ass out in that yard and tell our Archie his tea's ready!'

Rosa Brooks rolled her eyes. Marcie's mother had had some class. Babs was common.

Marcie's gaze dropped to Babs's finger.

'Crikey, Babs. Your finger's gone all yellow. Disgusting!'

Caught off balance, Babs looked at her fingers. All the red nail polish in the world wouldn't deflect attention from the yellow staining following years of smoking.

The freckled face of Arnold, the youngest of her half-brothers, appeared from under the table. Remains of dried jam encrusted his face and his mouse-brown hair was dirty and dishevelled. His smile revealed a broken front tooth. Arnold was always scrapping. 'It's in the blood. Your grandfather was the same,' Rosa Brooks had declared.

Unfortunately for young Arnold it was not a milk tooth – he would always have a toothy smile and that mischievous look. He was also bright and curious, always asking questions.

'Mr Ellis's digging a hole. Why's he doin' that, Marcie?'

Marcie couldn't help smiling and was about to tell him the reason, but Babs interrupted.

'Because he's bleeding stupid. That's why! Like that stupid nephew of his – daft buggers the lot of 'em.'

'You shouldn't say that,' Marcie snapped. 'Garth Davies can't help it!' She turned to her grandmother for support. 'He can't help it, can he, Gran. It was God's will, wasn't it?'

Her grandmother, Rosa Brooks, was small but mighty; if she said something was God's will then that was it.

The fierce glower returned. She pointed a warning finger.

'Barbara, you will not say such things. What God has made is good. And you will not use that language in my house. I have told you this before. I will not have it!'

'She riles me,' said Babs, her thick lips pursed into a sulk. Her eyes fell back to the lurid pictures and over-large print of her magazine.

Marcie's surge of triumph was short lived.

'Marcie. Get your brother.' Her grandmother's tone was ripe with authority. Her keen eyes, dark as black beads, missed nothing. Her look said it all. *I'll have no disobedience in this house.*

They were frequently reminded that they lived under her roof. Rosa Brooks made it clear to them all that this was her house bought with her money. Anyone who didn't respect her and her ways could get out. The choice was theirs. But she'd keep the children. She frequently reminded them of that particular fact. 'My blood is my blood, and I have the money.'

No one knew for sure whether she really did have money in the bank or even stuffed under her mattress. But they took it that she did. Gran wouldn't have no prying into her business just as she would have no arguing. The one thing they did know was that the house, a small terraced cottage dating from Nelson's time and within sight of the sea in Blue Town, was hers. She'd bought it with the sum of money she'd brought as a dowry to her marriage. Her husband, Cyril, Marcie's grandfather, had been a sailor in the Royal Navy in the 1920s. He'd met Rosa in Malta, the headquarters of the Royal Navy Mediterranean Fleet and hinted to her that he had estates in Kent where hops were produced for the finest brewery in London. It was an outright lie, of course.

All he'd had was a room in a downmarket hotel around the corner from where they lived now. He hadn't even owned an aspidistra in a pot, let alone fields of Kentish hops.

Clinging on to her inheritance, Rosa had had no intention of living in a hotel room for the rest of her days. She had used her money to purchase the little cottage from the landlord. He'd been reluctant to sell at first as the whole terrace had once belonged to his wife's family, but for some reason he'd changed his mind. Nobody quite knew why except that it had something to do with a favour being done by Rosa Brooks.

It was pleasant to be out of the house, away from the smell of home cooking and the liberal stink of nicotine.

The sun bathed the back yard in a rosy glow that made the dusty vegetation look greener, the powdery earth darker. Even the tough marsh grass that hadn't quite been obliterated from its place along the fence looked as though someone had painted it with copper and brass.

A slight hum came from the direction of the cranes and derricks that serviced the docks. So did the smell of metal, marshland and burning oil. It only happened when the wind was blowing in a certain direction. Sometimes all Marcie could smell was the sea. She liked that. 'That's how your grandfather smelled,' her grandmother had told her when she'd mentioned it. 'Black tobacco, strong rum and the North Sea.'

'Archie?'

Archie was peeing into the chicken run. The chickens looked curious, not sure whether to keep away from the perfect arc of urine or investigate the wormlike spout from which it was streaming.

'They'll think it's a worm and peck it off,' Marcie shouted and couldn't help laughing.

The lean-to lavatory was just outside the back door. She asked him why he hadn't used it.

'Cos Gran's put Chlorus down it. Can't stand the smell of that.'

Marcie sympathised. Gran was a stickler for having things clean and germ free, but was a bit heavy handed on the bleach, and a demon with the scrubbing brush.

Rosa Brooks had standards. The net curtains hanging at the shiny windows were the whitest in the terrace. Her door knocker gleamed and flashed like gold in the sunlight, her path was the best swept and although she admitted to not being a skilled gardener, the tiny square that she called the front garden was tidy.

Except for the pot of growing herbs, the back garden was a different matter, a place of dusty vegetables growing in rows. The chicken run occupied the far end close against the fence and the back lane.

Grandma had kept chickens – mostly cockerels destined for Christmas dinner – for years. The chicks arrived in spring and were slaughtered two weeks before Christmas. Grandma did the slaughtering.

There were also two rabbits in a cage. These belonged to the boys.

'I've got a load of dandelions for Twinkle and Bobby,' Archie said.

He picked up the bundle he'd gathered from down by the railway line. Marcie gave him a hand.

'Here. Let me.'

As they pushed dandelion leaves through the wire mesh of the rabbits' cage, Marcie spotted Mr Ellis from two doors down. He was mopping his very red and sweaty face with a large handkerchief.

'Alright, Mr Ellis?' Marcie shouted by way of greeting.

He shouted back, his loud voice easily carrying over the other gardens.

'Yes, love. Thanks for asking. It's a bit warm for digging, but it has to be done. Sneaky devils, them Russians. You never knows when they're going to invade us, you know. So I'm one that's going to be ready for them.'

Marcie nodded and said, 'I see.' In fact she didn't see at all. She knew the Russians were frightening, but didn't really understand what this Cold War business was all about. More general things were important to her, things closer to home – like sneaking off to the café tonight, saving up for a new pair of shoes or listening to *Pick of the Pops* at Sunday teatime.

Anyway, how could a war be called cold or hot? What did it mean?

The sound of a radio and a news bulletin sounded from two doors up in the other direction, just beyond a row of runner-bean canes. Something similar came from the television set that the old couple next door had on too loud.

Marcie ignored both sets of news, concentrating instead on the song running round inside her head, her current favourite. 'Things We Said Today' by The Beatles. Paul was her favourite.

Humming a snatch of the song she watched Archie's rabbits feeding their faces. Her grandmother interrupted, calling for both of them to come in and eat.

As she walked back to the house Marcie looked up at the back bedroom window. The curtains were closed. Her little half-sister, Annie, was already put to bed.

Annie was the youngest and thus the most demanding. It was obvious to Marcie that Babs had no patience with babies and toddlers. She didn't have much patience with older kids either, but at least they could look after themselves.

Annie got put to bed early whether sleepy or not. It had occurred to her that Babs wasn't as keen on baby girls as she was on boys.

Her thoughts went back to the newspaper article. Would Babs have had an abortion if she'd had the choice? Without the boys and Annie she would have had a bedroom to herself. All the same, while she might have wished them not here more times than she could count, the boys were funny and the baby was sweet. Marcie couldn't help loving them.

Mealtimes in the Brooks household were silent except for the sound of scraping plates and clattering cutlery. Everyone ate at breakneck speed.

'Finished,' exclaimed Archie.

His grandmother caught him in the act of pushing his chair away from the table.

'Stay right where you are, Archie. I have an announcement to make.'

All eyes looked furtively up from their plates.

Rosa Brooks had tried on various occasions to have them say grace at mealtimes – hence the hurry to eat and leave the table. Wary eyes flashed from one sibling to another.

The nut-brown face creased into a wrinkled smile. The dark eyes, as black as the clothes she wore, danced from one family member to another.

'Your grandfather and I have spoken.'

Unseen by her grandmother, Marcie rolled her

eyes. That old thing again! Grandfather coming back and telling her grandmother things!

Marcie was at an age when her grandmother's eccentricities embarrassed her. It was bad enough to be Maltese and foreign. But imagine a woman who claimed she received visits and talked to her dead husband? It was stupid. Stupid, stupid, stupid.

Drawing herself up to her full five feet two inches, Rosa Brooks clasped her hands in front of her and pronounced, 'Your grandfather assures me that your father – your husband,' she said with a sideways glance at Babs, 'will be home shortly.'

Babs looked down at her plate so it was impossible to read her reaction.

The boys, however, were over the moon.

'When? When's he coming home, Gran? When?'

Archie's face was bright with excitement. All thoughts about leaving the table before his grandmother could inflict a prayer on him were totally forgotten. His eyes were round as saucers at the news. He missed his dad the most – more than his mother did, that was for sure.

Adopting an attentive expression, though her mind was elsewhere, Marcie fixed her gaze on her grandmother's face. She glanced swiftly at the clock when she thought she could get away with it.

'Soon, Archie,' said Rosa Brooks. 'Sit down and listen.'

Archie sat. So did everyone else, their eyes locked on this diminutive woman dressed in black, her black hair slicked tightly back into a firm bun.

'My son, Antonio, will be home shortly. Your grandfather assures me of this.'

She paused. Nobody said a word. Nobody moved.

Marcie gritted her teeth and hid her clenched fists beneath the table. Like the rest of the family, she'd got used to these pronouncements from her dead grandfather. They were usually about how well or how badly they'd been behaving, or to watch out for a windfall, a dip in fortune or the threat of imminent temptation; the latter pronouncement was usually aimed at Babs who had the reputation of being a bit free and easy with her charms, given half the chance.

But this was different. This was one pronouncement Marcie wanted to believe, that her father was coming home.

The last visit had been seventeen months before and that was only fleeting: Marcie had only seen him for a matter of minutes. The police had been right behind him. Before that he'd been away for five years.

She wanted her father to come home and see her as the young woman she'd become, not the child he'd glimpsed on the run. She told herself that things would be different. He'd say nice things and bring her more presents.

'Just like your mother,' he'd say, while smoothing her naturally blonde hair back from her face. Her blue eyes would look up at him adoringly.

Oh yes. Everything would be wonderful and he'd call her his little princess again. She vaguely remembered him calling her that when she'd been a lot younger. Then he'd gone away too. She'd put on a brave face and although she proclaimed that he was away working, she knew the truth. Sheerness was a small place and rumours travelled quickly. She'd chosen not to acknowledge them. The lie protected her against being hurt.

Her grandmother had her own views. 'It was all a mistake. He is innocent. Your grandfather told me this.'

The Marcie that believed and the one that did not fought in her mind. She gritted her teeth. When she'd been Arnold's age she'd believed it with the same innocence as he was showing. But she was older now and times were changing. It was 1965 and she wasn't a child. She didn't believe in that stuff any more, and yet . . .

She was sorely tempted to ask if this was true and if her father was innocent of inflicting grievous bodily harm on someone, then who had done it? Did her grandfather know that?

The modern, grown-up Marcie argued that this was not going to happen, that her grandmother was an old woman who only *thought* she could hear or see her dead husband. All the same . . .

Her half-brother did the job for her.

Arnold's hand shot up into the air.

Rosa Brooks looked at him and shook her head.

'Arnold. You are not in school. You do not need to put your hand up in order to ask me a question.'

His brother Archie grinned and slapped him on the head. 'Stupid.'

His mother fetched Archie a clout around the ear. 'Knock it off, you little sod.'

'Barbara!' Calling her daughter-in-law by her full name was a sign that Rosa Brooks meant business. 'When will you learn to curb your language?'

Looking suitably chastised, Babs lit another cigarette, even though the ash from the old one had only just disintegrated into the lid of a pickled onion jar that served as an ashtray.

Marcie's gaze alternated between the clock and her grandmother. Could she get out tonight without having to climb out of the window and shin down the drainpipe?

Rosa Brooks was looking at Arnold.

'What did you want to ask me, Arnold?'

Arnold sat on his hands. 'Tommy Smith's granddad died last week. I told 'im he'd come back and visit his gran. He said I was a liar. That when people is dead, they're dead and buried in the ground and ain't never comin' back. But I said I wasn't lying and that my granddad comes back to see you. Ain't that right, Gran?'

His grandmother's expression was unchanged. 'Only if she has eyes to see. Not everyone can see those that have passed over. Only people like me can do that.'

Marcie took it all in, but said nothing. The clock ticked on. Could she get out tonight without getting lumbered with babysitting young Annie? She loved the baby best of all her half-siblings, but Johnnie had promised her and she was sure he wouldn't break his promise.

Johnnie came down most Friday nights with the rest of a motorcycle gang from London. He'd made eyes at her a few times but it was only on the last occasion he'd finally spoken to her. He'd promised to buy her a bottle of Pepsi the next time he saw her. She wanted to hold him to that and had already decided what to wear.

The only thing curbing her impatience was that she wanted her grandmother's pronouncement to be true. She wanted to see her father again. It had been so long and although her father had sent her presents – like the transistor radio – she missed him. She wanted at least one parent – one *real* parent in her life.

'We will have to make ready,' Rosa Brooks said to

Babs. 'The boys will move into the attic room. The baby in with you and my son, Antonio. I will share with Marcie until I can get a bed for the box room. Marcie needs a room to herself.'

Although the box room wasn't very big, Marcie was grateful. The boys had been in there for a while so a lick of paint wouldn't come amiss.

'We can start sorting things out tonight,' said her grandmother. She was looking at Babs when she said it.

Babs looked startled. 'Tomorrow would be better. There's a ladies' darts team match . . .'

'That is not important. Your husband is coming home. We need to make ready for his return.'

Marcie said a silent prayer. Thank you, God. No babysitting tonight. It was difficult not to smirk at her stepmother's expense.

Babs grabbed hold of her just as she was emerging from the bathroom.

'Not so fast, you little tart. Sneer at me again and I'll smack it off your face, I will. Get it?'

Marcie shook her off. 'We'll see about that. And don't call me a tart.'

'I will too!'

Eyeing her stepmother's appearance brought a mocking smile to Marcie's face. 'OK. Call me that if you like, but just remember it takes one to know one!'

Babs's slap was well aimed, but Marcie was quick, ducking beneath it and racing for the stairs.

'You wait, Marcie Brooks,' Babs shouted after her. 'I'll cook your goose, my girl. You just see if I don't!'

Chapter Three

Marcie got on the bus in Sheerness. Rita was waiting at the halfway point just down the road from her house.

On seeing Marcie, her rosebud lips, liberally coated in Honey Beige Pan Stick, broke into a grin.

'You got out OK, then?'

'My wicked stepmother's was given a task to perform by the queen of the castle. So she's doing her own babysitting,' she added.

'So she should,' said Rita, slumping down into the bus seat beside Marcie. 'She 'ad the pleasure so she should 'ave the pain.'

'It's no real pain, really. Annie's a cute little thing.'

Rita wasn't impressed by kids. 'Here. Have a chewing gum.'

Marcie took a tablet of gum from the small packet. Nothing could daunt her spirits tonight, which made her say something she hadn't meant to say.

'My dad's coming home. Gran told Babs to sort herself out. She said me dad would get in a right stew if he thought she wasn't looking after our Annie properly, or putting on me. Told her she was to start staying in more and not meeting up with her mates down the Sailor's Arms. That told her good and proper.'

She'd been in two minds about saying anything about her father. There was no guarantee that he was coming home. No little brown envelope had arrived from the Prison Service saying that he would be. It was only on the say-so of her grandmother and a dead grandfather. What sort of confirmation was that?

But there it was – she was living on hope and hope had raised her spirits to such an extent that she couldn't be careful about anything, including what she said. And not just about her father coming home. Johnnie was going to buy her a Pepsi.

Their conversation turned to the things closer to their hearts.

'That's nice,' said Marcie referring to Rita's red corduroy dress. It looked expensive and probably was. It had a bib top and straps going over her shoulders. She was also sporting her signature tartan cap. It wasn't in Marcie's nature to tell Rita that she was too fat for the outfit and that the colour clashed with her rosy red cheeks. Saying it was nice was safe.

Rita preened. 'Me dad bought it for me in London. Your frock isn't bad either,' she said. She jerked her chin at Marcie's outfit. 'Made it yourself, did you?'

Was Rita being derogatory or flattering? Marcie was never quite sure whether Rita always meant what she said. Rita's dad had money and a flash car. She was always having new clothes. Marcie wished she could, but she couldn't. Luckily she was a dab hand with the sewing machine and had a good eye for fashion.

She took the course that Rita was her friend and chose to believe that she was being nice.

'I saw the dress in a magazine designed by someone called Mary Quant. I just copied it.'

The black dress had a scooped collar and short sleeves, both banded with white. It was sharp and slim, the skirt short and suiting her long hair and low-heeled shoes.

'Handy that you can sew,' said Rita. 'Bit short though.'

'It's the latest fashion,' said Marcie. She wanted to add that it only suited girls with long, slim legs, not Rita's tree trunks.

Rita did not consider herself fat, merely curvy. She also had the confidence to carry it off.

She grinned. 'Better watch going upstairs. You'll be showing your stocking tops or giving the boys a flash of yer knickers!'

Marcie declined to blush, but she did flash Rita a dismissive look.

'Stockings are old fashioned. Tights are coming into fashion so you can wear your skirt as short as you like.'

'I bet there's none in Sheerness, though.' Rita giggled. 'Well, not any good quality ones. I'll ask Dad to get me some in London.'

Marcie turned away so that Rita wouldn't see a trace of envy in her eyes. Rita, her father and her mother lived in a detached bungalow. They were so wealthy they placed orange and green striped sunblinds over the windows and front door. To Marcie, orange and green striped sunblinds were unimaginably posh.

The drive in front of the house was bordered by rose bushes and a lawn that in the month of May was dotted with daisies. Gardens front and back were looked after by a part-time gardener. Rita's home was imposing, though brash rather than elegant, a bit like Rita in a way. Marcie considered the garage was only fractionally smaller than the ground floor of the cottage her own family was crammed into.

Rita had a father who could buy her everything she asked for. More importantly, he was always around. OK, he did go away to Deal and London and other places on business, but only for short periods.

Perhaps it was because her father provided so well that Rita didn't harbour much ambition to be anything special in life. She hadn't been that good at school, mainly because she had the attention span of a newt. Whatever life threw at her was OK as long as she didn't have to work too hard.

Marcie wanted something better, though she didn't know what. Not yet. It was her fancy that her father coming home would be the turning point in her life, as though on his return her father would advise her on the best course. She was sure of it. It never entered her head that he hadn't done himself much good. He was her father and that was enough.

Her spirits had lifted by the time they alighted from the bus in Leysdown. The mix of sea air, multi-coloured flashing lights and laughing people out to enjoy themselves added an infectious quality to the exciting atmosphere of a Friday night.

The arcades of slot machines jangled, beeped and clattered. Beach balls and inflatables bobbed around in the breeze, and a queue had already formed outside the chip shop. The smell of frothy coffee wafted out from the Lucky Seven Café. Best of all a battalion of shining motorcycles were lined up outside, their front wheels nudging the kerb. Triumph, BSA, Norton and Matchless; names that breathed speed and sheer masculine vigour; the leather boys from London were in town.

Marcie felt Rita's elbow nudge her arm.

'They're here.'

She sounded excited. Marcie felt the same.

'How do I look?' said Rita, setting her hat straight.

'Great,' Marcie responded.

'I feel great,' said Rita.

Rita would never admit to it, but Marcie was the magnet most boys headed for. Rita benefited from that. By herself she might not have been so lucky.

Most of the boys were inside the café. Buddy Holly's

'Peggy Sue' was playing on the jukebox. The jukebox was playing loud and the café was too small to contain the sound.

Only two leather-jacketed boys remained outside. One was sitting on the railing against which the bikes were parked. The other – the one that interested her the most – was sitting astride a Triumph Bonneville with a blue and silver tank. Marcie knew the model name because Johnnie had told her so.

'It's a 1964 unit construction model,' he'd explained, his face glowing with pride. 'Unit construction gearbox. It's a new piece of engineering they've come up with.'

She didn't have a clue what unit construction meant, only that it seemed very important as far as Johnnie was concerned. But she made herself remember because it pleased him when she looked impressed. She wanted to remember everything he said to her.

He had dark hair fixed into a loose quiff, so loose that it flopped over his dark-blue eyes when he bent forward. There was a carelessness to his smile as though he was only inclined to smile when it suited him, never anyone else.

Her heart thudded in her chest as she willed him to look her way.

At last, just as he was tilting a bottle of Pepsi into his mouth, he spotted her.

Their meeting would have been perfect and she would have been flattered if he'd raced over to her

straight away. But Johnnie liked to play it cool. He
eyed her casually and for one awful moment Marcie
wondered if his promise was worthless. After all,
buying her a Pepsi was no great thing, was it?

Resting his elbow on the bike's chromium headlight, he turned away and said something to his friend.
Their foreheads were almost touching and they
laughed as though sharing an intimate joke.

Marcie bristled with indignation. What if it was
about her? She should blush; she should care and
perhaps she should turn her back. But she couldn't
do that. Johnnie was irresistible and she had to know
if he really meant what he said.

Rita had also weighed up the situation. 'Don't wave.
Don't look too keen,' she warned in a low whisper.

Too keen?

Marcie didn't entirely understand the changes she
was going through – the mood swings, the pining for
things and people that were out of her reach.
However, she did know that her heart was jumping
fences. If that meant she was keen, then so be it.

She'd met Johnnie only two weeks before at the
same spot. He and his friends were based at the Mile
End Café on the North Circular Road in London.
He'd told her that they often journeyed out from
London to explore new places, make new friends.
'They look at us lot arriving as though we're fucking
Marlon Brando and gonna bust the place up,' he'd

bragged, then grinned. 'We like them thinking that! We're the boys for trouble. You can bet on that.'

He'd winked when mentioning the making new friends bit. Instantly adding to his wild-boy appeal, strands of brandy brown hair had dropped over his eyes. He'd almost smiled – a kind of half smile, one corner of his mouth turned up as though he was torn between a smile or a scowl.

'Relax.' Rita was giving advice again.

'I'm trying,' Marcie whispered back. It wasn't that easy. A knot of barbed wire was rolling into a tight ball in her stomach. Her legs felt as though they were full of wet sand. She was rooted to the spot and couldn't have gone anywhere if she tried.

She'd never felt like this about any other boy. Plenty of local lads had shown an interest – she had the looks, she had the figure, but she just hadn't been interested.

The truth was that Johnnie was so different to the local boys. He'd been places; towns and villages around London and the south-east where the arrival of a leather-jacketed gang riding motorcycles had worried the local *older* population, though it had probably done wonders for young females.

His surliness made her toes curl up, and despite the fact that he appeared very dangerous she couldn't help being drawn to him. Behind the surly surface lurked a lovely boy; she could see it in his eyes.

'Hi, babe.'

He played it cool, taking another swig from the uniquely shaped bottle. He lowered the hand holding the bottle and ran the fingers of the other through his hair, pushing it back onto his scalp. He winked.

'Don't I know you from somewhere? Now let me think. Mary?'

How could he forget that quickly? A second too late Marcie began to suspect he was making fun and wanted to hit him.

'No! It's not!'

He exchanged a brief look with his companion then looked back at her and grinned.

'Must be Maria then.'

'No!'

Now she was getting mad. He WAS making fun of her. She tossed her head and began to turn away.

'Sorry, Rita. I'm off home. It's boring here.'

Her friend's jaw dropped. 'Marcie! You can't! It's too early.'

Johnnie took his cue. 'Marcie,' he said suddenly. 'Your name's Marcie.'

Yes, he had been teasing her. One half of her said 'Go away. Have nothing to do with him.' The other half was in danger of falling head over heels in love with him and believing everything he said. But she couldn't let him have it all his own way. She had to do something that would make him realise he couldn't mess her about. An idea came to her. Turn the tables. That's what she would do.

Wearing a haughty smile, she turned round and said, 'And your name's Fred, isn't it?'

'Johnnie Hawke.' He said it with a grin. 'Wanna Coke?'

'I thought you promised me a Pepsi.'

He shrugged. 'Whichever you want. Coke. Pepsi. I'll even buy you a coffee.'

She pretended to think about it – though not for long. 'OK.'

She was aware that Rita was eyeing up Johnnie's companion and posing for all she was worth. Amazing how provocative Rita could look when a boy she fancied came on the scene.

Johnnie must have seen Rita looking too. He leaned across and said something too quietly for them to hear. His companion said something back. Marcie fancied he didn't look too happy.

Johnnie appeared to have another word. His friend jerked his chin in response as though something had been agreed. Johnnie turned back to face them.

'My mate Pete wants to take your friend for a ride on his bike.'

Rita was overjoyed. 'Oh, yeah! Fab.'

Pete didn't look half as enthused as Rita. He threw Johnnie a frail scowl. 'Thanks a bunch, mate. See you later. Come on, then,' he said to Rita.

Pete threw his leg over a bike with a bright-red petrol tank embossed with the name 'BSA Rocket Gold Star'. He lunged up and down over the bike as he booted the kick start. Three attempts and the machine threw out a throaty roar. He backed it out and Rita climbed aboard, her red skirt bunching up over her generous thighs.

'See you later,' Johnnie called out.

Pete raised a hand in acknowledgement before driving off.

Marcie struck a casual pose; hand on hip, head tilted to one side and handbag swinging. *You don't impress me, Johnnie Hawke.* That was the message she wanted to send. The truth was something else.

'Your friend wasn't wearing a crash helmet,' she observed.

'So?'

When it came to casual, Johnnie was king. He flicked a comb through his hair as he turned his back on her and headed for the café. 'Come on then, girl,' he said over his shoulder. 'I'll stand you a bottle of Pepsi.'

Johnnie walked ahead of her, holding the door open just long enough for her to slip through. He had a strutting gait, as full of bravado as the way he spoke.

The coffee bar was crowded. Faces burned with wind and sun looked up. On seeing him with the gorgeous blonde, Johnnie's mates tipped him the wink.

'Pick of the crop again,' said one of them, his eyes raking her legs. 'Is that a skirt she's wearing or just a belt?'

Another grabbed her hand and pressed her fingers against his mouth.

'Marry me. You're too good for Johnnie and he's too fast for you – if you know what I mean. He'll eat you for dinner, though I will too if you like.'

The last comment was met by roars of laughter from the rest of the gang.

Marcie felt her face reddening. 'I think I should go.'

Johnnie took hold of her hand. 'Come on. Over here.'

In his other hand he held two opened bottles of Pepsi with straws sticking out of the top. He manoeuvred her into a far alcove of bench seats and a Formica-topped table.

Resting his palms on the table, it seemed deliberate when his fingertips almost touched hers.

She wondered if he could hear her heart thundering along like an express train. She hoped he was going to ask if he could take her home or see her again.

'Strange,' he said, tapping a nicotine-stained finger against surprisingly white teeth. 'I thought you'd be a mod dressing like you do.'

This was not the opening subject she'd expected. Her face must have betrayed her surprise.

'Don't look like that. I weren't meaning to be

cheeky or anything. Just wondered 'cos you really do look the business, girl. I mean gorgeous. Top-drawer crumpet – sorry – I mean young lady.'

She blushed at the compliment.

'You certainly know how to knock a girl off her feet. Anyway, I just like nice clothes,' she said, tossing her head as though she couldn't care less what he thought.

Lowering her eyes, she concentrated on sucking at the red-and-white straw sticking out of the bottle. In a matter of minutes this leather-jacketed rocker with his glossy hair and true blue eyes had got well and truly under her skin. Rita was right though. She had to hand her that. The secret was not to appear too keen; she'd also read that in one of her step-mother's cheap magazines. Would it work? And why did she want it to work? What did she want to happen?

The melodic sound of Johnnie's voice penetrated her thoughts. He was remarking on her appearance.

'Can see that,' he said. 'You look smart. I thought that the first time I saw you . . . though . . . come to think of it . . .'

His smile made his eyes twinkle. 'Reckon it was yer legs I noticed first. Long and slim, just as I like them!'

More compliments! This was unbearable.

'Stop it,' she said suddenly. 'You're embarrassing me.'

He looked surprised. 'Because I'm speaking the truth?'

'I bet you say that to all the girls.'

His eyes held hers as he slowly shook his head. 'No, I don't. I saw you that first time and said to myself, "Johnnie boy, that's a right corker if ever there was. You're going to ask her out, and if you don't you're going to regret it for the rest of your life – or at least until you get drunk."'

He laughed at his own joke. Marcie didn't think it was that funny, but overwhelmed with a need to please him, she laughed anyway. She wanted him to like her.

'Another Coke or Pepsi, or whatever?'

She shook her head. 'One's enough, thanks.'

'I'll get myself another. Be back in a minute.'

Marcie twirled the bottle between her hands as she waited for him to come back. The shivers she'd experienced earlier were gone. Thanks to his compliments she was now feeling all warm inside – until someone slapped her on the shoulder.

'What the fuck do you think you're playing at, making eyes at my fella?'

Brown eyes glared down at her from beneath a peroxide fringe. Equally platinum tresses cascaded over the shoulders of a leather jacket. The girl wore jeans and knee-high motorcycle boots. She was chewing gum.

Marcie frowned. Having her daydreams interrupted was annoying. Her tone betrayed that fact. 'What do you mean?'

The girl obviously hadn't expected so strident a response. She hesitated but soon got back on track.

'Exactly what I said. Johnnie's spoken for. Me and him go way back.'

The girl chewed as she spoke. Marcie smelled her cheap perfume mixed with spearmint breath.

'How about way forward?' said Marcie. 'Maybe you and him have a history but are you and him likely to go traipsing off into the sunset in future?'

The girl looked nonplussed at first, but her mouth soon turned into a snarl.

She pointed a surprisingly clean finger. 'Cut-being-clever-with-me.' Each word was accompanied by a jab to Marcie's shoulder.

'I'm not that clever,' said Marcie, adopting a lofty manner like the girls at the grammar school seemed to do. 'Still, there's always someone LESS clever, isn't there? And you're it, I take it.'

The girl frowned. Voiced as it was, the insult was wasted on her. Her face contorted this way and that. Marcie guessed she was wondering whether she should get angry or not. Just in case it was the former, Marcie tightened her hold of the bottle. If this did get nasty she was ready.

'Jane. You're in my way.'

Johnnie pushed past the girl who'd expressed a claim on him.

The girl's frown vanished. The heavily made-up face became wreathed with smiles and her eyes were all for Johnnie.

Marcie studied the sallow complexion, the brown eyes so innocuously teamed with bottle-blonde hair. It was easy to see she was in love with Johnnie. It was also obvious that he wasn't in love with her.

'I was just explaining to the mod that you and me go back a long way.'

'Yeah, yeah, yeah,' said Johnnie as he ripped open a packet of crisps. He pushed them towards Marcie. 'Her dad and my dad are old pals. They used to knock around together apparently. But if you believe what she says, you'll believe anything.'

Jane looked indignant. 'Well, there's a nice way to treat a girl!'

'Sod off, Jane.'

It was barely possible for Jane's sullen expression to turn more sullen, but she managed it.

'She's not one of us. She's from around here and that makes her a peasant!'

What he said next made Marcie's head spin.

'This girl is no peasant, Jane. This is Marcie. She and me are going steady. Ain't that right, Marcie?'

Fingers slick with salt and crisp crumbs covered Marcie's hand. His palm was surprisingly soft. She hadn't expected that, not from a boy who messed about with motorbike engines.

She returned his smile. 'Yes. That's right.'

Jane's face clouded. 'Is that so? Well, at least I know where I stand. Never thought I'd see the day when Johnny Hawke was going out with a mod!'

She strutted off, eventually lolling all over a thin boy sporting a DA haircut and a jacket plastered with metal studs.

Marcie declined Johnnie's offer of crisps. The evening that had started so well had suddenly turned sour, although it had improved since Jane's exit.

Johnnie dipped his head in an effort to look up into her face. 'You OK?'

She nodded. 'Sort of. It's this mod business. Just because I like modern clothes don't mean to say I'm a mod or am only going to go out with blokes in suits and riding Lambrettas. It's stupid. Who does she think I am? Cathy McGowan?'

His hair flopped over his eyes. 'No. You're better looking. Point taken though. I like modern clothes.' He winked. 'Especially when you're inside them.'

His smile was so sincere that she couldn't help blushing with pleasure. She looked at her watch. 'Better not stay too much longer or I'll miss the last bus.'

'That don't matter. I'll give you a lift. Come on,' he said, easing out from the bench. 'We'll go for a bit of a burn up first. Ever done a ton up?'

She shook her head.

'It means going fast.'

'I know what it means,' she said, perhaps a tad too sharply.

'I suppose you know what a burn up means too.'

'Of course.' She responded more calmly this time – at least that was how she hoped she sounded.

She swigged back what remained of her drink, this time straight from the bottle. The straw had sunk to the bottom.

His eyes sparkled. She wondered if it was the advent of scorched tyres along the road or the prospect of getting her alone.

Of course she shouldn't go. But wanting to go overrode the rules she was supposed to adhere to. Besides, riding fast on the back of a boy's motorbike – doing a ton as the boys called it – sounded exciting.

She'd heard local lads talking about blasting along the roads as fast they could go. Mind you, they didn't have powerful bikes like Johnnie had. None that would do one hundred miles an hour – that was for sure.

He jerked his head sideways at the door. 'What are we waiting for?'

What were they waiting for?

With a swivel of her slender hip she sidled between the counter and the tightly packed tables with their spindly metal legs, and the booths where couples hugged and boys huddled and talked of bikes.

There weren't exactly catcalls, but there were low whistles and a clicking of tongues.

'Ride on,' somebody said.

Someone else laughed.

Marcie kept her eyes on the night and the lights beyond the glass-panelled door. She had no wish to meet the leering looks of those presuming she was fast and loose. She wasn't that, she told herself. She could handle this.

'Don't let him get carried away,' one of the girls called out.

Johnnie gave no indication that he heard what was said or saw the lascivious looks. He opened the door. She followed.

Once away from the milky warmth of the coffee bar, her tension grew.

You don't have to go, she reminded herself. You know he'll try it on, she thought as she buttoned her coat and tied a scarf over her head.

A nice girl who was saving herself for marriage would see the danger and say no, thank you very much. But she liked him. She liked him a lot! And besides, it was 1965, not 1865.

She put her head through the strap of her shoulder bag so it sat on her left shoulder.

'I promised Rita I'd go home on the bus with her.' What a lame excuse!

'Look, if you don't want to come for a ride, just say so.'

'I want to come,' she blurted out.

The mixed emotions were still doing battle.

'Suit yourself.'

Johnnie carried on pulling on his leather gloves, and then winding a white silk scarf around his lower face before putting on his crash helmet. The gleam of the café lights caught the red flames painted on the front of it. He pulled the white scarf up a bit higher. There was a zinging of metal as he zipped up his leather jacket.

He spoke through the scarf, his voice a trifle muffled. 'Don't worry about your mate. Pete will take care of her and take her home when she's ready.'

Marcie opened her mouth and started to ask how he could be so sure, and what did he mean by Pete 'taking care' of Rita. There was more than one way of interpreting that. She wasn't that daft.

Her voice was drowned out by the throaty roar of the 650 Triumph. She was about to go off with Johnnie and it was likely she might share the same fate as Rita.

Stop now!

But she couldn't stop because she was young and she liked him, and forces as old as time pumped through her body. She *had* to go with him.

The acrid aroma of burnt fuel filled the air. The

engine throbbed and escalated into a sound resembling rumbling thunder. It was like a challenge, meant to draw her forward, to throw caution to the wind and take a ride with a boy she was fast falling for.

She took a deep breath and made up her mind. Johnnie was waiting for her.

Chapter Four

Before her conscience persuaded her otherwise, she swung her leg over the pillion. The passenger foot pedals were mounted quite far back, so to keep her balance she had no choice but to wind her arms around him, her breasts flattened against his back.

Turning away from the sea front, he headed for the main road that eventually led to Sheerness. The warm night air was a heady mix of sea and salt marsh, leather and oil. The whole was like a great stew, the stew of life, and she wanted to hold it tight, just as tightly as she was holding him.

They took a turning off the main road to a place where the wind whipped straight from the sea and across the marshes, unfettered by trees or dwellings.

The place would have been pitch black but the moon was bright and the lights of Southend blinked like fallen stars from across the water.

After turning off the engine, Johnnie pulled the bike up onto its stand. Marcie watched him strip off his gloves, his helmet and the white silk scarf. There was something about the silk scarf that was strangely alluring, like a slinky snake as he furled it into his empty helmet with his gloves.

He took out a cigarette and offered her one. She declined. It was something she had tried once and not enjoyed. There was no point in persisting.

He tilted his head back as he exhaled. The smoke curled upwards in front of the moon.

She felt she should be saying something. This was one of those initially awkward moments when both knew something would happen. It was just a case of what form it would take.

Neither said a word. They both knew what came next. It was for him to make the first move. She couldn't possibly do that – shouldn't do that – but she wanted to. She truly wanted to.

Just as she was about to suggest something, he invited her to sit down.

She looked down at the ground. There was grass mostly but also bare patches where footsteps had worn the grass away.

'I don't think so.'

As she brought her head back up and faced him he kissed her.

She closed her eyes. His chin was slightly rough against hers. Boys felt so different, she thought. And they smelled so different. And felt so different. It was all so wonderful.

After he'd unzipped his jacket, he hugged her. She

responded, running her arms inside and around his warm body. Her hands ran over the tautness of his chest, the straight back, the slim hips.

'You've got a great figure,' he murmured against her ear.

Flattery will get you nowhere, she'd heard say. At one time she might have believed it, but not now. She wanted him to want her. She wanted him to say how the thought, the feel and the sight of her inflamed his desire. It was wonderful to be desired. She pitied the girls that were not and she felt special. Very special.

All girls promised to be good until they married. Gran expected her to be. Marcie had vowed that she would, but nothing had prepared her for such intense desire.

Hot masculine breath sighed against her ear. 'Oh, Marcie.'

She bit her lip to stop from crying out when his hand covered her breast. No one had ever told her it would feel as stupendous as this. She closed her eyes and vowed to remember this feeling for the rest of her life. Not the feeling of being with him, but the intensity of her own desire. How was a girl to resist such delicious feelings? Overcome with the urges of her body, she dropped her hand tentatively down his front, though only as far as the waistband of his Lee Cooper jeans. The desire to go further was hard to resist.

Hesitantly she thrust her hips that bit closer to

him. His hardness pressed against hers, and she was surprised enough to gasp out loud.

His fingers were tweaking her nipples. Her nipples responded. Like two hard rosehips they thrust against the bodice of her dress.

She gasped as what felt like a sharp electric current radiated outwards. It was funny, but it seemed her nipples were like super-sensitive buttons; press button to go and wham! Like a lunar module, she was up there in orbit.

A warning voice told her to come down to earth, But she was loath to do that. She didn't want him to stop, and yet . . .

She remembered Nancy with her bruised face and arm, pushing her baby along and looking so alone, so downtrodden. Did she want to end up like that? No! No, she did not.

His hand moved from her breast and was now sliding down her thigh, bunching up her dress as it went.

She clapped her hand over it. 'No!'

He moaned against her ear. 'Please . . .'

'No.'

'Aw come on, baby. Don't you love me enough?'

For a second she did nothing. That was before Jane the gum-chewing girl came to mind. Had he said the same thing to her? Had she given in? Had he dumped her afterwards?

Again his warm palm slid down her thigh. The

temptation to give in was incredibly powerful, but Gran's warning frown was in her mind. So was Jane.

This time she slapped his hand away.

'Ouch! That hurt.'

'It was meant to. No! I said, no! I'm not that sort of a girl.'

She pushed him away.

He threw up both hands in surrender, palms towards her. 'OK. OK.'

The dress she'd loved now seemed indecent. She vowed to let the hem down – if there was enough material to do so. She heard herself breathing heavily and felt ashamed. It wasn't with the effort of knocking him away. On the contrary, it was with the effort of regaining her self-control – that and the blood racing through her veins.

Resting back on his bike, Johnnie cupped his hand around a lighted match and lit a cigarette. He didn't offer her one this time. Not that she would have taken it. His chain-smoking reminded her of Babs and her yellow fingers. Her stepmother had put her off smoking. She didn't want to end up like Babs in any way, shape or form. She'd made a career out of disliking her and wasn't about to stop now. Babs might have physically replaced her real mother, but not emotionally. In her mind she wanted to believe that Babs was responsible for her mother going away, but she had no proof of that. No proof at all.

Smoke rings rose in bluish whirls then fused with the darkness. Johnnie's gaze was fixed on the sea. A silver path led out across the water to the moon.

It was a beautiful night. The situation was dangerous. She wanted this boy. Although a small voice said it was wrong, she wanted him to want her.

'I need to get home,' she said and knew she sounded in a panic. She *was* in a panic.

He turned and looked at her.

Instead of meeting the disappointment in his look, she glanced over her shoulder. If she remembered rightly there was a bus stop back there, a lonely spot but the bus shouldn't be too long.

Johnnie said nothing, but just kept on smoking, his gaze fixed on the distant glow in the sky above the Isle of Grain.

She looked at the bus stop, then at him, then back to the bus stop again. She didn't want to wait there too long. She didn't want to be left alone out here. He'd stay as long as she had something to say.

'Was Jane your girlfriend?' she blurted.

He shrugged his square, leather-clad shoulders. 'She thought so.'

'I see.'

That meant he hadn't considered them that way. Jane had thought more of him than he'd thought of her.

She tried to see the time on her watch. It was a

neat watch which meant it had a very small face and tiny hands. Her dad had sent it to her last Christmas. She often forgot to rewind it – like now. What was the time?

'I need to get the bus. Would it be too much trouble to take me to the bus stop? It's up on the main road. I should be alright from there, but if I don't get the bus I'm going to have to walk home.'

He tossed his head in response. 'For Christ's sake!'

The force and tone of his voice made her jump.

He flicked the half-finished cigarette into a clump of couch grass then turned and glared at her. 'What kind of bastard do you think I am?'

She glared right back. 'There's no need to swear, just because you didn't get your own way.'

Doing quick movements helped her keep her nerve. She hastily rearranged the strap of her shoulder bag.

'Damn!' she shouted as the buckle got entangled in her scarf. The scarf came off and was stuffed into the bag.

'Now you're the one who's swearing!'

'No, I am not,' she said indignantly. 'Well – not as badly as you!'

'If you were going to find fault with me, I'd never have taken you for a ride!'

'If you were going to behave like an octopus with eight arms . . .'

'Tentacles! Eight tentacles.'

'OK! Eight tentacles. If you hadn't tried to put your hand up my dress . . .'

'What do you expect wearing an outfit like that? Everything's on view!'

'Only my legs.'

'Well, you should cover them up.'

'No, I should not. It's the fashion, you bloody moron! Get with it, why don't you!'

The eyes looking at her narrowed. He was trying to dig beneath the surface; she hated it when people did that.

'You can be a right cow when you want to be.'

She didn't regard that as a worthy or accurate appraisal and it threw her off guard. If he got to know her better . . .

'Well, there you are,' she retorted. It was a nothing kind of comment but was all she could think to say. For good measure she added, 'You'll have to find someone else who'll let you put your hand up her dress!'

Feeling let down she hugged herself and turned away, unwilling to show her face in case he saw that her eyes were turning misty. Getting home was now her number one priority. Gran would kill her if she missed the last bus. If Johnnie didn't take her home, or at least get her to the bus stop, that's exactly what would happen.

It would hurt her pride but there was only one

thing she could do. She had to get him to take her to the bus stop.

Hugging her shoulder bag to her chest like some medieval breastplate, she turned to face him. Her mouth was dry but she was prepared to beg – or at least almost beg.

He was winding the white scarf around his face followed by the rest of the gear. He started the bike.

Her heart thudded. Surely he wasn't going to leave her here?

'Johnnie! I need to get to the bus stop!'

Pleading didn't come into it. Neither had please. Worried she might not get home on time, and angry at him, she did the only thing left to her. Clutching his arm with both hands, she shook him.

He looked surprised. 'No need to get violent. Hop on.'

Without bothering with the scarf or securing her shoulder bag strap, she got onto the bike, her arms around his waist, her head lying against his back.

The night air was turning damp and clouds were now hiding the moon. A light drizzle began to fall, stinging her face as they sped towards the main road. Without a moon Sheppey took on an eerie loneliness that had something to do with its flatness that was basically on the same level as the sea. Prone to flooding, it was as though the sea was merely waiting to reclaim the land it had begrudgingly given up. On nights such as this, without moon or stars and a drizzle-misting distance, it was easy to imagine the sea swallowing the whole island in one easy gulp.

Wind and rain sent her hair in tangled strands across her face making her wish she'd worn her scarf. Her knuckles were chaffed and cold from hanging on to her bag at the same time as hanging on to her escort. Burning up was not all that it was cracked up to be; she was cold, wet and would be glad to get home.

Ahead of them was the bus stop standing solitary on a small patch of pavement, an island amongst stunted shrubbery and rough grass.

The bike slid to a stop, gravel flying up from the front tyre and hitting her in the face.

She got off and looked down at her wet, dirt-spattered clothes. 'Look at the state of me. I look like something the bloody cat's dragged in.'

Johnnie glowered and said nothing, not even good night. Bracing one leg to one side, he turned the bike towards Leysdown where his mates would still be gathered.

She waited, half expecting him to look in her direction, perhaps even say goodbye. He did neither. The bike roared off, the engine's sound gurgling through the exhaust bafflers.

'Pig,' muttered Marcie under her breath, staring after him, willing him to come back for her. She shouted it, louder and louder.

'Pig! PIG!'

The rear light on his bike swiftly became a lonely spot in the distance. All alone now, she shivered. By itself the darkness was intense; coupled with the mist and the rain the night lay like a wet blanket in a damp, steamy room.

Suddenly she found herself craving a light – any light. Her thoughts turned to Rita. At least Rita would get home. She was probably already there. Rita would do whatever a boy wanted to do. She didn't have the best of figures, so made the best of what fate threw her way.

Forgetting that her watch had run down, she pulled back her cuff and attempted to check the time. It was too dark and the dial wasn't luminous. There was a good possibility that the bus was already gone. What would she do if it didn't show up?

She answered her own question.

There's only one thing you can do, Marcie. You walk.

She turned her face towards home. Land and sky had merged into one black sheet. What with the rain as well, it would be difficult to see her way. There was no light at the bus stop but at least she was on firm ground. She had no choice but to wait and hope that the bus would turn up. Otherwise she would have to wait until it got lighter and that would mean dawn. It would also mean trouble when she got home.

Chapter Five

The rain that had started as a fine drizzle came down in stinging stair-rods. Wet and miserable, Marcie peered into the darkness in the direction the bus should come from. Her hair was soon plastered to her head like a swimming cap and her short dress clung to her thighs, revealing her legs from there down. Thank goodness for the darkness, she thought. The clinging fabric left nothing to the imagination.

She wiped her face with the back of her hand and blinked into the driving rain. Something glimmered. Something shone.

Pushing her wet hair back onto her head she narrowed her eyes. Her spirits rose. Coming out from behind her hand she saw – headlights!

Not sure she was seeing things, and unable to judge whether it was a bus, she blinked again. Another light had appeared just beyond the first then seemed to overtake.

At the same time she heard the throaty roar of a motorcycle. It could only be one of the London boys. None of the local boys had big bikes, though they wished they did.

A single headlight bore down on her. The bike slowed and began to do a 'U' turn across the road.

The headlight lit up the road in front of her and the ground at her feet. By its light she recognised the painted flames on the front of the crash helmet and knew it was Johnnie.

'Hop on.' He jerked his head at the space behind him.

No apology. No explanation that he couldn't possibly leave her here all alone. And was his intention to take her home directly, or would there be a price to pay?

She asked him outright. 'How do I know you'll take me straight home?'

He shook his head. 'Aw, come on. Get on or get lost!'

'What did you say?'

Her bile was up! Oh boy! Did he have a nerve!

She was about to cross her arms and tell him to sod off, but could see other headlights. If that wasn't the bus coming along the road she'd have to walk home. She'd be late. She'd be in trouble and wouldn't be allowed out for a week.

It had to be the bus! If it wasn't then she'd thumb for a lift anyway.

Waving her arms and shouting, she ran out into the road.

'Stop! Oh please stop!'

She didn't hear what Johnnie was shouting at her

and didn't care. Besides, she could guess at the words. He was angry, just as angry as she was now.

The headlights of the other vehicle lit up her face. It was a car not a bus. Obviously the driver had seen her frantic waving and was slowing down.

The long bonnet and chromium wheel spokes were instantly familiar. No one, absolutely no one on Sheppey had such a super Jaguar car except for Alan Taylor, Rita's dad.

The passenger window was wound down. He poked out his head and even though it was raining, still managed to smile.

'Is that you, Marcie Brooks? What are you doing out at this time of night, girl?'

'I missed the bus.'

'Thought as much. Best get you home, I think. Do you want a lift?'

She didn't hesitate, opened the door and got in.

A headlight flashed over them like a wartime searchlight. Johnnie and his motorbike swept past.

Mr Taylor noticed.

'Was he bothering you?'

He was referring to Johnnie Hawke; Johnnie who had had second thoughts about taking her home.

'Just offering me a lift.'

'Was he now?' Mr Taylor sounded sceptical. 'You need to be careful of young chaps offering you lifts, my girl. You know that, don't you?'

'Of course I do. I'm not a child.'

'Glad to hear it.'

On the short drive home he asked her how come she and Rita were not together.

'She got the bus,' Marcie blurted. 'I got talking to some friends and missed it.'

'Boyfriends?'

'Just friends from school.'

Marcie was sensitive to him glancing at her in an intermittent fashion, as though he wanted to ask her something, or was merely surmising what she and his daughter had been up to.

She waited for him to press her further on where Rita was, but he didn't. She reminded herself that he wasn't the old-fashioned type of father. Rita had said that he had a very modern outlook.

They stopped at the main set of traffic lights in Sheerness. The lights took a while to change. While they waited she caught him staring at her.

'How old are you, Marcie?'

'Sixteen.'

'My God. Where have the years gone?' Do you know what? You've grown into the spitting image of your mother.'

'Have I?'

The statement embarrassed her. Should she be flattered? Or should she be as close mouthed about her mother as her family was? Her mother had run off with another man. That's what they all said.

Alan Taylor had soft blue eyes, light-brown hair and strong features. When younger he'd probably looked older than his years, the boy who got in the pub when he was fourteen. Now well into his forties, there was a lack of loose jowls, his jaw-line was still firm, his eyes had not yet sunk into folds of surplus eyelids. Middle age was slow coming to strong features.

Alan Taylor was well respected. People locally strived to get into his good books. Old codgers toasted his health with the drinks he bought them. Alan liked to flash his money around. He had plenty of it.

Marcie pushed her hair back from her face. 'I'm soaked. Like a drowned rat.'

'You'll do,' said Alan. He patted her knee. 'A bit of rain never hurt anyone. Anyway, didn't I hear somewhere that it's good to wash your hair in rainwater? Softer so I hear say.'

Marcie played with the ends of her hair. 'I did hear that. But people say a lot of things. They say young girls shouldn't wear short skirts and show off their legs.'

'Take my word for it, Marcie,' said Alan, raising one hand from the steering wheel and shaking a finger to make his point. 'Never take too much notice of what people tell you. Suit yourself. Promise me you'll always do that. Right?'

His smile was infectious. She smiled too. 'Right! I'll always suit myself.'

'Good girl. That's what I like to hear.'

He pulled up outside the front door of number ten, Endeavour Terrace. Marcie thanked him.

'Here you are, fair damsel. Your knight in shining armour has brought you straight to your own front door. Courtesy of his fiery steed.'

Marcie laughed. The evening had had its ups and downs but had ended on a high thanks to Rita's father.

'I don't know what I would have done if you hadn't come along.'

Johnnie returning didn't count and she didn't mention it.

Alan's smile was warm and made her feel good.

'Any time,' he said laying his hand on her shoulder and giving it a quick squeeze. Just make an old man happy and promise me one thing when you get indoors.'

'What like?'

'Promise me you'll get out of those wet clothes and wipe yourself down with a dry towel. Will you do that?'

She smiled at his consideration. This was what it was like to have a father around. Rita was *so* lucky.

'Of course I will.' She flicked her fingers at her hair. 'I need a towel for my hair too. I look such a mess.'

When he smiled deep creases appeared at the outer corners of his eyes. She couldn't help smiling back at him and wondered what he would say if he knew what she was thinking. Alan Taylor looked quite attractive, quite good looking for an old man of at least forty.

'You look good even wet, but take my tip for the state of your health. Strip everything off and dry off.'

'I will.'

She ran off down the garden path thinking what a kind man he was. She told herself that her father was kind too but tended to buy her things rather than show affection.

'Gran! I'm home,' she shouted up the stairs.

There was no reply. There never was, but the ritual was adhered to and Marcie knew that the first time she didn't call up those stairs her grandmother would be down looking for her.

Alan Taylor watched Marcie running up the garden path, her long legs kicking out behind her.

His eyes fixed on the soaking wet mini dress clinging to her young body. And what a body it was! He'd admired Marcie's legs when she'd called round to see his daughter. Up until this evening he'd never had the opportunity to touch them. Tonight he'd also taken in the swelling of her breasts. The wet dress had been the icing on the cake.

Tonight was not the first time that he'd mused on the idea of seducing his daughter's best friend. But tonight the idea had firmed up in his mind. She was ripe for the plucking and he had every intention of being the first in line.

'Take it slowly,' he said as he checked his reflection in his rear-view mirror. 'Some things are worth waiting for.'

Chapter Six

At last the days of incessant rain had cleared and the sun came out, making the wet pavements breathe steam. Holidaymakers down from London for their annual jamboree were queuing for popcorn and sticky rock shaped like bacon and eggs.

It was lunchtime when they were allowed to shut for half an hour before Marcie could ask Rita about the weekend.

'So how was Pete?'

Rita swallowed a mouthful of pasty and grinned from ear to ear. 'Snogged each other to a standstill.'

'Just snogged?' Marcie eyed her sidelong at the same time as biting into her cheese and pickle sandwich.

Rita managed a snigger even though her gob was filled with pasty. 'One thing led to another. Yes, of course I let him have a feel of my tits. In fact I wanted him to have a feel. I couldn't help myself.'

'It was that good?'

'Good for him and good for me. He's coming down again next weekend from Friday to Sunday night. This time he's bringing a tent!'

She said it with a sparkle in her eyes. Marcie could

read where this was going. When a boy took an interest in her, Rita was putty in his hands.

'Rita, you're not going to camp out with him, are you? You're not going to – you know – go all the way?'

Rita sniffed and tossed her head. Her tongue smacked the crumbs from her lips before she laid it bare – that is, as truthfully as she knew how.

'He fancies me. I fancy him. So why not do it? What about you and Johnnie. How far did you let him go?'

Marcie had been feeling superior and downright smug, but mention of Johnnie made her uncomfortable.

'Rita, I hardly know the bloke!'

Rita knew her father had given Marcie a lift home, but that was all he'd told her. He didn't seem to have mentioned Johnnie lurking around at the bus stop. Marcie was grateful for that.

Rita's pink cheeks bunched like apples when she grinned. She leaned close as though about to impart a secret. 'Bet he wanted to, though, didn't he. Bet he was up for it.'

Marcie was indignant. 'But he didn't get it. I'm not a five-bar gate, you know!'

'What's that supposed to mean?' said Rita, all indignant, even though her mouth was full of flaky pastry.

'My legs don't easily swing wide open.'

'Christ, Marcie! You are such a bleeding prude!'

Marcie threw a piece of crust at a seagull. 'No I'm not. It's you being too quick off the mark. One night and you're in love and willing to give him everything.'

Rita sprang to her feet, pasty crumbs scattering around her.

'Are you calling me a tart, Marcie Brooks?'

'I didn't say that.'

Rita pouted, rosebud mouth in a plump oval face. 'That's what you meant, though, but it's a bleeding cheek. You were tempted yerself, so don't give me that whiter than white stuff. You're no saint yerself, Marcie Brooks. And neither is that family of yours. Your dad's spent more time in clink than a cuckoo in a clock! As for your mother . . .'

Marcie leapt at her. 'Shut your big fat face, Rita Taylor, and leave my mother out of this.'

'She went off with another bloke! Must have been a bit of a tart herself!'

Marcie swung a clenched fist. Rita ducked.

They might have tussled, but a scrawny mongrel chose that moment to swipe the remains of Rita's pasty.

'Oi!'

Marcie fell back down to where she'd been sitting and rolled with laughter. Rita was livid. Boys were pretty important in Rita Taylor's life, but came a poor second to food.

The dog had intervened just in the nick of time. There was no scratching and pulling of hair, not this time anyway.

Rita's attention was diverted to the remains of Marcie's sandwich. She'd left it to one side, sitting on the paper bag she'd brought it in.

'Are you going to eat that?'

She didn't wait for an answer but picked it up and wolfed it down.

'Hope you choke on it,' muttered Marcie.

Once the sandwich was demolished, Rita sucked each finger in turn.

'I *love* Branston pickle.'

Marcie picked up her bag and transistor radio. The Beatles were singing 'Hard Day's Night'. Normally she and Rita would have jigged around and sang along together, but not now. Rita's remark about her family had touched a raw nerve. Was it true that everybody knew about her father? That in itself had dented her pride, but mention of her mother had hurt in a different way. Her father was all she had because she could barely remember her mother; except for her smell: violets. She remembered her softness and the smell of violets. Funny, she didn't recall remembering that before. In fact, she remembered little – so very little.

She'd tried asking her grandmother about her mother. But Rosa Brooks's thin lips had set into a straight line.

'She is gone. Life goes on. Do not trouble your-self about her.'

Marcie realised early on that she'd get no straight answers from her family so never asked anything again. On the surface she appeared to have taken her grandmother's advice not to trouble herself, but inside was a different story.

It was close enough to two o'clock to be back at work. Marcie marched off. Rita was her best friend. She should not have made the remarks that she did.

'Are we still friends?' Rita called after her.

Marcie didn't answer. Sod Rita. She was never going to speak to her again.

Chapter Seven

'Weee!'

Baby Annie squealed with delight each time Marcie sent the pushchair wheels racing along the pavement.

It was Saturday morning and a whole week since Johnnie had dropped her off at the bus stop.

Her stepmother had the day off from Woolworths and had gone out the night before leaving Marcie to babysit. Ten o'clock and she was *still* in bed. It had been down to Marcie to feed, wash and dress the toddler. The boys could manage without their mother and their grandmother ensured they were fed a hearty breakfast. Rosa was biased towards boys – they got the bacon and eggs while Marcie and the baby only got toast. Marcie considered this unfair seeing as she was the one out at work, not the boys. She wouldn't dare challenge her grandmother. Rosa Brooks didn't see things the same way as she did. She'd been brought up to regard men as the breadwinners even if they were not. Nothing could change her now.

Marcie pulled up outside the shop and engaged the brake with her foot.

'Won't be long, poppet,' she said and stroked Annie's cheek.

She collided with Rita just outside the shop door. Rita was carrying a brown carrier bag full of food. On seeing Marcie she flushed bright red.

'Hello. Um . . . just in case you see my mum or dad, I stayed at your place last night – and tonight,' she added quickly.

Marcie glanced behind her. She hadn't noticed the shiny motorcycle waiting at the kerb, but she did now. Pete was sitting on it sideways, blowing smoke rings.

There wasn't much chance of Alan Taylor calling at Endeavour Terrace to check on his daughter. Rita could do no wrong in his eyes. She wished she had the same freedom but it wasn't likely given the old-fashioned views of Rosa Brooks.

Bearing in mind their argument, Marcie was tempted to be awkward. The comment about her mother still stung. But Rita was her best friend.

'Sorry about what I said,' said Rita as though reading her mind.

Marcie wasn't sure of her sincerity. 'OK. So how was last night?'

Rita's eyes sparkled. 'We did it three times last night and twice more since breakfast.'

Marcie was about to say it was a wonder Rita could walk or Pete could ride a motorcycle, but didn't. Instead she counselled Rita to be careful.

Rita grinned in response. 'He's got some johnnies. I went with him into the chemists. He was too scared to ask for them by himself. But I did though.'

Marcie shook her head in disbelief. 'You've got some front, Rita Taylor.'

Rita giggled. 'See you in work on Monday then.'

Gone was the angry Rita she had argued with. She was gushing and looking pleased with herself.

She watched Rita mount the motorcycle, her skirt riding high. She cuddled the carrier bag between her breasts and Pete's back, and waved as the bike moved off.

It's none of your business, Marcie said to herself as she went into the shop, bought the bread and came out again. 'Here,' she said to baby Annie. 'Hold on to that loaf of bread until we get home.'

Podgy hands reached out for the bread.

Marcie began to push. Annie gurgled and dribbled over the crusty corner of the bread. Marcie thought about stopping her, but held out against it. The poor kid was hungry. Her mother should look after her better. Her thoughts went back to Rita.

'It's none of your business,' she said again, though out loud this time. If Rita got into trouble she only had herself to blame. She found herself wondering if Babs had ever been like Rita when she was younger. How could Rita face her father if she did find herself with a bun in the oven? Johnnies, French letters or whatever they were called, were known to split. Everybody knew that.

'Silly cow! Silly, silly cow!'

'You shouldn't do that, you know.' The voice that took her by surprise was slow and jerky.

Marcie knew who it was. 'Alright then, Garth?' She said it without looking round. Garth was over twenty-one but had the mind of a ten-year-old. He looked what he was – ungainly, awkward and scruffy.

She felt sorry for him, but he was hardly good company. Besides, she preferred to be alone with her thoughts.

Being offhand might put him off following her. Garth Davies. He lived with his mother in rooms above the shop. His mother being a bit of a gadabout, he was usually there by himself. Lonely and scruffy, he latched on to people like a stray dog pining for attention.

'You shouldn't be doing that,' he said again. His voice was slurred as though his tongue was too big for his mouth. And he dribbled. Annie dribbling she could cope with. A grown man dribbling was something else. It made her feel a bit queasy.

Marcie rolled her eyes in exasperation. She wasn't going to get away with it. Might as well stop long enough to put him off. She brought the pushchair to a standstill.

'What's that I shouldn't be doing?' she asked, eyeing

the scruffy young man as though she might clip him around the ear.

Well used to admonishments, Garth turned sheepish.

'You was talking to yerself,' he said in that same slow tone. 'Shouldn't do that, you shouldn't. Ma don't like it. My Ma says people think you're mad if you talk to yerself.'

Marcie was irritated. 'Do I look mad, Garth? Do I look scruffy and speak in a stupid slow voice and follow people around?'

Her voice petered out. A strange glazed look came to Garth's eyes. It was as though he had heard all this before and was now retreating to some secret place deep inside. The fingers of one hand intertwined with the other in nervous anticipation. People treated Garth cruelly just because he had the mind of a child.

In Marcie's opinion Garth was a person to be pitied and that was how she felt, plus some guilt on behalf of herself. The tall gangly lad had watery blue eyes and a nose that seemed continuously to be running. He was supposedly the product of a wartime liaison with a Polish aviator, who had taken off when he'd found out about Edith Davies's pregnancy. On top of that misfortune, poor Edith had gone through a difficult birth – or at least so ran the tale.

'Well, I wouldn't want to be thought mad, Garth. I'll bear that in mind in future.'

When Garth smiled his teeth flashed like a row of lopsided tombstones. He began giggling inanely and only stopped when he wiped his nose on his sleeve. Once the snot was wiped away, he recommenced giggling.

Marcie began heading for home. Just as she'd feared, he began to follow her.

'Where are you going?' he asked, his head held to one side, almost as though he were trying to rub his ear against his shoulder.

'Are you following me, Garth?'

Again he asked her where she was going.

'Home.'

'To your mother and your father?'

She shook her head. 'To my grandmother. You know her, don't you? Her name's Auntie Rosa. She comes to your mother for a cup of tea now and again.'

His giggling stopped abruptly. 'Auntie Rosa and the man.'

'Auntie Rosa.' She presumed the man was either a figment of his imagination or his mother's latest man friend. Edith Davies took in lodgers now and again – difficult seeing as she only had one bedroom and a box room. Garth slept in the box room. His mother took up one half of the double bed in the other.

Garth rambled on, so Marcie didn't pay too much attention as he went on to describe the man and what he had done or said.

'My mother's got a red dress, one like your mother's.'

'I don't think so, Garth,' she muttered, her mouth set in a straight line. Why had he mentioned her mother? He couldn't possibly remember her and certainly not a red dress.

'I saw her in it.'

'No, Garth! You did not!'

She instantly regretted being snappish, but Garth had unnerved her. For the second time in a few days someone had mentioned her mother. For ages there'd been no mention and now there'd been two. Coincidence or something more? Coincidence, she decided. What else could it be?

People avoided Garth. He was one of life's cast-offs, rejected from the moment he was born. His mother paid too much attention to her lodgers and not enough to her son. Poor Garth. There were moth holes in his pullover and the cuffs of his shirtsleeves flapped around his hands. His trousers were grey and shapeless and there was a line of grease around his shirt collar. He ponged a bit. Poor Garth had been named after a strong man in a comic strip, but didn't – in fact, couldn't – live up to his namesake.

Jabbering and giggling, he followed her all the way home and looked surprised when she came to a stop outside number ten.

He stared at the front door. 'You going in there?'

'Yes. This is where I live.'

She had been unfastening the straps holding Annie in the pushchair.

On looking up, she saw him stare at the house then wave. She looked to see who he was waving to. The window panes upstairs reflected the sky. Light to the downstairs windows was blanked out by the privet hedge. They reflected nothing; in fact they looked as though they weren't glass at all – more like black bitumen squares.

She turned her attention back to Garth. A trickle of saliva oozed from the corner of his mouth. Her pity was like a lump in her throat.

'Would you like to see the chickens, Garth?'

She didn't really want to see the chickens herself. They were stupid creatures fit only to be eaten.

Garth's slack jaw firmed up. He clapped and gasped like an excited child. 'See the chickens! Cluck, cluck, cluck, cluck, cluck!'

'Come on then.'

He followed her as she manoeuvred the pushchair up the garden path. She ordered him to stay there while she got the pushchair through the door.

Once inside she got Annie out of the pram.

'Keep hold of the bread, Annie,' she said.

Annie obeyed, her gummy mouth returning to suck at the corner of the loaf.

She heard raised voices. Gran was giving Marcie's stepmother a piece of her mind. Cupping her ear against the door, she tried to hear what was being said. There was something about Babs being underhand, something about her being devious behind her mother-in-law's back. Babs sounded as though she might be on the verge of tears. This I have to see, Marcie decided. She grabbed the door knob and pushed the door open.

'Here we are,' she said.

Her grandmother was sitting at the kitchen table. Silver-framed photographs, a duster and a can of silver polish were spread out in front of her. The family photographs usually sat on the high mantelpiece above the stove. Marcie's grandfather dressed in his naval uniform smiled out from one. Another was of both grandparents on their wedding day; another still of Marcie's father as a toddler. Regular as clockwork, Saturday morning was when her grandmother took them all down and polished the frames.

At the sight of her mother, Annie began to howl. Her little arms reached out for her grandmother.

Marcie smirked. 'Annie loves her granny. Isn't that sweet?'

She couldn't help throwing a look of triumph at Babs who scowled back, picked up a duster and began polishing a photo frame.

Annie was cooing and chuckling in her grandmother's arms.

Marcie placed the bread on the table plus the change from half a crown.

'It's chewed,' said Babs on glimpsing the corner of the crusty loaf. 'What did you let her do that for?'

'She was hungry,' said Marcie. 'You need to feed her more often and not go out to the pub so much.'

Babs began to ease her wide backside out of her chair. 'Less of your cheek . . .'

'Barbara! Make your child some porridge!'

Rosa Brooks fixed her with a hard stare.

Marcie smirked. She loved hearing Babs being told what to do, but her grandmother's eyes were everywhere. Her smirk was noticed.

'And you, young lady. We will have some respect in this house.'

Marcie turned to leave.

'Where do you think you're off to?'

Small she might be, but Rosa Brooks could fill a room with her voice.

'I'm taking Daft Garth to see the chickens.'

She'd presumed her act of compassion would save her from a telling off. She was wrong.

'Do not call him that. Garth is a human being and one of God's creatures, as are we all.' She made the sign of the cross on her thin chest, her voice softer now. 'Go on. Show the poor boy the chickens.'

Babs did as her mother-in-law directed, fed her child and made her a bottle. Soon the little brat was asleep and Babs was free to sit down with a magazine and have a smoke. However, it was difficult to concentrate. Her mother-in-law's boot button eyes were boring into her.

'You would leave and live in a council house rather than stay here with your family?' Rosa's voice was cold. Her daughter-in-law had done the unthinkable. She'd applied for and been given a council house. And all done without her – Rosa Brooks – knowing.

Babs stiffened but didn't take her eyes from the words on the page. 'I want my own place.'

'Antonio will not allow that,' Rosa exclaimed. She had great faith in her son. He put his family first above everything and cared about his mother's welfare. That's what she told herself and that is what she believed. Unfortunately he had not been lucky as far as matrimony was concerned. If Barbara was intending to take the whole family with her, Rosa would be left alone. Rosa did not want that; besides, she saw trouble looming. Babs was not the best of mothers. Things would fall apart. She was sure it would.

'Antonio will want what I want,' said Babs, blowing a cloud of smoke from pouting pink lips.

'I will write to him,' said Rosa.

'Yeah! You do that.'

'I will.'

Rosa threw down the tea towel and made her way to the living room and the dark oak bureau sitting in the corner. That's where she did her letter writing.

Babs allowed herself a small smile of triumph. This

time she had won the battle with the old witch. Soon she and Tony would have a new beginning – and a new house.

Throwing the magazine back onto the yellow-topped table she took a big puff on her fag and threw her arms in the air. That old bat – Rosa could write all the letters she liked. Tony was on his way home, though neither his mother nor his family knew that.

The old girl had supposedly received a message from the other side – pie in the sky as far as Babs was concerned. She, however, *knew* beyond doubt that Tony was coming home.

Reaching into her bra cup she withdrew the letter he'd sent her. Actually the letter was addressed to his mother, but Babs had got to the post first, recognised what it was and who it was from, and decided to keep it for herself. She was fed up of being bossed around, fed up of that cheeky little cow Marcie and her stuck-up ways. Not letting them know he was coming home was her way at getting back at them all. She would be there at the station to greet him.

Chapter Eight

Humbled by her grandmother's reprimand, but relieved to be out of the house, Marcie rejoined Garth. He was standing where she'd left him, staring up at the front bedroom windows, with a stupid smile on his face.

'This way.'

She got as far as the front gate before realising that he might not have heard her. When she looked he was still smiling stupidly up at the bedroom windows.

'Garth!' she called out.

It was as though the gangly, misshapen young man was a wooden puppet and someone had suddenly pulled a string. His head jerked round before his body. Another string and his body followed his head.

She led him along the front of the rank of houses, turning at the end into the lane that ran along the back of the terrace. He made clucking sounds all the way and flapped his arms in a childish interpretation of a chicken.

It irritated her. She looked over her shoulder, mouth open ready to tell him to shut up. One look at his face and she clamped her mouth shut. He reminded her of Annie – happy and trusting, lost in a world of his own.

Tall nettles grew in big clumps the whole length of the stony lane. Too narrow to take a car, the back entrance was mainly used for coal deliveries, the coalmen carrying sack after sack along the lane and up the garden paths to the coal house.

Beady-eyed chickens strutted up and down their run, watching them approach. The back garden was empty, Archie and Arnold out playing along the beach with their friends.

Mr Ellis from two doors down was taking a rest from digging his nuclear fallout shelter. He mopped his brow and waved.

'I'm going down a lot deeper than I planned,' he called. 'Got to be ready for the enemy now old Churchill is gone. I reckon I'll be more ready for them than anyone else on Sheppey.'

'That's good,' she called back, and wondered if he were right to be so diligent. Yes, she was aware that Sir Winston Churchill had died earlier that year but he'd been an old man who'd done well in the war. She also wondered if he was digging it big enough to take everyone in Endeavour Terrace seeing as no one else was bothering. Or would he lock them all out if the Russians did come?

Marcie used the tree stump at the side of the

chicken hutch to get up on the roof. Garth declined her offer to join her there. He was absorbed in the chickens, clucking in response to their clucks and dipping and darting his head in the same manner. Being a chicken quite suited him. His hair was the colour of dark corn and formed what resembled a cock's comb on the top of his head.

Poor thing. No dad and not much of a mother to speak of. Was it just getting pregnant and not being married that had made Edith Davies the way she was?

It occurred to her that if Rita didn't watch herself she could end up the same way as Garth's mother – what a chill thought that was. Though Alan Taylor did have the money to put things right.

The roof of the chicken hutch had soaked up the warmth of the sun. Marcie lay back against the single slope, her arms folded behind her head. She closed her eyes and pretended that her surroundings had melted away. That she was lying on a tropical beach and surrounded by blue sky and fluffy clouds. At least that bit's true, she thought, squinting up at the sky with one eye.

'There used to be a tree 'ere,' Garth said suddenly.

With that same, single eye, she saw the top half of his face regarding her from above the ridge of the roof.

'Well, that's hardly earth-shattering news,' she muttered. The stump was testament to that.

Garth went on talking in his slow way as though he hadn't heard her.

'And grass was here. And a little seat was here. And a flower bed full of flowers. And a bird bath . . .'

'Chickens, Garth. There's only ever been chickens.'

'And people used to sit here.'

She blew out a gasp of frustration. 'Shut up, Garth.'

The world blurred. Her mind drifted.

Garth gabbled on.

'That was back when you were small. You and your mother used to come out here to sit under the tree. And she wore a red dress.'

Yes. A red dress with tiny brass buttons . . .

Her eyes blinked open. Perhaps it was the sun, or perhaps it was that he'd snapped her out of the edge of sleep, but she could see – *actually see* – the scene he was describing. Not physically of course, but in her mind's eye as though it had really happened.

Bolt upright she looked down at this slow-speaking excuse for a man. He was clucking again, folding his arms against his side like chicken wings and going around in a circle, legs bent, head dipping backwards and forwards.

'What was that you said, Garth?'

'Cluck, cluck, cluck—'

'Garth!'

His limbs jerked to stillness. Round eyed he looked up at her, his lower lip sagging.

'You told me I was sitting here with a woman in a red dress.' She couldn't help the trembling in her voice. 'Did I?'

Swinging her legs to the edge of the roof she got down onto the tree stump and from there to the ground. The grass was springy beneath her feet, as though the earth was made of sponge.

'You said I used to sit here with my mother and that she was wearing a red dress. How do you know that, Garth? Did you see her sitting here? Do you remember seeing me sitting on her lap?'

He stared at her with pale, ill-focused eyes. A sliver of saliva trickled from his drooping lower lip. 'I don't know.'

'What do you mean, you don't know?'

It was hard to control her anger – or perhaps it wasn't anger – just a kind of craziness because she wanted to know the truth – a truth – about her mother. She'd had no picture in her mind until now. There was no photograph in a silver frame sitting on the mantelpiece. What had her mother looked like? Had she really worn a red dress with small brass buttons?

He shook his head like the fool he was, drooling, eyeballs popping, neck hanging forward at an awkward angle. How ugly he was. He looked like a tortoise warily emerging from its shell.

Questions buzzed like wasps around Marcie's head.

They blinded her to her calmer self. They brought about a temper and strength that she didn't know she had.

She grabbed the shoulders of his greasy shirt, the cotton feeling gritty in her hands. Her eyes blazed and her hands had balled into tight fists.

'Did you meet my mother, Garth? Think! Did you really see her? REALLY see her?'

She was aware of how tense she'd become – and how loud.

Her shout had unsettled Garth. She wasn't aware of that either or how terrifying a picture she presented. Neither did she see the alarm in his eyes or the quivering of his jowls. It wasn't until he began to shake like a man on the verge of a fit; only then did she realise.

'Garth! I'm sorry.'

She let go of his shirt. She wiped her hands down her skirt.

'I'm sorry,' she repeated.

Garth's shaking lessened into an all-over shiver. He blinked as though he'd just woken up. His shoulders slumped and his spine seemed to curve as though in minutes he'd aged years.

'I'd better get home for my tea. Beans on toast,' he said thickly. 'Beans on toast.'

Once the old gate had creaked shut behind him, she went back up on the roof. It didn't matter that the midges were biting her arms or that the sun was still hot enough to burn her face. There was a lot of thinking she needed to do. Most of all there were questions she needed to ask.

It wasn't until teatime that she had the chance to ask the only person who would know whether what he'd said was true.

Her grandmother was sitting outside the back door knitting when she finally climbed down from the roof. Annie was playing with some water at the bottom of a galvanised bucket and chuckling as though it were the best game in the world.

The clicking and clacking of the knitting needles slowed or sped up in response to Rosa Brooks's swiftly moving fingers, the sound echoing between the rank of houses and the factory wall on the other side of the back lane.

Mouth dry and mind confused, Marcie settled herself on the back step. She stared silently at the chicken run where the young cockerels were pacing up and down in anticipation of food.

Finally turning away from them she looked at Annie. Annie was only a baby. How much would she remember of being a baby?

Her grandmother's voice broke into her thoughts. 'You are thinking something?'

It came as no surprise that her grandmother was

reading her mind and knew she was having deep thoughts. That's the way she was. People said she had the gift to look into people's lives, their problems and their futures, and give them sound advice. There was also the small matter of being able to communicate with her deceased husband, Marcie's grandfather.

'I was wondering,' Marcie began hesitantly. She took hold of the chubby fingers Annie offered her. 'I was wondering if Annie will remember being a baby or even a small child.'

The needles stopped clicking. She felt her grandmother's dark eyes scrutinising her.

'She will remember little.'

The eyes continued to scrutinise. Marcie chose not to meet her grandmother's steadfast gaze, but turned away when she felt a prickling sensation run down her spine.

'How did Garth enjoy the chickens?' asked her grandmother.

It seemed an odd thing to say seeing as they'd been discussing Annie.

'He said he remembered the garden being different, something about a tree and a seat . . .'

Marcie's voice trailed away. Her intention had been to ask about her mother and whether they had sat beneath that tree. Surely it was a very innocent question?

But was it?

A flock of seagulls flew screaming and wheeling overhead. Marcie watched one as it dived from a great height and attacked one of its own. The attacked bird fell to earth, quickly revived, then flew off again.

A plucky bird, thought Marcie. Go on. Be plucky yourself.

She dived in.

'Do you have any photographs of my mother?'

There was silence. No wise response, no nothing. And still the knitting needles were silent.

'I want to remember her,' Marcie said.

She looked up at her grandmother. What she saw in the tanned face and jet-black eyes alarmed her.

Her grandmother looked away. 'We will go in now,' she said, rubbing at the small of her back as she got up from her chair. 'Bring in the baby.'

Before bending down to do as ordered, Marcie took a deep breath. Her gaze strayed to the chicken house and the tree stump; all that remained of the pleasant scene that Garth had described. But was it real, or was it imagined? And what about her grandmother when she'd asked for a photograph? She had seen something unreadable in those Mediterranean eyes. It could have been fear, it might just as easily have been intense sadness. No matter how hard she tried, she could not remember ever seeing such a look before.

Chapter Nine

The prison officer grinned wryly as Tony Brooks stepped out of the gate and into his first bout of freedom for eighteen months.

'Goodbye for now, Brooks. See you again some time?' His tone was sarcastic.

Tony threw him a scowl. 'Of course, Mr Carter, sir. I'll stand you a pint sometime. Always willing to do that for screws, I am.' Tony could do sarcasm too.

He knew very well that the screw thought he'd be back in the nick before too long. Stuff him! He'd taken a fall this time, but was damned if he would again. Alan Taylor owed him and he'd hold him to it.

His eyes searched the road running along the front of Wandsworth Prison. He saw the pale-green Jaguar parked tight against the kerb, smiled to himself and shook his head.

Alan Taylor never failed to amaze him. He was the prince of Jack the Lad types and lived the life of Riley; an out-and-out ducker and diver who always managed to keep his head above water.

A bit further along he saw the two-tone Ford

Consul of the Cazuna boys. The choice was his: back to working the clubs and whorehouses for the Maltese Mafia, or doing a bit more for Alan.

Working for Alan Taylor meant going back to the Isle of Sheppey and the questionable bosom of his family. He'd miss London of course, the buzz, the good money and the tarts who'd give him a blow job for nothing. But even in stir he'd heard the word that things weren't going so well for the Maltese. Trouble was brewing big time and he'd considered things carefully. And there was the money to consider. He got a 'finder's' fee for nightclub owners who were ripe for a touch. He'd introduced Alan – though Alan wouldn't exactly know that. They were mates, but this was business. Anyway, he'd done enough of a favour for Alan Taylor, not mentioning his involvement in a little wage snatch at a factory in Dover.

Working for the Cazuna boys in future meant getting involved in something he didn't want to get involved with. Collecting protection due from pubs and clubs for them had been a worthwhile career up until now, but a turf war was brewing. Two East End brothers, the Kray twins, were muscling in on Maltese territory. Things were about to get violent and if there was one thing Tony was not it was violent. At least, not when faced with geezers with guns.

He hot-footed it to the Jaguar.

'Tony! Me old mate!' Alan gunned the engine the

moment Tony was in. 'See you've got other friends waiting for you.' He nodded at the two-tone Ford as they passed.

'There's no place like home, mate,' said Tony. 'Especially when it looks as though there's a bit of trouble coming off with the Krays. I ain't getting my knuckles cracked for nobody.'

'Don't blame you, old son. Don't blame you at all. Word is they're a pretty nasty pair. You're best out of it.'

Tony didn't offer that the Maltese were pretty nasty too. Of course, his mother didn't see things that way. They were all family and she believed that they were all legit – the landlords of business premises. The truth was they collected protection money not rent; that was besides running tarts. The prostitution had been a natural progression for the Maltese in London, seeing as they'd catered for the Royal Navy in Malta. The boys had done well, but he'd made his choice. He knew which side his bread was buttered.

They drove the streets of London heading for the roads that would take them east and along the south side of the Thames estuary.

Tony enjoyed the scenery, even seeing the shops again and men out of uniform. The women were best though. He'd missed seeing women.

'Bloody hell! Would you look at those skirts!'

'Legs are everywhere,' said Alan with a laugh.

Tony asked if Alan minded him opening a window. 'I stink. I've brought the stink of prison with me. Can't you smell it?'

Alan shook his head. 'Can't say I've noticed.'

'I can smell it,' growled Tony. 'It's a stink I've lived with for nearly eighteen months. Bloody hard to stop smelling it even when you've left it behind.'

'That might help,' said Alan, nodding at the glove compartment.

Tony's eyes lit up. He'd been expecting this, in fact he'd dreamed of this moment every night when sharing a cell with a poof called Roderick. Roderick had learned early on to keep his feelings to himself. Tony had chucked him out of the top bunk and claimed it as his own. He held the view that the top bunk was easier to defend should Roderick decide to get friendly in his sleep.

With fingertips worn smooth from sewing mail-bags, he unlocked the glove compartment and brought out a bulging brown envelope, opened it and flicked at the wedge of money.

'Five hundred quid,' said Alan. 'Never let it be said that I don't appreciate what people do for me.'

Tony stuffed the money into the inside pocket of his brown suede jacket. The jacket was shiny in places. He'd had it years. He could now afford a new one.

'Thanks.'

'No need to thank me. You earned it.'

Tony settled back into the warm leather seat. 'My old lady's going to be surprised.'

'You told her you were out, didn't you?'

'Yeah.' Tony stroked his chin and a wide grin split the prison pallor. 'I wrote to her and me mum and gave them the train time. My mum will make sure that Babs will be there, waiting for me at the station.'

'That's OK. I'll take you round there and run you both home. You two must have a lot of catching up to do.'

Tony's black brows frowned. 'Too bloody right we have. I'll be wanting some answers. Rumours get round in prison.'

'Is that right?'

Tony failed to notice that Alan's expression had turned wary.

'Yeah.' Tony's gaze fixed on the road ahead. 'I've been hearing she's been messing around. Better not have or I'll have to set her straight – her and the geezer she's been messing with.'

As they got closer to the Medway and the River Swale, the fertile fields of Kent gave way to acres of flat marshland. Once they'd crossed onto Sheppey a forest of metal pylons sprouted like giant pines. In the distance dockyard buildings loomed between the low-lying land and where the Thames and the Swale met the sea.

'Breathe that air,' said Alan. 'Nothing like it. Good to be home, eh?'

'Good! Real good,' Tony responded.

His mind was beginning to wander. He wasn't just thinking of Babs and coming home. He was thinking of the last time he'd been in prison before this one. It had been for a longer stretch back then and yet the time had passed more quickly. He'd been brooding back then, brooding about a dark night and his first wife Mary, with her clothes disturbed and the scent of sex about her.

He was still brooding on that time when Alan slapped him on the shoulder. He blinked, surprised to see that they were parked outside the railway station.

Tony breathed deeply. He'd missed the tangy air, fresher he reckoned than anywhere else. He took another gulp and another. At last he sighed with satisfaction.

'It's good to be home.'

He suddenly spotted his wife. Babs was crossing the road on her way to the station entrance, unaware that they were watching her.

She was done up to the nines in a black blouse and a check skirt that barely reached halfway down her thighs. OK, she was carrying a bit of extra weight since he'd gone inside – too much for a mini skirt and a button-up blouse. Still attractive, though, and he had been inside for a year and a half – a lifetime as far as the lack of sex was concerned.

'Look at the sight of my missus,' he said out loud. 'You know, Alan, I'd have her right here and now if I could.'

Alan laughed. 'Easy, mate. There's no big rush.'

Alan was right, thought Tony. Tonight was soon enough. Tonight she'd have the full benefit of his bottled-up lust. Tomorrow he'd ask her the name of the bloke she'd been messing around with and after he'd given her a good hiding, he'd go round to give him one as well.

Chapter Ten

It was a Friday night and Rosa Brooks dropped a pan when her son walked through the door.

'You did not tell me,' she exclaimed.

'Yes I did!'

The penny dropped and she threw an accusing look at Babs.

Tony decided to lie. 'A last-minute thing, Mum. Time off for good behaviour, and you know what a good boy I can be when I try.'

Tears in her eyes, Rosa patted her son's face. 'My, my, Antonio, you look so thin. See? Your cheek-bones are so prominent.'

Tony Brooks still wore his hair Teddy Boy style. The deep quiff quivered when he laughed. His side-burns were still coal black and without a trace of grey. The room always smelled of cigarettes and Bryl-creem when Tony was in the room.

His sons stared at him, until the eldest, Arnold, threw his arms around his father's waist.

'Dad. Don't go away again. Promise.'

'Bet your life, son.'

Archie hung back. Eighteen months was a long

time in his young life, but he came round, adding his hug to that of his brother.

Marcie was up in her bedroom when she heard his voice. Her father was home! She had to look her best.

She fetched out her favourite black and white dress, brushed her hair till it gleamed, put on her make-up and then her black patent shoes. A quick glance in the mirror and she was ready to show herself.

Not quite satisfied with leaving her hair long, she pulled it back into a pony tail, then added a pink gingham bow that she'd found up in the attic on the day the boys had moved their beds up there.

She flung open the door to the kitchen.

'Dad?'

Wearing a happy expression, he turned round to face her, the boys still clinging to his waist.

For a moment the happy expression seemed to freeze on his face.

Rosa Brooks saw his eyes and understood. Marcie Brooks looked like her mother.

The look passed. 'Come here!'

Tony Brooks hugged his daughter.

She buried her face in his chest, wrinkling her nose against the strange smell of mould and disinfectant.

'I've missed you, Dad! Promise you won't ever go away again.'

'Promise, darlin'. I promise.'

He said it easily like he said everything easily and

because he spoke so casually people thought he was a pushover. He was enjoying being in the bosom of his family where they didn't know the half of what he did up in London.

Marcie certainly didn't know. He was her dad. She loved him. And he was home.

All the kids got much the same treatment – hugs and reassurance that he was back for good. Later on he gave the boys money for fish and chips and five pounds – a whole five pounds to Marcie.

'Buy yerself something nice. Then put yer glad rags on and go out and have a good time tonight.'

After she'd gone, Tony turned to his mother. His face was like thunder. He pointed at the door Marcie had just gone out of. 'I don't want her going out tonight looking like that.'

'That is how all the girls dress,' his mother responded.

'I don't care how the other girls dress. I'll not have my daughter going out on a night wearing a dress that barely covers her arse. Is that clear? Short skirts make a woman look like a tart.'

Babs butted in. 'Hey, steady on there, Tony . . .'

He spun round on her. 'As for you. I've been hearing rumours while I was in prison. Is there something you want to tell me, Babs? Want to tell me how lonely you've been, or haven't you been lonely at all? Want to tell me about that?'

Chapter Eleven

With five pounds in her hot little hand, Marcie didn't need telling twice to go out, spend on clothes and then go out on the town tonight and enjoy herself.

Heels clattering on the broken pavement, she headed for the phone box on the corner. The door was heavy but her heart was light. The interior of the cramped phone box smelled of stale chips and other things she didn't want to think about. Someone had stuck a blob of pink bubble gum over the slot where the pennies went in. She tore out a page of the telephone directory, wrapped it over the gum and pulled it off. After screwing it up and shoving it to the rear of the box where the directory was stored, she got out her pennies and rang Rita's number.

Even a grotty phone box couldn't dampen her excitement. Her dad was home and he'd given her a fiver. It was so rare she had money for new clothes. It made a change to buying material and getting out the old treadle sewing machine.

Rita was the only person she knew that had a phone. Mrs Taylor answered.

As usual Stephanie Taylor's tone was offhand,

bordering on downright rude. Marcie knew she thought girls from detached bungalows shouldn't mix with girls from Endeavour Terrace, or anywhere else in Blue Town for that matter.

Blue Town was called that because most of the dockyard workers who'd lived there in times past and had painted their front doors blue. The paint was nicked from the old Royal Navy Dockyard. And that, as far as Stephanie Taylor was concerned, said it all.

Rita came to the phone.

'My dad's home,' Marcie blurted excitedly.

'Good for you.'

'He's given me some money to spend on new clothes.'

'How much?'

'A fiver. Isn't that great?'

'Great. I'll get a tenner from my dad and meet you outside Woolworths. Give me twenty minutes.'

Typically for Rita, she would have more money to spend than she did. But Marcie didn't care. She could do wonders with five pounds.

She began making her way into town right away. Excited beyond belief, she would still have started walking even if she hadn't been meeting Rita for another hour. New clothes she could afford, and new clothes she was going to have.

She held her head high as she walked along. Nobody could point the finger and say her dad was in prison now. Not that he would admit to it himself.

'I've been working away for your sakes,' he'd said to the boys. 'See? Look at the money I've earned.'

He'd pulled a bundle of cash from his pocket. The boys had been impressed. Their mother had almost glowed with pleasure. Her grandmother had remained silent and watchful.

At other times she'd seen her grandmother's black eyes flash with the anger of a possessive mother who would hear no wickedness spoken about her son.

'Who are these people who accuse my son? My Antonio is a good boy. He has done nothing to be ashamed of. Nothing at all.'

Rita looked smug when they met.

Marcie plumped for the obvious. 'You've been eating cream cakes, Rita Taylor?'

'No. What makes you say that?'

'You're grinning like a Cheshire Cat.'

Rita's grin widened. 'I'm seeing Pete tonight. There's a party above the Crown in Leysdown. It's Johnnie's birthday. I wasn't going to tell you seeing as you and him had a bit of a fallout.'

'I'm not that easy,' Marcie said hotly.

'That fast?'

'Too fast for me.'

'You're a bit of prude, Marcie Brooks. Get with it. This is the sixties.'

'So people keep telling me,' Marcie grumbled as they walked along. Why was it so difficult to be what she wanted to be at the same time as living up to the modern image?

Rita's mind was already onto other things. She waved two five-pound notes in front of Marcie's face. My dad told me to buy something nice.'

'So let's get spending,' said Marcie. She flashed the fiver. It was difficult to stop herself grinning like a Cheshire Cat herself, so she let it spread unimpaired over her face.

Bouncing with enthusiasm, the pair of them headed for the shops. Sheerness was far from being Carnaby Street; in fact it didn't have half of what a lot of high streets across the country had, but they managed to find new outfits.

Rita bought a purple mini dress with a zip down the front. Marcie thought it made her look like a large Victoria plum, but she didn't say so. Rita felt good in it and that was all that counted. She bought a corduroy cap to match. Rita had a thing about caps.

Marcie bought a pinafore sheath fastened with laces at the front. It looked like suede but wasn't really. She matched it with a yellow polo-necked sweater. The skirt was very short.

'How do I look?' Marcie asked Rita.

'Nice,' said Rita. 'How do I look?'

Rita preened like a peacock, one hand behind her

head, one on her hip just like she'd seen the skinny models do.

'Just like Twiggy,' said Marcie.

It was hardly the truth. OK, the pose was like Twiggy in a glossy magazine, but Rita was more branch than twig.

They made arrangements to meet at eight.

'As long as the bus is on time, I'll be there,' said Marcie.

'No need for a bus,' said Rita. 'My dad said he'll pick you up and take us both there.'

'Fab! And us in our new gear.'

'I'm going to get my mum to trim my fringe,' said Rita. Eyes outlined with black pencil blinked through a straggly fringe.

'Mine stays as it is,' said Marcie.

Like Cathy McGowan on television's *Oh Boy!* Marcie's hair was long and thick, though she was blonde rather than brunette. Her fringe was dead straight and easier to trim than Rita's flyaway wisps.

She bought a Revlon eyeliner pencil and a block of mascara with some of the money. She had everything she needed. Now all she had to do was get ready and go out.

On her way home she bumped into Garth coming from the other direction. He was totally absorbed in eating something big and round. On seeing her, a wide toothy grin split his face in half.

'Look at what I've got!' He shoved what turned out to be a large home-made pie at her. She immediately recognised her grandmother's cooking.

'Auntie Rosa,' he said before taking another bite.

The way he was eating and chewing and talking made her feel slightly sick. Crumbs scattered in all directions. Poor Garth. His mother had probably left him to his own devices for the weekend. He'd got hungry and headed for her grandmother.

'That's nice,' she said and prepared to rush on. She had no wish to linger. 'The man was there too,' Garth added in his slow, deliberate way.

Marcie turned round, her face wreathed in smiles. 'That's my dad, Garth. My dad's home and he's here to stay.

'He's always there,' said Garth.

Marcie shook her head and smiled. Garth was daft. Plain daft.

Chapter Twelve

Marcie loved her new outfit. She turned this way and that in front of the full-length mirror on the wardrobe door.

The short pinafore dress made her legs look even longer. Yep! Cathy McGowan eat your heart out! She looked fabulous – or fab, as Rita kept insisting.

A small speck of mascara had fallen onto her cheek. Using her small finger she brushed it off. Leaning close gave her the opportunity to check her make-up once more before going downstairs. She wanted to show her father what she'd bought. She wanted him to be proud of her and say that she looked pretty. So far he'd seemed a bit distant, although he wasn't like that with the boys. He played pretend boxing with them, and promised to take them to a cricket match, then down to the beach to flick pebbles across the water in a game of ducks and drakes.

He didn't do the same with her. OK, she didn't want to fight with him or play rough and tumble around the floor. But she did want him to warm to her, and for some reason he did not.

The smell of disinfectant and mould pervaded the

kitchen. Marcie realised it was coming from the clothes that Babs was pummelling into the galvanised boiler in the corner. The steam was rising in smelly clouds. Her stepmother's carefully lacquered bouffant hairdo sat deflated, like a bird's nest on her head.

Apart from being smothered in steam, it wasn't often Babs got stuck into housework.

Marcie couldn't help commenting.

'My. Things have changed since me dad came home.'

Babs turned round. 'It bloody well has.'

Marcie's smile froze on her face. Babs was not looking her best – one eye was partially closed, and her lip was split and smudged with blood.

Her father came in from the bathroom at the back of the house. The bathroom was downstairs and next to the outside privy. He'd shaved and had a big bath towel wrapped around his waist.

A wave of embarrassment swept over her. She felt too grown up to be seeing her father like that.

Marcie twirled. 'Do you like it,' she asked, her face bright with pleasure.

He stared at her.

She waited for his reaction, suddenly fearful that it might not be the one she expected.

Suddenly his face was flushed with anger. He pointed an accusing finger. 'What do you think you look like? No daughter of mine is going out dressed like that!'

Marcie felt herself colouring up. She'd taken such care with her appearance.

'This is what I bought with the money you gave me. I thought you'd like it. It's really modern.'

Her voice trembled. Her legs shook.

'Like it? It's what tarts wear. Tarts like her,' he said, pointing a finger at Babs.

Babs kept her head down.

'There was no one,' she muttered. 'No one. It's all lies.'

'Shut your mouth,' her father shouted. 'I'm talking to my daughter. Now,' he said, again wagging the warning finger. 'You go back up them stairs and put on something that doesn't show your knickers. Get it?'

She couldn't remember her father ever speaking to her like this. She caught Babs looking at her, a sly smile on her torn lips.

But Marcie didn't care what Babs might think. It was her father's good opinion she wanted and needed.

She tried again. 'It's the fashion, Dad.'

'I don't bloody care what it is. You're not going out dressed like that! Get back upstairs and put something else on.'

'But Dad—'

'You're only a kid. And I want you back in this house by ten.'

'Ten!'

She felt hot tears stinging the back of her eyes. By ten o'clock things would only just be getting interesting.

She turned on Babs, blaming her for souring her father's mood and his opinion.

'This is your fault, you bloody cow!'

Her father intervened. 'Get back up them stairs, get that warpaint off your face and get into a decent length of frock!'

Frock! Who ever referred to their clobber as a frock nowadays?

She threw a last glower at Babs before going back upstairs. Once up there she looked at her reflection in the dressing-table mirror. The dressing table had three mirrors, a big one in the middle and a smaller one at either side. Three Marcie's from three different angles were reflected back at her. If it hadn't been for the fact that Rita and her father were coming to pick her up, she would have flung herself down on the bed and cried. As it was she got out her black and white dress, the one she had made. It wasn't as short as the one she had on, mainly because her grandmother had supervised the making of it. She wiped most of the heavy make-up off her face hoping it would be enough to pass her father's inspection. Once it was all done, she sat on the bed, not daring to go back downstairs until the Taylors arrived.

Annie was now sleeping in the cot in the corner of her parents' room. Marcie went in there – looking down at her half-sister helped her calm down.

The curtains were drawn against the last of the sunset. Annie looked so peaceful and without a care in the world. Perhaps it might be better to remain a child for ever, she thought to herself. Being sixteen was more difficult than she'd ever bargained for. She'd expected her father to be proud of her, to think she looked pretty. Only now on reflection did she remember seeing his look of surprise when he'd first come home. Oh yes, he'd sent her presents that any teenager would love. But he'd failed to face the truth. She was no longer the little girl he'd doted on. She was a young woman.

Hearing footsteps on the stairs, she went back into her own bedroom and closed the door.

The footsteps crossed the landing. Her grandmother entered the bedroom without knocking and went straight to the wardrobe. As a widow and true to Mediterranean tradition, she always wore black, though the black dress she wore during the day was a different one to the dress she wore in the evening. Whereas her day dress was plain, the one she wore in the evening was trimmed with black beads around the scooped neckline.

She began to speak as she brought her best black dress out of the wardrobe. 'Marcie. Do not be angry with your father. He has not seen you in a while. Now he sees you and is very much afraid.'

Marcie slumped down on the bed. 'He's treating me like a child!'

'He's surprised. You are different than when he went away. You have left school. You have grown. He thinks only of what is best for you and you will do as he says.'

'I am doing that,' Marcie said sulkily, arms folded across the dress she had once loved. How things had changed. It now represented her father's dictate, the suede mini-dress her own rebellion.

Her grandmother seemed to be thinking deeply. The sound of her voice suddenly interrupted her thoughts.

'I presume your stepmother did not tell you she had received the offer of a council house?'

Marcie looked at her in surprise.

'No,' said her grandmother, shaking her head. 'I did not think so.'

Marcie couldn't help smiling. Was that why Babs was sporting the beginnings of a black eye and a split lip? She wondered if they'd always fought and she'd just forgotten how bad it could get. Perhaps she'd been too young to notice or regarded overheard arguments as merely that – arguments, not out-and-out fights.

'Your father will not move from here,' said her grandmother resolutely. 'He will not leave me here alone. This is where he was born. This is where he will stay.'

'So was I – I mean I was born here,' said Marcie. To her own ears her voice sounded far away. Thinking of her birth, she suddenly felt a great urge to ask her grandmother if her father had ever hit her natural mother. Was that why she'd run away? It occurred to her that her grandmother was not the right person to ask. Antonio – Tony Brooks – could do no wrong in her eyes.

'No. You were born in hospital. He brought you here.'

'With my mother?'

Rosa Brooks slammed the wardrobe door and turned the key. She had a tight smile on her face when she turned to face her granddaughter.

'Come along, Marcie. No more questions. Out while I dress.'

Marcie frowned. Her grandmother had never before insisted she go outside while she changed from her day dress – except on those occasions when she asked questions about her mother – as she had now.

Alan Taylor's sleek Jaguar slid to a stop outside the Brooks's place. He kept the motor running while he checked his appearance in the rear-view mirror, combing and patting his hair to hide areas where it was thinning.

He smiled. 'Not bad for your age, old son.'

Satisfied that he was still the ticket, he jumped out of the car, smoothed his hair back one more time and rapped on the door.

Babs answered. The state of her face threw him for a second – not that he was all that surprised. Tony was the sort of bloke who liked to think he was in charge of his family. He got pissed off when anyone tried to prove otherwise. He guessed Babs had been pushing her luck with someone, though she must have kept quiet about their own brief fling – he'd have heard from Tony before this if she hadn't. Full marks to her for keeping her mouth shut. Maybe he should slip her a few quid for that.

'Fell down the stairs, girl?' he said blithely as he breezed into the tiny front room of Tony's gaff.

Babs threw him a meaningful look that he chose to ignore. Now to test Tony's frame of mind.

The bloke who'd helped him with a very profitable job down in Dover came in from the back somewhere.

'Tony! You're looking better, my old china! And smelling like violets,' he said with a wink to denote that he was joking. 'Your girl ready to go out and trip the light fantastic, is she? I've left our Rita waiting down at the Crown in Leysdown.'

Tony looked surprised, but also better at ease. 'She didn't say you were giving her a lift.'

'There and back, old son. Got to make sure they're safe, haven't you. Never know what perverts are about nowadays. I said I'd pick them up and take them home afterwards.'

'Good of you to give her a lift.'

'No goodness about it, mate. Glad to do the favour.'

Everything was OK. Alan had known Tony Brooks for a while and before that by reputation. Not the brightest bloke he was ever likely to meet, though not the thickest either. Alan prided himself on being a good judge of character and hand-picked the blokes he had working for him. He worked out their strengths and their weaknesses, then used them accordingly. He could play blokes like a violinist could play a violin, though more profitably. They carried the can, he reaped the proceeds.

Tony Brooks had one big flaw: his pride. He was the sort who could get well out of order if his pride was hurt. Alan made sure he never dented his pride. Couldn't count Babs of course; just a moment of weakness on his part – a few quid in her pocket would keep her sweet and her mouth shut.

'How about I come with you and we have a pint or two?' Tony suggested.

Alan shook his head. That was the last thing he wanted. 'Can't, mate. Got a little errand to do after dropping off your girl. Could pick you up after though. How about that?'

'Suits me fine,' said Tony, looking and sounding sincerely grateful. 'Gives me a chance to settle in like.'

He threw a meaningful look at Babs. Alan got the gist of it – Tony was making up for lost time and the lack of female company in Wandsworth. Poor cow would have trouble walking by the end of the week. Likely have a bun in the oven as well.

His attention was diverted to Marcie who had just come down the stairs. Sweet sixteen and never been kissed. That was the saying that came to mind, though he was after a bit more than that. Women were glorious no matter what age they were, but there was nothing like a young piece of fruit that hadn't yet been picked.

At the sound of the door opening, he turned round and adopted his most disarming smile. 'And here comes Tony Brooks's little princess. My, my, girl, all the young fellahs in Sheppey are going to be after you. You'll have your old dad out there with a shotgun if you're not careful.'

Tony Brooks responded by saying that his daughter had to be in by ten.

Marcie groaned. 'Oh, Dad. Get with it!'

'Keep yer cheek to yerself!' His eyes, as dark as those of his mother, were wide with warning.

Marcie winced and took a step back. Even Babs looked away. Luckily the kids were out, the baby in bed and Gran Brooks was in the kitchen.

It was Alan who calmed things down.

'Come on, Tony. Give the girl some slack. Tell you what, make it half eleven. I'll pick the girls up at eleven and get your Marcie home by half past. How's that?'

For a moment her dad was reticent, though not for long. It was difficult to refuse Alan anything. He knew how to handle people.

Marcie couldn't believe how 'with it' he was. In fact he was the only proper grown-up she'd met who really understood teenagers. Rita was so lucky.

Tony's expression relaxed as he began to see things Alan's way. 'We . . . ll . . . I'm still not happy about her being out so late, things being the way they are nowadays, but seeing as it's you, it's OK. Just don't think you can make a habit of it, my girl,' he finished, wagging a warning finger before Marcie's face.

Marcie sighed as she finally settled in the passenger seat of the smartest car on the island. She was glad to be out and would have burst into song if it hadn't been for the fact that she'd had to change outfits and scrub off the make-up.

Alan smiled at her. His eyes were shiny and friendly.

'Well? Are you going to thank your Uncle Alan for getting you extra time?'

She managed a self-conscious smile. 'Thanks.'

'Just here. You can kiss me just here,' he said indicating his left cheek.

She darted a quick kiss as directed.

He began to drive.

'You look smashing, by the way.'

Coming from any other bloke his comment might have made her blush. But Alan was her dad's age. And he was so nice and so easy to talk to.

'This old thing,' she said disparagingly. 'I wanted to wear my new outfit. It's suede and looks lovely, but Dad said it was too short. He wouldn't let me wear it.'

'That's a shame,' said Alan. His attention flickered between the road ahead and her. 'Can't have been that short surely. How short was it then?'

'Only a few inches shorter.'

'Show me.'

She placed her hands sideways on to where the hem would have reached. 'That short.'

'I can't tell that well from here what with having to keep my eyes on the road ahead. Fold the hem of that dress up to where you reckon the hem of the other one came to. I'll tell you whether it's too short or not.'

Marcie didn't question his reasons for asking her to do that. He was on her side. There might even be a chance that he'd tell her dad there was no harm in wearing her skirt four inches shorter than the one she had on.

'Like that,' she said.

Alan took his eyes off the road long enough to take in the fact that her legs were long and slim, and that she was wearing stockings and not those terrible tights that women were beginning to get keen on.

'Can't see anything wrong in that. You're young and you've got a gorgeous pair of legs. Show them off. That's what I say.'

He patted the leg nearest him.

'I've got an idea,' he said suddenly. 'What if I was to look after this new outfit for you? I could hide it in the boot of my car and when you wanted to wear it you could give me a ring and I'd come along and pick you up. You could change in the back. Then I could drop you off with our Rita or whoever you're with that night. How would that be?'

'You'd do that for me?' She couldn't believe her ears.

'Course I would. I'll persuade your dad to come round. He will if I've got anything to do with it. Trust me. Do you?'

She looked at him. 'Sorry?'

'Do you trust me?'

She thought about what he'd suggested. She thought about the swift change in atmosphere since her father had come home. What was it that had changed him? She didn't hate him yet, but in time . . . who knows?

Alan noticed her wistful expression. He nudged her arm as though he was her best mate, not her best mate's dad.

'I asked if you trusted me, sweetheart. Well do you?'

'Yes.'

'Go on. Say it as though you mean it.'

'I trust you.'

He looked extremely pleased. 'Right,' he said. 'That's settled. Let's get you to our Rita.'

Chapter Thirteen

The party was being held in the room above the Crown, a big pub at its busiest on a Saturday night.

Johnnie's birthday party!

'Are you sure I'm invited?' she'd asked Rita as they did a last-minute check on their make-up in the ladies.

'Of course you are,' Rita had replied. 'He's expecting you to be there.'

Her manner had been flippant. Perhaps if Marcie had been older and wiser she might have reserved judgement, but she wanted to be invited. She wanted to see Johnnie again.

Her heart was beating in time with the thumping sounds coming from upstairs. The ceiling in the ladies loo was high and had ornate plasterwork along one wall. The rest of it had disappeared long ago when the toilets were first installed.

Bits of loose plaster fell like snow from the ceiling. People up above were stamping their feet to the sound of the Dave Clark Five playing 'Bits and Pieces'.

Coming out of the toilets meant passing the public bar on her way to the staircase. Noise and cigarette smoke poured out of the bar in equal measure each time the door swung open.

A middle-aged woman pushed the door open and held it there. With her free hand she held on to a man of similar age, obviously her husband.

'Alfie Metcalfe, you're coming home! You've had enough!' she barked, her expression not dissimilar to an out-of-sorts bulldog.

Her husband was holding on to the door. 'Bugger off! Give me another pint.'

She tried prising his fingers off. It did no good. Leaving smudgy sweat marks in their wake, his fingers found a new holding place.

Drinkers at the bar turned to laugh at the unfolding spectacle. The door remained open.

'Marcie!'

She peered between the heads of the warring couple. Rita was waving from the bar.

'Wanna pint or a port?' Rita called out.

Pushing between Alfie and his wife, Marcie shouted back that she'd prefer a port and lemon.

'Are you old enough to be in here, young lady?' someone said as she squeezed past.

'Course I am.'

The man was old enough to be her father. His grin exposed broken teeth and bad breath.

'That's alright then. I'll buy you one any time.'

'Shove off!'

There was always the chance of being refused a drink as they were under age. Not that they'd ever let that worry them.

Rita could sink a pint as quickly as a bloke and had the belly to prove it. Marcie preferred shorts of any kind rather than pints.

'Don't know how you do it,' she'd often said to Rita. 'If I drank pints I'd be out on the lavatory all night.'

Pete was leaning on the bar looking the worse for wear. His lank fair hair was hanging in grease-slicked stripes over his forehead and he was having trouble focusing. He waved a hand in a desultory manner.

'I'm out of cash or I'd buy you one,' he said with a stupid grin on his face. Shoving both hands into the pockets of his jeans, he brought out the linings.

'Look,' he said, still grinning. 'Not a penny in the bloody world. Brassic I am. Absolutely brassic!'

Rita intervened. 'Here. Have another,' she said, opening her purse.

She was wearing the plum-coloured dress with the zip down the front that she'd bought earlier. The sight of it almost made Marcie wince with pain. She would so loved to have worn the suede pinafore dress.

Rita didn't appear to notice that Marcie was wearing her familiar black and white number. Wrapped up in her own world, she leaned close and whispered in Marcie's ear. 'Pete wants me to sleep with him tonight.'

Marcie nearly choked on her drink. 'How are you going to work that one? Your dad's coming to pick you up.'

Rita wrinkled her nose as she worked her mind around the problem. Plump fingers drummed against the side of her pint glass. Suddenly she grabbed it, tipped it up and downed the lot.

'I know,' she said, wiping her mouth with the back of her hand. 'He can drop both of us off at your place. I can say I'm stopping with you and then Pete can pick me up from there. Right, Pete?'

Pete didn't look as though he could pick himself up if he fell down, let alone drive a motorcycle to her place and pick Rita up.

'Anything you want, babe,' he slurred.

'You know what I want,' Rita murmured. She laid her head back so it rested on his shoulder. Pete's hand slid beneath Rita's armpit and proceeded to grope her breast and pinch her nipple.

Marcie looked at her drink rather than watch Pete's hand kneading Rita's left bosom.

'For goodness' sake,' she muttered.

'You're just jealous,' said Rita wearing a hurt expression.

'Of what?'

'Me and Pete. We were made for each other. Ain't that right, babe?'

It was obvious from Pete's bleary-eyed expression

that he didn't have a clue what she was on about.

'I don't think Pete's driving anywhere,' Marcie observed. 'Besides, my dad's home. Him and your dad are going to be drinking pals in future. Something's bound to get said, then you'll be in for it.'

Rita shook her head. 'Nah! My dad believes in live and let live. Course he'll be mad at first, but I'll get away with it.' Her face became wreathed in smiles as she cuddled Pete's paw against her breast and gazed lovingly up into his eyes.

Pete's fingernails were black, his hands calloused. Couldn't help it, of course: he worked in a garage, according to Rita.

Pete bent close to Marcie. She winced as a fog of boozy breath smothered her face.

'So! What you giving Johnnie for his birthday?' he slurred, a salacious grin curling his mouth.

Marcie gritted her teeth and held her breath.

'I bought him a card.'

Pete threw his head back. He nearly fell over with the force of his laughter. 'A card! A bloody birthday card!'

She'd bought the card when they'd gone shopping and without Rita seeing. It had seemed the right thing to do.

Pete was not her favourite person. Fist resting on hip, Marcie glared at him. 'And what's wrong with that?'

His breath fell over her again. 'I think he wants to do more than open an envelope, darling.'

Marcie found herself wishing she hadn't come. She'd been angry and mortified when Johnnie had left her at the bus stop, but at least he'd come back for her, otherwise she wouldn't have come tonight.

'I've come to his party! He should think himself lucky for that.'

Pete was frowning as though some sober thought had swum through his muddled brain and was puzzling him. He turned to Rita, his lips brushing her nose as he murmured, 'Is it really Johnnie's birthday? I didn't know that. I should have stood him a pint.'

'Course it is.' Rita laughed. 'Don't you remember?'

There was something about Rita's expression that put doubt in Marcie's mind. Rita did have a habit of bending the truth to suit her purpose. Marcie bristled. Rita was her mate. They'd been at school together and now they worked together. They exchanged make-up, clothes and snippets of gossip, and they'd rarely argued. Things had changed since Pete's appearance on the scene, but if she was really honest with herself Rita had always been much the same.

'Better go on up to this tatty party,' Marcie muttered as she turned away. Again she threaded her way between the Saturday night drinkers, both locals and holiday-makers, determined to acquire at least one hangover before they returned to the job and familiar streets.

Alfie, the man who'd been hanging on to the bar door, was nowhere to be seen. No doubt his wife's persistence had paid off and he was now snoring comatose in his own bed.

When she glanced over her shoulder Rita and Pete were having a snog and oblivious to everything and everybody.

Ignoring the offer of drinks she marched out, her face blazing red. Rita was not the only friend she'd ever have and she certainly wouldn't be her bloody last!

Out in the corridor one of the leather boys had a girl pressed up against the wall. Their lips were suctioned together like a couple of sink plungers.

Another couple were panting and groaning at the end of the corridor almost beneath the stairs and next to the payphone, where it was darker and more private.

She stood and stared. There was something fascinating about watching people doing something so private in a public place. But two strangers doing it weren't so arousing as the vision invoked in her mind – her and Johnnie, entwined, breathless and heaving against each other.

The tingling stayed with her as she made for the stairs.

Pausing halfway up she considered tearing the birthday card in half, but decided against it. She couldn't be sure whether Rita was lying or not.

The room heaved with music and cigarette smoke.

Parchment shades on scattered wall lights diffused the light. A jukebox lit up one corner and the earnest faces of those hanging over it.

'Groovy Kind of Love' had replaced 'Bits and Pieces'. The stamping had stopped, but no one was responding to the slower number as avidly as they had the previous. No one was dancing.

Girls dressed in leather, trying to look tough and unconcerned, talked in small groups, their mouths working chewing gum at the same time as speaking. Girls like Marcie, their hemlines at least six inches above their knees, couldn't hide their interest in the boys. It didn't matter that they were leggy and modern; the leather boys had the look that attracted them.

The girls in leather, faces thick with make-up, threw menacing looks. Their targets were the girls in mini dresses, their hair falling thick around their shoulders, fringes hiding eyes outlined in black liner.

The menacing glares turned en masse on the newcomer.

Marcie ignored both their looks and their snide remarks.

Johnnie wandered over to the jukebox. A group of girls in leather gathered around him, eying him like willing slaves.

So much for their pretence of being tough; they'd do anything for him and probably had.

Tarts! The lot of them!

You're jealous, said a little voice inside her head. It was true. She couldn't deny it.

She overheard the conversation of two girls close by. One of them was writing something in a small diary. 'I've had fifty-three. Wouldn't mind a go with Johnnie though,' she said, her smile directed in his direction. 'He's got a big one. I'd love a go on that.'

Marcie felt her jaw drop. Her face must have been a right picture because one of the girls caught her shocked expression and burst out laughing. 'We're not talking about what you think we're talking about.'

Two other girls giggled.

'It's the bikes we like,' said the girl who had spoken first. She had shoulder-length red hair and a pleasant, round face. A white silk scarf – similar to the one Johnnie wore – was wound around her neck. 'What's your name?'

'Marcie.'

The girl jerked her chin in acknowledgement. 'My name's Suzy.' She did the same chin-jerking motion at the other girls. 'This is Tina and that's Pauline.' The other two nodded a greeting then carried on with their conversation.

It made Marcie feel like an unimportant outsider. She was split between standing there looking stupid or pushing between the girls surrounding Johnnie – almost as though she were claiming him for her own.

'I've got my leg over enough BSAs,' said one of

the girls. 'I'd like a go on a Bonnie. Had a go on other Triumphs, but never on a Bonnie.'

Marcie couldn't believe what she was hearing. She wanted to laugh out loud. They were talking about cadging rides on various makes of motorbikes! Was that right?

'Excuse me . . .'

The girls looked at her in disbelief as she asked the question. Then they burst out laughing. 'Yeah. That's what we do. We see which of us can get a ride on the most bikes. Whoever wins . . . well . . . they win. And that's it!'

She should have guessed. They were like a strange kind of club, all wearing denim jeans, leather jackets and black sweaters.

'You with Johnnie?' Suzy asked.

Unknowingly she had interrupted Marcie's thoughts about how some girls never stopped being tomboys.

Marcie shrugged defensively. 'Not really. What makes you think that?'

Suzy jerked her chin at Johnnie. He was standing watching her. Their eyes met. She sucked in her breath. What now? Give him the card? Toss her head and leave?

And then he smiled.

'Better go and wish him happy birthday,' she murmured.

'If you like,' said Suzy looking more than a little puzzled.

Marcie tossed one side of her mane of blonde hair back over her shoulder. There was no need to be nervous, she told herself. You look good despite the old dress.

She flashed Johnnie a pink-lipped smile and fished the birthday card out of her bag.

'Happy birthday, Johnnie.'

He looked bemused when she gave him the card and even more so once he'd taken it from its envelope. It had a picture of a motorcycle on it plus a pair of crossed fishing rods. She didn't know whether he was into fishing or not, but it was the only card she'd managed to find sporting a motorcycle.

'A birthday card.'

'I didn't buy you a present, but perhaps this will be enough.' She cupped his face with both hands and kissed him. The contact went on longer and deeper than she'd intended. Deep down she didn't want it to stop, but her pride wouldn't let her carry on. She mustn't appear too keen. A boy like Johnnie would take advantage – just like Pete had taken advantage of Rita.

'Well,' he said somewhat breathlessly. 'That was nice.'

Yes it was, but play it casual she told herself.

'I'm glad you think so, but don't think there's

anything more than a kiss coming to you. I've only made this exception 'cos it's your birthday.'

The blue eyes blinked in an amused manner. 'It's not my birthday.'

Marcie was taken aback. 'Oh! Did I get it wrong? Rita said it was and so did your mate Pete.'

At the mention of Pete he burst into laughter. 'Take no notice of him. He was just pulling yer leg – that's all. Stupid sod!'

She wasn't sure whether the stupid sod bit was aimed at her or Pete. She certainly felt stupid. And disappointed. And angry.

'If that was his idea of a joke . . .' she said huffily and took a backwards step. 'Hey,' said Johnnie, reaching for her with both hands.

This whole evening was not turning out as well as she would have liked. First there was her dad not allowing her to wear her new mini dress, now there was Rita and Pete making fun of her.

'I'll kill that bloody cow,' she muttered, already turning on her heel.

'Don't take it so seriously,' said Johnnie. 'It was just a joke.'

Marcie's eyes flashed with anger. 'The joke being that I was supposed to give you something special for your birthday, a lot more than a kiss, in fact. No prizes for guessing what THAT was!'

Livid and smarting, she turned her back on him

and prepared to march off. She was disappointed and what's more she felt a bloody fool! Well Rita bloody Taylor was going to get a piece of her mind!

'Hey!'

She knew he was behind her, following her down the stairs. Although she was hurrying she spared the time to glance at where the couple had been making whoopee under the stairs. They were still there. The girl was patting her hair and making sure her skirt was down where it should be. The boy had his back to her. She heard the sound of a large zip. He was zipping up his jacket.

All over, she thought! Just like her and Johnnie, though in their case it was all over before it had even started.

The crowd in the public bar was spilling out into the corridor. She squeezed through. Someone stepped on the strap of her shoe and pulled it off. She did a rushed hobble to the door and out into the night.

There was a lot of shouting as a new surge of drunks fell out of the public bar behind her. Johnnie was bound to get caught up in that.

Once outside Marcie bent down to adjust her shoe strap. It was still early. Alan Taylor would be picking her and Rita up at eleven thirty. She didn't want to wait that long; neither did she want to go home early.

She weighed up the alternative. The prospect of

going for a drink by herself didn't appeal. The alternative was quickly dismissed, leaving her with nothing else to do but to head for the bus stop and home.

Purple clouds streaked with salmon pink hung low in the sky. The smell of late summer – fish and chips, candy floss, hamburgers and the sea – hung in the air.

Johnnie made a grab for her. His fingers brushed her arm as she jerked away.

'Leave me alone.'

'No. I don't want to leave you alone. If I'd wanted to leave you alone I wouldn't have come back to that bus stop the other week.'

'I managed.'

'So I noticed. Well, there you are,' he said, his tone turning surly. 'A bloke with a Triumph Bonneville don't hold a candle to a Jag when it comes to picking up girls.'

She read the look on his face.

'I was not picked up. It was Rita's dad.'

He looked surprised at that.

'Look,' he said. 'This party was just a general thing we've been having for three years now.'

Her silence and arms stiffly folded across her chest was enough of an answer.

'Pete can't resist a joke. Sorry about that.'

Marcie turned and walked slowly away before stopping and pretending to study the skyline – not that Leysdown had that special a skyline – low-rise buildings that never failed to look vulnerable against the dark water lapping at the beach.

Ice-cream banners flapped in the sea breeze; paper bags rustled in wire bins advertising Lyons Dairy Maid.

'How about going swimming tomorrow?' he said suddenly. 'I've brought my trunks with me. You up for it?'

She thought about tossing her head and telling him to go and take a running jump. Instead she tapped her finger against her lips as though she were thinking it over. The taste of him still tingled on her lips.

She eyed him from beneath her deep blonde fringe. He looked as though he was holding his breath in case she declined his invitation. She didn't.

'Yeah. OK.'

'I'll pick you up from your place.'

She detected the frisson of excitement in his voice.

'You don't know where I live.'

'If you let me take you home tonight I'll know then. Right?'

It was in her mind to tell him to get lost, but she liked the way he looked at her. There was respect in his manner.

'I'll have to tell Rita that I won't be coming home with her. Her dad was going to collect us. In the Jag.'

'OK.'

'What do you mean? OK.'

He shrugged. 'What I said. I'll take you home.'

'I'll have to tell Rita.'

'Go on then.'

Rita was annoyed when she told her. 'What about my alibi?'

'I thought you said your dad didn't care what you did.'

Rita chose not to comment on that particular statement. 'Oh Christ! I'll phone him. I'll tell him I'm staying with one of the girls. You'll back me up, right Patsy?'

The tall thin girl with long ratty hair and a sallow complexion said that she would. 'It'll cost you a pint.'

'Done!'

Rita turned her back on her and shook hands with Patsy.

'I'm sorry.'

Rita wasn't listening. Marcie knew when she'd been given the brush off.

'She's not happy,' Marcie told Johnnie when she got back to him.

'Because I'm taking you home.'

She shook her head. 'No. Because she needed an alibi.'

Johnnie put his arm around her and whistled through his teeth. 'Your mate Rita likes to live dangerously.'

'Is Pete dangerous?' she asked.

She didn't really care. Johnnie's closeness would

make her tongue stick to the roof of her mouth if she didn't say something.

'In a way. Never mind them. Don't know about you, girl, but I've had enough of this party. How about me and you take a walk along the beach?'

She smiled. 'Yes.'

Close and warm they strolled off beyond the beach huts. Tiny lights from hundreds of caravans herded into coastal sites twinkled like fireflies.

'Hang on.'

Johnnie unzipped his motorcycle boots and socks. He also took off his jacket. 'Too warm and too heavy,' he added. He was forced to carry both. The jacket he slung over his shoulder; the boots he carried beneath his arm. He shoved his thick socks into his boots.

Marcie slid her feet out of her shoes. They fitted inside her shoulder bag.

The clouds had fallen like a wad of rolled-up bedding onto the horizon. The stars had come out. The evening that had not started so well now turned magical as they walked and talked their way in one direction along the beach, then changed direction and headed back again. The sand was damp beneath their bare feet.

'Am I forgiven?' he asked her.

'For leaving me at the bus stop?'

'Yeah. There's nothing else to forgive me for is there?'

She shook her head and smiled. 'I can't think of anything.'

'Great. We can kiss and make up.'

'Can we?'

Her voice trembled with laughter.

They turned to face each other.

'I'm sorry,' he said.

His voice was soft.

'Apology accepted.'

He took hold of her hand. They began to walk.

Her hand was warmed by his. Her toes were cooled by the wet sand.

'I liked the card by the way.'

'Even the fishing rods?'

He laughed. 'I've tried fishing. I'm not very good though. You'd starve if you had to depend on me for a fish supper, I can tell you.'

'Chips only?'

He laughed, a big, throaty, infectious sound that got her laughing too.

Time flew. They talked of their families. Marcie told him that her father had been abroad working and had only just come home.

'It was all to do with the Navy,' she said.

Thankfully, he believed her.

'My dad's away at times too. That's nothing to do with the Navy.' He looked away. She fancied he was unwilling to tell her what his father did and she wondered if he too had done something to be ashamed of.

Now the ice was totally broken, it seemed only natural that they should kiss and hug a lot more. By the time they'd put their footwear back on kissing and hugging had become something they just *had* to do.

Johnnie had left his bike in the pub car park. A church clock struck eleven. She'd be home by eleven thirty as agreed with her father. She told herself that it didn't matter that Johnnie would be taking her home and not Alan Taylor. It would be alright; she had to believe that.

Chapter Fourteen

It was gone ten o'clock and Rita had been drinking heavily when she finally got round to calling her father. She told him that she was staying with Patsy, another friend.

'Marcie's got a lift home so there's no need for you to pick her up. Marcie can be a right little tart when she wants to be,' she added with a slurred laugh.

'Sure, sweetheart. That's fine. As long as you're OK,' said her father. Alan Taylor put the ivory coloured phone back in its cradle.

He didn't believe a word of it, of course. He loved his daughter but she could be a right little baggage at times. She knew what she wanted and went after it no matter what anybody else might think. A bit like himself really.

However, that wasn't what had set his teeth on edge. He'd been counting on Rita making up a different excuse for staying late at the party. It would have been a lie, but he didn't care. He would have had Marcie to himself. But maybe Rita was already lying about Marcie having a lift home. Sometimes it was hard to tell with his daughter. It depended whether it suited her to lie.

Stephanie was thumbing through a magazine. A glass of gin and tonic plus a lit cigarette sat on the coffee table in front of her. 'Is your little princess staying out again?'

She said it in a desultory, lazy manner while continuing to study the stick-like fashion models. One was called 'The Shrimp'. Another 'Twiggy'. In Alan's opinion they both had as much charisma as a wire coat hanger. Too skinny by far.

He swigged back his own drink. At the same time his eyes strayed to his car keys.

'She's staying over with a friend. Somebody called Lynette.'

He'd already forgotten what the friend's name was. It didn't matter.

Stephanie picked up her glass of gin and eyed him over the top of it. 'Do you know this girl?'

'Of course I do!'

He congratulated himself on making it sound as though Rita really did have a friend named Lynette. The truth was he didn't have a clue who Rita's mates were – except for Marcie. Marcie was not the sort of girl you could easily forget. She was like her mother – just as irresistible. Even now all these years later he still thought of Mary. Shame she'd never agreed to play ball, but there you are. But with Marcie it seemed he was getting a second chance.

'Where's this Lynette from?'

The cock and bull story was ready and waiting. 'Convent educated, but hey, you can't hold that against her.' Alan laughed at his own joke. Stephanie was unmoved.

'Her old man's a big noise up in Battersea. Owns a big Ford dealership and another forecourt a few miles away dealing in second-hand motors. Well wedged up, he is. I could be doing a bit of business there.'

Stephanie had the face of a china doll – cold, shiny and devoid of any expression except one: aloofness. Stephanie made a hobby of being aloof.

'She's your problem. That girl takes no notice of me at all. Cocky little cow.'

Stephanie's voice was as deadpan as her face.

'You're the one she worships, so you're the one responsible for her. And if ever she brings trouble to our door then it's your fault.'

Alan looked at his watch. He didn't want to argue with Stephanie. Things between them were fragile, but he wasn't ready to tell her to clear off just yet.

'I promised to have a pint with Tony.'

'Please yourself. As long as I don't have to mix with him and that blowsy wife of his.'

Alan narrowed his eyes. Stephanie never had a

hair out of place and was always immaculately dressed. She sometimes forgot that it was thanks to the likes of his graft and employing blokes like Tony that she could have the things she had.

He didn't tell her that he'd already been for a drink with Tony. Living with Steph was claustrophobic at the best of times. She was hardly the only woman in his life, but she kept a nice home and knew how to dress. She looked the part at the legit side of his business and for social events where local bigwigs attended.

'See you later,' he said after collecting his keys from the onyx-topped table in the hallway.

He wasn't sure whether she responded and didn't care. Their golden years were long over.

The inside of the Jag always smelled of leather. The seats were tan coloured. Walnut veneer lined the dash and parts of the door. There was a lot of chrome both inside and out. Alan loved his car. No matter what other car he ever owned in his life, he would always love this one more than any other.

'Better than a woman,' he said to anyone who would listen.

He'd always prided himself on having a feel for cars, one of the reasons he'd started dealing in them from an early age. Things had progressed from there of course; nowadays he had his fingers in other more lucrative pies. But the old respect for a good motor was still there. He normally made it a rule never to gun the engine from cold, but tonight he broke that rule.

Slamming his foot to the floor he hightailed it along the road from the upmarket bungalows of Leysdown to Blue Town and Endeavour Terrace.

There was a light on in a bedroom window when he got there. Rather than rushing in he turned off the engine and sat thinking about the best course of action.

The first option was to go banging on the door and pretend that he'd gone to pick Marcie up but she wasn't around. That should get old Tony worried.

He gritted his teeth at the prospect that the lad on the motorbike was venturing where he wanted to go. So far as he could tell, little Marcie was virgin territory, territory he'd earmarked for himself.

An idea came to him. How about dropping him in the proverbial?

Alan Taylor was good at getting what he wanted without people suspecting what he was up to. Owning a nightclub in London had led to dealing with some of the hardest criminals in the East End. The secret was to appear that you were doing them a big favour when in fact you were only taking care of number one. Oh yes, he was good at that.

'Here goes, my darling,' he said as he swung his legs out of the car.

Tony answered the door, looking as though he'd been sleeping in a chair. Waiting up for his daughter?

You have to trust them, mate, Alan wanted to say, but decided to save that pearl of wisdom for another day. It helped to have a few ready lines in the arsenal of useful platitudes.

Tony blinked. 'Alan.' He threw an expectant look past Alan's shoulder. 'Where's our Marcie?'

Alan adopted the concerned expression he could do so well.

'That's the problem, mate. I don't know. I didn't tell you before but the other week there was a toe rag on a motorbike trying to pick her up. I scuppered his chances driving past when I did. But I saw him again tonight. He forced your Marcie to go with him. I followed as best I could but you know how it is with motorbikes; shot off down between two bollards along by the beach.' He sighed a deep, meaningful sigh. 'Sorry, old son. I lost the bastard.'

His expression a mix of alarm and anger, Tony pushed Alan aside and shot down the garden path like a greyhound from the trap.

'Hold on, mate,' Alan called out behind him. 'What you going to do?'

'Kill the bastard if he lays a finger on my Marcie! I'll fucking kill 'im!'

'Hold on there.'

Alan congratulated himself. He'd easily wound Tony Brooks up into a state. It wasn't just his tall tale about the kid on the motorbike that had done it. Tony could see the same thing in Marcie that Alan saw: she looked like her mother – a *lot* like her mother.

A low rumble of violence sounded in Tony's voice. His look was pure evil. 'Are you taking me to look for her in that road burner of yours or what?'

Alan nodded and kept nodding, anything to calm the stupid git down. 'Course I will. What are friends for?'

At the very moment when Alan turned the ignition key, a single headlight came into view at the end of the terrace.

'Could be who we're looking for,' suggested Alan.

Tony was out of the car before Alan could tell him to calm down. He had no option but to follow. Not that he'd get too involved at first, not until getting involved was likely to work to his advantage.

The bike slowed then stopped.

Alan had been right. Hair tangled over her face, skirt way above her thighs, Marcie alighted from the pillion.

She looked terrified when she saw her father. There was pleading in her eyes when she turned to Alan.

She opened her mouth to explain. Her father grabbed her arm and swung her in a wide semi-circle towards the gate.

'Get into the house. Now!'

It was Johnnie he was after.

'You!'

His shout was enough to wake up the whole terrace.

Johnnie looked at him in disbelief. 'What's the score, mate? There's no harm done. She's home safe and sound.'

Alan managed to catch Tony's raised fist before he had time to use it.

'Steady on, Tony mate. Think of the consequences. Anyway, like the boy said, she's home safe and sound. That's all that matters. Get going, kid,' he said to Johnnie.

'See you tomorrow.' The cheeky little sod blew Marcie a kiss.

Alan saw the kid's grin and guessed it was done on purpose to wind Tony up.

Tony saw it too and was livid. 'You stay away from my daughter! Hear me? Stay away or I'll rip your fucking head from your body!'

'Get going, get going,' Alan repeated.

Bedroom lights were being switched on in some of the cottages. It was only a matter of time before the police were called. Tony couldn't afford that to happen. He'd only just come out of nick. If he went on like this he was likely to end up back inside and Alan didn't want that to happen. Too bloody right he didn't!

As Tony lurched out of Alan's grasp and towards him, Johnnie spun the bike in a half-circle, opened the throttle and roared away.

Marcie's hair had tangled into long strands around her shoulders. It flew out behind her when, wild eyed, she headed for her father, still trying to explain.

'Dad, he didn't do anything wrong. I wanted to go with him. Honest I did. He just gave me a lift home. Rita phoned her dad and told him he was going to—'

'She didn't phone,' explained Alan, not wanting Marcie to explain any further. He lied easily. Rita wouldn't mind. 'Head like a sieve that girl of mine. Still. No harm done.'

Tony didn't notice what was being said. His attention was firmly fixed on his daughter.

'You're not going to meet that boy again and that's that!'

'Yes I am!' she snapped, uncaring of how disrespectful she sounded. 'What are you going to do? Keep me prisoner?'

His meaty paw lashed out and caught her cheek. 'You're just like your mother!'

Face smarting and eyes streaming with tears, Marcie stared at him.

'I hate you!' she shouted. Then she ran off, her feet slapping the broken pavement at the front of the cottages. She heard Alan shouting at Tony to knock it off but she didn't stop running. Her sight was clouded with tears.

The darkness of the back lane felt cool and safe.

No one could see her crying here. No one could hear her sobbing.

Squeezing her eyes shut she tried to reason what had gone wrong. She'd been so looking forward to having her father home, to being like everybody else. It was bad enough not to have a mother. Her father was supposed to have made up for that.

She thought of Babs and her cut lip. How long before she sported the same?

A cold breeze sent the weeds and rubbish rustling around her feet. Footsteps sounded from the end of the lane. They sounded quick and heavy. Her first thought was that her father had come to fetch her. He was likely still angry, still intent on having her do what he wanted, not what she wanted.

Her heart began to race. She flattened herself against an old stone wall. It wasn't that cold an evening except when the breeze clocked in. All the same, she shivered.

'Marcie?'

The sound of Alan's voice calmed her. She sighed with relief and her whole body began to relax like a rag doll with too little stuffing.

'Here,' she said breathlessly.

It was dark and she could barely see his face, but she could smell him – a mix of expensive cologne, good clothes and cigars.

'Never mind, sweetheart,' he said gently as he

pulled her against him. 'Your Uncle Alan will kiss everything better.'

His voice was soothing. She sobbed against his chest as he stroked her hair and patted her head.

'It's going to take time for your old man to adjust to life outside. But don't you worry. He won't be doing stir again. Not if his mate Alan Taylor's got anything to do with it. But remember this: your old man's his own worst enemy. He can't help what he is and deep down he loves you. Honestly he does.'

There was truth in Alan's words. Her dad was flawed; far from perfect. She wished with all her heart that he could be more like Alan.

'I wish I had a dad like you,' she blurted.

He laughed, a low self-conscious laugh. He said it was nice that she thought so.

'I mean it.'

Alan even smelled different: fresh, clean and expensive. Tony Brooks tried his best to emulate his better-off friend, but failed. His sand-coloured suit might look similar but it was cheap, a snip in the summer sale at the fifty-bob tailors. On top of that he smoked like a chimney and smelled like an old ashtray. But he was still her dad even though he'd changed. In an effort to rekindle old feelings, she reminded herself that he'd sent her presents each time he went away. Sometimes he'd been in prison. Sometimes he'd been in London working for people he knew. Being younger back then, all she'd cared about was him coming home.

'He shouts at me more than he used to. Is it because I'm grown up? Is that why he's like he is?'

Alan patted her back as he held her close against his fresh-smelling cashmere sweater.

'There, there, now.'

She closed her eyes, felt herself drifting away and imagined him smiling as gently as he was speaking.

At first the words seemed to float over her head. And then she heard them – heard what he was really saying as her brain made sense of them.

'You being grown up now has got a lot to do with it, that and the fact that you remind him of your mother.'

Her eyes snapped open. 'My mother.'

His comment surprised but also pleased her.

'I can't remember her. I can't remember what she looked like and there are no photographs. They're not allowed.'

She couldn't see his face clearly; she merely guessed that he was taken aback.

'Why is that?' she asked in a forlorn voice.

He paused as though taking an extra breath before answering.

'Your dad must have good reason.'

'They said she ran away with another man. Would my mother do that? Would she?'

Again that hesitation.

'I don't know, Marcie. Honest. I don't know.'

'But I want to know,' Marcie said forlornly. 'I want to know where she is. I want to know whether I really do look like her.'

'You do. Honest. No matter what she was or she wasn't, you're just as gorgeous as she was and I think you bring back a few aching memories,' Alan added.

Mention of her mother suddenly made her less aware that her face was stinging. 'I want to know what happened when she went away. Who did she go away with?'

'I don't know. Honest, Marcie, I don't know. Now come on. I'll take you home. I presume the back door's locked so we'll have to go round to the front.'

Marcie hesitated. She was thinking of her mother. No matter how hard she tried she couldn't visualise her features. Sometimes in the night she lay in bed trying so hard to remember. Some tiny things came back, but for the life of her she could not see her mother's face.

'I don't remember her and I feel I should.' Her voice teetered on the edge of a sob.

Alan attempted to reassure her.

'Now, now. No need to worry. Everything's going to be fine. I've had words with your dad. If he ever lays a finger on you again then you tell me and I'll sort him. Right?'

'Right.' She smiled at him through her tears. 'If you think so, Mr Taylor.'

'If anything really bad happens, you know you can live with me.'

She was so grateful for his kindness that she didn't notice he'd used the singular; she could live with *him*.

He kept his arm around her all the way back. Every so often he squeezed her a little more tightly.

'Just like your mother,' he said softly. 'And call me Alan. Just Alan.'

Marcie liked him saying that and liked the closeness and the fact that he stood up for her. She wished her father was the same, though it no longer seemed to matter quite so much. At least she had someone to run to, someone who cared.

In order to give her parents some privacy, Annie and her cot had been moved back into the room Marcie shared with her grandmother.

Assured that her grandmother was fast asleep, she knelt at the side of the baby's cot, her fingers entwined around the bars.

The baby was fast asleep, her tiny hands clinging to a small brown teddy bear that one of the boys had won at the fairground. She looked so small, yet so peaceful. Suddenly Marcie found herself envying her for one thing above all others.

'At least you know your mother – even though she's not much cop.'

The bravado with which she'd voiced the comment swiftly died. She bit her lip and a tear squeezed out from the corner of one eye. She brushed it aside, but the thought that came with it wouldn't go away. It needed to be said out loud if only in a whisper.

'Know what, Annie? I'm going to find my mother. Yeah! That's what I'm going to do.'

Annie made a snuffling sound in her sleep.

Marcie smiled. 'God bless,' she said softly, went to her bed, undressed and fell asleep.

Rosa Brooks, supposedly asleep, had heard Marcie's heartfelt vow to find her mother.

Over my dead body!

She could not allow that to happen. Much as she loved her granddaughter there were other family members she loved just as much. Her son, Antonio, she loved above all others. She could not allow him to be hurt.

Chapter Fifteen

It was gone eight o'clock the next morning and Marcie was wiping dishes. As she wiped she watched her father follow her grandmother down the back garden to the chicken run. Her grandmother was carrying a small axe.

The axe was frequently waved to emphasise whatever it was her grandmother was saying. She wondered if they were discussing her.

By the time they came back to the house her father's hands were buried deep in his pockets. His chin almost touched his collar bone – he was hanging it that deeply.

Her grandmother was carrying a dead chicken in her right hand, the bloodied axe in the other.

Marcie guessed that her grandmother had given him a tongue lashing. She wanted to smile at that. Perhaps unknowingly she did. Her father glared at her sidelong as he passed.

The atmosphere was electric. She guessed he didn't want her to go swimming, but her grandmother had persuaded him to let her go.

The other thing that helped matters along was

that clouds were totally absent from the sky. A summer day had dawned though the year was swiftly sliding into autumn.

Adding more joy to the day, Alan Taylor's sleek green Jag pulled up outside. Rita got out and rushed through the front gate, leaving it thrashing around behind her. She was wearing a turquoise mini skirt with a crocodile leather belt and ankle-strap shoes. Another figure sat in the front passenger seat: Stephanie, Rita's mother.

'Come on, Marcie. Get your costume. We're going to the beach. And the boys will be there,' she added in a conspiratory whisper.

'And last night?' Marcie questioned.

Rita giggled. 'I got in at three this morning.'

'Did your dad go mad?'

'No. He wasn't home either. Steph was, but what the hell . . . it's no business of hers.'

It continued to be a mystery to Marcie how Rita managed to get away with what she did. Her parents let her do anything. Marcie looked hesitantly at her own father, asking with her eyes before even daring to open her mouth.

His lips cracked into an insincere smile. 'Go on. Enjoy yerself. You're safe enough with Alan.'

And that was it. He was agreeing to this because Alan was here to look after her. Not that she was going to look a gift horse in the mouth. Two minutes and she had costume and bath towel. She'd also managed to change from jeans into the suede pinafore dress and a pair of snow-white elastic knee-length boots. Neither the dress nor boots were exactly suited to the beach, but she didn't care. Damn her father. She was going to wear her new outfit despite him. She ignored his grimace, sure she could get away with it.

Out in the car Stephanie Taylor looked at Marcie as though she had the smell of drains under her nose. 'Look at that bloody skirt. And those boots. Tart's boots. That's what they are. Tart's boots!'

'You should know,' said Alan. He threw her a warning look.

Stephanie swiftly changed the subject. 'Wouldn't have been so bad if you hadn't insisted we brought a packed lunch.'

'A picnic!' Alan exclaimed. 'What could be better on a day like this?'

'I hate picnics. I hate beaches. I hate sand. It gets everywhere.'

Alan leaned closer and whispered in her ear. 'So why the fuck did you come?'

He hadn't planned to bring her. His plan had been to have a day out with the girls. Rita would have done her own thing – he knew she had a boyfriend. That daughter of his was an open book and he'd have been more than happy if she went off with her bloke.

Her going off meant he could have had Marcie to himself. As it was, Stephanie was the proverbial gooseberry – and just as prickly.

He watched Marcie, her long legs in those shocking white boots kicking out behind her as she ran to the car. Just like her mother. What the hell had Mary Morse been thinking of marrying Tony Brooks, he'd never know.

Stephanie came out with what he was thinking. 'She looks like Mary.'

He pretended to be offhand. 'A bit, I suppose. Can't say I noticed.'

The last thing he'd wanted was for her to notice that. It unnerved him only momentarily. Nothing could throw him off the course he'd planned. Nothing at all.

The two girls had laughed when they'd ran down the garden path to the car. The car was only two door, so Rita's mum had to get out of the front seat to let them clamber into the back.

The leather was warm and filled the car with its own particular smell.

Marcie said hello to Alan Taylor, being careful to call him mister. She also said hello to Rita's mum who she would never ever call anything except Mrs Taylor. Stephanie always looked so sour.

Alan Taylor responded with undisguised exuberance.

'Glad you could come, Marcie. Lovely day for the beach.'

Rita's mother was as icily polite as the inside of a fridge. Once she was sitting back down she folded her arms and stared at the road ahead.

'Well! Let's get going then,' she snapped.

'Temper, temper,' Alan muttered.

Marcie wondered whether they'd had a row. None of your business, she thought to herself. Anyway, Rita's mum was a funny cow at the best of times.

The beach was crowded, with everyone taking advantage of the fine weather, the last they were likely to get at this time of the year.

Babies in pushchairs were being trundled over the damp sand. Teenagers were everywhere accompanied by the tinny blast of pop music picked up from Radio Caroline. It was a well-known fact that the pirate radio station, so proud of the fact that they were cocking a snook at Government taxes, were rolling around on an old ex-dredger somewhere beyond the three-mile limit.

As they entered the water, shrieking at the sudden shock of coldness, Rita and Marcie waved at the Taylors, both of whom had opted not to enter the water. Alan was quite affable about it.

'Count me out, darlings. I don't mind floating on top of it or having a hot bath in it, but I don't do swimming.'

Rita turned to her mother. 'I don't suppose you want to come in, do you.'

It was a statement rather than a question.

'No, I bloody well do not,' returned Stephanie. 'The sand's bad enough without getting my hair soaking wet.'

She'd brought a pile of magazines with her, picked up one and began to read.

It seemed totally unnatural, but Marcie sensed there was no love lost between mother and daughter. She couldn't help wondering if things would have turned out like that between herself and her mother. Hopefully not, but then how could she be sure about someone she'd never known?

Shielding her eyes against the glare of sunlight on sea that was usually grey, she looked to where a group of teenage boys were swigging from bottles of Coke. They didn't notice her as their eyes were fixed on a group of mods. The mods were playing it cool, which was difficult when dressed in fur-lined Parka jackets. Sunlight sparkled on the mirrors sprouting like cabbage leaves from the fronts of their scooters.

Her gaze moved back to the rockers. Hard as she tried she couldn't see Johnnie.

They were out of earshot of Rita's parents, sitting on a low wall eating ice creams. The distance was safe enough for Marcie to ask her if she'd arranged to meet Pete.

Rita chortled. 'Well, I'm not here to build bleeding sandcastles, am I?'

'Knowing you, Rita, it's not likely.'

'Not bloody likely at all,' said Rita, almost choking over the very thought of it. 'Pete said he'd be here. I dream of him all the time, you know. I even dreamed of him before I actually met him. Funny that.'

'Have you got some kind of instinct that tunes you into a bloke you fancy? Is that it?'

'My dreams always come true,' Rita said smugly. 'Witches run in our family.'

Marcie's first thought was of her grandmother and her herbs and superstitions, but then she cast a curious glance over her shoulder to where Rita's mum was spreading out food and drink on a grey army blanket.

Rita saw where she was looking. 'Not that old cow! I mean my real mother.'

'Your real mother!' Marcie couldn't believe what Rita had just said. 'Are you having me on?'

Rita shook her head. 'No. Course not. My mum died. Dad married Steph when I was really little because he thought a girl should have a mother figure. It was alright early on, but now she's just a pain in the ass.'

An instant thought came to Marcie that witches weren't the only thing running in Rita's family. Rita told tall stories. And she didn't like being outdone. Strange as it might be, Marcie not having a mother was something to be equalled, or even bettered.

On the other hand Stephanie not being Rita's real mother explained a lot. It was Alan who took full responsibility for his daughter. Stephanie only put her oar in now and again, though her advice was rarely heeded.

The day was too perfect. Marcie decided not to spoil it and to take what Rita had said as the truth.

'Do you ever think how it might have been if she was still around? Your real mother I mean,' said Marcie.

'Yeah. I fancy having somebody to go shopping with and have secrets with.' Rita said it a little sadly. 'But then,' she said, her face suddenly wreathed in smiles, 'I wouldn't be able to twist me dad round me little finger then, now would I?'

'I wish my mother was around,' Marcie said wistfully. 'I wonder where she is. I wonder what she's doing.'

'Does she ever get in touch?' asked Rita.

Marcie shook her head. The act of mulling over the question had left what felt like a lump of lead in her throat. 'No. Never. You'd think she would, though, wouldn't you.'

'Depends,' said Rita. 'Might have a new family or be living in some other country. Like America! I'd like to live in America,' she said throwing back her head and looking up at the sky. 'It seems a lot more exciting than Sheppey.'

Marcie squinted against the harsh light shining from the sea. Rita wouldn't know that what she said had hurt her. She didn't like the thought of her mother having a new family. How could she possibly think more of them than she did of her? And she must think more of them seeing as she never enquired after her daughter. There'd been a film on at the local fleapit where a woman had lost her memory and couldn't remember that she'd once been married and had a child. Perhaps her mother had lost her memory too and didn't know who she was. It was a thin hope and yet Marcie wished desperately that it was true.

She voiced her desire out loud. 'I wish I knew where she was. I'd go and see her.'

'But you don't, so that's that.'

Rita's exclamation sounded so final, so curt. Marcie was having trouble dragging her thoughts back from a dark void that she couldn't quite see into. She wanted to see her mother again. She wanted her mother to want her. She sighed. There was no cure for the feeling of emptiness she sometimes felt. All she could do was forget the past and live in the present.

Meanwhile, they'd changed into their swimming costumes. Marcie threw off her towel.

'Race you!'

She dashed off before Rita could get up from the wall they'd been sitting on. Her kicking feet left a shower of grit and pebbles in her wake.

The water was cold. On first contact it took her breath away. There was a swimming platform some way out, perhaps 300 feet. Marcie prided herself on getting there first. Rita followed but was puffing and blowing by the time she made it.

A group of boys were already there along with two or three girls. The boys were lean and had the first beginnings of contoured muscles. The girls pretended not to be self-conscious. Through the wetness running down her face, Marcie recognised Suzy, one of the bike girls she'd met at the Crown.

'Nice day,' said Suzy.

'Yeah. Real nice,' said Marcie.

It occurred to her that Suzy was far too staid to be a leather girl – or whatever it was the girls called themselves. Suzy was wearing a red bikini. Marcie wished she had a bikini – her black one-piece that she'd worn for swimming lessons at school seemed so old-fashioned in comparison.

Someone wearing a pair of blue swimming trunks crouched down beside her. A kiss she recognised landed on her cheek.

Her heart skipped like a thrown pebble. Johnnie was here!

He grinned, looking pleased with the fact that he'd taken her by surprise. 'You made it.'

With his help she heaved herself up onto the platform.

Droplets of water dripped from his wet hair and into her eyes. She laughed as he yanked her more vigorously forward and into his arms. Again she felt his lips on her cheek. He only briefly moved to her lips.

'People are watching,' she whispered. 'Rita's parents are on the beach.'

They sat with their legs in the water. Rita had found Pete. He'd tried pulling her aboard like Johnnie had pulled her. Twice he tumbled into the water before both he and Suzy dragged her on.

Rita's shrieking laughter caused Marcie to glance over in time to see that Pete had yanked open the front of Rita's costume and was peering inside. If Johnnie did that to me I'd be mortified, she thought. But Johnnie hadn't.

'They'll end up getting married if they carry on for long like that,' observed Johnnie.

Marcie wasn't so sure and said so.

'If he gets her up the duff, they will,' Johnnie pointed out. 'Her old man is bound to make sure of that.'

'You could be right. Alan's a very kind person. My dad would have killed you if it wasn't for him.'

'Nah!' said Johnnie shaking his head. 'I'm too fast for your old man. Open the throttle and I was gone!'

'OK, show off. But you're right. Alan would make sure Rita was taken care of if she did get pregnant, and that includes making the bloke marry her.'

'Is that so?'

'Definitely.'

'Would you marry me?' he asked suddenly. 'Even if you didn't have to,' he added.

She felt herself colouring up, laughed and tossed her head so that fronds of wet hair flicked across her face. 'Now there's a question to ask a girl you've only just met.'

'We've met a few times,' he countered, sounding quite hurt.

'Not that many.'

'You still haven't answered my question.'

'Which was . . . ?'

'Would you marry me – even if you didn't have to?'

'I'll think about it.'

His smile disappeared and a dark almost wild look chilled his dark-blue eyes. 'It doesn't matter much. I wasn't really being serious.'

She sensed by the sudden petulance around his mouth that he hadn't liked her answer. Johnnie was used to girls fawning over him, agreeing to anything he said. She was under no illusions – they mostly said 'yes' to him no matter what it was he was asking.

Deep down she knew she was no exception. That was the way Johnnie got to you. He was like Brando in *The Wild Ones*, good looking, petulant and a challenge to tame. No girl could resist.

Marcie tried. She told herself that she wasn't

besotted, so why did she want to please him? Why did she so readily speak the words she thought he wanted to hear?

'I knew you were only joking. If I'd thought you were being serious I would have said yes.'

She laughed and his look brightened. Marcie suspected that women would pander to Johnnie's every need all his life. Any girl who did marry him would have a lifetime of other women wanting him.

Jealousy was not a familiar emotion, but still it came. Deep down she realised that if she wanted him she'd have to live with it. Johnnie was irresistible to women and what was more, he knew it!

Stephanie Taylor watched the young people out on the swimming platform through red-rimmed sunglasses.

'They're with boys,' she observed.

Alan merely grunted.

Stephanie adjusted her sunhat. She hated to burn. In case the sunhat wasn't enough to keep her pale and interesting, she was sitting beneath a large pink and white sunshade.

'That boy Rita's with is taking a few liberties.'

'Only natural,' murmured Alan against the rim of his hat. Unlike Stephanie he adored the sunshine. Luckily he browned easily and knew he looked good with a tan. A brown skin emphasised his white teeth – and made him look like Alan Ladd, he always thought.

He was lying flat out on a blow-up lilo bed, his straw Panama pulled over his face, arms folded behind his head.

'What are you going to do if Rita gets knocked up?' Stephanie asked him.

'Deal with it.' Alan shifted his body as though what she said had made him feel uncomfortable. 'Now cut the rabbit, will you? I'm trying to get some kip.'

He was only pretending to sleep. The sight of Marcie in that short skirt and white boots was the stuff of fantasy. He'd been pretty discrete watching her as she peeled her kit off and revealed the swimming costume beneath. The end result had been worth waiting for, though to see her in a bikini would have been even better.

Chapter Sixteen

The rain that had started on the Monday after the trip to the beach continued through Tuesday. Wednesday saw it pausing for breath and a glimmer of sun peering from behind the thick clouds that rolled in like coal dust from the North Sea.

Marcie arrived home at six and went straight through to the kitchen. After shaking the rain from her coat she hung it behind the back door to dry off.

The two boys were sitting at the big square table in the middle of the kitchen, eating bread and jam.

'Where's Gran?'

'Down with the chickens,' said Archie between bites of jam sandwich.

The stew simmering on the gas ring left a steamy haze over the kitchen window. Marcie rubbed at the misted pane and looked out. She could see a small figure leaning over the chicken run and heard the squawking and flapping of the birds.

Babs came in from work looking disgruntled. Her bouffant was plastered to her head in a sticky mass like a broken pancake. Her mascara ran in black rivulets down her cheeks.

'Bloody rain,' she muttered.

Once her coat was shaken and had joined Marcie's behind the door, she turned her attention to the children.

Baby Annie was strapped firmly into her high chair. There was raspberry jam around her mouth and a sticky pink goo was running down her chin. The reason for this was that Arnold was letting her take turns to suck a large pink gobstopper which he held between finger and thumb.

Babs fetched him a belt around the ear. 'Oi! Stop that! She's only a baby. You'll choke her, you silly sod.'

Alarmed by the sudden loud voice, the baby started crying and slid to one side. Babs gave her a bottle. 'Drink that.'

Marcie started to get the plates out plus a large tin loaf ripe for slicing into thick doorsteps.

Her dad came in just as she was stirring the soup. He was working for Alan Taylor. 'Charge hand,' he responded when asked what his job was. 'Like a foreman. I'm in charge of other blokes,' he explained when Arnold had pressed him.

Marcie felt her father's eyes on her.

'Going out tonight?' he asked.

There it was again, that forced good humour that set her teeth on edge. It was so false. Not like Alan who really meant what he said and had her best interests at heart.

'Might be,' she replied in an absent-minded manner.

'Should go out, girl,' he said.

He'd been doing his best to make amends for his former behaviour, for slapping her. Marcie remained reticent.

His mock joviality failed to impress and he knew it. She didn't care if he looked crestfallen when she continued to freeze him out. Her father had let her down. His feeble attempts at making up merely left her cold. There was also that nagging question at the back of her mind: where was her mother? Was he telling the truth about her going off? The trouble was she couldn't quite bring herself to ask him outright and couldn't work out whether it was because of how he might react or her fear of the truth.

He tried again. 'Here. I've got ten bob in my pocket. You can have it. Go out. Enjoy yourself.'

His eyes followed her hand as she reached for the bread knife. 'What you going to do with that?'

'Slice bread. Gran's busy.'

'Where is she?'

'She's out killing the chickens,' young Arnold interceded. 'She's taken her chopper, the little one she uses to chop the chickens' heads off.'

'Bags I get a butcher's at that,' cried his bright-eyed younger brother. His skinny legs had been dangling from a chair while he stuffed a doorstep-sized jam sandwich. Archie loved food but remained as skinny as a rake.

His father grabbed him. 'Not so fast, son. What the hell is your gran thinking of, out killing a chicken just before we have our meal?'

Arnold took on a self-important look as he explained. Shoving the gobstopper over to one side of his mouth where it bulged against his cheek, he said, 'She's doing away with all the chickens and their house, and reckons she's going to grow peas and beans. I don't like vegetables very much, especially beans. Do you think we could dig a big hole when the chicken house is gone and have a nuclear shelter instead, like Mr Ellis? We could if she burns it down like she says she's going to.'

'Bloody good job,' Babs sniffed, most of her attention fixed on filing her thumbnail.

Tony's dark features stiffened. 'What the bloody hell . . .'

No one really understood why he wrenched the back door open so forcibly, sending it crashing against the wall.

Marcie was curious and made a move to follow. Babs got to the door before she did.

'Don't go out there. Take my advice: never get between mother and son. You'll only live to regret it.'

There was no way Marcie was going to take orders

from her stepmother. She wrenched the door from her grasp. 'Don't tell me what to do!'

She dashed out.

'Wilful little cow!' Babs shouted after her.

Her grandmother was gathering up the half dozen birds she'd killed, their claws sticking through her fingers like yellow twigs. Her son, Marcie's father, was a picture of agitation, a look of absolute dismay on his dark, rugged features.

'But you've always had chickens, Mother. You always said we'll eat well if we keep chickens.' He sounded dismayed, even puzzled.

'That was in the years after the war,' she said without turning to acknowledge his presence.

She straightened, rubbing her aching back with one hand despite the meat cleaver she still held in it.

'We had to grow and rear our own food back then. We do not need to keep chickens now. They make too much noise in the morning and people are beginning to complain.' Her eyes seemed to light up when she looked at him. 'It is nothing for you to concern yourself with. They are my chickens. It is my shed. I will do with it as I please.'

He frowned when he saw Marcie. 'What are you doing out here? Get on in.'

She stood her ground. 'The boys said Gran was getting rid of her chickens. Is that true, Gran?'

She didn't add about wondering why he'd dashed out at the news. Why should he get concerned over dead chickens? Her grandmother had been raising and killing chickens for years.

Tony Brooks turned back to his mother, a fearful look in his eyes.

'But there's no need to burn the coop down,' he said, slapping the side of the hutch. 'It's a strong old lot. I could use it to keep tools in and the lawn-mower.'

She noticed he was using the same forced light-hearted tone he'd used with her in the kitchen.

Her grandmother noticed something else. 'We have not got a lawnmower. I cut the grass with a pair of shears.'

'I'm going to get a lawnmower,' he blurted out. 'I was only thinking about it the other day. Save you getting down on your knees, Ma. But I will need somewhere to keep it. This shed should do the job nicely.'

It occurred to Marcie that her grandmother was fixing her son with a very suspicious eye. Her father saw it too, blinked and looked away. There were few people who could meet a look from Rosa Brooks. She had a way of eyeing people that made them feel naked, as though she were reading their thoughts.

'Everything is arranged,' said Rosa Brooks.

She went on to inform him that the chickens were

already sold – her grandmother was shrewd enough to make sure she could dispose of them before she'd killed them.

'You're not plucking and drawing them tonight!' Tony said with a grimace.

'Yes. Once I have eaten my meal.'

Rosa Brooks was true to her word. She had six chickens to prepare for her customers and at ten shillings and sixpence a time she certainly wouldn't leave them to waste. 'Chickens are best plucked when they're warm,' she pointed out.

Later on after they'd eaten she asked Marcie to get her chair from the front room. 'I was using it to hang up the clean curtains after I'd washed them.'

The same rickety old chair that she sat on outside the back door to do her knitting had many uses, hence being used as a stepladder for hanging curtains.

Just for a change Babs had put young Annie to bed herself. Marcie's father was sitting at the kitchen table reading a newspaper, though it looked as though he was having trouble concentrating.

The two boys were preparing to assist their grand-mother.

'I like pulling out the giblets best,' said Arnold, rolling up his shirtsleeves.

Archie said he preferred the feathers.

When Marcie went to collect the required chair

Babs was standing in the middle of the room quietly contemplating the right-hand alcove to the side of the fireplace.

'What are you doing?'

Babs was startled at first. 'That wasn't funny! What you doing spying on me anyway?'

'I wasn't spying.' Marcie went to the window where the chair had been left. 'I came for this. Gran wants it so she can sit outside and do the chickens.'

Babs sniffed. For once she seemed placated. 'That's alright then. Just don't tell her you found me in here,' she added somewhat worriedly. 'Promise?'

Marcie frowned. Babs had never been easy to deal with. Hostility had always simmered between them. 'Why should I promise?'

Babs made a face. 'Look. There's something that I want to buy. I was just in here looking to see where it will go. I've decided on that place there.'

She pointed to the alcove.

Marcie was curious. 'What are you buying?'

Babs grinned and her eyes sparkled. 'Promise you won't tell? I'll gladly tell you if you don't tell. I know you'll be pleased.'

'OK. Tell me.'

Babs took a deep breath. 'I'm going to buy a radiogram. A Pye radiogram. A Black Box they call it. It's all glossy wood with thin black legs. What do you think about that then?'

'With a record player?'

'Of course it'll have a record player. Wouldn't be a radiogram without one, would it!' She sounded indignant that Marcie might have presumed otherwise.

'Right.'

Marcie headed out of the door without committing herself to secrecy. Babs grabbed her arm.

'Don't tell your grandmother. And don't tell your dad. Right?'

Marcie chewed her bottom lip as though she were thinking about it. 'Right,' she said at last and Babs was happy.

She wondered how come her stepmother was able to buy something so expensive.

'There you are, Gran.'

Her grandmother settled herself on the chair. The boys hunkered down. Arnold waggled a chicken leg at her.

'Yuk! Boys are so disgusting.'

'We are being watched,' said her grandmother.

Marcie looked around her.

'At the back gate,' said her grandmother.

Someone large and awkward was peering over the back gate. Realising he'd been discovered, he backed away then dipped back again, his head appearing around the side of a straggling buddleia.

'Garth. The boy is lonely.'

Her grandmother's voice broke into her thoughts. Her lips had barely moved and the fingers nimbly plucking feathers did not pause. Neither did she look up.

Rosa Brooks had often told her that you didn't need to see people to know they were close. You could sometimes feel them.

The last thing Marcie wanted was Garth following her around in that persistent and pesky manner of his.

'I fancy a night at the pictures,' she said, pulling thoughtfully at a strand of long blonde hair. She was contemplating going by herself if she had to. Without Garth seeing her she could dash out through the front door – he wouldn't be able to get round from the back lane in time to follow her.

As usual her grandmother was in tune with her thoughts. 'Take Garth with you. Remember that good deeds done on earth are remembered in heaven.'

It was far from Marcie's thoughts, to be remembered in heaven. Hoping by some chance Johnnie had stayed on in Sheerness was her uppermost thought.

Babs chose that moment to poke her head out of the back door. 'Marcie, love, can you look after Annie, only me and your dad want to go down the pub? There's a darts game tonight and he fancies his chances.'

Her wheedling voice was annoying, but that's how she could be when she wanted something done.

'You're too late,' said Rosa Brooks. 'I have given Marcie five shillings to take herself and Garth to the pictures.'

'Oh!' Babs's face dropped. 'Well . . . I put her to bed—'

'Once Annie is asleep you may follow your husband to the pub.'

Marcie pulled on a coat with a big collar and turned it up around her face.

Newly shaved, her father came out of the bathroom at the back and regarded her quizzically.

'Bit warm for a big coat, our Marcie.'

She snuggled her head down inside the collar. 'It might rain later.'

What if any of her friends saw her out with Garth on her way to the pictures? Hopefully nobody would see her once she was inside and cloaked by darkness. She couldn't bear the leg pulling she'd get if they did.

The coat she wore covered the very short suede pinafore. Her dad looked her up and down before turning and making his way back to the bathroom to finish his shave.

That was something she'd got away with! Garth was a burden she had to bear. She groaned inwardly, her fingers playing with the coins her grandmother had given her.

Garth was already waiting at the front gate.

'We're going to the pictures, Garth.'

She swept straight past him. Best if he walked behind a bit.

'Is it a cowboy?' he asked excitedly, his gangly legs and shuffling gait struggling to keep up with her.

'I don't know.'

Marcie could have kicked herself for not checking what was on.

With a bit of luck it might be a love story, she thought, as she hurried along with her head buried in her coat collar.

The collar was doing its work and her face was partially hidden. No one glancing at her would recognise her as Marcie Brooks. Not if she kept her head down.

It was sometimes difficult to believe that Garth was twenty-one, old enough to join the Army and fight; old enough to get married without his parents' consent. Due to the circumstances of his birth he acted and sounded like a ten-year-old, and would never do things like others of his age.

He continued to prattle on in his inimitable manner as they marched along. He was chattering nineteen to the dozen and darting around from one subject to another until they all seemed to run into one subject – which couldn't possibly be right. She caught snatches that made some sense, but not much

– until he said the one thing above all others likely to catch her attention.

'Your mum used to take me to the pictures with you when you were small. I was bigger than you. You were smaller than me.'

'What did you say?'

He continued to prattle on.

She grabbed him with both hands so he had to stop, had to face her.

'You remember my mother. You do, don't you!'

It was a statement not a question. He'd mentioned her twice. He couldn't be storytelling. He really did remember.

His sudden whimper made her realise she was holding him too tightly.

'Are – you – going – to – to – hit – mmmeee?' he stammered.

She released her grip on him, aware suddenly how intimidating she must appear to someone used to being bullied.

'I'm sorry.'

They walked on. Garth was silent at first, a little wary of what she might do. A few yards and he was off again prattling on about digging holes and planting cabbages.

Occupied with her own thoughts, Marcie took little notice. She'd wanted to talk to someone about her mother, someone who would speak freely and openly.

It had never occurred to her that Garth would actually remember her mother. She'd half expected his account of the woman and child sitting beneath a tree was some kind of story; her grandmother hadn't confirmed whether it were true or not.

She slowed her pace until he caught up and was shuffling along beside her. He had a strange, loping gait, similar to the crabs she'd seen on the beach. Desperate as it seemed, he was the only person she could ask about her mother.

'Do you remember my mother?' she repeated.

He had a donkey-like action when he nodded his head, almost as though it were too big for his body.

'Yes. She was kind. She took me to the pictures with you – when you were small. And I was bigger than you—'

'Yes. So you said. And my father? Do you know my father?'

'Yes. He isn't kind.'

She didn't argue with that. 'My mother went away. Do you remember the time when she went away?'

He nodded.

'Did you see her leave?'

He shook his head. 'Your dad had a shovel. He said he was going to plant potatoes.'

Marcie's head jerked round. 'But you didn't see my mother?'

'I saw your dad with a shovel. Going to plant potatoes.'

'But you remember my mother went away?'

He nodded. 'She was hurt. I saw her hurt.'

Marcie's blood ran cold. 'Who hurt her?' Had her father hit her mother like he hit Barbara? Or worse, perhaps.

Garth hung his head, his eyes fixed on the broken pavement and his shuffling footsteps.

'Can't say,' he said at last. 'Can't say.'

She didn't need him to answer. Each word was part of a puzzle, a puzzle of suspicion that was swiftly coming together. The look on his face was enough to convince her that her mother had good reason for leaving home.

'Even if she left with another man, I can't blame her for leaving,' she murmured mostly to herself, though Garth heard her.

'She got hurt,' Garth said again.

Marcie frowned. He'd said that just now.

'How? How did she get hurt, Garth?'

But Garth was already in a world of his own.

'I love Hopalong Cassidy.'

It was no use telling him there was no cowboy showing that night, and certainly nothing as old as Hopalong Cassidy!

It was only a five-minute walk to the Ritz. They were outside and there wasn't much of a queue for the stalls – there rarely was this early in the week.

While they queued she tried pressurising Garth, asking him how her mother had got hurt.

Garth's eyes flickered. 'I like cowboys and Indians.'

She could see how excited he was and that the chance of getting a logical answer was extremely slim. However, she had to try.

Taking a deep breath she asked him the question that now haunted her. 'Where is she? Where is my mother? Do you know where she went?'

He hung his head again, so deeply that his chin rested on his chest. She fancied his spoon-deep eyelids were closed and presumed he was trying to remember. She prayed he'd come up with an answer.

The answer when it came didn't make sense and was certainly not what she'd hoped for.

'She's lying down somewhere dark. It's very dark and she doesn't want to be there. And then we built a chicken coop. I helped.'

Marcie stared. Garth looked as though he'd scaled Big Ben, while she felt more like throwing herself off it. She removed her coat, not realising that she was being watched.

Chapter Seventeen

Marcie tossed her head, an action which sent her hair falling like a velvet veil onto her shoulders. She was wearing a honey-coloured mini dress – a very short mini dress which showed off the shape and firmness of her young, coltish legs. Alan Taylor sighed with longing. He'd watched as she'd taken off her coat, wishing he was in the position to ask her to take off more.

He sighed as he ran his fingers through his thinning hair, hair that had been corn coloured and thick as a lion's mane when he was younger. Still, you're the same man inside, he told himself, and let's be fair, you're not bad for your age.

He clicked an appreciative sound at his reflection in the rear-view mirror before turning his attention back to Marcie.

He'd been driving quickly but had slowed down rapidly when he set eyes on her. At first he hadn't seen the chap she was with. Now he did. Who was that scruffy looking sod with the shuffling gait? It wasn't the rocker he'd seen before. He couldn't be her new boyfriend, surely? And she didn't have a brother who was a bit slow; Tony would have told him. They were great friends, right?

He narrowed his eyes in order to see the bloke a bit more clearly. He'd been told he could do with glasses. He'd got glasses. Trouble was he couldn't stand wearing them. It made him look old – older than he should look. He decided she was going to the pictures with the decrepit-looking guy out of pity. Poor girl. Now what sort of a night out was that?

The billboard advertising the film 'now showing' caught his eye. *Some People*. Judging by the leather-jacketed boy, the motorcycle and the sexy-looking girl, it was aimed at teenagers. No harm in keeping up with the times, he told himself and made a snap decision, parked the car and crossed the road.

'Marcie!'

His heart almost stopped when she smiled at him and he couldn't believe the blueness of her eyes. And they were wide, so wide and full of innocence.

'I'm her dad. She was keeping our place,' he said to those about to protest that he was jumping the queue.

Marcie giggled.

'You're not going to see this film, are you,' she whispered.

His smile was broad and his wink was wicked. 'Why not? I heard it was good. Steph don't like the pictures.'

He glanced at Garth. 'Who's your friend?'

Marcie adopted a long-suffering expression, conveying that she'd been put upon and didn't really want to do this. Nobody wanted to be seen with Garth. She'd only done so at her grandmother's insistence. Rolling her eyes she explained how it was, that her grandmother had insisted. All the same, she kept her voice low so Garth wouldn't hear.

She needn't have worried about hurting his feelings. He was far too busy counting out some grubby coins he'd found in his pocket, having promised he'd buy two ounces of jelly babies to share with her.

Alan squeezed her hand. 'You're a kind-hearted girl, Marcie. Wish my Rita was the same. I give her everything and she's not grateful. Definitely not.'

Marcie glowed at his approval. She'd always envied Rita and thought how wonderful it must be to have a dad who denied you nothing and was always there for you. Now perhaps she was the one to be envied.

'I'll pay,' said Alan. 'My treat.'

She'd intended to go into the stalls, the cheapest seats in the house and also the most crowded. Alan purchased three seats in the balcony. He even gave Garth enough money to buy four ounces of jelly babies. He bought Marcie a box of Maltesers.

Marcie felt privileged climbing the stairs to the balcony. The queue for the stalls had disappeared so no one saw her going up in the company of Daft Garth and Rita's father, though she wouldn't have

cared much if they had. Not with Rita's dad going
with her.

'Ladies first,' said Alan when they got to their seats.

She thanked him and thought how polite and
considerate he was, even more so when he stopped
a very excited Garth from leaning too far over the
balcony to wave at the less fortunate audience below.
Garth had far from an easy life and a lonely one too;
it was nice to see someone being kind to him.

Alan sat next to her, Garth in the aisle seat on
the other side of him.

'Now,' said Alan as the lights dimmed. 'Don't tell
our Rita I treated you and your simple friend. She'll
get a cob on and I won't ever hear the end of it. Right?'

She promised she would say nothing and took
another Malteser from the box.

The colours from the screen lit up Garth's face.
His mouth was chewing relentlessly, one jelly baby
after another swiftly disappearing. She sat back in
her seat feeling extremely happy. Alan took hold of
her hand.

'Just squeeze hard as you like in the scary bits,' he
whispered.

She muffled her laughter with her hand and whispered back, 'I don't think there are any scary bits,
only tearful ones.'

'In that case, take this.' He gave her a neatly folded
handkerchief.

She thanked him. Settling back in her seat she began wondering if she could confide in Alan Taylor. He and her dad were friends. How would he react if she told him the way her imagination was running wild. That she was daring to think the unthinkable – that her father had murdered her mother and buried her under the chicken coop? Would he believe her? Did she believe it herself?

He rested his arm along the back of her seat. It wasn't like a boy doing it and it made her feel safe.

Garth watched the film avidly. Marcie enjoyed both the film and sharing the box of Maltesers, though they only ate half of them. Garth had finished his jelly babies within half an hour so Marcie handed him the chocolates.

'That's it,' whispered Alan. 'We'll look after our figures and the lad can get fat.'

Marcie stifled a giggle.

After the film was over he waited outside with her while Garth went to the toilets – his third visit since they'd entered the Ritz two hours before. Alan offered her a lift home.

She shook her head. 'It's only five minutes. We'll walk. I'll tell Dad you offered though.'

Alan looked very concerned. 'No. No need to do that. You know how jealous he gets about you nowadays, now you're grown up. No need to tell him I was here at all, actually. Your old man can get nasty when he's been on the beer. Best say nothing at all until he's sober.'

'I'm sixteen and grown up,' Marcie said petulantly.

'Of course you are.' Alan saw his chance to charm and took it. Placing his hands on her shoulders he held her at arm's length and looked her up and down.

'Yes. You're certainly grown up now. Awkward age, sixteen. Nobody seems to understand how you feel. But rest assured any time you need a shoulder to cry on or someone to talk to, come see Uncle Alan. Right? Think of me as a second dad if you like; just like I think of you as a second daughter, you and my Rita being so close.'

Alan Taylor spoke affectionately and made Marcie feel extra special. She smiled at his words and agreed that she would come running if she needed to. It felt so good when he hugged her and kissed her on the head as he might a child. It didn't occur to her that a moment before she'd riled at being called a little girl. This felt good.

Garth came out of the Ritz, his eyes shining. He'd been totally engrossed in the film. Through the characters and events he'd entered another world, one far more appealing than the one he lived in.

'I'm going to ask my mum if I can have a motorbike. I'm going to drive fast. I'm going to race like the boys in the film!'

Marcie laughed. 'That's lovely, Garth.'

She knew perfectly well that Garth's mother would certainly not let him have a motorbike. He didn't even have a bicycle. She never bought him anything and quite frankly he wasn't really capable of riding a bicycle. His limbs didn't move like other people's did.

Alan Taylor eyed Garth with a certain misgiving. 'Tell you what, son. Tell no one that you saw me tonight and I'll see what I can do for you. I might be able to lay my hands on a BSA Bantam or something. How would that be?'

Garth's eyes shone even more brightly. His mouth gaped and his throat and chin moved as though he was trying to say something.

'I'll make sure he doesn't say anything,' said Marcie. 'Though now you've promised him a bike, I'm sure he'll say nothing.'

Relieved, Alan patted her cheek. 'You're a right little sweetheart, Marcie Brooks. A right little sweetheart, just like . . . you should be.'

Alan knew he'd almost blown it and said she was like her mother. Thankfully he'd got away with it.

'You knew my mother, didn't you?'

His mind worked quickly. If there was one thing Alan Taylor excelled at above all else it was the gift of the gab. It was said that Alan Taylor of the silver tongue could flog an Aston Martin to a geriatric. That was his reputation and it wasn't far wrong.

He gazed at her face which seemed to glow despite the fact that the Ritz had turned off most of its lights.

'Yes. I knew her.'

'What was she like? Do you know what happened to her? Did she run off like my grandmother said? Did my dad hit her too?'

Her questions took him off guard, but he rallied swiftly.

'Look, Marcie,' he said, his voice low and sounding genuinely sincere. 'I don't think we should be discussing family affairs in public.' He glanced meaningfully at Garth, as though that poor sod was likely to gossip about things. 'What say you we meet up in private and I could tell you all I know? How would that suit you?'

Marcie nodded avidly and told him how much it meant to her. 'You're so kind, Mr Taylor.'

'Alan. Call me Alan.'

'Alan.' She smiled then stood on tiptoes to kiss him on the cheek. He liked that.

'Get off home now.'

Garth ambled along beside her. She didn't want him to be there. Her thoughts alone were good enough company. But Garth was incapable of taking the hint.

'Can I come round and see you tomorrow night, Marcie?'

'I expect I'll have things to do,' she replied. She'd

arranged to look after Annie in exchange for half a crown. Extra money went into a china pig she kept on her bedroom window ledge.

'I'd like more things to do,' echoed Garth.

He sounded lonely. Her heart went out to him. All the same, she didn't really want him tagging along behind her everywhere she went.

'Tell you what. Why don't you ask Mr Ellis if he needs a hand with that shelter he's digging? It'll never get finished before the Russians invade if he's got to keep digging it all by himself.'

Garth brightened. 'Yeah! I know how to use a shovel.'

Marcie believed it. Although Garth wasn't too strong of mind he had a brawny enough body. And while he lacked co-ordination enough to ride a bike, he was handy enough with a brush or a spade. Digging would keep him occupied. She smiled to herself at the thought she may have done him a good turn.

Alan watched them walk away. It irked him to see her wander off into the darkness with the daft devil she'd come with. But never mind. The seeds were sown and the way was now clear as to how he could best gain her total trust – and ultimately much, much more.

Chapter Eighteen

Alan Taylor watched Tony Brooks pacing up and down. They were in his office, Alan was smoking his third Castella of the day and Tony was pacing. That was it.

'Tony, you're wearing out the carpet.'

Tony barely changed the tempo of his pacing. 'My mother wants to get rid of the chicken hutch.'

Alan Taylor burst out laughing. 'Is that why you're pacing up and down like an expectant dad in a maternity ward? Don't look so worried, Tony. She'll have to get rid of the chickens first.'

He slapped Tony on the back. Tony stopped pacing. His expression was grim when he looked at Alan. 'She's already got rid of them. Screwed their necks.'

Alan's humour departed. He pulled a face.

'Your mother's a tougher old bird than the chickens, I reckon.'

Tony resumed pacing the floor of Alan Taylor's office. Alan had the best new and used car dealership on Sheppey. Cars, premises and salesmen were all well presented. Even the mechanics with their oily black hands and greasy faces were expected to change their overalls once a week.

But he made the serious money from the night-club up in London – that and a few other less-than-lawful enterprises.

'I'm worried that she knows.'

'She's your mother. Family don't give you away – not unless there's something in it for them. Can she be bought?'

Tony shoved his hands in his pockets and shook his head. His mother was the last person on earth who'd take money to betray him. But this wasn't about that. He didn't *want* her to know, though some-times he truly believed that she saw a lot more than she let on. Never mind the talking to the dead bit, she was a shrewd old lady. You didn't easily pull the wool over her eyes.

'We could move it,' Alan offered. 'We'd have to wait for a grim night when there's no one about, but it could be done.'

Tony nodded. If the worst came to the worst, that was exactly what they would do.

Marcie's working week continued in a kind of limbo. She kept mulling over what Garth had said and wondering what to do next. Should she confront her father? Ask her grandmother? But ask what? And on Garth's say-so? The poor sod wasn't all there.

She couldn't help but be churlish, especially to her father. In fact, she couldn't bear to look at him.

'I hate my dad,' she blurted out to Rita.

They were in Woolworths at the time, perusing the array of bottled hair dyes. Rita had used one the week before on her mousy brown hair. She'd been disappointed when her hair had stayed its mousy self, and her parting and ears had been stained navy blue.

Rita was in a world of her own. 'I still want it dark. P'raps I should try a mid-brown or a chestnut brown. What about deep auburn?'

'Not before you've tried Sunlight soap and a scrubbing brush on your ears.'

'Ouch!' said Rita with pretend pain.

The girl behind the counter looked directly at her. 'Are you that bird going out with Pete Risdon?'

Rita pouted. 'Might be. I know a lot of Petes. Might have to check my little black book.'

'Rides a motorbike. Comes down from the smoke at weekends. I used to go out with him. Didn't last long though. Hands like a bleeding octopus.'

The girl was chewing gum. Marcie wondered how she got away with it. Babs was a supervisor and always going on about how the girls should appear neat and tidy in front of customers. Chewing gum, Marcie recalled, was strictly forbidden.

Rita puffed up with pride when she answered. 'I've

been going out with him for a while. We're quite serious as it happens.'

The girl sniffed. 'As I said, I went out with him, but turned it in when I realised he only wants what he can get, and I'm not that free and easy.'

Rita's face looked punctured along with her pride. 'What you trying to say? That I'm cheap? Is that it?'

She was poised as if to gatecrash around the back of the counter. Marcie grabbed her arm and attempted to drag her away.

'Leave it, Rita. It's not worth it.'

Rita tried to shrug her off, but Marcie clung on.

'Tart yourself,' Rita shouted out. 'Wait till you're outside work. I'll have you, accusing me of being a tart!'

It was on the tip of Marcie's tongue to say that the girl wasn't far wrong. She herself had been surprised at Rita's total abandonment of self-control. She was besotted with Pete; whether he was besotted with her was another matter entirely. Boys being boys bragged of their conquests and Sheppey was a small place; word was bound to get round. Rita was lucky that Pete came down only intermittently from London. Still, if the girl behind the counter at Woolworths knew, how long before a lot more people did?

She told herself that Johnnie wasn't like that. He made no attempt to have his way with her – not since that first time. She liked to think she had his respect; in fact she was sure she did.

A loud voice interjected. 'What's all this racket?'

Babs had arrived.

The salesgirl pleaded that Rita had called her names. Rita wasn't given the chance to explain.

'I want you out of here,' said Babs, who was showing an imperious side Marcie had never seen before. That, she thought, is what being in charge at Woolworths does for you.

'Out, out, out!' she proclaimed, a nicotine-stained finger pointing at the dark-framed doors.

'Come on,' Marcie said, dragging Rita towards the doors and the street. Her face was beetroot red. The last thing she wanted was to give Babs reason to repeat what had happened to her father.

'Promise you'll wait here,' she said to Rita, plonking her outside the door.

'Don't be so bloody bossy.'

'I have to be bossy,' Marcie grumbled. 'It's me that's got to apologise to Babs and stop her from mentioning it at home.'

'I don't care,' said a defiant Rita.

'But I do,' returned Marcie. 'I most definitely bloody well do! My dad's not like yours, spoiling you to bloody bits.'

Rita gaped at the comment. 'I am not spoilt.'

'Yes you are. Now shut up and wait here while I go back in and see Babs. Alright?'

Rita grumbled an agreement that she would stay.

Taking a deep breath Marcie pushed open one of the series of glass doors. She saw her stepmother straight away, exactly where she'd left her. The girl behind the counter seemed to be doing all the talking.

'Babs?'

She had never ever called her stepmother anything but Babs. They'd never been close enough for Marcie to call her mother.

Babs looked pretty formidable in her Woolworths uniform and you could see she was in charge.

'Well! Look what the cat's dragged in!' snapped her stepmother. 'Where's that cheap little mate of yours?' she asked, dodging her head from one side to another in an attempt to see past Marcie.

'She started it.' She pointed at the girl behind the counter. 'Rita likes Pete and he likes her too. That's all there is to it. She shouldn't have called Rita a tart.'

A lip-curling smirk preceded her stepmother's biting words.

'Is that so? Well, I'm not so sure about that. From what Maureen tells me she's been throwing her favours around a bit freely. That girl's going to end up in trouble if she don't watch it. Though I s'pose she'll get through that alright. Knowing Alan Taylor, he'll pay whatever it takes and any way he can to sort things out.'

'He's a good dad to her,' Marcie blurted out. 'Why

shouldn't he do what's best for her? Better that than being told what to wear, what to do and where to go by a dad who drove my mother away and set up with a . . . a . . . an old brass from the East End of London!'

It was only the fact that she was in work that Babs didn't blow her top. Marcie could see that she looked about to explode. So explode, she thought. Have it out right here and now in the middle of Woolworths.

Marcie became aware that all eyes had turned in their direction. Customers had stopped in the middle of paying for their purchases; shop girls' heads went together behind the wide wooden counters.

This had not gone the way Marcie had wanted it to go. She wished she could disappear into the cowl neck of her bright-mustard top.

Babs grabbed her arm, her red claws digging deep. 'Just you wait 'til your father hears about this!'

Marcie winced. The digging fingernails were bad enough. The wrath of her father was something she wished to avoid – at least for now. She wasn't ready to confront him with what Garth had said. It wasn't that she didn't believe Garth, but what he'd said was hardly proof. He got easily confused. She also didn't have the confidence to spill the beans. It took guts to accuse her father of murder. Somehow, each time she was on the point of accusing him, the words just wouldn't come. Leave it for now.

Marcie pointed. 'That girl's chewing gum!'

Babs sneered. 'So? I'm still going to tell your old man what you and your cheap meat mate have been up to.'

'I haven't been up to anything,' Marcie protested. 'Not like you. When my dad was inside you didn't exactly sit at home and knit.'

It was a shot in the dark. She'd heard rumours but had no evidence whether Babs had strayed from the straight and narrow while her dad was in prison. Judging by the look on her stepmother's face it was very likely that she had. Marcie didn't ponder about who she might have been unfaithful with. Babs had had the opportunity – once a week she'd gone out to bingo, or so she said, with girls from work. Maybe her father had had more than one reason to knock his wife around.

'Is her chewing gum one of your mates from bingo?' Marcie asked pointedly.

A silvery pallor shone through the thick Pan Stick on Babs's face. Marcie knew she'd hit a raw nerve. Was Babs going to admit to anything? Not likely, she thought.

Lashes clogged with black mascara flickered. She prayed that her stepmother was definitely thinking things through.

Suddenly she knew things had changed. Babs spun on the girl chewing gum.

'You should know better than that. No chewing

gum behind the counter. Now get it out of your mouth or you'll find yourself out of a job!'

'You look pleased with yourself,' said Rita when she got back outside.

'I fixed her good and proper,' Marcie said, her grin widening. 'Fixed the girl chewing gum too. Likely she'll get the sack.'

Far from being grateful, Rita looked terrified. 'Do you know who that is? Maureen Phelps. Her and her mates were bullies at school. They'll come after you now – and me. You might be able to cope but I certainly can't. Christ! What am I going to do?'

Marcie didn't know quite why but no way was she afraid of Maureen Phelps or any of her mates. She'd fixed her stepmother good and proper, and that alone made her feel good. The one aspect of her denunci-ation that stayed with her was that her stepmother had played around while her dad was away. She couldn't help wondering who she'd been playing with.

Chapter Nineteen

Rosa Brooks watched her son mowing the front lawn, although the effort was hardly worth it considering that the dingy patch of grass was barely enough to stretch out on.

The boys sometimes played on it but not very often. Babs sometimes put Annie out there in her coach-built pram. It was more to do with showing off the 'Pedigree' pram with its fringed canopy and cat net rather than for Annie's benefit, which was understandable really: the child was a reminder that Babs wasn't all that she should be – fur coat and no knickers, as they said up in London.

Tony had caught her out with a brawny Dutch sailor and had given her more than just a good hiding. Annie was the result – that, at least, was the story Rosa's son had spun her.

The child could not help it, but continued to be a brooding reminder of what her mother had done. Babs didn't hurt the child – Rosa would not stand for that – but she had less affection for her than for the boys. Not that she showed that much for the boys.

Rosa tilted her head sideways as she gave the lawn

further contemplation. Tony was only mowing it with his new lawnmower so she wouldn't get rid of the chicken house. He'd put other stuff in there as well, even an old deckchair he'd 'borrowed' from the beach.

Marcie was the only member of the family likely to lie on the lawn. She'd seen a tanned Bridget Bardot in a magazine and decided she wanted to be bronzed and blonde like her. Rosa had refrained from advising that the starlet's eyes were dark brown and her hair was no doubt the same colour, therefore she tanned easily. Marcie's hair was naturally blonde and her eyes were blue. Just like her mother's. She'd inherited little from the Maltese side of their family.

Rosa's lips tightened at the thought of her daughter-in-law. She'd thought over the years about asking Cyril whether Marcie's mother was in spirit, but didn't have the courage. She preferred to believe that she had run away with someone rather than face the possibility that her son's temper might have got the better of him. In the meantime she found herself wishing that she hadn't got rid of the chickens. It occurred to her that killing them had masked other blood that stained the ground. Blood was life and a life taken violently echoed through the years. Of course she could be mistaken; in fact she wanted to be mistaken – for the sake of her family – and especially for the sake of her son.

*

It was Friday night. Marcie knocked at the door of the Taylor bungalow. Rita opened the door swiftly and dragged her in.

'Quick,' she whispered. 'Steph's in the bath and Dad's not home yet. Pete's promised to phone and Johnnie's going to be there with him.'

Just recently Marcie had noticed that Rita was calling her stepmother by her first name more and more.

Whatever Rita wanted to do, that was up to her. Marcie was here for Johnnie. She was trembling with excitement. Johnnie had been in her thoughts all week. New sensations that were all part of growing up made her think differently than she had done. It seemed her thoughts and reactions were changing from week to week, as though her body had a mind of its own. Thinking of Johnnie filled her with a strange tingling that made her legs turn to jelly.

Rita was asking her whether she'd brought her overnight bag and suitable clothes for camping.

Marcie held up her brother's navy blue duffle bag. It looked out of place in the palatial bungalow with its thick square of carpet, black leather furniture with stick-like legs and room dividers glowing with orange, green and dark-red glass ornaments. They even had pelmets above their windows. Pelmets were something only posh people had. At home in

Endeavour Terrace the curtains were threaded onto cheap wires Babs had 'acquired' from Woolworths.

Rita pointed at a square-shaped plastic bag decorated with pink flowers. 'That's mine.'

Marcie relegated her hands and the grubby duffle bag behind her back.

Rita was grinning. 'Your dad was OK then. Told you he would be if my dad told him you were sleeping here with me. My dad's all right, don't you think?'

Marcie couldn't help agreeing.

'He's great. You are so lucky. My old man's a right misery. I'm frightened to ask him anything. He only says no or shouts at me as though I've done something really terrible – he never used to be so mean.'

Marcie had been amazed when her father had agreed to her request so easily. She'd been getting her courage up all week to ask him, worried that he'd slap her again merely for asking. But he hadn't. Rita had got her dad to ask and them being old mates . . . it was easy.

'Alan Taylor's a good mate of mine so I'm not worried about you staying at his gaff. But listen here, girl, and listen good: don't you go bringing any trouble home to my door. Hear me? No buns in no ovens or I'll knock you to kingdom come. Right?'

She truly believed he would. It seemed such a short time ago when he'd sent her presents like the pink transistor radio. Back then she'd missed him and wanted him home. Not now though. The father who'd gone away was different to the father who'd come home – though deep down she knew she'd changed too. Alan Taylor was no doubt right. The coltish girl was gone to be replaced by a woman who very closely resembled her mother.

Rita's face was pink with excitement as she checked her watch. 'Pete promised he'd ring at seven. One minute . . . thirty seconds . . . fifteen seconds . . .'

The phone rang just once. Rita pounced on it. 'Pete?'

Of course it was Pete. Rita spoke to him in an enthusiastic whisper.

Marcie waited. Rita's conversation was sparse and low – a series of monosyllabic whispers continued.

At last she swiftly and quietly placed the receiver back in its cradle.

'They're coming here. They won't be long. Pete said they've got a tent each.'

Marcie headed for the door. Rita shouted a hasty goodbye to her stepmother.

'Doubt whether she heard. But never mind. She thinks I'm going to an all-night party. So does my dad.' She giggled. 'And I'm all set.'

She took an oblong of foil-wrapped pills from her pocket. 'My dad got them for me. Reckons I'm going to do it anyway so might as well be prepared.'

Marcie's eyes opened wide. 'Birth control pills?'

Smiling broadly, Rita nodded. 'Correct.'

Marcie could hardly believe it. Rita's dad was as far from being an old square as it was likely to be.

'I wish he was my dad,' she said wistfully. 'My dad wouldn't allow me to take them. Besides, my gran would kill me. She'd kill my dad too.'

Rosa Brooks was an ardent Catholic. Babs had mentioned the birth pill within her grandmother's hearing and said how it would change everything for women.

Her grandmother's face had stiffened to the consistency of cold marble. 'Not in this house!'

So her father resorted to quick visits to the local chemist for a packet of Durex or Babs herself got some during her lunch break.

Marcie knew because she'd bumped into her on the landing. Babs had dropped the evidence. 'I don't want any more bloody kids,' she'd hissed when they'd fallen out of her folded headscarf.

Giggling and talking about the boys and how things would be, they made their way to the corner of the street where the boys had arranged to pick them up.

Waiting made Marcie nervous. She kept pulling at the hem of her skirt – as if by some miracle it might lengthen and cover a bit more thigh. Fat chance! When that didn't work she began biting her lip. It had seemed a great idea and she'd bubbled with excitement. Now she wasn't quite so sure.

'Rita, I don't know that I can go through with this.'

Rita looked at her. 'What do you mean?'

'Staying out all night. Sleeping in a tent with Johnnie.'

'Course you can.'

'It's all right for you. You've got the pill.'

Marcie herself thought she might give in if she knew for sure that she couldn't get pregnant. She couldn't help being curious. Only natural, wasn't it?

'I can't give you any,' said Rita. 'It's a twenty-eight-day course. It's too late to go to the chemist. Get him to jump off at Sittingbourne instead of going all the way to Victoria.'

Marcie looked at her not comprehending. 'What?'

Rita's plump face wobbled as she giggled. 'Get him to withdraw before he comes.'

Marcie winced. Talking about the sexual act so casually was downright off-putting. Where was the romance in all this? Where were the sweet words of love and the affectionate kisses that could take her to heaven?

'It all sounds so . . . I don't know . . . like a shopping list. Not exactly *True Romance*, is it.'

Rita let out a loud guffaw. 'They're just stories. They're not real.'

Of course they weren't. They were stories, but Marcie had believed in them. True love always won in the end. She tensed. Should she go or should she stay?

Two black dots appeared in the distance, fast speeding towards them. The sound of powerful engines and the smell of Castrol 'R' filled the air.

The two motorcycles were silhouetted against a salmon-pink sunset. It was as though the London the boys had left behind had shot showers of alabaster up into the air to herald their approach. Just a little romance left, thought Marcie.

Johnnie pulled his goggles up onto his helmet and the white silk scarf down from his face. The smile in his eyes made her heart leap.

'Hi, beautiful. Hop on.'

What a smile! She couldn't possibly let down a boy who could smile like that. Slinging her duffle bag over her shoulder, she got on.

'Chip shop first,' he said before readjusting his goggles and scarf.

'Oooow! Lovely,' said Rita.

Marcie noted that Pete had not greeted Rita as warmly as Johnnie had greeted her. Rita, she decided, was treading on dangerous ground.

Chapter Twenty

The grey sky merged with the slate-grey sea. The brightly coloured buckets and spades, beach balls and rubber rings hanging from shop fronts stirred in the breeze. The air was warm and the breeze would likely keep the rain off. September was giving way to October.

Alan Taylor was feeling pleased with himself. Steph had gone off to visit her mother – the old cow had fallen and twisted her ankle. Shame it hadn't been her neck but at least the phone call had come in time to get Steph onto the next train to Sittingbourne. Shame he hadn't known earlier then he might not have smoothed things over with Tony for Marcie and the all-night party.

He decided to drive over to Endeavour Terrace and perhaps stir the waters a bit; say that Rita had told him she was sleeping over with Marcie, not the other way round. Now that would put the cat among the pigeons. Tony would go mad, but never mind, his old mate Alan Taylor would be there to pour oil on troubled waters. Marcie would be grateful for that.

He leered at some girls down from London, their

bottoms pert and thrusting inside yellow and pink shorts.

'Don't get many of them to the pound,' he muttered, started the car and headed towards Tony's place.

It could have been a street scene any place, any place at all in any town in the country, but this was happening in Sheppey. A gang of kids, most of them no older than ten, were baiting the limp-looking lad – Garth, was that his name? – who'd accompanied Marcie to the pictures. They were hitting him around the legs with sticks; not big sticks, just whippy saplings they'd snapped from over somebody's garden wall.

The big loon was trying to fend them off, holding his arms across his head as he hopped from one leg to another.

Alan Taylor slowed the gleaming Jaguar. An upright citizen would interfere and stop the kids from baiting the poor chap. Even though he wasn't that upright he might have done so except for one thing: he didn't want to remind Garth that he'd gone to the pictures with him and Marcie. Five to one he might not remember him being there at all. Evens favourite he might. Alan couldn't risk that; not at this stage.

His own fault, of course; thinking below the waist. He was going to have Marcie Brooks. She was a cock tease if ever he saw one and he'd tell her so when the time was ripe. Her mother had been much the same, enticing him with those big blue eyes of hers, that supple body. What the bloody hell had she seen in Tony Brooks? He looked what he was, a bit of a spaghetti, his dark looks inherited from his Maltese mother. He bragged about being related to the Maltese Mafia that was presently having a run-in with the Kray twins. Yes, old Tony certainly looked what he was.

'A downmarket Tony Curtis,' he said out loud and laughed at his own joke. He'd decided of late that his own looks were more like Steve McQueen: dark blond, blue eyed and laconic rather than fiery Latin in temperament.

He drove on finally coming to a stop outside number ten Endeavour Terrace. Tony was mowing the front lawn of the old cottage he shared with his family. Alan grinned and stuck his head out the window.

'Never thought I'd see Tony Brooks doing a Percy Thrower. Where'd you get the mower?'

On seeing him Tony let the mower handle slam to the ground. Wiping his hands with a piece of old rag he came out onto the pavement.

He brought his face level with Alan. 'A mate got it for me,' he said in a low voice. 'I asked him for one with a motor, but he couldn't get one. Got me this bloody thing instead. It's doing my back in something rotten.'

Alan's ultra-white teeth flashed as he choked back his laughter. 'I s'pose you didn't keep the receipt.'

'Are you kidding?'

They exchanged a swift grin. Both knew there was no chance of it being legit.

'Someone's bound to be missing it,' said Alan.

'They could have it back if I knew who it was,' said Tony, his grin echoing that of his boss.

'That's alright then. Your Marcie's staying at our place tonight. That OK with you?'

'Course it is. Fancy coming in for a cup of tea?'

Alan's eyes flickered for a moment. He liked having a chinwag with Tony because Tony had respect for him and Alan enjoyed being looked up to. The poor bloke made him feel good. He might have stayed and stirred the mud just as he'd planned but he'd seen the front door open. A pram complete with swaying canopy emerged from the doorway. Babs was bumping the pram down the two steps and into the garden.

He smiled apologetically. 'Sorry, old son. I've got work to do. How about we meet down the pub later? Just you and me?'

Tony grimaced. 'Can't do that, mate. We're going out in a foursome. There's a bit of a sing-song down the Britannia. Can't put it off. Saturday night is music night for my old woman. Got to keep her sweet.' He winked. 'You know how it is – do them a favour and they might do you one.'

Alan winked back. 'Absolutely, old son. See you, mate.'

His wheels squealed a bit when he sped off, but needs must. Tony's wife was number one when it came to doing men favours – though not it seemed too often in Tony's case. Funny that Tony couldn't see that, but then Babs didn't hold a candle to his first wife, Mary. No wonder Tony had been so possessive. He'd have been the same. And now there was her daughter. Marcie had grown up and perhaps he was in with a second chance.

Chapter Twenty-one

Pete and Rita had favoured pitching their tent close to the beach. Johnnie protested that the breeze was too strong coming as it was from off the sea.

'What about up by that old church?' he suggested. 'I drove past there a few times. Looks alright. There's trees to give us a bit of shelter from this poxy wind and the grass looks greener. And there'll be no one to trouble us . . .'

He meant Minster Abbey.

'I vote for that,' said Marcie. She knew it was illegal but the churchyard would be less exposed. She tried not to think about the fact that the churchyard was also the cemetery.

The wind was whipping her hair across her face despite the fact that she was wearing a helmet Johnnie had brought for her.

'It's my old one. Just in case,' he'd told her.

'That's fab! Thanks.' She kissed his cheek.

'It's only an old one,' he'd said, turning gruff.

Marcie wasn't fooled. He was a typical bloke and didn't want to be thought soft.

'You could still get your head cracked open if you come off,' he added.

Pete insisted they go down to the shoreline first just to test the wind. After a bit of arguing they found themselves near Garrison Point.

Johnnie began throwing pebbles into the water. He made a comment that the old forts standing high up on metal legs looked like the Martian machines in *War of the Worlds*.

'I ain't seen that film,' said Pete.

Rita echoed his comment.

'It isn't a film, it's a book,' said Marcie.

Johnnie winked at her over his shoulder. 'There is intelligent life on earth!'

'I don't read books,' said Pete.

Again Rita agreed with him.

Pete didn't return her doting looks, in fact he seemed to be in a bit of a mood. He began doing the same as Johnnie, picking up pebbles and sending them skidding into the incoming water. All three of them watched. Rita remained jolly but Marcie knew her friend well. Even she could tell that Pete wasn't his usual self.

'We'd better go,' said Johnnie. 'It's too windy here. Told you it would be. And we've got tents to put up.'

It was getting dark and the breeze from the sea

had freshened. Marcie wrapped her arms tightly around Johnnie's waist.

The road up to the Abbey hadn't altered much in its history. OK, it had a modern surface, but it still wound about a bit and had twisty bends in nasty places.

Johnnie loved bendy roads. She could tell that by the way he threw the bike over this way and that, the toes of his boots barely missing the tarmac.

They arrived at the Abbey during the last glimmer of twilight.

The boys parked their bikes on the grass against the crumbling perimeter wall. The gatehouse loomed large to their right. The grass was long and rustled when the wind blew.

Johnnie concentrated on getting the tent and Marcie's duffle bag from the back of his bike. Pete was doing no such thing. He was sitting astride his bike messing with the fuel intake.

'Hey, mate,' shouted Johnnie. 'Give me a hand getting this tent up, will you?'

Pete nodded. 'OK.'

'I'll get the food,' said Rita grabbing her pink plastic bag. 'I've brought loads.'

No surprise there then, thought Marcie. Trust Rita to think of her stomach.

'Pete's very quiet,' she whispered to Rita. 'Is anything wrong?'

Using her hand to shield her mouth, Rita leaned close and whispered in her ear. 'I told him I was late.'

Marcie gasped. 'But it's not true, is it? You told me you were on the pill!' she hissed, careful that Pete didn't hear.

Rita took on that silly smug smile that was beginning to get irritating. 'Yes, but I didn't tell him that. I know what I want. I want Pete. I want us to get married.'

'But Rita, you're forcing him to ask you.'

'I thought I'd make the first move.' Her round face turned petulant, pink lips pursed like a tight rosebud. 'I want to get married. I want a nice-looking bloke like Pete. Anyway, I've given him what he wanted so it's only fair that he does the same by me. Right?'

'No – that's wrong!' Marcie barely resisted the urge to take her friend by the shoulders and give her a good shaking. 'You shouldn't have been so free and easy—'

'But everyone's doing it. That's what boys expect.'

'That don't mean you should trick him into proposing.'

'I thought you'd agree we should be responsible for our actions,' Rita said slyly. 'Pete wanted it. He's got to pay the price.'

Marcie restrained from retaliating. Besides, Rita had a point. She'd been letting Pete have his way

224 • *Mia Dolan*

for a while. It was a wonder she hadn't copped out by now. Her dad getting her the birth pill may have happened just in time. Still, what she was doing was wrong, lying just so she could get Pete to marry her. But lying might not be such a good idea. No wonder Pete was in a mood.

'That's not fair,' Marcie warned. 'Tell him the truth, Rita. It's only right.'

Rita tossed her head and folded her arms. 'I thought you were my friend. I thought you'd understand.'

Marcie sighed. Rita could act childishly at times. And this was certainly one of those times. 'Look,' she said, still keeping her voice to a whisper. 'You could frighten him off. I know you always reckon there's plenty more fish in the sea, but—'

'I love him!' Rita blurted out.

The statement took Marcie by surprise and for a moment she was speechless. Rita was always so brash and full of herself. Even in the dimming light she could see that her eyes were glassy.

'I'm sorry.' She gave Rita's shoulder a reassuring squeeze. 'It'll be alright ... I'm sure.' She tried to hide her doubts with a change of subject. 'How about we try and get some music on my tranny?'

Rita sniffed and managed a weak smile.

They sat on the grass, flattening it like a pancake, Marcie got out her beloved pink transistor and turned it on. The batteries were due for replacing but with a bit of manipulation Radio Luxembourg fizzled and crackled into being. Caroline seemed unavailable. With a bit of knob fiddling she got Cilla Black and 'Anyone Who Had a Heart'.

The lyrics had Rita sighing and moving her head dolefully in time with the music – apt for the occasion.

Marcie looked up at the stars as she listened. She thought about what Rita had done. Would she do that in order to keep a boy? All week she'd thought about Johnnie. Thinking about him blotted out the animosity she felt towards her father. Between serving holidaymakers sticks of rock and plastic shuttlecocks, she'd closed her eyes and dreamed of Johnnie Hawke. Every feature was imprinted on her mind, even the smell of him, a subtle mix of leather, fresh skin and the greasy smell of engine oil.

The boys seemed totally occupied in putting up Johnnie's tent. Normally they ribbed each other at a volume easily overheard by everybody. Tonight they seemed more restrained, yet they were still speaking, though more quietly as though they too were discussing what Rita had said.

'There. All done,' said Johnnie.

Marcie had trouble reading the look on his face, but it was getting dark. Pete had wandered back to his own motorbike, but instead of unloading the tent he was making it more secure.

Rita joined him. 'Pete? Aren't you going to put our tent up now?'

Their heads seemed to merge as words were said between them.

Johnnie put his arm around Marcie. 'Alright, babe?'

She nodded. 'Is Pete leaving?'

'Yeah. He wants to camp on the beach, preferably a beach with a pub close at hand.'

There was a catch in his voice. Marcie didn't believe him. Even though she hadn't known him that long she'd latched on to the honesty in his voice. She knew when he was lying.

'We're going up to Warden,' Pete said. 'There's a nice beach there.'

'You'll have to walk down to it,' said Marcie and frowned. Pete's motorcycle had a red fibreglass tank, clip-on handlebars and a lot of shiny chrome. He was very proud of the way he'd customised it and rarely let it out of his sight. She couldn't see that he could get it down to the beach and he certainly wouldn't leave it unattended.

Rita was all smiles when she grabbed her pink plastic bag. 'He wants us to be alone so we can talk,' she said breathlessly. She rushed off. Marcie watched her go, feeling mildly apprehensive.

The throaty roar of the big bike echoed against the ancient walls of the old Abbey.

Something bad was going to happen. Marcie was

sure of it. She looked up at Johnnie. 'Where is he really taking her?'

Johnnie gave her a reassuring hug. 'That's their business. Let's get down to ours, shall we?'

One arm followed the other. He embraced her, his hair falling over his eyes as he bent his head and kissed her.

His lips were warm and soft as velvet. She held her breath, luxuriating in his kiss. Boys had kissed her before, but not like this. And what was happening to her body? It wasn't just that he was holding her tightly against him, it was as though they were merging into one. Except that his body was harder, especially against her belly, and she didn't care, she just didn't care. The warnings instilled in her by a Catholic grandmother were overcome by something much older and stronger than religion. For the moment Marcie was lost. But years of being told to 'look after herself' were not easily dismissed.

'Crikey! Are you sure your name's Johnnie Hawke? Sure it isn't Johnnie Octopus.'

He laughed when she pushed his hands away. 'Aw come on, Marcie. It's just us here and we can do what we want.'

He lunged for her.

She sidestepped. 'No we can't. Besides, we haven't known each other that long.'

Placing a finger on his bottom lip, Johnnie tipped his head back and looked thoughtful.

'Now let me see. It's about three months since I first clapped eyes on you. You were sharing a bag of chips with your mate Rita and you were giggling. That was back at Whitsun, I think.'

Marcie couldn't believe what she was hearing. 'At Leysdown?'

'Leysdown. Whitsun.' His smile was sheepish. No boy could adopt a smile like that unless he was telling the truth.

'You saw me and I didn't see you.'

'Didn't you?'

He sounded disappointed.

'Well . . . not exactly. You had a girl with you.'

He grinned. 'A blonde with big . . . blue eyes.'

Marcie laughed derisively. 'You mean big bosoms! That's what you mean, isn't it!'

'She was just a friend.'

'But you remembered her bosoms more than her friendship.'

He was cornered. His cheeky grin was enough for her to forgive him anything. She wanted him to want her for more than her body, but that was difficult. Boys just seemed to notice the physical more so than anything else. Girls didn't, she told herself. They just didn't, but my, he had the loveliest smile and given the right circumstances she would gladly nibble at his ear and possibly . . .

He kissed her again, longer this time.

How do I handle this? I want him. I really want him.

Johnnie's mouth left hers. He regarded her with a look she couldn't quite interpret. He wasn't smiling. He was looking deeply into her eyes. She'd thought only the actors at the pictures looked at women like that, as though they were the only girl in the world.

'Nothing's for ever,' he said suddenly. 'And it's a lovely night. We could have something to tell our grandchildren.'

She raised her eyebrows. Laying her palms flat against his chest, she leaned away.

'Are you suggesting we have children?'

He grinned. 'We have to have children if we're going to have grandchildren.'

She laughed. That was the great thing about Johnnie. He made her laugh. It was difficult to say no to someone who made you laugh. Easy to relax and think the moment would last for ever.

He took hold of her hand. 'Come on.'

She willingly went into the tent with him. This was the real thing, she told herself. It really was!

The sleeping bags were soft beneath her. She vaguely thought about getting into one, but what was the point? She was warm enough. Johnnie's body was covering her. His erection pressed painfully against her abdomen. His hips began to move in a slow rhythmic action – not unpleasant, but his weight and the angle of his erection grew painful and had a detrimental effect. It reminded her that she was supposedly a good girl.

'No! No more,' she said suddenly, her hands pressing against his biceps.

His hand was already beneath her jumper, beneath her bra cup. The feel of his fingers on her nipple was delicious, but she couldn't let this happen.

'Not yet,' she gasped. 'Please! Not yet.'

He rolled off of her and she sat up.

'I've left my tranny outside,' she said abruptly and went out to get it. The air was several degrees chillier than it was inside the tent. She took great gasps of it as she fought to regain control of her body. She couldn't stop trembling and her legs were shaking. When Johnnie's body had been on top of her she'd wanted nothing more than to give in. Responsibility and concern over the consequences of sexual inter-course – her very first time – had flown out of the window. Aroused to fever pitch, she hadn't cared about the result of such an act. Had her mother been carried away by passion just as she had been? If so, then her running away might be the truth and her father was innocent of having killed her. After all, what proof – what *real* proof did she have?

'Marcie?'

Johnnie had followed her out. His voice was soft.

'It's here,' she said, picking up the transistor radio from among the long grass. It had fallen on its back.

The music had been replaced by the crackling sound of a radio station that refused to be captured. Marcie turned it off.

Johnnie lit up a cigarette. The smell of strong tobacco drifted skywards along with a spiral of blue smoke.

For a while neither of them spoke. Marcie had expected him to pack up the tent and tell her to sod off and find her own way home. He didn't. He seemed pensive as though he were waiting for her to make the next move.

'The moon's coming out.'

They both looked upwards. She was right. The moon had totally escaped the girdle of cloud that had kept it at half glow.

'The man in the moon sees everything,' said Johnnie and laughed.

Marcie turned and looked at him. 'What do you mean by that?'

'Well,' he said before taking another puff on his cigarette. 'The man in the moon's a bit like God, isn't he? Sees everything and knows when you've been a bit naughty. Ain't that right?'

Her jaw dropped. 'What?' He didn't really believe that surely?

A wide grin split his face in half. 'And the moon makes men go mad. Or worse still, they change into werewolves.' With that he tilted his head back and howled.

Marcie burst out laughing.

Johnnie shrugged off his jacket. He grabbed his throat; his legs crumpling beneath him.

'Oh no! I think it's happened! I've got to get my clothes off before I go all hairy and out of shape. Watch out! Watch out! I'm turning into a werewolf.'

Marcie tried to stifle her giggles as he dropped forward onto all fours. She squealed as he crawled swiftly towards her.

There was a ripping sound as he tore off his black tee shirt. Moonlight silvered his back. He snarled. 'I'm hungry!'

He rushed at her, grabbed her leg and, snarling, pretended to take a bite out of it.

'Stop it,' she squealed, unable to scream properly because she was laughing so much.

Johnnie tilted his head back and howled again.

Still laughing, Marcie attempted to disentangle his hands from her leg. She gave him a push, not vigorous enough to send him sprawling the way he did. Raising himself up onto his elbows he eyed her mournfully.

'I'm hungry,' he whined.

'Well you're not taking a bite out of my leg,' she replied brusquely.

He let out a deep heartfelt sigh. 'That's a shame. But I'm not fussy. In fact, I could murder a corned-beef sandwich.'

They ended up rolling about laughing. After that

they sat inside the tent eating sandwiches, pies and crisps and taking it in turns to swig from a full-size bottle of lemonade.

Marcie's thoughts turned to Rita and Pete. 'Pete's going to dump Rita, isn't he?'

Johnnie stopped chomping on the pork pie he was eating. He swallowed and appeared to be inspecting its crust.

On receiving no reply, Marcie said. 'I thought so.'

She got up and made to go outside. Johnnie grabbed her wrist and looked up at her.

'I wouldn't do that to you,' he blurted.

She smiled. 'That's nice to know.'

Again she made a move to go outside.

'Are you leaving?'

She nodded. 'I need to water the grass.'

He frowned before the penny dropped. 'Oh! Yeah! Sure!'

By the time she came back he'd tidied up the debris of crisp packets and pie wrappings, and was laying full length on his back, his eyes closed, his hands folded behind his head.

Wary about lying down too close to him, she sat against the wall of the tent, hugging her bent knees.

'You're right,' Johnnie said suddenly, his eyes flashing open. 'About Pete, I mean. He's going to dump Rita. He don't want no kid. Don't want no wife either. Reckons he's too young for all that malarkey.'

Marcie bit her lip. Johnnie noticed.

'What's up?'

She gulped. It wasn't nice to betray a friend, but Marcie firmly believed that what Rita had done was wrong. 'She's not pregnant. She only said that because she wants to get married.'

'Oh shit! The stupid cow!'

Marcie was inclined to agree with him. What he said next worried her.

'Then that's it. She won't ever see him again. Her fault though. She shouldn't have lied.'

'He won't ever come to Sheppey again?'

'Not bloody likely!'

'Poor Rita.'

'Poor Rita, my ass! She deserves to get dumped.'

'She only did it because she loves him.'

'People in love don't lie to the people they love. I wouldn't lie to you and wouldn't want you to lie to me. I'd hate that.'

Marcie stared at him in the flickering light of the paraffin lamp. He'd pulled his ripped tee shirt back on; most of his chest remained bare. But it wasn't his body that made Marcie stare. It was what he'd just said.

'Do you mean that?'

'Of course I do! What?' he added as though the question had only just sunk in.

She looked down at her hands. Her fingers were intertwined and incessantly moving. She couldn't stop them doing that. Johnnie had sent shockwaves through her emotions. He'd said he loved her. He'd said he meant it.

'I would never lie to you,' she said softly.

He brought his hands out from behind his head and sat up. His eyes were fixed on her face.

'Listen,' he whispered. 'I would never lie to you. It's not in me to lie to you. You're the only girl I've ever loved, Marcie. Honest. I mean it.'

For one starry-eyed moment their gaze seemed to lock together. It didn't last. She almost smiled as a touching thought came to her: Johnnie had reminded her of Archie and Arnold – tough exteriors but on the inside they were as soft as butter. Boys weren't good at receiving affection and even worse at dishing it out. Saying 'I love you' had taken guts. Throwing caution to the wind, she eased herself close, reached out and stroked the nape of his neck.

'Do you mean that?'

His eyes were full of longing when he looked at her. 'I wouldn't say it if I didn't mean it.'

All the love scenes in all the films she'd ever seen flickered through her mind. Now what did they say in such situations before the big fade out, the big scene when you knew they'd committed for ever and ever.

'That's lovely.'

It was hardly the stuff big scenes were made of,

but her mouth was too dry and her brain was too dizzy to think of anything else.

They sat staring into each other's eyes for what seemed minutes but must only have been seconds. Gradually the distance between them lessened until once again his mouth was on hers, his lips warm and moist, his tongue darting between her teeth.

Perhaps it was the scent of him, the hint of fresh male sweat and the warmth emanating from his body like the heat from a fire, but suddenly she reached out and touched his bare flesh.

Her fingers burrowed beneath the torn fabric to explore the slight sprinkling of dark chest hair and the hard nipples. She might not have been so bold if she hadn't glimpsed his flesh through the rip in his tee shirt. Glimpsing just a portion of his chest was erotically enticing.

Despite all the warnings in the world, she couldn't overcome her own curiosity and the powerful forces driving her on. She lay down beside him, breathed in his scent and revelled in his hardness.

His hands began to explore her body, tentatively at first, as though he were half expecting her to tell him to stop as she had before. This time she did not.

She winced at the initial pain. The inevitable could not be stopped. A warning voice whispered to her to turn back. *Think what could happen!*

No! If it hadn't happened to Rita despite the number

of boys she'd gone all the way with, then it wouldn't happen to her. Besides, hadn't someone told her that you couldn't get knocked up on the first attempt?

Closing her eyes she determined to remember this first time, not just him, his smell and his actions, but the process of desire and its ultimate conclusion. Her blood, her nerves seemed to be rushing together like a raging whirlpool, faster, faster and faster ... spinning upwards in tighter and tighter circles until forming a pinnacle, until making her feel that she was on top of a mountain and all she could do was jump off and soar ...

The sudden glare of car headlights flashed over the hill but dimmed swiftly. Alan Taylor turned off the ignition and glided to a stop. He could see the ridge of the tent above the long grass. The tent shone brightly, bathed as it was in moonlight.

He gripped the steering wheel so tightly that his knuckles turned white. His jaw stiffened and he had to take deep breaths in order to control himself. He was feeling angry – very angry. That boy had likely taken Marcie's virginity. It should not have happened. That right should have been his. He was owed that.

If he'd arrived earlier he might have caught them at it. He could have watched for a while as their young bodies writhed together. At least that would have been some compensation. He smiled at the thought and was calmed. Besides that another angle had sprung to mind: Marcie wouldn't like her father to find out about this and he could help her prevent that from happening. He could also demand that Rita keep her mouth shut – she'd told him and that was quite enough. *'You wouldn't want to damage your friendship, now, would you, Rita?'*

'And you, Marcie. You wouldn't want your old man to know, now, would you? So be nice to your Uncle Alan. Be nice or he could get you in bad trouble. Very bad trouble.'

Marcie knew what sort of day it was going to be the moment she walked into work. Besides the fact that it was beginning to rain, someone had broken in and taken a box of peppermint lollipops. Worst of all Rita was pouting.

The rain put off all but the most hardened day trippers, mostly the elderly who marched resolutely along wearing plastic hoods and eating home-made sandwiches. The younger generation headed for the amusement arcades or an amble around the shops.

The owner of the stall was not best pleased that a box of lollipops had gone missing, and even less pleased that the intruders had ripped a hole in the boxwood back wall.

'Little sods. If I ever lay my hands on them . . .'

Mr Tytherington, the owner, ambled off, shoulders hunched, fists clenched like pork chops swinging at his side.

The weather and Mr Tytherington were bearable; Rita and her glum countenance would be more of a struggle. The rounded peak of a tartan cap hid the look in her eyes, but not the rosebud pout.

Marcie had decided by Sunday evening that she wasn't going to admit to Rita that she knew Pete had dumped her. She and Johnnie had made love twice more before lying naked in each other's arms, his fingers tracing silkily across her back. Johnnie wanted to see her again and, of course, she wanted to see him.

'Fancy coming away with me for a weekend in Ramsgate? We can take the tent.'

She knew what he was saying. He wanted a repeat performance of tonight. There was no denying that she wanted it too. But, despite him promising that he'd be careful, there was a risk . . . unless . . .

'So Rita won't need her birth control pills.'

Johnnie was taken aback. 'She's on the pill? But I thought . . .'

'She lied.'

'I thought only married women could have the pill.'

'Her dad got them for her.'

'Wow! We wouldn't need to worry, would we?' He cupped her chin in his hand. 'Cos I can't stop loving you – and wanting to show you how much I love you.'

She'd caught the excitement in his voice. If Rita wasn't seeing Pete, chances are she wouldn't need to take the birth control pills. Now if only she could get Rita to hand them over . . .

'So! How did it go?' she asked, feigning innocence as she spread pink sticks of rock over the area designated for the missing lollipops.

'How did what go?' Rita snapped.

Marcie pulled a face and managed to hold back an exasperated sigh. This was never going to be easy but she had to try.

'You and Pete. Did you tell him you were up the spout?'

'Nope!' said Rita as she handed an old gent change from the half a crown he'd just tendered for three sixpenny sticks of rock. 'I said I didn't want to see him again.'

There was a lying look in Rita's eyes, but Marcie went along with it. 'I thought you loved him.'

Rita scowled at her accusingly. 'Yeah! You deaf or something?'

'But I thought . . .'

'Rockers are out. Mods are in. I've decided that I'm only going to go for lads on Vespas or Lambrettas.'

'Scooters?'

'Whatever. They're more with it. I might even ask my dad if he'll buy me a Lambretta. I've seen girls riding them. Don't see why I can't ride one. How difficult can it be?'

Marcie wasn't at all sure how difficult it was, but she couldn't see Rita's wide girth balancing on two wheels of any sort. Still, knowing Alan Taylor, if his daughter wanted a scooter, his daughter would have a scooter.

To Marcie's relief she didn't ask about her and Johnnie. Marcie had expected at least an 'I know what you've been up to' kind of smirk.

On-and-off silences were the order of the day, or at least the morning. Lunchtime and the smell of fish and chips lured Rita out from the deep pit she'd dug herself.

'I could eat a horse,' she said, three feet in front of Marcie as they made their way to the chip shop.

Marcie accepted a solitary chip when it was offered. After a liberal sprinkling of salt and vinegar, Rita scoffed the lot, her gaze fixed on a freighter chugging its way through the rippling sea.

'I'm going spending this weekend. I want some new gear. I've still got the twenty quid Dad gave me for my birthday. I saw Roslyn Coates wearing the same skirt as me. I hate that. Time to splash out, I reckon. Wanna come?'

Marcie swallowed the mouthful of chicken sandwich she'd brought from home. 'OK.'

She didn't add that there were so few shops catering for young style on the island that wearing the same as someone else was likely to happen again. She hadn't banked on the rest of the plan.

'We'll have to leave on Thursday night and come back on Friday, so that means we'll both be off work.'

'What are you on about?'

'London! Dad's taking me up to London to do some shopping. Well? Are you coming or not?'

Was she? Of course she was! 'I hear the King's Road is the place to go.'

'Nah! My dad says forget that. It's overpriced. There's other places around – even in Battersea, according to my dad. Boutiques. That's what they're called. *Booo-tiques!*'

Marcie wasn't sure where Battersea was as opposed to the King's Road, but perusing racks and racks of clothes was instantly appealing.

'No need to worry. My dad will tell your dad that you're coming with me and staying overnight at Aunt Kitty's.'

'What about Mr Tytherington? He won't like both of us being off at the same time.'

Rita sniffed dismissively. 'He'll just have to lump it then, won't he!'

The prospect of a shopping trip to London lifted the subdued atmosphere that had pervaded all morning. The rain kept falling and even that turned matters to their advantage. The roof sprung a leak. Droplets of water dripped onto the nougat display. More rain dripped through a secondary leak. Soon there were five or six buckets and bowls strategically placed to cope with what had become a deluge.

Mr Tytherington pulled up in his dark-blue Ford

244 • *Mia Dolan*

Zephyr. By the time he'd surveyed his small business and saw the damage he was almost pulling his hair out.

'This is really terrible, Mr Tytherington. It's going to be raining all week,' said Rita.

She sounded and looked genuinely concerned to his face. Behind his back she threw Marcie a conspirational wink. They'd made most of the holes themselves. If the stall wasn't fit for opening then they needn't come to work.

Mr Tytherington ran around swearing under his breath, his usually stiff grey hair sticking like plaster to his head.

'Box up everything! And I mean everything! Store some under the counter. I'll take the rest in the boot of my car.'

'Quick as lightning, Mr Tytherington!'

'Like Jack Flash,' echoed Marcie.

They jumped to it. If Mr Tytherington had not been so agitated he might have noticed that they were uplifting his goods with far more enthusiasm than when they were selling them.

'You've done a good job,' he said gruffly. 'Now get off home and don't come back 'til Monday. I'll have everything fixed by then. Damned nuisance though. I could do with every bit of trade up until the end of October. You do know you girls will be laid off early, don't you?'

They said they did. A summer job was a good filler after leaving school at fifteen. They'd had a whole summer to work out what they wanted to do, and selling candy floss and speciality rock to summer visitors wasn't it.

After shrugging themselves into their coats, the girls ran off giggling as they jumped the puddles.

'Silly old sod! Now who's going to buy rock in this weather?' Rita laughed.

Marcie laughed too. As they headed for the bus stop Marcie considered asking Rita about the birth control pills. Rita seemed outwardly to be her usual bouncy self, but Marcie wasn't totally convinced. Beneath the surface she might still be hurting. It was pretty obvious that she hadn't dumped Pete at all. She'd told him she was pregnant – which she most certainly was not – and he'd told her to get lost. Perhaps she'd flushed them down the lavatory, but perhaps she had not.

'I've five pounds in my piggy bank. I'd like a black and white dress and pair of strappy shoes with a chunky square heel. I'm seeing Johnnie again on Saturday and it would be nice to wear something new.'

Usually Rita would have bounced back with something like, *'What's the point of wearing anything. You're only going to take it off.'*

There was a telling pause before Rita responded. 'Oh yeah.'

Oh yeah.

It was all she said. She sounded as though the words had scratched her throat.

Marcie made an instant decision. There was no gentle way to do this and Rita must realise how much it would mean to her. They were friends. Right?

It all came out in a rush.

'Look, Rita. Those pills. You don't need them now you've split with Pete, do you . . . ? So how about letting me have them.'

An ominous crack sounded as Rita opened her umbrella. The rain was starting to fall heavily again. Marcie put hers up too.

'Well?' she asked as they hurried along. It worried her that Rita was taking her time answering.

'I've only got three months' worth and they cost a lot of money.'

Marcie thought of the five pounds she'd saved over a period of three months. Three months' savings. Three months' supply of pills. Three months of blissful and carefree lovemaking. Should she offer it?

Rita made the decision for her. 'Five pounds.'

It meant going without the dress and shoes she craved, but Marcie didn't care. She was giddy with desire. Every night alone in her bed she lay with closed eyes reliving each caress, each spiralling thrill.

'Alright. Five pounds.'

It meant watching enviously as Rita chose new

clothes in the London boutiques, but Marcie reckoned she could get over that. She had something that Rita would dearly love to have. She had a boy who loved her.

That night before she went to bed, Rita stood before the bathroom cabinet mirror. A scowling face looked out at her. Rita was used to getting everything she wanted. She'd wanted Pete but Pete hadn't wanted her. His rejection had hurt her deeply. Especially as he wasn't to know she'd been lying about missing her period. The hurt had turned into anger and now she wanted revenge. Pete was the one who deserved to be hurt now, but he wouldn't be back to Sheppey. He'd told her that in no uncertain terms. The need to lash out and take revenge would not go away. Someone had to suffer and it shouldn't – it really should *not* be her. She was hurt enough.

Before scrutinising her reflection she had taken the three packets of birth control pills and a large jar of aspirin out of the cabinet. She'd thought of an easy excuse to give Marcie for taking the pills out of their original packaging – she would suggest that Marcie's dad and her grandmother would have a fit if they thought she was taking birth control pills. As a kind and considerate friend Rita would say she'd put the pills in an empty aspirin jar to disguise them. Then if anyone did discover them they'd be none the wiser. What Marcie wouldn't know is that she'd substituted the pink birth control pills for aspirins which were white. She knew Marcie wouldn't have a clue what the pill was supposed to look like. She was such an innocent in so many ways. Well, now Miss Goody Two-Shoes would be playing with fire and might even get burned.

She'd give the jar to Marcie on Thursday and in return would get five pounds. Someone had to share her pain. It might as well be her best friend.

Chapter Twenty-three

Marcie picked her way along the back lane rather than go through the front garden where her father was mowing the patch of grass he called a lawn. He hadn't seen her pass and she didn't want him to. Just lately she'd made a point of avoiding contact simply because it was difficult to be civil. Every time her eyes met his she saw a man who might have done something terrible to her mother, and still she couldn't confront him. She kept asking herself why that should be so, but couldn't come up with an answer.

She exchanged a wave with Mr Ellis as she passed his back gate. The smell of turned earth was strong in the air. No big surprise really. Mr Ellis, his bald pate gleaming with sweat, was leaning on his shovel. He was dwarfed by a mountain of earth excavated from his nuclear fallout shelter. She wondered whether the shelter would ever be completed in time for the Third World War that everyone insisted was coming.

The back garden of number ten, Endeavour Terrace, was a lot quieter than it used to be since the demise of the chickens. Tony Brooks was now using their shed for storage and his new lawnmower. Marcie had never known him do any gardening whatsoever before and certainly not mowing a lawn.

The old wooden gate gave its customary squeal as she pushed it open. Raindrops trickled from the shed roof and brushed onto her skirt from the rough grass growing against the fence.

On a fine night her grandmother would be sitting outside knitting, popping peas or shredding cabbage. The rain had kept her inside this evening.

Marcie wondered what she would say about her going up to London – not that she was quite so keen on going now that she had no money to spend. She had to consider telling Rita that she wouldn't be able to go. Somehow she didn't think she'd be that disappointed. Her father, Alan Taylor, would spoil her rotten. He doted on her, as her gran would say. She only wished her father was like that. At least Rita knew for certain that her mother had died of an illness. She must have been as lovely a mother as Alan was a father, she decided. Just like her mother. From what everyone said she was lovely too.

A sound from the chicken house made her slow her steps. There was giggling coming from inside. Resting her hand on the rough wood, her ear close to the felt-covered roof, she heard the giggling again plus low, boyish laughter.

Archie and Arnold were in the shed. They'd been talking about making a den out of it – that's if their father couldn't be persuaded into digging a nuclear fallout shelter. Tony Brooks was of the opinion that the Russians were *never* coming; the Kennedys had scuppered their game, he reckoned. Besides, they'd probably bypass the Isle of Sheppey. In fact it was likely they didn't even know it existed.

Marcie smiled. The boys hadn't heard her approach so she decided to surprise them.

The hen house roof had a flap that could be opened. Carefully, so they didn't hear, she undid the catch, counted to three and snapped the flap open.

'BOO!'

Two startled boys nearly jumped out of their skin. Two sticky faces – two very sticky faces – looked up at her. Each was holding a lollipop. A few more lay in a small box on the ground between them. The situation was plain as day.

Marcie pointed an accusing finger at the evidence. 'Archie! You little thief! I know where you got those.'

'Don't tell, Marcie! Please don't tell!'

The wire enclosure leading off the chicken coup had been removed. Marcie went round to the front of the hen house and opened the door. Leaning forward, she snatched the box from between them.

'We're not the only ones,' Arnold protested. 'All the kids have got some.'

Marcie slapped each of their faces. 'That's for stealing.'

'We didn't steal them,' said Archie, his eyes misting over as he rubbed the red spot her hand had left on his cheek.

'Don't lie to me. A big box of lollipops just like these were stolen from where I work. What am I to think?'

'All the kids have got some. Bully Price said to come quickly and take what we wanted.'

Bully Price lived up to his nickname. His real name was William so he should have been called Billy, but Bully suited him better.

'Right,' said Marcie, heading back towards the gate. 'I'm going to have a word with Bully Price and then I'm taking him to see his parents. If they don't sort him out I'll leave it to the police!'

She could hardly believe what she'd just said. Bully was not easily intimidated – he was best avoided. At thirteen he was the size of an eighteen-year-old.

The boys were impressed.

'Great! I've got to see this.' Archie scrambled to his feet.

Equally thrilled to watch his sister face the local answer to Al Capone, Arnold followed.

Marcie was full of trepidation. She didn't like confrontation and Bully Price had a reputation. As well as being big for his age, he swore like a trooper. His parents were as offensive as he was. But she couldn't back down now. Her brothers were expecting some drama and her being brave. She had to go through with it.

Bully Price was smoking a cigarette when she found him hanging around in the bus shelter. The tips of three more cigarettes peeked from a grubby-edged breast pocket. Four other boys accompanied him.

'Hey, Bully. You got a bit of skirt come to see you.'

Marcie cuffed the speaker's ear. 'Less of your cheek! I'm not a bit of skirt. I'm a young lady!'

The others gasped and looked at Bully for a lead.

A slight movement crimped the corners of Bully's mouth.

Marcie tensed. Would he lash out at her, set his gang on her? Archie and Arnold, bless their cotton socks, stood firmly close to her side. Although Arnold must be quivering in his boots, he braved voicing a warning.

'This is our Marcie. Touch her and you're for it.'

The gang members laughed – all except Bully. He eyed her far too brazenly for a thirteen-year-old. He was so big for a lad of his age. Determined not to be intimidated she folded her arms and held her head high.

'Touch me if you dare.'

Bully's square chin seemed to bristle for a moment before his small mouth cracked into a grin.

'You've got spirit! You can be my girlfriend if you want.'

'I don't want,' snapped Marcie, blushing profusely despite herself. 'I don't go out with schoolboys and this isn't a social call. I work for Mr Tytherington. We had a box of lollipops go missing. We've reported the theft to the police and the damage done to the stall. Now I come home to find my brothers eating the evidence. They tell me you were the thieving little sods who stole them. Oh, and besides not going out with schoolboys, I do not associate with common thieves.'

Bully eyed her through the smoke he'd exhaled. His eyes narrowed and he certainly wasn't looking at her like a thirteen-year-old should, the cocky little sod!

She waited.

He flicked a dog-end into a stained corner of the bus shelter. 'You got it wrong. I'm no thief. I'm just the distributor, if you know what I mean. Got it?'

Marcie knew Bully mostly by reputation; he was younger than her so wasn't a kid she'd had much to do with. He was the sort she mostly avoided, but still she knew better than to show fear. On the contrary, she had to do the opposite. It wasn't easy.

He looked shocked when she snatched the three cigarettes from his pocket.

'So tell me who did pinch them and you can have your fags back. Tell me now or I'm off to the coppers. Got it?'

She could see by his face that she'd taken him off guard. A lazy eyelid flickered. His smile was slow to spread over his face and once in place was more like a sneer.

'The dope,' he snapped. 'Dopey Davies.'

Now it was Marcie who was taken aback. 'Garth Davies?' She shook her head. 'I don't believe you. He wouldn't do something like that. And how would he get there? On the bus?'

Bully grinned. 'He would if we were holding his cat hostage. And no problem getting there and back. Not if I was driving my old man's van. We wouldn't let him have his cat back until he did the job.'

'You're too young to drive!'

'So?'

The gang members laughed along with him and stopped when he stopped.

'Now give me my fags back.'

He wasn't smiling now, but Marcie didn't care. Her fingers tightened around the three cigarettes. He'd probably stolen them from his parents. It might not be so easy to get any more. I hope not, she thought, I really hope not!

She purposely crushed them in her hand. Bits and pieces of tobacco and cigarette paper crumbled to the floor. She ground the bigger pieces into the ground with her toe and thoroughly enjoyed doing it.

Bully's face turned from pasty white to purple. He

was furious and like all bullies he targeted the weakest. Rather than threaten her, he turned to her brothers. 'Me and my mates will get you, Brookses. We'll get you in school, you just see if we don't!'

His threat was ended abruptly with a swift right hook from Marcie. She wasn't easily roused to violence, but unluckily for Bully Price he was a softer target than her father.

Bully looked at her in amazement. 'I like a girl with spirit,' he repeated as he rubbed his chin.

'But I don't like bullies,' she said, purposely stamping on his foot.

'None of them will be bothering either of you two,' she said to Archie and Arnold as they marched smartly away. 'Head up. Chin up. Start as you mean to go on.'

Marcie added that her half-brothers should not look back. 'They'll think you're a coward if you do and the Brookses are never cowards!'

Testing her courage against someone like Bully Price was bound to flood her with feelings of triumph. However, that triumph was tempered with surprise and sadness. Poor Garth had been bullied into doing what they wanted. She knew he had a cat and that he was fond of it. Sometimes he could be seen sitting on the steps leading up to the miserable flat he called home, the cat lounging across his lap. There had to be a way of keeping Bully and his mates off Garth's back for good. She could tell his mother but doubted that would do any good. Despite her age she went around dressed like Marilyn Monroe; mutton dressed as lamb according to Rosa Brooks. Not that her grandmother condemned her for that. 'She's had a difficult life,' she'd said.

No, it needed a man to sort Bully Price out, a man who knew how to handle himself. She was unwilling to approach her father for obvious reasons. Even if she didn't still harbour suspicions that he had done something to her real mother, or had, at the very least, driven her away, he was hardly the sort to ensure justice was done for Garth. Despite what he was, she'd still been brought up to respect him. However, she couldn't help believing that he'd probably started out stealing sweets himself, before graduating on to bigger and more valuable property.

Marcie thought about the coming Thursday and the weekend to follow. The fact that she was seeing Johnnie at the weekend made up for the fact that Rita was taking her hard-earned savings in exchange for the course of birth control pills. The prized pills outweighed the cost – what was a new dress and shoes in comparison to a weekend of bliss with Johnnie?

As work was out of the question at the moment due to the renovations needed to the stall, she and Rita met for a coffee on a day out at Leysdown.

Marcie had expected her to bring the pills with her.

'I'll give you them when we go up to London.'

Marcie had no choice but to agree. It seemed that Rita was going to relish spending money, including her five pounds. She looked more cheerful than she had for days except when Marcie attempted to mention Johnnie. Rita turned curt when she did that, cutting across with her views that boys who rode motorbikes were disgusting and that she'd made her mind up to 'get with it'.

Rita's father was driving them up in his sleek Jaguar. Apparently he had business to attend to. Her father was fine with that.

'Alan knows how to handle himself. He'll take care of you.'

In more ways than you think, she thought to herself. He's the one who can take care of Bully Price. If anyone was going to set the little sod to rights it was him.

Chapter Twenty-four

They were in Rita's bedroom, a pink and white concoction of laminate furniture, sheepskin rugs and white plastic chairs, when the deed was done. A three-legged tubular standard lamp sat in one corner. Marcie had always envied her friend having a bedroom all to herself. Now the pink and white surroundings made her feel quite sick.

Alan Taylor knocked on the door before coming in.

'Won't be long, girls. Are you both ready to go?'

They both said that they were.

'Marcie's buying my birth control pills,' said Rita without an iota of embarrassment. She waved the five pound note in front of her father's face.

Marcie went scarlet.

Alan noticed the container. 'What happened to them? Why are they in an old jar?'

'Marcie's gran won't like it if she found them – so I disguised them for her.'

Marcie didn't care what sort of container the pills came in as long as they worked. Rita's idea had been a good one, though – heaven knows what sort of trouble she'd get in if her gran or even her dad found out she was on the pill.

She shoved the jar to the bottom of her handbag, still sporting a bright-red complexion. Whatever would Rita's father think of her? Rita telling her father about their deal was the last thing she'd expected. Nobody told their parents things like that – not normally.

Alan Taylor gave no sign of being shocked or embarrassed by his daughter's statement; only interested. His deep-blue eyes narrowed when he looked at her. 'Is that right, Marcie, girl? Must be someone special.'

A smile creased the corners of his mouth. Marcie half wondered if he were making fun of her – a silly little girl who thought she was in love.

Rita bulldozed the information to him.

'She's in love with a leather boy named Johnnie. He's a rocker. Rockers ride motorbikes, wear leather and are always tinkering with engines and oil.' She wrinkled her nose. 'Actually they stink. I've gone off them myself. I prefer my boyfriends to be well dressed and drive a car or a Vespa.'

Marcie couldn't help feeling a bit hurt at Rita's tone. She was saying that Johnnie was downmarket and so Marcie was too. It was hard not to retaliate. She consoled herself by thinking of the weekend – she wanted to go away with Johnnie and needed Rita to cover for her.

Alan raised his eyebrows in a knowing way and grinned at his daughter. 'Trust you to want the best. But if that's what you want, then that's what you shall have. Please yourself in this life, my girl. It's a pound to a penny that no one else will.'

Alan carried their luggage out to the car and laughingly noticed that they were travelling pretty light, both girls having only one bag each.

'I'll have more bags when I come back,' crowed Rita.

Marcie said nothing. She wouldn't be bringing anything back with the exception perhaps of a pair of tights. She'd seen some red ones that she thought would look good with a black mini dress in the winter. She'd seen a dress pattern she liked and the material – an old dress she'd spotted in a battered brown suitcase up in the attic.

Rita had forgotten her favourite red nail varnish so had to rush back into the house to fetch it.

'Sit in the front with me while we wait for her Royal Highness, Marcie love,' offered Alan. He stretched across the front seat to open the car door. 'You can sit up front all the way if you like. There's not a great deal of room at the back and our Rita normally falls asleep after thirty minutes of travel.'

Alan patted the length of leg above her knee. Normally she went bare legged at this time of year. Today, because they were off to London, she was wearing tights and a lilac-coloured crimplene mini dress with a full-length zip down the front.

'Don't let our Rita's openness get to you. There's no secrets between me and Rita. None at all. She tells me everything.'

Having him try to reassure her did nothing except make her plunge to a deeper shade of crimson.

Alan leaned closer. 'Look, love. What the eyes don't see the heart don't weep over. Your dad would prefer you not to bring any trouble to his castle, know what I mean? And you're in love with this bloke and can't help yourself. No need to be ashamed, you know. It's only natural. Men and women have been doing it for ages.' He grinned widely at the same time as taking a sliver of her hair and brushing it gently behind her ears. It felt nice, very soothing.

'Let's face it, Marcie, if your mum and dad and my mum and dad hadn't been hot for each other, neither you nor me would be here, now, would we? But you're not ready for family commitment, so it makes sense to take precautions. Relax. This is the nineteen sixties not the eighteen sixties. Science has provided the birth control pill. Make the most of it, darling. Go out and enjoy yourself.'

Despite his reassurances, Marcie still felt as though her face was on fire. In fact her whole body was burning with embarrassment. She badly needed to change the subject.

'I wanted to ask you something. A favour,' she said. Her long straight hair swung like skeins of silk as she jerked her head round to face him. 'You remember Garth Davies, that funny bloke at the pictures?'

Alan nodded. 'Yes.'

'He's been in a spot of bother, but it's not his fault.'

She went on to tell him about Bully Price threatening to hurt his ginger cat if he didn't do as they said. 'I told him I'd tell on him if he didn't leave Garth alone.'

'Sounds like a boy working his way up to bigger things – like protection rackets and even a spot of larceny,' said Alan. 'So what did he say to that?'

'He was cheeky at first. Then he threatened to beat my brothers up in school. I got angry. So I hit him.'

Alan threw his head back and laughed. 'Good for you.'

'The trouble is he might not take any notice of me. It needs someone who knows how to handle people like him.' Marcie looked at him with pleading in her eyes. 'Can you do anything?'

So that's why the kids were ganging up on the spastic lad. Poor sod!

He grinned and patted her leg again. 'For you, Marcie Brooks, I'd do anything. Like I said to you before, you're the second daughter I never had.' On seeing Rita on her way back to the car, he dropped his voice to a whisper. 'And far less expensive!'

Alan Taylor had the sort of mind that twisted this way and that. They didn't call him 'The Dodger' for nothing. Even as he drove he was thinking on how best to turn what Marcie had said to his advantage. From what she'd said, Bully Price had potential in some aspects of business he himself was involved in. Of course he'd need a bit of guidance and likely as not he'd do a stint in borstal before qualifying as an out-and-out incorrigible. Incorrigible! He liked that word. He'd read it somewhere, or likely Steph had and passed it on to him. Yeah. That was it. 'That's what you are,' she'd said to him. 'An incorrigible. That's what they used to call criminals that refused to mend their ways.'

He'd laughed it off. He felt like laughing out loud now. Everything as regards the seduction of Marcie Brooks was going to plan. She trusted him more than she trusted her own dad. Couldn't blame her really. Old Tony was a bit of a loser. Lost his wife, lost his job, lost his freedom. Pretty soon, if Alan played his cards right, he'd be losing his daughter.

And goodbye to Sheppey.

Alan wanted a cut of the big time. He had a club in the East End that was really doing well, but success came at a price. At present he was paying 'insurance' money to the Maltese Mafia – relatives of Tony Brooks. It was Tony who'd introduced them to him.

'It's normal procedure around these parts,' Tony had explained. 'Might as well keep it among friends. Right?'

Alan Taylor was no fool and realised he had no choice. The Maltese mob was in control – or at least they had been. Now the Kray twins were in the ascendant, taking over swathes of what had once been Maltese mob territory, including prostitution and protection money – insurance as they termed it.

Being a shrewd operator, Alan knew that if he didn't pay his place could be torched. What he did know was that it was better to throw your lot in with the gang that was on the rise. He reckoned he could get a good deal if he went to them direct, asking them for 'insurance' before they came demanding it. It made sense.

He hadn't told Tony, of course. Why should he? First as last it was his business. Anyway, Tony was a bit of a spent force, weighted down as he was with that family of his. Buried alive in Sheppey! Well, he wasn't going to be that. He wanted to move onwards and upwards. He wanted to open more clubs and get in on the big time.

The only way he could get that was to move up to the smoke – the big city – London. The pavements weren't exactly paved with gold, but that depended on what you were doing. Oh yes. Alan Taylor was poised to move up in the world. He'd leave Steph behind and Rita too, but he'd take Marcie, just as he'd once planned to take her mother.

Chapter Twenty-five

The shopping turned out to be better than Marcie could have anticipated. Alan insisted on buying her a black and white dress she very much admired, plus a pair of black patent shoes with a low Cuban heel and ankle straps.

'But don't let our Rita know. She'll only get jealous.'

Rita bought herself a pair of elastic-sided Chelsea boots and a pair of cream-coloured jeans to wear with them. By the time she'd bought herself a black top sprinkled with psychedelic swirls and a black felt hat, she didn't have enough for the Crombie coat she wanted. Her father obliged.

'And that's your lot,' he warned her. 'No more shopping. I've got business to attend to.'

He drove them to a narrow cobbled street in the East End of London. The street was lined with terraced houses built of dark-red brick.

'Won't be long. There's some blokes I've got to see.'

Kids stopped playing hopscotch or swinging from improvised swings – lengths of rope flung over lamp posts. En masse they milled around the posh car and made faces through the windows.

A giant of a man came out of the house Alan Taylor had disappeared into and told the kids to shove off.

They didn't need to be told twice. The big man stood on the pavement with his hands folded in front of him. The kids went back to their games.

Marcie lowered her head and looked beyond the man standing guard over the car.

'Whose house is it?'

Rita shrugged. 'No idea.'

She was sitting in the back taking each item out of the bag, scrutinising it and jabbering on about how good it was going to look on her and how much she was going to enjoy being a mod.

Marcie made no comment. Rita's father had hidden the dress and shoes he'd bought her in the boot.

He'd smiled and winked at her. 'We'll meet up later – just the two of us. You can collect them then.'

She sighed. Alan Taylor was the most generous and kindest man she'd ever known.

Alan Taylor sat in the chair that was offered him. The twins sitting opposite nodded a swift greeting. Their faces were pale, their eyes unblinking and seemingly without any variation in colour. Their mother

268 • *Mia Dolan*

had placed a tray containing a pot of tea, sugar, milk and cups and saucers on the table.

'I'll leave you boys to it,' she said cheerily once she'd added a plate of mixed biscuits. It was as though her sons were boy scouts, not two of the most vicious gangsters in the East End.

Reggie took a biscuit from the plate. 'I hear you're a mate of Tony Brooks.'

'Kind of. He does a few odd jobs for me – cleaning cars mostly.' He gave a little laugh. 'Just about all he's fit for nowadays.'

He was feeling nervous, but knew it was unwise to show weakness. He got a cigar out plus a gold-plated lighter.

Ronnie shook his head. 'Sorry, no smoking. Mum doesn't like it.'

Alan didn't like being told what to do but recognised when he had no choice. Both cigar and lighter were put away.

The big guy sent out to guard his motor came back in, went to Reggie and whispered in his ear. Then he went out again.

Alan wondered what was said. He wasn't long finding out.

'You've got two girls in your car.'

Alan nodded. 'My daughter and her friend. They wanted to do a bit of shopping.'

Ronnie appeared to relax. 'Glad to hear it. Should

always take care of the family, Alan. Know what I mean?'

'I do indeed.'

'Good.' He leaned back, exchanged a look with his brother and laughed. 'For a moment I thought they might be a couple of tarts.'

'No offence,' said Reggie, his teeth set in something between a grimace and a grin.

'No offence taken,' returned Alan.

He had no problem persuading them that his intentions were genuine. They expressed satisfaction that he'd come to him.

Alan congratulated himself. He struck a good deal and was told in no uncertain terms that their own boys would be waiting the next time his present 'insurers' came calling.

Alan congratulated himself. He was one step ahead of the game. His club was safe. His only problem was dealing with Tony's reaction when he found out. There were tight family connections involved, but it couldn't be helped. This was business. Tony had to understand that.

Heart in mouth, Marcie broached the subject she was dreading. 'Look, Rita. Johnnie's picking me up on Friday. We're going away to Ramsgate, but I can't go unless you cover for me. I'm sleeping over at your place. Right?'

Like a cat that's stalking a sparrow, Rita narrowed

her eyes. 'For two nights? That's a big lie for your dad to swallow. Besides, I don't know whether I can.'

The fact that Rita was being awkward roused Marcie to anger and caused her to blurt out the unspoken truth. 'Don't be such a cow, Rita. I've done the same for you often enough. I still would be if Pete hadn't dumped you.'

Rita's soft-skinned complexion turned stiff. She might as well have been fashioned from stone.

'He did not dump me! I dumped him!'

The damage was done. Marcie decided to go the whole hog and tell it as it was.

'You are such a liar, Rita Taylor! You told him you were pregnant when you weren't and he didn't want to know. He dumped you. You did *not* dump him!'

Rita's natural bravado melted like a chocolate mask. Suddenly she burst into tears. Marcie felt immediate remorse.

'Oh, Rita. I'm so sorry. I didn't mean to say that. I know he meant a lot to you.'

Rita sobbed on her shoulder while Marcie patted her back.

Her dad came back, saw her crying and asked what the problem was.

His daughter straightened and promptly lied. 'I got all overcome suddenly. We were talking about our mothers – our real ones, that is, not Babs or Steph. Old cows the pair of them.'

'I wouldn't exactly say that . . .' Marcie couldn't believe what she was saying, sticking up for her step-mother. They were hardly close. Rita was becoming aggravating of late. And selfish – very selfish.

Rita butted in. 'Marcie wants me to lie for her on Friday and Saturday. She wants me to tell her dad that she's staying with us, but she isn't really. She's going off with Johnnie, that rocker down from London.'

Alan turned in his seat. 'Is that what you want?'

Marcie didn't know what to say. Once again she was mortified that Rita was so forthright with her father.

He laughed. 'Why not? Old Tony's getting to be a miserable old sod. A girl deserves a bit of fun, I reckon. Of course we'll lie for you.'

Rita looked dumbstruck. 'But it wouldn't be the truth.'

Alan grinned at his daughter. 'Let's face it, darling, you don't always tell your dad the whole truth, do you now!'

Rita made a humphing sound and folded her arms across her ample chest. She pursed her lips. 'You love Marcie more than me. And that's the truth!'

'Don't talk rubbish. You're my girl. Always have been, always will be. Tell you what, Rita. Come and sit in the front with your old dad.'

He patted his daughter's plump knee just as he'd done to Marcie – though not so high up.

Rita jumped at the invitation. Marcie was ejected from the front seat and forced to sit in the back, not that she was worried about that. She watched as Rita flung her arms around her father's neck and kissed his cheek.

'You soft cow,' said Alan and kissed her back. 'Now let's get going, shall we? Back to Sheep Dip by the Sea.'

He laughed at his own joke. Marcie had never heard him call Sheppey that before and in such a derogatory tone. He actually sounded as though he hated the place.

Still, none of her business.

It had been a long day. She slept all the way back, her head resting among Rita's many purchases.

'Come on, sleepy head. I want my stuff.'

Rita dragging the carrier bags from under her head woke her up.

'Wait a moment, Marcie. I'll get my girl and her stuff into the house then I'll run you home. OK?' said Alan, and winked at her.

She knew what he meant when he winked. Somewhere on the way home he'd stop, open the boot and hand over her new dress and shoes.

Marcie watched somewhat enviously as father and daughter approached the front door. They were so close. The only way to keep the envy at bay was to remind herself that he regarded her as a daughter too.

It made her feel better, enough to throw him a welcoming smile when he returned.

When he invited her to sit beside him in the front passenger seat before they set off, she jumped at the chance. The rear seat was small. Falling asleep there meant a stiff neck and knees.

'Don't you worry about our Rita and you staying out the weekend. Go on and enjoy yourself. Leave your dad to me. I'll make sure he's kept busy.'

Marcie's eyes shone with gratitude. 'That would be great. I can't thank you enough.' The gratitude was echoed in her voice.

Alan stopped the car next to a farm gate. Straggly-coated sheep chewed the long salt-laden grass. On the other side of the road a barren piece of beach stretched between old concrete pilings. Offshore the old fortresses stood rusty and barren, the sea lapping at their rotting legs.

'Let's stretch our legs,' said Alan.

He winked again.

She laughed. She knew what he meant. Let's get your new purchases out of the boot.

'Here you are.'

He took them from the boot and offered them. She hugged her two purchases to her chest.

'You're so good to me,' she said sighing with satisfaction.

'If you really want to show your appreciation, you

can give me a kiss. A great big one. Is that possible?'

She laughed again. 'Of course it is.'

He held out his arms. She knew she had to do the same. They hugged mutually, and while they did so, she kissed him on the cheek.

'A real kiss,' he added, suddenly holding her at arm's length. 'Seeing as I'm lying for you this weekend.'

It embarrassed her to kiss his lips and to feel the pressure of his teeth against his mouth, kissing her back. He hugged her like a grizzly bear.

He didn't force her to kiss again but stood looking pensive as he stroked her hair back from her face.

'This boy, Johnnie. What do you know about him?'

'He's from London.'

'And?'

She had to admit she knew nothing much except that he'd had a motorbike for two years and that his dad was employed full time and was sometimes away. He'd never told her what he did for a living. Come to think of it, Johnnie had never told her exactly what he did for a living either.

'I push bits of paper about and sometimes work in a motorcycle shop,' was all he'd admitted to.

'His name's Johnnie Hawke.'

Alan narrowed his eyes. The name meant nothing.

'I'd like to see you in that dress and shoes,' he said suddenly. 'How about you give me a fashion show, right here and now?'

Marcie blushed. 'But I couldn't undress here.'

'There's no one around – except me, that is. Oh,' he said pulling a face. 'You're quite the young lady, but I promise I won't peek. Honest I won't. Tell you what; I'll pull the boot up. You can change behind there and I'll sit here in the front. You can shout out ready or not, if you like. On the other hand you can come round to the front of the car and give me a fashion show.'

His suggestion seemed innocent enough.

'Alright! I will.'

Excited to show off her new outfit, she waited until he'd opened the boot and lifted the lid. As promised, he went back and sat in his place at the wheel.

After checking to make sure there was nobody around, she stripped down to her undies. Back at the shop she'd noticed that the dress had cut-back sleeves which meant her bra straps were exposed. She removed her bra and pulled the dress over her head. Then she tried on the shoes. They were burgundy patent and had low enough heels to be the height of fashion.

Dancing round to the front of the car, she could see that Alan held his hand so it shaded his eyes. He'd kept his promise not to peek.

'What do you think?'

She twirled on the spot.

'Very nice. You've got the figure for it.'

Alan Taylor was telling the absolute truth about the dress suiting her figure for he'd seen her strip down to her pants and take off her bra. Thanks to the strategically placed rear-view mirror, he'd seen her sweet young breasts in all their rounded beauty. It was tempting to press himself on her right now, but he knew it wasn't the right time. Let her have her fun with this Johnnie bloke. It wouldn't last – he'd make sure of that. And once it did come to an end, he'd be offering his shoulder to cry on – and much more besides.

Chapter Twenty-six

Alan Taylor was true to his word. Picking her up in his car he confirmed she was spending the weekend under his roof with Rita.

Rosa Brooks was trimming the privet hedge when the sleek green car came to a halt at the kerb. She stopped when she saw him, her eyes narrowing as she attempted to study his face through the gleaming glass windscreen.

He got out and gave her a wave. 'Keeping well, Mrs Brooks?'

She nodded. 'Well enough.' No matter how hard she tried she couldn't warm to Alan Taylor. Yes, he'd been of some assistance on her son's release from prison. He'd even provided him with a job, if you could call cleaning cars and sweeping the showroom much of a job. For Tony's sake she had not criticised, but smiled as though she agreed with him when he said that Alan Taylor was the salt of the earth. Too much salt can be poisonous.

A smiling Marcie hurtled out of the house clutching her brother's navy blue duffel bag which seemed to be stuffed to bursting.

On her way to the gate her granddaughter leaned over the navy blue Pedigree pram where Annie was just stirring from an afternoon nap.

'Bye, bye, Annie. See you on Sunday.'

She stopped to kiss her grandmother.

Rosa nodded an acknowledgement. Her brows knitted in a troubled frown as she watched Marcie get into the car. Deep inside, she knew beyond doubt that her granddaughter would be leaving the family nest before very long. Something brushed against her arm. Anyone else would say it was just a privet twig catching her sleeve. But she knew better.

'She is too young to leave home, Cyril.'

The breeze snatched her voice along with the snipped leaves and twigs, sending them dancing over the grass.

'Did you say something?'

She turned to see Tony standing behind her. He'd lifted young Annie from the pram. Somewhat forgetting what she'd been thinking, she smiled at the blue-eyed, fair-haired child. Her son was so different in colouring from his daughters. He was typically of Mediterranean origin, whereas Annie and Marcie both had blue eyes and blonde hair. And yet Marcie's features bore a resemblance to her father and grandmother. Whereas Annie's features were . . .

Her head swivelled back round in time to see

Marcie waving from Alan Taylor's car. She caught a glimpse of Alan Taylor waving at her through the windscreen. He had fair hair and blue eyes.

'I was speaking to your father,' referring back to Tony's question.

It was a family joke that she could often be heard talking to herself. Whenever she was asked she always said that she'd been talking to her dead husband.

'And what did he have to say?'

Rosa Brooks pursed her lips. She could tell by her son's tone that he was wearing an amused expression. *Humour the old girl.*

'He said that it wasn't only chickens that lost their heads.'

Everything else about that Friday night paled into insignificance once Marcie was on the pillion of the Triumph Bonneville, her head leaning against Johnnie's back, her arms around his waist.

The evening blue washed into indigo as they sped along the road to Ramsgate, reaching the campsite by about eleven that night.

Putting the tent up was a feverish exercise and done with the least amount of fuss or conversation. Eventually they fell onto their sleeping bags. Their arms wrapped quickly around each other by the light of a battery operated torch.

'I've got something to tell you,' said Marcie after

extricating her lips from the first deep kiss of the night.

'Don't tell me you're up the spout,' said Johnnie. 'We haven't done it enough for that to happen.'

'Of course not.' Marcie too had heard that you couldn't possibly get into trouble right away. 'I bought Rita's birth control pills seeing as she won't need them any more.'

'That's great!'

'I started taking them last weekend so it should be OK.'

He showered her with kisses. 'Even better.'

'I think I'm supposed to be careful until I've taken a week's worth,' she managed to blurt between kisses. Rita had been less than forthcoming with the instructions.

'That's a shame.'

He stopped kissing her and sounded very disappointed. It made her feel as though she was being a spoil sport and she certainly didn't want to be that. She'd been looking forward to this weekend and knew he had too.

'I'm not sure if it's true, though. You know what Rita's like. If it's not dinner time she doesn't always pay attention.'

Johnnie laughed. 'She does like her food, doesn't she? Pete reckoned she ruined his back suspension with her weight.'

'That's not a nice thing to say.'

'But it's true.'

Marcie sat up. 'Don't say that. Rita's my friend.'

Johnnie lay looking up at her. His hand reached for the nape of her neck. As he began drawing circles with his fingers, his touch had the desired effect. Shivers of delight ran like cold water down her spine.

'Can we forget Rita?'

Marcie shrugged.

'Everyone else can go to hell,' Johnnie went on. 'Tonight's for us. Right? We'll just have to be careful.'

He ran his hand down her back and back up but beneath her jumper this time. His fingers found her bra fastening.

She didn't know how he did it, but with a flick of one finger the hooks parted from the eyes, the bra became loose and her breasts were free. The hand that had been drawing circles on the nape of her neck now slid between her arm and her ribs and cupped her breast. A thumb and forefinger tweaked her nipple.

Marcie closed her eyes and shivered. Sexual longing was indescribable. It was like being devoured whole; and she wanted to be devoured. She wanted everything her body wanted. She wanted Johnnie, now and for ever.

Chapter Twenty-seven

Tony Brooks was polishing cars at the showroom when the phone rang. Alan was down at the pub having lunch with someone he described as an old friend, which in Alan's parlance probably meant it was his bit of stuff on the side – or rather *one* of his bits of stuff on the side.

Tony knew him well. Alan had always had an eye for a nice piece of skirt. He'd been much the same himself when he was younger, which was why they'd clicked years back and were still friends now.

Joyce who manned the switchboard waved at him from behind the glass screen that shielded her office from the car showroom where Jags rubbed shoulders with Ford Zodiacs. Signs saying 'One Careful Owner' meant they were all ex-company cars, their mileage turned back to make the statement more believable.

Joyce was pointing her finger at the receiver and then at the black phone hanging on the wall in the corner. The call was for him.

After downing his polish and cloths, Tony wandered over to the corner, picked up the phone and said hello.

'It's me. Your cousin Xavier.'

Xavier wasn't exactly a cousin, more a second cousin about twice removed, but he was family – of more than one kind. Xavier regarded Rosa as his aunt, mainly because his grandfather had lived a stone's throw from her father back in the old country.

'What's up?' said Tony. It wasn't usual for anyone from the East End to contact him unless there was a job in the offing. He wondered what it was.

'Your friend has gone over to the opposition.'

The line went dead. Tony put the phone down. He didn't need to hear any more. Alan had jettisoned his Maltese relatives and arranged to pay his regular protection money to the Krays. Now where did that leave him? Pissed off! Very pissed off! Unbeknown to Alan he'd been getting a ten per cent kickback from his Maltese 'cousins'.

Grinding his jaw in frustration he walked back to the half-polished Jaguar, Alan Taylor's pride and joy, opened the driver's side door and snatched the keys from the ignition.

'Taylor! You bastard!'

Metal squealed against metal. The ignition key cut deeply into the paintwork. The car was scratched from bonnet to boot.

He heard Joyce hammering on the window at him. She'd obviously seen what he'd done. Well, sod her too. He was finished with this job, and it wasn't just Alan's car he would damage. He went back to the phone, picked up the receiver and dialled Alan's home number. Stephanie answered.

'This is Tony Brooks. I thought you'd like to know that your old man's out giving some old scrubber a length of his tool.'

He heard her intake of breath. What she said next surprised him.

'Alan's obviously upset you. You know and I know that he's been putting it about for years.'

The fact that his declaration had not resulted in the desired effect made him more livid.

'Have you got no pride, woman, allowing your old man to knock around like that?'

'Have you?'

She'd confused him. He frowned at the receiver. 'What's that supposed to mean?'

'Have you no pride allowing your old woman to knock around. Ask Babs! And while you're at it why don't you take a closer look at your youngest?'

Tony Brooks roared into the house, his face flushed with anger.

His mother recognised all the signs. She'd known intuitively that soon – very soon – he would find out the truth, the truth she had suspected long ago; the truth confirmed the day Annie had been out in her pram in the front garden and Alan Taylor had come to pick up Marcie.

'Where is that fucking slapper?'

'Antonio! Not in front of your children!'

'Children? Whose children? Are they mine? Do I know that for sure?'

He pointed up at the stairs. The baby having heard the sounds of anger was wailing for attention.

'That one's not mine and I want it out of the house. Out of my sight! Is that clear?' He looked at his sons. 'And what about these two, I wonder . . .'

The two boys were sitting at the dinner table in the kitchen. They stared at their father round eyed, afraid to say anything, afraid to take another bite of their sandwich.

'Where is she?' he bellowed.

Hearing her father's shouting, Marcie came down from upstairs where she'd left little Annie sitting on her bedroom floor playing with a plastic duck.

'What's up?'

Her father stared at her, blinked, then raised a warning finger. 'Just you listen here, my girl. If I catch you putting it about like that fucking whore that calls herself my wife, I swear I'll kill you. Do you hear me? I'll fucking kill you!'

Marcie looked at her grandmother. Her grandmother's eyes were firmly fixed on her son. She'd always been a tower of strength to the family, but now, for the first time, Marcie saw the tiredness in her face. Her grandmother was getting old. Her strength was going.

Babs came in from the back garden burdened with a pile of laundry that had dried in the salty air and was now brought in for ironing. Her eyes widened when she saw Tony lunge at her. He hit out, his hand catching the side of her face and sending her reeling. Her head hit the wall. He hit her again. Only the fact that the laundry had piled up before her face stopped the blow from breaking her jaw.

The boys leapt from their chairs and crawled under the table, all the time shouting 'Stop! Stop! Stop!' They held their hands over their ears, desperately trying to shut out their mother's cries and their father's angry shouts.

Though her stepmother was hardly her favourite person, Marcie couldn't stand by and do nothing. A freshly laundered bra had got caught around Babs's neck. Her father was using it to strangle her.

Although only a fraction of father's size and bulk, Marcie tried tugging at her father's right arm, using her weight to pull it down and away.

'Get off,' she shouted. 'You're killing her.'

'Too fucking right I'm killing her . . .'

Hot tears of anger and frustration began trickling down Marcie's cheeks. All her pent-up emotions about her mother finally broke like a dam no longer able to cope. She hit his arm, his neck and his head, her puny fists driven by anger. 'Stop it! I won't let you! Not again! You killed my mother!' All the dark thoughts she'd been keeping to herself spilt out, the tears pouring faster now. 'And you hid her under the shed! I know you did. You killed my mother!'

Only the last sentence seemed truly to get through to him. Still with the bra straps in his hands, he turned his head and looked at her. There was amazement in his expression, but also something else.

She didn't have time to analyse that other look. There was a dull thud of metal against bone.

Unseen by Marcie, her grandmother had grabbed her biggest and heaviest frying pan and brought it down on her father's head. Eyes rolling in his head, he slowly but surely sank to the ground.

Rosa Brooks accompanied her son to the hospital. The old iron frying pan had opened a cut in his head and he was out cold. An ambulance had been called. Grandma told them that her son had taken a fall. Nobody questioned the explanation of a tiny old lady dressed in black. Nobody suspected her of physical violence towards her only son.

The moment they were gone, Babs went into immediate action. Her cork-heeled mules thudded up the narrow staircase to the bedroom she shared with her husband.

'Marcie! I need your help!' she shouted down.

Once all the noise and excitement were over and done with, Annie had fallen asleep in Marcie's arms. Curious to know what Babs had in mind, she lay the child on the settee, covered her with her cardigan and followed Babs.

The boys were cowering in the bed they shared, pretending to sleep. Marcie could tell they weren't really sleeping by the quivering of their eyelids. To her surprise, Babs went in and pulled back the bedclothes. The boys were still dressed, complete with shoes and socks.

'Splash some water on your face,' Babs told them both. 'And hurry up about it.'

'We couldn't find our pyjamas,' said Archie.

Marcie knew the pyjamas were among the laundry that Babs had brought in, but Archie and his brother had been afraid to come back downstairs. Just for once they'd scuttled off to bed without being told to do so.

Babs dragged a spindly-legged chair over to the wardrobe. Kicking off her mules she stood on it and brought two suitcases down from on top of the wardrobe.

'Right,' she said, throwing open the wardrobe door. 'I'm off.'

'Off?'

'Well, don't sound so surprised,' said Babs on seeing Marcie's expression. 'Your dad has always had a bit of a temper but look at this! Look what the swine's done!' She pointed to the red mark around her neck. 'This is too much. The bleeder's gone too far and I'm not staying here for him to kill me or the kids. I'm off. Well, get moving then,' she added on seeing that Marcie was standing open mouthed. 'You'll be alright with your gran, but me and the kids are off.'

'No! You can't go!'

'Yes, I bloody well can!' Babs was all action, tugging open drawers, throwing things into the suitcases.

The shock she felt took Marcie by surprise. Although she'd never got on with her stepmother, the fact that she was leaving and taking the children came as a blow. The house would be so empty without them and she'd come to love little Annie. From what her father had said, she also now realised why Babs had always been so offhand with the child. Annie was her guilty secret.

'Where are you going?' Marcie asked as she helped her pack.

'London. I'm going to my mother's, but don't tell your father that. Just tell him I never want to see him again.'

The two boys looked at each other. Marcie could see from their expressions that they were upset at the prospect of not seeing their dad again. She could understand their feelings – he'd been away in prison for long enough and they'd been overjoyed when he'd come home. Now it was they who were off to live without him. Life is so unfair, thought Marcie.

Babs insisted that she walk with them to the train station.

'I can't manage by myself.'

Marcie decided she had no alternative. Even if she refused to help, Babs was determined to leave anyway.

They were in time for the last train to Sittingbourne where Babs and her children would have to change for the train that would take them to Victoria.

'I'll get a taxi from there,' said Babs. 'It's sure to be too late for a bus.'

With a sinking heart and cuddling Annie on her lap, Marcie waited. There were no words to describe what she was feeling. Even thinking about Johnnie failed to raise her spirits. Everything in her life was changing. Nothing, she realised, ever stayed the same, not even her grandmother, though her skill at wielding a frying pan was quite impressive.

The train came and the last farewells were said. The boys took charge of the suitcases. With Annie in her arms, Babs paused before getting onto the train. There were dark lines beneath her eyes, a small cut mark that had healed at the corner of her lip. A pink chiffon scarf hid the mark around her neck. She looks worn out, thought Marcie, like a woman of forty, though she wasn't much more than twenty-seven.

'Take a tip from me, Marcie. Never marry a man

for love or fall for a handsome face. Find a bloke with a kind heart. No matter if he does look like the back of a bus.'

She smiled at that, a weak regretful smile as though she wished she'd done the same.

'Ta-ta, love.'

She was gone in a rush.

Marcie stood and watched until the last puff of steam no longer stained the night sky. Then she was off home, not sure what she would find there and not really sure she wanted to return.

Chapter Twenty-eight

'Would you like a cup of coffee, Mr Taylor?'

Alan resisted the urge to grind his teeth and tell her to sod off. Joyce was middle-aged, wore big glasses and had fine, fuzzy hair that vaguely resembled a halo. She mothered him, stuck up for him and was totally ignorant of the fact that he was a little less than honest.

'No thank you, Joyce.'

His eyelids puckered at the corners as he surveyed the damage done to his prize possession. Perhaps if he'd told Tony what he was going to do, this might not have happened. But that was probably rubbish! Tony was hardly snow white himself; it stood to reason that he'd been making a bit on the side at his expense, taking a cut from the protection money he'd been paying.

Joyce had explained about the phone call. She said the caller hadn't given their name, only said that they were family. Alan nodded, said nothing but knew they were a family alright. One big *criminal* family.

'Thank you, Joyce,' he said.

Joyce Fielding studied his face. His eyes were

narrowed. He did that when he was thinking deeply. His thin lips looked thinner and straighter. She knew when he was angry and he was certainly that now. Unlike other men he didn't shout and bawl and throw his fists about. He analysed things carefully before taking action. He knew how to do things properly.

'Are you sure you don't want me to call the police?'

'No. I'll take care of it.'

She nodded and went back to her little kiosk and her switchboard.

Grandma Brooks didn't know her own strength. She'd done more damage with the frying pan than most people would have believed of an elderly woman who was less than five feet two and light as a feather. The hospital insisted on keeping her son in for observation.

'About a week should do it,' said the young black doctor with the pock-marked skin and the horn-rimmed spectacles.

Marcie made her grandmother a cup of tea and handed her the blue and white striped biscuit tin.

Rosa Brooks took the tea but refused a biscuit. She was having trouble taking in what Marcie had told her. Babs and her darling grandchildren had left, seemingly for good. She thought about the many times she'd prevented her son's second wife from having a home of her own. Would things be any different if she'd acted otherwise? She took a sip of the hot, sweet tea and considered. Whether it would have made a difference or not was beside the point. While her family lived under her roof she couldn't help but do her utmost to cling on to them. The thought of them not being here was unbearable. She'd grown up with close relatives living all around her and she'd hoped to do the same in her adoptive country. Things had not worked out that way.

Her grandmother was quietly eyeing the places on the mantelpiece where photographs of her grand-children had smiled out from silver frames.

'I suppose she has gone home to her mother in London,' she said suddenly.

Marcie shrugged. 'I don't know.'

'You are not a good liar, Marcie. Your mother was not good at lying also.'

Marcie's heart skipped a beat. Her grandmother rarely mentioned her mother.

'What happened to my mother? Did my father . . . ?' Under her grandmother's fierce dark gaze, Marcie's question withered.

Eventually, her grandmother sighed, rested her head against the back of the chair and closed her eyes.

'She went away.'

Marcie held the warm teapot against her. Her grand-mother's statement sounded so final. She could see from the firmly shut mouth and tight jaw that her grand-mother had no intention of saying anything else. The house would be quiet this week until her father came home and his ego would fill the whole house. He would rant and rave about how Babs had let him down, and how it was her at fault – not his. Never his.

Best to keep out of the way, Marcie decided. She liked the empty house no better than he did. The summer season was ending on the Isle of Sheppey and her job would also be ending. Perhaps she'd never get the answers that she sought here. Not from her grandmother or her father. Maybe she too should go to London. It seemed to be the place to head for if you were running away from something. The thought appealed to her, though it wouldn't be easy. Leaving would never be easy.

He came home at the end of the week just before six in the evening. His mother gave him an outline of what had happened.

He paced the house like a wolf in a cage. 'She's gone to her bloody mother's!' He turned to his own mother. 'I'm going to London.'

'Count to ten,' said his mother. 'Think before you act.'

'I'll do as I bloody well please!'

His mother had been standing between him and the stairs. He pushed her roughly aside. Rosa Brooks staggered and half fell against the wall. Marcie was livid.

'Look what you've done!' she yelled as she helped her grandmother to her feet. 'You are such a pig. Why don't you just leave or go to prison again? We were better off without you!'

He raised his fist as though to strike her.

She stood her ground. 'Go on. Do it. You're pretty good at hitting women, aren't you!'

His eyes flickered. His fist dropped. 'I don't want to hurt you, Marcie. I never wanted to hurt you.'

His shoulders began to shake as he sank onto his haunches, elbows on knees, hands covering his face. And he cried.

There was a strange feeling of helplessness when a man cried. Marcie would never forget it or get used to it. She had never heard her father cry before. She'd never seen him look so desolate, so totally despairing.

A hand brushed against hers. A voice murmured, 'I will take care of him.' Her grandmother's old eyes were full of love for her son. 'Antonio?'

The world that was her home was changing too fast. A sudden craving for fresh air turned her footsteps towards the front door, the street and the way into town.

The pubs were just opening their doors. Boys and girls she knew from schooldays waved to her. Some invited her to join them. For the most part she refused their offers.

'Oh come on. You look as though you could do

with a drink or two. Come on. For old times' sake.'

The girl asking her had red hair and a freckled face. Her eyes were heavily made up with black eyeliner and green shadow. Marcie remembered that her name was Jennifer Page and that at school she'd got picked on because of the colour of her hair.

'I came out in a hurry and didn't bring any money with me,' Marcie explained as she followed her into the pub.

Jennifer jerked her chin in understanding. 'You needed to be alone by the looks of you. Still, you might find that it's easier to cast off your worries in good company than dwelling on them all by yourself.'

'You're a brick, Jennifer Page.'

A smile displayed a gap between Jennifer's front teeth. 'I've been called worse than that. Carrot Top was the one I hated the most.'

It was difficult not to blush. Marcie was sure she might have been one of those who'd called her that. In return the girl was treating her with kindness. How guilty did that make her feel?

'Are you still going around with Rita Taylor?' asked Jennifer.

'I was up until just lately,' Marcie explained. 'We've kind of gone our separate ways. She's decided to become a mod and not to bother with anyone who isn't one.'

Jennifer laughed. 'She always was a bit dippy. That's

what comes of being spoilt. Daddy's little girl who thought she could be anything she liked and have anything she liked – especially doughnuts!'

'Her father loves her too much. That's all,' said Marcie, a tad defensively. 'He's a nice bloke. Wish my dad spoiled me.'

'Wish mine did,' said Jennifer after taking a swig from her port and lemon.

Being with other people turned out to be more refreshing than she'd envisaged; Jennifer was as warm as her hair colour. What was more, her open face and kind comments showed up just what a bitch Rita could be at times.

The press of old friends, the gaggle of laughter and one drink after another went a long way in raising her spirits. By the end of the evening she was laughing along with the rest of them.

'You'll have to come out with us again,' said Jennifer once last orders had been called.

'I'll do that.'

'By the way, did you know that Maureen Phelps got knocked up?'

'No.' Marcie didn't add a sigh of relief. No wonder Maureen and her cronies hadn't come after her and Rita following the incident in Woolworths. 'Is she getting married?'

Jennifer shook her head. 'I heard she got rid of it. A back-street job.'

'Want anyone to walk you home?' asked one of the boys.

She shook her head. 'No. I need some fresh air. I might take a walk along the prom.'

The breeze blowing in from the sea sent her hair flying out behind her. She stood staring out at the flashing lights of Southend and the ships wending their way up towards the Medway.

The breeze also made her aware of just how much she'd had to drink, but she didn't care. She'd needed a few shorts to chase away her blues. She'd also needed good company far more than she'd realised.

After what seemed like over half an hour, she turned back the way she'd come, down over the grassy bank to where the locked-up tea stalls sat square and black against the lights of Sheerness.

Car headlights swooped suddenly around her feet and she recognised the chromium spokes of Alan Taylor's Jaguar coming to a stop beside her.

He stuck his head out through the window. 'What's a lovely girl like you doing out all alone on a night like this?'

His teeth flashed white. She reasoned that her falling out with Rita didn't mean she'd fallen out with him. She got into the car.

'Let me take you away from all this,' he said.

She laughed.

'Have you been drinking?'

She felt his eyes on her and couldn't lie.

'I met some friends. I needed a few drinks. I was feeling bad. My stepmother's shot off, you know. She's taken the kids with her.'

Alan nodded slowly as he sped around a right-hand turn. 'Any reason?'

He didn't let on that he suspected he knew what was probably at the bottom of it. The fact was that he didn't possess the full details.

'He reckoned she's been knocking around with some other bloke – or even more than one other bloke – I don't know. Anyway, he tried to strangle her and when he wouldn't let go my gran hit him over the head with a frying pan.'

It must have been the drink making her feel more relaxed because the funny side of it got to her. She burst out laughing.

'Whack!' she said, raising her arm in a pretty good imitation of her grandmother bringing the pan down on her father's head.

'Serves him right, the silly bugger!'

Alan threw back his head and joined in her laughter. At the same time his arm snaked around the back of her seat. He gave her a hug.

'Marcie, you deserve better. Ever thought about leaving the Isle of Sheppey?'

She made a so-so face. 'Not really . . . Well, sometimes.'

'How about we have a talk about it; have a chat about your options now the summer job's come to an end. Our Rita's joining me in the local business, but I reckon you could do well in my place in London. I could give you a job. What do you reckon to that?'

She paused. Was it merely coincidence or was fate pointing her in the direction of the big city. 'I might like that. I've been thinking about London.'

'Right. That settles it,' he said withdrawing his arm and starting the engine. 'We'll go to my place now and talk it through. Steph's gone to Brighton to see her mother and our Rita's going on some trip to Margate with a group of scooter riders. I've got the place to myself.'

Tonight had been great and she was in no hurry to rush home. It was long gone ten o'clock, but curfews had gone out of the window. Her grandmother and her father had weightier concerns. They didn't care much about what she did at this moment in time. Strangely enough, it hurt to think that they were less caring now about what time she came home. She looked at Alan. He smiled at her and she smiled back.

At least she still had him taking an interest in her life.

All except for the kitchen and bathroom, the Taylors' place was wall-to-wall carpet throughout. Thick Wilton and Axminster fitted carpets cushioned her footfall. The Taylors were the only people she'd ever met with fitted carpets. It just showed how rich they were.

Alan invited her into what he termed 'the lounge'. She'd been in here before. Once again she was impressed. The furniture was modern and flashy, and included a cocktail cabinet. Nobody else she knew had a cocktail cabinet. It was made of creamy coloured plastic with pinkish tones and gold-coloured fretwork around the top.

'Lemonade,' she said when he asked her what she'd like to drink.

'Not in this house. A cocktail! I will mix you a cocktail, young lady, that will blow your socks off – or at least make you feel very, very happy.'

It was easy to laugh. Her drinks at the pub made sure of that. She couldn't stop giggling as he poured the mixture into a tall glass with a thin stem and a cone-shaped bowl. The mixture was blue.

'It looks funny.' She giggled.

'It's a kind of daiquiri,' he said.

She didn't have a clue what that was. 'It looks pretty.'

'And tastes even better than pretty,' he said.

He slid along the brown leather settee until he was beside her, watching as she took the first sip. It tasted good.

'Lovely,' she said. 'Just like lemonade.'

The fact that Alan was hiding a triumphant smile

behind his hand or that his eyes were shining with anticipation, did not register. The drink was pleasant to the tongue and refreshing, its alcoholic content smothered by bitter lemon and blue Curaçao.

'Don't just sip it. Drink it. Down in one. It'll do you good.'

She took a deep breath. 'OK.' The drink went down smoothly. Just like lemonade, though lemonade never made her feel as though she'd turned into a marshmallow.

'Good?' He was smiling at her through a silky haze.

Feeling as though she were floating up to the ceiling, she nodded and smiled back.

He made her another cocktail and sat with his arm around her until she had drained her glass.

It felt as though she were floating and her body, which had felt so warm, seemed cooler. Eyes bleary and half closed, she fancied her bare breasts were being tickled with a bunch of feathers. Perhaps she'd fallen into the hen house by mistake and the old shed was still full of clucking cockerels being fattened for Christmas.

She vaguely remembered lying full stretch on the settee and something heavy covering her; she presumed a blanket, though it didn't smell like a blanket.

In the morning Marcie found herself alone and feeling woozy. The night before was just a fuddled memory.

All she could think about was getting home and explaining why she was so late.

Carrying her shoes in her hand, she let herself out of the front door. If the ground was stony, she didn't feel it. Not until she was sitting at the bus stop halfway between Leysdown and Sheerness did she notice that her feet were bleeding. Besides that, her head ached and she felt sick. She groaned. What a mess she must look.

A sudden retch made her reach for the grassy area behind the bus stop where she left the contents of her stomach.

Once it was up memories of the night before came back in a fragmented, piecemeal manner. First she remembered going out drinking with old friends and how good she'd felt when she'd left them. After that she recalled starting to walk home and then Alan Taylor picking her up. After that . . . she wasn't sure, but the Taylors' bungalow was close to the bus stop. How embarrassing! Had she been ill at the Taylors' house?

Walking home seemed like a good idea. She needed the fresh air. She also needed to concoct an explanation as to why she was so late. Her legs were like jelly. Her throat was as dry as the bottom of a bird cage. Despite the early morning air her head maintained its drumming beat all the way home.

She went around the lane at the back of the house,

lingering beside what was now just an old shed. The wood was rough and dry beneath her fingertips. Leaning her head against it, she strained to hear some echo of her brothers giggling on the other side, but there was no giggling, no sound at all.

Staggering slightly, she made her way up the garden path and into the house.

No bacon and eggs were being fried and no kettle being boiled. The kitchen was coldly bare and empty. Where was her grandmother? Where was her father?

She remembered her father saying that he was off up to London but that didn't explain her grandmother's whereabouts. On the other hand she didn't really want to bump into either of them creeping in at this time of the morning.

As if to confirm that she'd been out all night, the old walnut clock ticking away on the wall struck six. Six o'clock in the morning and nobody was around. And nobody had thought to go looking for her.

She made her way to the bathroom and ran the taps. Although her head still felt as though a drummer was beating a strict tempo, fragments of her time at the Taylor place came flooding back. She giggled at the thought of the cocktail cabinet; what a hideous piece of furniture – presumably Steph's choice.

She let herself into the outside lavatory and slumped down on the pan. At first it didn't seem unduly odd that only one hook out of three was fastened on her bra. It was then she noticed that the pink gingham panties she'd put on yesterday were on the wrong way round – and inside out.

She slumped forward.

Nothing had happened at the pub to explain this; she'd merely had a good time. Her memories about that were pretty clear. There was only one other explanation, an explanation that was difficult to face.

She didn't want it to be true that the man she'd thought so much of wasn't deserving of her respect.

Twenty-nine

Tony Brooks hammered on the dull brown door, his anger beating like a drum inside his head. A net curtain lifted briefly in the bay window. He hammered again and kept hammering until Barbara's mother came to the door.

She looked nervous but also hard as nails, her cheeks two red splodges on a heavily powdered face – mutton dressed as lamb, just like her daughter. Tony had met plenty of her type before, most of them pacing the streets of Whitechapel in search of clients.

'Where is she?'

At first Mrs Sanderson looked reticent, her lips pursing tight as a duck's ass. Her fingers tightened over the edge of the door. He briefly noticed her fingernails were as red as her cheeks. But he wasn't here to scrutinise her attempts to hold on to her youth. There was only one thing in his head. He wanted his family back.

The door shuddered under the impact of his size ten boot. 'Don't even think about it!'

'It's no good you keep coming back here,' she

snapped, the tautly stretched face breaking into movement.

'I want to see Babs! I want to see my kids!'

'Well you ain't seeing any of them. Worse day's work my Barbara ever did was meeting you. Now clear off or else.'

He pushed into the doorway. She couldn't close the door at all now without it knocking him backwards and she wasn't strong enough to do that.

'Or else what?'

He glared down at her.

She gave a little gasp as she looked up at him, her eyes round as gobstoppers. The red rouge was joined by a fast-moving flush spreading up from her neck and over her cheeks. But she didn't give in. Instead she seemed to gather herself up, like a snake rising and about to spit venom.

'I'll set my Donald on you!'

Donald was Barbara's father and too old and decrepit to stop Tony coming in. Tony jeered at the thought of it.

'Just the man I want to see. Send him out.' He peered over her head along the dark passageway leading to the scullery at the back of the house. 'Come on, Donald. Let's see what you've got to say.'

Mrs Sanderson glanced over her shoulder. 'He'd come out and protect his wife and daughter – if he was home. But he's not.'

'Is that so?'

He saw a shadow move somewhere deep in the darkness behind her and knew she was lying.

Donald would not come out and there was no point in staying, though it did cross his mind to force his way in. But there was no point. It wasn't Donald he'd come to see – he wanted Babs and his kids.

'Just you take note, you old bag. I'll be back, and I'll keep coming back until I see her. Right?'

'Piss off!'

He swung away from the front door and heard it slam behind him. Barbara had to be there, or they knew where she was.

Back on the Isle of Sheppey, Rosa Brooks had fallen asleep in her armchair. The chair was old and had been inherited from her husband's mother as had most of her furniture. Carved wood surrounded the stuffed headrest and the springs were pressing upwards through the seat.

But Rosa loved that chair because it had been her husband's chair. When she closed her eyes she could still detect the pungent aroma of Navy Shag tobacco from his pipe. It had faded with age but it was still there, the last remnant of his physical presence.

Tonight the scent overwhelmed her and in her dreams she was with him again. During her waking hours she was now longing to be with him. Life was not worth living without her son and all her grand-children. She had been brought up to value having her family round her. Now there was no one other than Marcie; and even she would be leaving home soon, Rosa fancied.

It often happened that she dreamed of things to come, though rarely with regard to her own future. Although she often saw the future of others, her own seemed shrouded from her sight. She accepted that this was the way of things and the will of the Almighty.

The emptiness of the house seemed to echo around her as though silence itself was a sound. A terrible darkness seemed to flood over her. She found herself gasping for air and smelled dark earth all around her; it felt as though she'd been buried alive.

She awoke with a start. Her gaze toured the familiar surroundings. Everything was where it should be except for those photographs that Babs had taken with her.

Shaking slightly, Rosa got to her feet. There was no real reason to rearrange the photographs of her and her son when he was still a babe in arms. Her fingers alighted and stayed on a photograph of her husband. She couldn't help but smile back for to her he would always be young, and always be alive.

The smile dropped from her face as she recalled the dream and attempted to interpret its meaning.

Could it be that she'd witnessed her own death?

She spoke of her concern to her husband's photograph.

'It seems I could be joining you soon, Cyril.'

She smiled at the thought of it. In the back of her mind she tried to recall all the details. She frowned. She'd *felt* and *smelled* earth all around her, yet she hadn't seen herself lying there.

A shiver coursed down her spine as she retrieved what she could remember. There was a body, but not her own. It was a man's body but she couldn't see his face. She jumped to the obvious conclusion, closed her eyes and prayed.

'Please, God, spare my son.'

Chapter Thirty

There were days that week when Marcie could quite happily have murdered Rita. She was going on and on about the new friends in her life and how trendy they were.

'My new friend Sandie has got the most *gorgeous* pair of Courreges boots. *Courreges*,' she repeated. 'They're white with cut-out bits around the top. I'm going to get a pair.'

'Is that so!'

Marcie was deliberately offhand. It had taken someone else to point out that Rita wasn't such a good friend as all that. But Rita didn't seem to notice and went rabbiting on about her new friends, and how fashionable they were.

'Sandie looks a lot like Sandy Shaw. She doesn't sing, though, but she is just *so* fashionable. It's all shop-bought clothes, of course. She buys it up London in the King's Road. Her boyfriend does too. He wears a suit with a round collar like the Beatles and a yellow shirt with buttons on the collar. He smells nice too. Not like rockers and their dirty motorbikes,' she added, an obvious dig at Marcie and her relationship with Johnnie.

Rita's dad seemed to pick his daughter up from work nearly every night that week, on each occasion offering Marcie a lift home. 'I'm doing overtime,' she said.

'I can wait.'

'Don't bother.'

She refused even to look at him. Her face reddened at the thought of what he'd done. She'd told no one. How could she? They'd question why she hadn't reported the incident at the time. Besides, what kind of incident was it? She found she was wearing her knickers inside out, her bra not properly fastened. But you'd been drinking, they'd say. What can you expect? You went willingly with him to his house when his family was away. You're a prick tease. You were asking for it.

Once his car was out of sight she grabbed her things and marched to the bus stop with her head hanging. On the Friday she told Mr Tytherington that she didn't want to work for him any more. He said it was OK, but he wouldn't have minded keeping her on for a month or so, just to help him with the packing away.

'Have you got a job to go to?' he asked.

'I've been offered a job in Woolworths.'

She hadn't been offered any such thing, but there had to be a chance of getting a job there now Babs had left. The true reason was that she wanted to be away from where Alan Taylor had an easy excuse to run into her.

Johnnie was coming down every weekend, and Marcie was glad to leave the emptiness of the house. Her father was in London; her grandmother was like a lost soul. Many times she caught her staring out of the kitchen window. Perhaps like her granddaughter she was willing the garden to echo with her grandsons' laughter once again.

Alan Taylor never came to the house, but his car did pull into the curb in front of her on a few occasions and she knew he'd been following her.

'Marcie! I need to speak to you. It's important.'

She ran into the nearest shop rather than speak to him.

Rita never called, not even to ask why she'd left her job without saying goodbye. Sometimes she saw her riding pillion on a shiny scooter, its fairing festooned with a multitude of wing mirrors.

Woolworths weren't hiring but Marcie found a job working in a local record shop on the high street. It wasn't long after starting there that she began to be sick in the morning. She'd become friendly with Jennifer Page. Jennifer worked in the chemists nearby and was hoping to go a lot further than serving people rheumatic remedies and haemorrhoid cream.

One Tuesday lunchtime they met on a seat overlooking the beach. Unlike Rita who never ate anything unless it was with chips, Jennifer, like Marcie, preferred sandwiches.

Marcie took only one bite of hers. Just the weight of the bread on her tongue was enough to make her feel sick. She spat it out.

'Sorry,' she said to Jennifer. 'I don't know what's wrong with me.'

She felt Jennifer's eyes on her. 'You're looking very pale. Is everything alright, Marcie . . . you know . . . is everything as it normally is?'

'Of course it is!'

She regretted snapping. She valued Jennifer's friendship. Rita would have stormed off to nurse her injured feelings. Jennifer was more steadfast and there was genuine concern in her eyes.

Marcie apologised.

'I'm sorry. I didn't mean to snap your head off.'

'It told me everything.'

'What do you mean?'

'Are you sick most mornings?'

Of course she was. And her period was late. But she'd been tired lately and upset because of her family troubles. That was all it was.

She shook her head vehemently when she realised what Jennifer was suggesting. 'I can't be in the club. I'm on the pill. I can't be.'

Jennifer frowned. 'Did you follow the instructions?

You didn't miss one, did you? Or, have you been ill? I know if you're ill, they sometimes don't work.'

Marcie's eyes followed a young woman pushing a pram. Two toddlers with barely a year between them scurried along beside her. The young woman looked worn out. She could have been any age between eighteen and forty. It was hard to tell.

Marcie thought of Annie. She wondered how she was and hoped Babs was looking after her. Sometimes she'd resented having to look after her baby half-sister. Now she found herself missing her.

But to have a baby of her own?

'I'm not seventeen yet,' she said, her eyes still following the young family.

Jennifer sighed. 'You're going to have to get it checked.'

Marcie swung her gaze back from the sea front.

'I don't want to do that yet. The doctor would have to tell my father and he'll go mad.'

'Have you got your pills with you? Show them to me. It's easy to check if you forgot to take one,' said Jenny.

Marcie couldn't understand how it could be easy to check, not unless you counted each and every pill from the very start. She opened her bag and passed them over.

Jennifer frowned. 'Where did you get them? Why are they in an aspirin jar? They should be in a preformed pack with each day of the week imprinted underneath them.'

Marcie explained what Rita had done in order to disguise the pills.

Jenny frowned. 'They look a bit ropey,' she'd said. 'And they're white. I don't know for sure that there are any white ones. Most of them are pink. Are you sure they're real birth control pills?' she asked sceptically. 'I think I should get them checked out.'

They met the next day after Jennifer had shown the pills to her pharmacist.

'These aren't genuine,' she said gravely. 'These are aspirins that someone has filed down to look like a different kind of pill. Someone has deliberately sold you something that might cure a headache but it wouldn't stop you getting pregnant! It must have been your friend Rita.'

Marcie shook her head. 'No. She wouldn't do that.'

It was hard to believe that her old friend might have tampered with the pills, but Marcie knew it might well be the truth. The other option was Rita herself had been sold dodgy pills, but in Jennifer's opinion, that seemed less likely.

'It was done deliberately,' said Jennifer.

Marcie didn't meet her eyes. They were thinking the same thoughts, but it was so hard to face.

Would she have gone on being free and easy with

Johnnie if she hadn't had the birth pill? The question was a difficult one to answer. The responsible side of her would not, but the surging of teenage hormones was difficult to control.

The worse thing of all would be facing her family, especially her grandmother. Jennifer offered to help her have a pregnancy test. 'All I need is a water sample and we can tell you for sure whether you're in the family way or not.'

By the end of the week, Marcie had her answer. There was no doubt about it – she was nearly three months pregnant.

The weekend loomed bright and clear, one of those autumn days when the sky is blue and the air is crisp.

As usual Johnnie turned up on Friday night and picked her up from the corner of the street. They drove to Leysdown. The night was warm, and the atmosphere buzzed with laughter and the Mersey Sound bubbling from half a dozen transistor radios.

There were teenagers on motorbikes wearing leather jackets and jeans, and teenagers on scooters wearing cool-coloured trousers and double-breasted blazers – all drawn by the smell of fried onions simmering on the mobile hot-dog cart.

The cart was a Saturday night regular in Leysdown, occupying one corner of the car park. The leather boys were parked in the second corner to the right of the cart, the mods to the left. The little man dishing out burgers and hot dogs was nervously aware that his cart formed a kind of demarcation zone. In order to keep the peace he maintained non-ending cheeriness and he had very good reason to.

The queues alternated between mods and rockers so that there was never a mix, though the girls in mini skirts and summer dresses looked as though they might belong to either camp.

She saw Rita. Neither girl acknowledged the other – it was as though they'd never been friends at all. After what Jennifer had told her, all she wanted to do was walk over there and give her face a good slapping.

Pete turned up with a new girlfriend who introduced herself as Diane, the introduction dissected with the blowing and popping of pink bubblegum.

Pete said hello. 'Saw your mate,' he added, jerking his head to where the scooter crowd were gathered. 'Glad to see you haven't joined the opposition.'

'Course she hasn't,' said Johnnie, wrapping an arm around her. 'She's my girl. Always will be.'

She liked the way he hugged her. She was going to need a lot of reassuring hugs before the night was over – once she told him that she had a problem. What would be his response?

Johnnie offered to buy her a burger but she shook her head. 'Not for me.' Her stomach was rolling in response to the smell coming from the hot-dog cart.

The candyfloss stall didn't open at night, but the sticky sweet smell lingered and mixed with that of deep fat fryers containing everything from chips to doughnuts.

'Won't be a minute.'

He went off to the burger cart and came back with two. 'I thought you might change your mind,' he said. 'It's a well-known fact that women change their minds as regularly as they change their underwear.'

The comment was meant to be humorous. Marcie turned away. At the same time she hit the burger from his hand.

'No! I don't want it.'

Diane, the girl blowing bubblegum, asked if she was alright.

Marcie might have been fine if Diane hadn't blown another bubble. The sight of the shiny pink ball emerging from Diane's mouth was too much to bear. She threw up.

Pete gave Johnnie a knowing look and a sharp nudge from his elbow. 'I think you might have a problem, mate.'

Johnnie looked stunned. Then he put his arm around her. 'We'd better talk.' He led her to a quiet spot between two shops selling beach stuff and cheap mementos of Leysdown, made in Hong Kong.

She looked up at him. The look in his eyes and the slight frown said it all.

'I'm not stupid, Marcie. Have you got a bun in the oven?'

She nodded. 'I'm late.'

He frowned. 'You said it was safe. You said you bought the birth control pills from your mate Rita.'

She heard the suspicion in his voice. 'I did,' she said bitterly and looked down at the ground. She thought she'd been safe but she hadn't. She explained what she'd discovered, what Jennifer had told her.

'Shit!' Johnnie braced his legs, his back against the wall, his head hanging. Slowly, he raised his eyes and looked deeply into hers. 'Are you telling me the truth? You're not pulling a fast one like your mate Rita tried with Pete?'

'I bloody well am not!'

Marcie folded her arms, a defensive gesture. It wasn't her fault. She'd been responsible. The pills were the sign of that. None of it mattered now – the deed was done. And what was it they said? No good crying over spilt milk. All the same, the fault lay with the person who'd swapped the real pills with aspirin. Would Rita do that? She still didn't want to believe it.

'Let's walk,' he said.

They headed for the dunes.

'Seems like your mate Rita's not the good friend you thought she was.'

Johnnie's comment hit her hard. All these years

and she'd found Rita funny and opinionated and from the right side of the tracks. Was it possible that she'd been more influenced by Rita's lifestyle and that in itself had blinded her to the person Rita really was?

It seemed that Johnnie thought so.

He said something else that made her blood run cold. 'We're too young for this.'

She took a deep breath before voicing an obvious option. 'I suppose I can make enquiries about getting rid of it.'

'No!'

The suddenness of his response surprised her. She'd been bearing this burden by herself for some weeks. His rejection of the idea was all very well, but she was the one who was most *physically* involved. She had the right to be awkward about it.

'It's none of your business!'

'Of course it is! It's my kid, isn't it?' He paused before hurling the fatal barb. 'Or is it?'

She felt as though she were blushing from top to toe – even in the areas unseen beneath her clothes.

'What do you take me for? There's only ever been you.'

Her throat felt so dry that speaking actually hurt. How crazy was that.

'I'm going to have to tell my grandmother. I can't tell my father – at least not to his face.'

'We'll get married.'

He said it so suddenly that it didn't sink in at first. When it did she raised her eyes and looked up at him.

'You don't have to.'

'For Christ's sake!' He slammed the palm of his hand against his forehead. 'I don't have to! I don't need to! Has it occurred to you that I might actually *want* to marry you? Let's face it, we clicked from the word go. A few years down the line and we would have married anyway.'

To hear him say that was like a breath of fresh air.

'We'll have to live somewhere,' she said.

'Of course we will. We've got plenty of room at our place. We can live there and I can get a job instead of going to university.'

'University?'

He nodded. She joined him sitting on a low wall to stare at the sea.

'So that's what you meant by shoving bits of paper around.'

'It doesn't matter. I can either go full time in Sid Norton's motorbike shop or I can use my qualifications to get something in an office. I got offered a job in an insurance office; not something I'd choose, but if there's an extra mouth to feed . . .'

Marcie could hardly believe her ears. Johnnie had amazed her. He was reeling off future plans that he'd only thought up within the last minutes – even seconds! She found herself swept along with a strange kind of enthusiasm. They had some mighty hurdles to jump, the biggest of them being telling their respective families.

'When will you tell them?' she asked him.

He shook his head. 'I don't know. Not yet perhaps. Not till you've told your family. Mine are going to be disappointed. They had their hearts set on me going to university.'

The type of parents Johnnie had were a world away from hers. For the first time she had some inkling of his background. It frightened her that she might not fit in.

'You don't have to marry me.'

'No. I don't.'

'Then don't.'

The air seemed to bristle between them. Marcie turned her gaze back to the sea. It wasn't even grey any more. The nights were drawing in. The sea was turning darker along with the evenings.

The wet shingle crunched beneath his boots as he came up behind her, standing so close she could feel the heat of his body.

'Let's wait and see what happens. Things can happen, can't they?'

He meant a miscarriage. It was early days but it was possible she could lose the baby she was carrying. She nodded in answer to his question but deep inside she knew she didn't want anything to happen. This baby was unborn but already she felt a great love for it.

He sighed deeply. 'OK. Leave it until the bump starts to show, and then we'll sort it all out.'

They'd been gone barely five minutes when Rita Taylor sauntered over to the hot-dog stand. Pete was standing in the queue with a girl who was chewing gum and in Rita's estimation wasn't very well dressed. Her jeans were faded, her leather jacket was scuffed and her dirty blonde hair was a mass of tangled tresses.

Rita sniffed her disdain and addressed Pete.

'I really fancy another hot dog. I'll let you buy me one if you're a good boy.'

Pete barely glanced at her. 'Buy your own.' He looked pointedly at her stomach. It was obvious to anyone that she wasn't pregnant and never had been. Lucky for him that he had a mate like Johnnie who had told him what she'd been planning.

Rita followed his gaze and blanched. She swiftly recovered and tutted, shaking her head like a teacher she'd once known. 'Peter, Peter, Peter! There was a time when you'd do anything for me.' She stroked the leather sleeve of his jacket.

Pete grinned. 'Burgers and hot dogs are cheap meat, Rita. Just like you.'

While they'd been talking the girl with him had

blown a large bubble. On her bursting into laughter, the bubble popped and stuck to her face.

Rita got the meaning in Pete's comment, but she wasn't one to let it ride.

'They're not very big sausages anyway! A bit like you really! Greaser!'

He grabbed her by the hair. 'Let's get it straight, you slag! I wouldn't have touched you with a barge pole if Johnnie hadn't fallen for your mate. Get it?'

Rita lashed out and managed to get free. Her eyes blazed with anger and a sneer twitched at the corner of her mouth, making her jaw look lopsided.

'Well, it's her that's going to fall now. She's going to fall right good and proper!'

The bubblegum girl had taken an instant dislike to the plump mod with the flat shoes and the patterned smock. 'What do you mean by that?'

Pete frowned. Rita had been a ready and willing participant on the sex front, but he hadn't really liked her. She ran down her friends. He would never do that.

'She's up the spout! Or if she's not she soon will be the way her and your mate are carrying on. But then, what do you expect from one of the Brookses! Rough lot all round and from the roughest side of the island.'

Pete was rarely roused to temper, but he was now. He raised his hand. Diane hung onto it.

'No. She's not worth it.'

Heeding her advice he let his hand drop. They both watched as Rita sauntered off, head in the air, backside swaying like the back of an Indian elephant.

'What did she mean by all that?' he murmured.

Diane shrugged. 'Could be something. Could be nothing. But never mind. Johnnie's a big boy. He can take care of himself.'

Chapter Thirty-one

There was nobody at home when Johnnie dropped Marcie outside her house.

'Next weekend,' he said. 'And don't worry. We'll get through this.'

They kissed goodnight, then kissed again. She felt apprehensive as she watched him ride away. She had never planned for this to happen. There were so many 'ifs' and 'buts' attached to a situation like this. There were so many people they had to satisfy and so many considerations as to what might happen, where they would end up, and if they would end up together.

She thought all these things until the rear light of the motorcycle glowed red then disappeared.

Exclamations and a noisy interchange of conversation drew her attention to the other end of the street. A crowd was gathered outside the entrance to the back lane, but she felt no curiosity to go along and see what was going on. She presumed her grandmother was there and that's why their own house was in darkness.

She ran into the house and up the stairs. Babs had left one last suitcase. It was small, brown and battered, and barely enough for Marcie's things, but she made it enough. Another stupid thing, she thought to herself. Why pack a case now? It would be months before she left.

She looked round the old cottage where she'd been born and had spent her life. Leaving would be difficult; she'd never realised before how difficult. The cottage was part of her; her family was part of her. How would it be to live with Johnnie in London?

The bedroom was oddly cold without her small sister or her grandmother sleeping in there. She'd always dreamed of having a bedroom to herself like Rita, but now it had come to be she didn't like it.

Before climbing into bed, she looked out of the window. The window overlooked the back garden, a dingy place by day but transfigured by moonlight.

A full moon escaped from a circlet of clouds. The garden was bathed in silver clear light. Even the shed where the chickens used to live looked slightly magical, as though someone had splashed it with silver paint.

Just for a moment – a very fleeting moment – she fancied she saw a figure evolve between the fence and the shed.

After rubbing her eyes she leaned closer to the window pane. There was no one there, just black shadows falling like mats among the silver.

A sudden creaking on the stairs caused her to turn

round. Her grandmother was standing there, a small figure in black, eyes piercing even in the muted glow of the bedside light.

'Oh. Gran. I thought you were already in bed.'

Rosa raised one well-defined eyebrow in disbelief. 'Is that what you think?'

Her eyes were unblinking. Marcie felt instantly guilty.

'Did Dad find Babs?'

'I think you know the answer to that.'

Of course she did. If her father had found her step-mother he wouldn't be spending his days pacing around the house like a caged wolf.

'He will be going up to London for good, I think,' said her grandmother. 'It is best he is there so he can find her more easily, especially now he has left his job with Mr Taylor.'

Mention of Alan Taylor made Marcie blush. He'd caught up with her one day outside the shops.

He'd smiled as if nothing had happened, as if he'd done nothing wrong.

'And how's my little Marcie?'

She'd flounced on by, her face burning and a queasiness in her stomach. The events of the night when she'd gone to his place came back like a bad dream. Alarmed at the sight of her stained underwear, she'd washed them swiftly in the sink rather than adding them to the laundry bin where her grandmother would see them. Her face blazed at the thought of it.

'Leave me alone.'

He'd grabbed her arm. 'Me and you are made for each other, Marcie,' he'd hissed, his breath hot and moist against her cheek.

'People are watching,' she hissed back.

'They would do. Small-town mentality,' he said, his comment accompanied by the signature whiter-than-white smile. 'How about we go away up to London? Just you and me. I could show you a good time. A real good time.'

Jennifer had come to her rescue.

'Am I right in thinking that was Rita Taylor's dad?'

Marcie had confirmed it.

'Thought it was,' said Jennifer. She popped a crisp into her mouth. 'I hear he can't keep his hands off young girls – or anything in a skirt for that matter. Have you heard that?'

Marcie shook her head. She'd been shaking then, and she almost did the same now.

'I expect Dad will find something better in London.'

Her grandmother's eyes stayed locked with hers. 'You are leaving too.'

Too! The word made Marcie smart.

'I don't know what you mean, Gran.'

She told herself that it was too early to confide in

anyone about her condition. As Johnnie had said, what if something happened? She'd heard of women having miscarriages. It might happen to her, but if not, Johnnie had promised to marry her.

'There's not much round here,' she said. 'I might leave sooner or later.'

'There's a boy.'

Again her grandmother had startled her with her insight. This was how she was sometimes.

Her grandmother nodded and although a smile twitched at her lips there was sadness in her eyes. 'I can see it in your face.'

'I've got a boyfriend. I think I might marry him.'

Her grandmother blinked then shook her head. 'No, you are not.'

'Yes. Yes. Of course I am. It's just a case of getting Dad to sign the permission because I'm under twenty-one.'

'Your father will not like it.'

She's right there, thought Marcie. Her father wouldn't like her running off and getting married. Seeing as she was not twenty-one, he had to give his permission. She convinced herself that he would, but deep down she knew he would be furious. He'd be even more furious if he knew about the baby. Hadn't he said he would kill her if she brought trouble home?

Turning away she threw the bedclothes back. 'I'm tired, Gran. You must be too.'

She climbed into bed.

Rosa Brooks stood absolutely still, her expression unfathomable. 'You saw the people at the end of the street?'

Marcie made a big show of pummelling her pillows. 'I saw them. What was it all about?'

'Mr Ellis was buried in his air-raid shelter. It collapsed. He's dead. Garth was in there too, helping him.'

Marcie gasped.

'Mr Ellis is dead. Garth is safe. We should thank God for that.'

Rosa Brooks went back downstairs and made herself a cup of tea. Her heart was heavy and she was feeling drained. Perhaps if she hadn't been she might have sat Marcie down and talked with her. As it was, recent happenings had taken their toll.

'Cyril, so many things, so many bad things,' she murmured as she sat herself down in her favourite chair.

The dream about the dark earth falling in around her had been broken. The nuclear fallout shelter that had taken up so much of Sam Ellis's time had fallen in on him. The poor man had been buried alive. Garth had been lucky to get out. He was in hospital but basically fine.

The things she was seeing were jagged and piece-meal, like bits of jigsaw from more than one puzzle, all jumbled up together and needing a clear head to sort them out.

'I am tired, Cyril,' she said and closed her eyes. She imagined he patted her head and told her to sleep, just as he used to when they were sharing the same bed.

Wise words. She needed to sleep on it, though before falling asleep she prayed that her grand-daughter would survive the mishaps that fate would put in her way. Her instinct told her that although it wouldn't be long before Marcie left home, she was equally sure that one day she would come home.

Upstairs in her bed, Marcie lay staring at the ceiling. It was at her suggestion that Garth had offered to help Mr Ellis with his digging. The suggestion wasn't entirely from the centre of her heart. She'd wanted him to stop following her around. She countered her guilt with the fact that she hadn't done everything from selfishness. Alan had stopped Billy Price from bullying Garth. That was a good thing, wasn't it?

Even so she felt guilty. Tomorrow after work she'd go to see him in hospital. First she would go along to the telephone box to check that he was still there. If he wasn't she'd visit him at home. He deserved that at least.

Chapter Thirty-two

Tony Brooks wanted his wife back. He also wanted his job. Not the one with Alan Taylor cleaning his cars and sweeping his floors. He wanted his old job back up in London, but only temporarily.

They called him the rent collector. He called round at all the businesses – nightclubs, pubs and massage parlours – collecting the insurance dues. If anybody got shirty about paying, then he'd phone up for the heavy mob to sort things out.

There was an added advantage to it – if he was up in London it would be easier to call at his mother-in-law's on the off chance of seeing Babs and the kids. Once he found them he would bring them back to where they belonged. The Isle of Sheppey was where he'd grown up. He'd done the big city thing. He wanted to be home, but home was nothing without a family.

In between he had to lay the groundwork for returning there full time, which meant making his peace with Alan back in Sheppey. He'd regretted scratching Tony's motor; he told himself he wouldn't have done it if that bitch Stephanie hadn't wound him up. What did she know? She hardly knew Babs. OK, they'd had the odd night out in a foursome, but they hadn't said much to each other.

He had decided that Stephanie was jealous. He shouldn't have mentioned Alan being out with a bird, but then, he argued, Alan shouldn't have swapped sides and opted to pay the protection money on his club to the Krays – relative newcomers in the world of intimidation and protection.

The door had a notice on it saying 'Lounge Bar'. Tony Brooks pushed it open. It was a Saturday night. Someone in the public bar was singing 'Ferry Across the Mersey' and falling off more notes than he was hitting; the same applied to whoever was hammering the life out of the piano.

Alan Taylor was standing at the bar with three blokes. By the cut of their suits they looked as though they were down from London. He vaguely recognised them – not big players but blokes who dealt in dodgy cars. If he'd been sober he might have held back, but he'd just got back from yet another trip to London searching for his family, and he'd had no luck. Alighting from the train he'd immediately made his way into the nearest pub and had been supping in there for a few hours. Then he'd got word that Alan Taylor was in the Britannia.

'I want a word with that bastard,' he'd muttered.

Downing his seventh pint, he'd made his way out

of the pub he was in. Everything in his life had gone wrong lately. To a greater or lesser extent he blamed Alan Taylor, but he had to play this carefully, mainly because of the secret, the one they'd both been nursing all these years.

He staggered slightly as his eyes came to rest on Alan Taylor, who hadn't noticed him. His attention was focused on his business associates. Mr Conviviality of the Year. That was Alan. He was buying them drinks, laughing at their miserable jokes and generally being 'mine host', the man who was grateful for their patronage.

As Tony elbowed his way through the crowd, Alan saw him and his expression froze.

'Well! Look what the cat brought in.'

Three sets of eyes turned to look at him. The eyes were cold, emotionless – like dead fish on a slab.

Tony pretended they were real friendly types even though he knew they were far from that. Three blokes from the East End; hard types who talked with their fists rather than their gobs.

'Look, Alan old son. How about we have a quiet word?'

He hated the way Alan threw a smile at his new pals before sneering at his old friend.

'Do we have anything to say?'

Tony had sunk a skinful, but he prided himself on being able to take his drink and still think straight.

'Just remember, Alan. We've got skeletons in the same cupboard.'

He saw Alan blanch. His mouth closed in a thin, rigid line.

'Not so much my skeletons, Tony, as yours.'

Garth had recovered and been sent home. He was wearing a dark-red dressing gown when he answered the door of the dreary flat he shared with his mother. His face lit up when he saw her.

'Marcie! Have you come to take me to the pictures?'

'No, Garth. I came to see how you were after your little accident.'

'Accident?'

He looked totally blank. She wondered if being buried in Mr Ellis's back garden had erased his memory.

'The accident in Mr Ellis's garden. I heard you got buried under a lot of dirt.'

Realisation dawned instantly. 'Oh! Yeah! But I'm alright now.'

She wondered if he knew that Mr Ellis was dead. Somehow it seemed pointless mentioning it. Anyway, he might get distressed if she did.

'Do you remember what happened?'

His eyes rolled in his head. He looked skywards. 'I think so. We were moving some bits of wood to hold the roof up. And it all came down.'

'Is your mother looking after you?'

'She's out collecting.'

'Collecting?'

He nodded but didn't elaborate.

'I'll make a cup of tea,' Garth said suddenly.

Noticing the state of the place and working out that the cups wouldn't be much better, it occurred to her to refuse. She didn't have the heart.

'OK. But I can't stop for long.'

She followed him up the stairs. The kitchen was old-fashioned and smelled of old grease and overcooked cabbage. A dresser took up the whole of one wall. It was painted a dark green. The walls were brown.

Garth's cat was the only other occupant of the flat. The ginger-coated feline was curled up in an old orange box lined with paper. There was another orange box next to it filled with more newspaper and earth. Catching a whiff of cat's pee she guessed this second box served as a toilet.

Garth explained that the cat wasn't let out now since the incident with Bully Price.

'I don't want him to get hurt,' he said plaintively.

She could see that he wasn't very good at making tea and took over. The first thing she did was to wash the cups, getting as much of the stain out as possible.

'So when did your mother go out?' she asked by way of conversation.

'After Mrs Brooks left.'

Surprised, Marcie turned round. 'My grandmother's been here?'

'She came round to see how I was and then she had a cup of tea and a chat with my mother.'

The cheery way he mentioned her grandmother was very noticeable. 'You like my grandmother, don't you?'

'Yeah.' He chortled with joy as he said it.

Despite her own predicament, Marcie brightened too. 'She must like you too.'

He nodded vigorously. At the same time he dribbled tea down his chin and the biscuit he dunked in his cup sank without trace.

'She asks me what I see and I tell her.'

'That's good.'

Someone took an interest in him, asking what he saw on a day-to-day basis. It struck Marcie as odd that her grandmother, who was usually quite unapproachable, could be kind to someone like Garth.

'I do drawings for her.'

'You do?'

This was a surprise.

'Would you like to see some of them?'

Before she could answer either way, he'd set his tea down and was tugging open one of the dresser drawers. The wood was old, warped and stiff so made scraping sounds as he heaved.

There was a rustling of paper. Another smell was

added to that of the cat, though not nearly so pungent. Garth's drawings were done on butcher's paper, the sort used to wrap a pound of liver or a couple of pork chops.

'Here,' he said, straightening and flattening out the paper with stubby fingers. 'There you are.'

The drawings were childlike, but even so it was easy to see what they represented. The first was of two men. One was standing upright. The other was buried beneath a pile of earth. Both were waving what supposedly represented spades.

'Is this you and Mr Ellis?'

'Must be,' he said. 'I saw it in my head.'

She guessed he'd done the drawings on his return home. Like a camera he'd wanted to capture what must surely be the most exciting event in his humble, humdrum life.

He brought out more pictures, all of them done in crayons. One of them was very crumpled and fell to the floor. Garth dived on it.

'This is one of my old ones. My mum burns them on the fire when we're a bit short – but only the old ones. Not this one though.'

Marcie could tell it was old. The butcher's creamy coloured paper was fast turning to a tan colour.

She felt the blood drain from her face.

'Oh my God!'

She only whispered the words, but Garth heard.

His round eyes scrutinised her face looking for approval, but in this case she had none to give. Instead there were questions, questions perhaps that Garth could not answer.

The drawing was of two men digging. They were burying a third and smaller, less distinct figure. There was a shed just above the makeshift grave. It was as though Garth had juxtaposed one drawing on top of another.

There should be a number of interpretations, but as far as Marcie was concerned, there was only one. Suddenly she felt very, very sick.

'I have to go.'

Clapping her hand over her mouth, she ran out of the door and down the steps.

Garth watched her from the door.

'What about your cup of tea?' he called after her.

Marcie didn't look back. She needed air. She needed to talk to someone about what she'd seen and what it meant. The only person she could turn to on Sheppey was her grandmother. But she couldn't do that. Neither could she talk to Alan Taylor.

There was only her father. This was as near to evidence as she was ever going to get. The time had come to face him and beg him to tell her the truth. As soon as he came home, that was exactly what she would do.

Chapter Thirty-three

It was three o'clock in the afternoon in the East End of London. Tony Brooks looked the business in a light-grey Italian suit, sharp shoes and white shirt with button-down tabs. His hair was well cut and his tie was made of silk. If it hadn't been for the fact that he was where he was, he would have been taken for your everyday London businessman, a man of the City and worth a few bob. As it was, stockbrokers and commodity traders didn't stray much into places like Rotherhithe and Whitechapel and all the places in between.

He glanced up at the pub sign: a picture of a long-nosed king complete with crown and ermine-edged robe. The Royal George.

Most pubs round here were empty by closing time and it was past that. The patrons had wound their way back to the docks and factories. There might be a few old timers still sipping in the public bar, picking their horses and coughing up phlegm with each puff on their Senior Service.

The acrid smell of stale beer and fag ash flushed outwards as the door hushed shut behind him.

There were no lights on and no old blokes sitting at round tables picking the winner in that afternoon's three-thirty at Newmarket. There was only the landlord leaning on the bar. He was leafing through the *Daily Sketch*. He kept turning the pages even when he glanced up and acknowledged that Tony was there.

A load of unwashed glasses sat on the bar. Tony swept them to the floor in one swift movement.

'Ooops! They're a bit fragile.'

The landlord stopped reading the paper. Tony knew he had his attention. But something was wrong. He wasn't screaming at him; he wasn't offering to cough up what he owed either.

Tony started taking steps backwards, his eyes nervously darting this way and that for the attack he knew would come.

They were on him before he got to the door and he was buried beneath an avalanche of fists. The other side had got to him. He heard the name calling but was unconscious by the time the ambulance came.

The smell of antiseptic made Marcie's stomach heave.

'Don't worry,' said her grandmother as they waited for the visitors bell to sound. 'He will be better soon.'

Marcie said nothing. She wasn't worried about her father. On the contrary she was angry that this had happened. She'd been building up her courage prior to asking him about her mother as a consequence of seeing Garth's drawings. She couldn't tell him about the baby and getting married; she couldn't tell him she was going away. How could she go and leave her grandmother by herself? Though *he* would, she reminded herself. He would leave his mother all alone if it meant he could find Babs and the kids.

Visiting was the same week in and week out – he was unconscious for a very long time. At first it was touch and go, which meant joining her grandmother on her knees at the side of the bed, praying for her father's recovery.

In the meantime she considered telling her grandmother about her little problem, but somehow it didn't seem right. Surely it was her father who should be told first?

So that was how it went on, Marcie sighing away the weeks that her father spent in intensive care. Why had this happened now, just when she'd found the courage to ask him about her mother, plus telling him that she was pregnant?

Once a week she accompanied her grandmother. Visiting times were strictly controlled and the journey to and from London meant arriving back late at night. In time he would be transferred back to the local hospital on Sheppey. Until then her grandmother said more prayers to hurry this happening along.

He'd incurred such serious injuries from the beating that it was very likely he'd been left for dead. The doctors reported that a rib had punctured his lung and that it would be a long haul back to recovery.

The problem seemed to be that he didn't seem to care about recovering.

'You will come home soon and I will make you pasta and bolognese,' Rosa Brooks told him.

Marcie saw no improvement in her father's will to get better despite her gran's offer to feed him more nourishing meals than provided by the hospital.

It wasn't until he'd been in hospital for roughly five weeks that they saw a slight improvement – and found out that Babs had paid a visit.

A few weeks more and he was sitting up in bed and talking about coming home.

'Things will be different,' he exclaimed, a smile splitting his face from ear to ear.

There was something secretive in the way his glance shifted from his mother to his daughter. Marcie felt her grandmother tensing.

'You are not staying in London?' asked Rosa Brooks.

'No! Course not!'

A bright smile lit up her grandmother's face. 'That is good. That is so good.'

He sounded all exuberance and good humour, but Marcie wasn't convinced. There was something idling beneath the surface, something he didn't want to mention just yet. She wondered if it had something to do with Babs again. Maybe she was coming home with him.

'Get yourself something nice,' he said to his daughter as she stood at the side of the bed. He'd slipped a five pound note into her hand.

She bit her lip. Was it ungrateful to believe that he was giving her money as compensation for the way he'd treated her? Perhaps he was turning over a new leaf. The father he had once been began shining through again. In time, once he was home, she could tell him about her own problems – especially the baby. But not yet, simply because she was building up her courage. If her grandmother noticed how tense she was or that she was putting on weight, she didn't say so. Marcie was grateful for that. She would tell both of them once her father was home and back on his feet. She hoped that would be soon. Letting out seams and making shapeless shift dresses helped hide her condition, but couldn't go on much longer.

The income in the Brooks household had gone down since he'd been in hospital. Not that they were destitute – far from it. He'd left them a bit of cash and Marcie had the money from her part-time job at the record shop. And seeing as there was only the two of them living at home it didn't have to cover as much as when there was a house full.

Johnnie came down most weekends. She was wearing looser clothes now that she'd made herself.

She'd paid seven and six a yard for some plain black material bought with some of the money her dad had given her. So as not to arouse suspicion she trimmed the neckline and sleeves with white – just like the other dress she'd made. The pattern was pure Mary Quant, the idea created from a picture in a magazine.

Perhaps one day I'll be able to afford a real Mary Quant mini dress, she thought, though goodness knows when that would be.

On the night when they found out that Babs had visited and her father was in such good spirits, her grandmother was strangely morose all the way home.

Marcie didn't question why. Although a bank of clouds was gathering over the sea beyond Sheppey, Marcie was feeling happier than she'd been for a long time.

It appeared her grandmother wasn't so happy.

'She has made him promise something,' she said when pressed.

Nothing more was said. Marcie wondered idly if Babs had agreed to come home if her dad had promised not to hit her any more. Or even if the promise was something to do with the radiogram Babs had set her heart on months ago.

Marcie kept Johnnie informed about what was happening, but there was one particular subject she kept avoiding. Johnnie voiced the obvious question.

'So when will you tell him about the baby?'

They were sitting on the sea wall in a bracing breeze that was blowing straight at them in indiscriminate gusts.

'Soon.'

She turned away so he wouldn't see her confusion.

'What does that mean?'

She shrugged. 'I'll tell him as soon as he's been home a while. He's been very ill. I can't present him with a shock like that just yet. He needs time to recover.'

'Damn!'

The single word was delivered with undisguised exasperation. Johnnie was losing patience and she knew it.

But he had to understand how she was feeling; how important it was that she and her father be on good terms. That was the way things had to be if she were ever to approach him about her mother. She hadn't forgotten Garth's drawings and his odd references to a time she herself found difficulty in remembering.

'How about you? Have you told your parents?'

She already knew the answer, but she'd still had to ask. Johnnie had promised to tell his parents immediately after she'd told hers.

He grimaced. 'I've already told you I won't. Not until you do. First as last, it won't be easy.'

His expression clouded. Not for the first time she

sensed there was something he wasn't telling her. It wouldn't be easy for either of them, but Johnnie was very cagey about his parents. Even his best friend Pete seemed to know little about Johnnie's background.

'He arrived at the café on the North Circular all alone with just a bloody great bike between his legs, told us his name, challenged us to a burn up and that was it. Never been to his house, not even sure where it is. Never heard him speak of his mum and dad neither.'

Marcie had given up trying to get any information out of him. He got ratty when she persisted. She had her own reasons to explain why he was uncomfortable discussing them.

She was aware that her belly was getting bigger – she'd have to give up her job soon lest her boss begin to suspect. It would pay if she could stay on for six months. At least then she'd get Maternity Allowance. It wasn't much, but it would help. After that . . .

The time was coming when they *had* to tell their families. Marcie gathered her thoughts and laid them on the line.

'Your family'll disapprove of me. I'm not the same class as you. That's the truth, isn't it? They're going to think that I'm not good enough for you and that I've spoiled your chances of going to university.'

'No! That's what they want for me, not what I want for myself.'

He didn't meet the searching look in her eyes. Without confirming or even looking at her, in a way he was admitting that what she said was the truth. She didn't want it to be. It hurt like mad that they'd think she wasn't good enough for their son. But she was pretty certain she'd hit the nail firmly on the head.

Chapter Thirty-four

When Tony Brooks told his mother that he, Babs and the three kids were moving into a council house, she refused to believe it.

'You are leaving home?'

The pitch of her voice rose in disbelief. The small face, still a light shade of coffee and cream despite the fact that she'd lived with rain and damp for years, looked dumbfounded.

'I reckon I'm big enough,' he grumbled. He'd sorted things out about baby Annie. Babs had explained that reddish blonde hair ran in her family. She also reminded him of a night just before he'd got arrested. They'd been to the pub, had a bloody good time and had bought a fish and chip supper on the way home. Halfway home they'd paused in the bus shelter where the passion of their courtship returned with a vengeance.

'Annie was only a bit early,' Babs had added. 'And anyway, your Marcie is blonde – she and Annie are very similar. Marcie takes after her mother, Annie takes after me,' she'd said, patting her platinum blonde bird's nest.

All the same, he'd never expected telling his mother he was moving out would be easy.

He couldn't bring himself to look at her. She would most likely be heartbroken, but he had to do this. His marriage depended on it. Babs had told him to make a choice: live with her and the kids in a council house or with his mother, but without his family in the old cottage.

'And may you both be very happy together,' she'd tacked on to the threat.

The prospect of living with his mother all his life did not appeal – certainly not if his family wasn't there too. He'd agreed to move into the council house they'd been allocated as soon as he was out of hospital.

'Our Marcie will like it,' he'd added. 'Especially if I buy you that radiogram you want. You can both play records on it.'

He sounded gleeful at the prospect. Babs was more reticent. At first he couldn't quite work out why – until she dropped the bombshell.

'Your Marcie would appreciate a room of her own – especially now she's in the family way.'

At first he thought he was hearing things, either that or Babs was being spiteful seeing as her and Marcie had never got on.

The hospital wouldn't cope with a bloke with a temper. They'd likely call the police. Instead he turned sullen. His teeth ached with tension when he spoke.

'Run that past me again.'

Babs told him again. 'I saw her on the way out with your mother. I'm surprised the old bird hadn't noticed herself. But I did. The breeze caught your daughter's frock and I could see the outline of her belly. Five months by the looks of it.'

Tony placed a hand over his racing heart as his anger rose with his pulse.

Babs knew very well what was coming next, but she didn't care. She was getting her own back.

'Who's the father? I'll break his fucking neck!'

A nurse threw him a look of reproach. He ignored her, his brown eyes boring into his wife's face. 'Well?' he snapped. 'Who is it?'

She shrugged. 'I don't know. I haven't been home, have I?'

No. Of course she hadn't. But his mother had. His mother must have known. Surely she must!

His mother had cried off from visiting of late, citing the fact that she was old and in need of a rest. The real reason was that she couldn't contemplate him leaving home and was punishing him for taking his wife's side. In lieu of visiting she wrote terse letters briefly outlining what had been happening on the Isle of Sheppey.

The last one he'd received had told him that his father had visited and said to look out for increasing family. The news wasn't entirely unexpected. He'd be home and lying in his wife's arms before long which might very well result in an extra mouth to feed.

Babs was rabbiting on about the new house all the time. It was wearing him down a bit but he was finished with London. Broken ribs didn't suit him.

'Does Mum know about this?' he asked.

'How the bloody hell would I know? I've been putting up with my own mother these past months, not yours. Be glad to get shot of the pair of them and have my own place.'

'I thought our Marcie would have been smarter than to get herself into trouble.'

'She fell in love,' said Babs in a dreamy voice. An avid reader of *True Romance*, she reckoned she knew about these things.

'Silly cow. What did she want to go and do that for?'

Babs fluttered her eyelashes at him. 'I did. I was five months when we got married.'

Tony wasn't listening. 'Just wait till I get home. Whoever it is has to marry her, or they'll have me to reckon with.'

Marcie had never expected to be lonely. The cottage in Endeavour Terrace had been alive with the sound of her half-brothers arguing and little Annie crying for attention. She even missed the sound of Babs drinking her tea from a saucer, and that was saying something. Babs used to suck the tea into her mouth in such a way that her lipstick wouldn't be washed away.

Her grandmother had told her that her father and the family were not coming back to the cottage. They were moving into a council house.

'What about me?' she'd asked.

Her grandmother had replied in much the same vein as Babs had done to Marcie's father.

'You will need a room to yourself, you and the little one, unless the father is going to marry you.'

'Yes. He is,' Marcie blurted. Then she stopped. 'You knew?'

Rosa nodded sagely like old people do. 'Then I will write to your father and tell him so. He will understand and not blow his top if I explain that all will be well. What is the father's name?'

'Johnnie. Johnnie Hawke,' Marcie said softly.

She shook her head in disbelief. This episode was passing like a dream. She really couldn't believe how easy this had been. She'd expected arguments resulting from a pretty hot confrontation. It hadn't happened.

'Putting the position down on paper is always better in these situations,' said her grandmother. 'Hot anger needs time to cool and become reflective.'

The first thing she had to do was to tell Johnnie

when he came down on Friday. The working week would pass slowly until then. She resigned herself to that fact – after all, what was worth having was worth waiting for and what she wanted most was Johnnie.

Chapter Thirty-five

It was Thursday night, the wind was getting up and the air smelled of rain. Earlier that evening Marcie had accompanied her grandmother up to the hospital in Wards Hill just around the corner from Minster Abbey. His condition having improved, her father had been moved there so his family could visit more easily. They'd only been able to manage once a week when he'd been in London. Marcie had avoided doing even that and he wasn't happy about it.

'You should know why,' she said when he asked her the reason. Her belly made it obvious.

He reacted just as her grandmother had said he would. The letter and time had made him see sense.

'I can't say I'm happy but what's done is done. As long as that young man is going to marry you, that's fine by me. I'll let bygones be bygones.' He raised a warning finger. 'But I'll not have you living with him without a ring on your finger. You've been brought up a Catholic and even though we don't attend Mass that much, we do things right.'

The fact was that Rosa Brooks was the only one

who did attend Mass regularly, the rest of the family only attending baptisms, marriages and funerals.

Marcie told him that Johnnie wanted to marry her.

'Then that's alright then.'

Relief rolled over her. Everything was working out fine as far as her father was concerned.

Up until now her grandmother had been loath to mention the matter, but on the bus on the way home she added her own brand of approval to that of her son.

'You and your young man can live with me,' announced Rosa Brooks, 'but only if you get married,' she added with a hint of warning.

'I'll see what he wants to do,' Marcie replied.

Expecting a new baby in the family – a great-grandchild – always raised her grandmother's spirits, more so now that Tony and his brood had moved out.

Rosa Brooks was round at Edith Davies's. At present she was eyeing Garth's latest artwork while waiting for Edith to make the tea, which was spread out on the drop-down flap of the kitchen unit. Garth was sitting on a wooden kitchen chair, totally absorbed in what he was doing.

'You are a very good artist,' Rosa said to him. 'These pictures come out of your head?'

He nodded but did not look up. The tip of his

tongue protruded from the corner of his mouth. His fingers clenched the crayons tightly.

'I don't know where he gets it from,' said his mother.

'No. You would not,' returned Rosa brusquely.

The gossip that Garth's father was a Polish airman during the war wasn't necessarily the absolute truth. His mother had been pretty free and easy with her favours. Blokes in uniform were like a drug – she couldn't resist them and she couldn't say no.

Edith Davies had few friends she could confide in and Rosa Brooks was one of them. It did not matter to Rosa that Edith had a very bad reputation. Out of Christian charity, plus the promise of silver if she read the tea leaves or the cards, she called in regularly.

The tea was drunk, the cup tipped upside down and turned the requisite number of times in the saucer. As usual a few male strangers lurked in the tea leaves. Edith was always happy with that kind of news.

By the time they'd finished talking it was nine-thirty. Rosa rubbed her aching back as she got up, stretched and reached for her coat, her hat and her stout walking cane.

She hadn't let the rest of the family know that her knees were playing her up and she didn't go to the doctor. Instead she relied on prayer to see her through. It would clear up in time – she was sure of it.

Edith Davies showed her the picture that Garth had only just finished.

'He gets tired out after one of his sessions,' said Edith. 'He's not like it all the time with his drawing. Just now and again he'll go hell for leather at something and come out cream crackered.'

Rosa nodded in understanding. Garth was sitting quietly in a tatty old armchair, his chin lolling on his chest, his eyes flickering as though he were about to fall asleep.

'Garth. Get to bed,' ordered his mother.

At first he didn't seem to hear her. She repeated herself, this time accompanying her brusque words with a slap at his head.

He responded to this, getting up slowly and without a murmur shuffling off to his tiny room.

Rosa picked up the crumpled piece of paper he'd been drawing on. It smelled of haddock. She reached the obvious conclusion – on this occasion Garth's drawing paper had come from the fishmonger.

She frowned at the drawing. It seemed to be mostly black. There was a female figure in the middle wearing something pink spotted. She was surrounded by blackness. A figure resembling a man lurked at the edge of the blackness. The figure in pink did not seem aware of the second figure. The second figure, definitely a man, appeared to be watching.

'He's got a very vivid imagination,' said his mother.

Rosa let the paper fall back onto the drop-down ledge.

'I must go. I have left Marcie by herself.'

She hurried out as though the devil himself was on her tail. She'd left Marcie by herself many times before. Despite recent events, Marcie was usually sensible and reliable, but Garth's drawing had unnerved her. She prayed as she hurried along; prayed that she'd be in time.

There was no doubt in her mind. The girl in pink was Marcie. She could only guess at the identity of the man in the shadows. All she knew was that she had to get home. Fast!

Chapter Thirty-six

Marcie was sitting at the old treadle sewing machine at the kitchen table, dressed in a pale-pink maternity dress. Her grandmother had persuaded her that there was no need for her to stay on at the record shop.

'We can do without charity,' she'd exclaimed.

It cut no ice telling her that the Maternity Allowance was not charity. Marcie did as ordered, though she hadn't told her boss the real reason why. At her side were piled the leftover pieces plus a scrap of broderie anglaise. She smiled as she fondled the silky material.

'Pink for a girl,' she mused. Her fingers went to the blue cotton scraps she'd found. 'And blue for a boy.'

Annie's cast-offs were stored in a box in the attic, but Marcie was determined that her baby would have a few new things even though they were only home made.

She didn't realise how badly she was squinting until her head began to ache. The nights were drawing in. The small windows of the old cottage let in little light which meant there were always dark corners where daylight never reached. Once the sun went down it seemed as though the darkness crept out from those corners to cover the whole room.

There was no electric light above the sewing machine, the only recourse being to bring over the old oil lamp that usually sat in the middle of the 'best table' in the centre of the living room.

Once a match had been held to the wick, the flame came to life, its rosy glow falling over the tiny garments.

Just two more seams and the last of the baby clothes would be finished. She was pleased with her efforts, holding each one up and imagining the tiny person that was presently only a bump in her belly.

She quite often studied the lump, trying to deduce by its size and shape whether she was expecting a boy or a girl.

'I don't care what you are,' she said as she cuddled her bulge. 'Boy or girl. It doesn't matter.'

Being under twenty-one, her father had agreed to sign the necessary forms that would enable her to get married. Now all she had to do was get hold of Johnnie and tell him to go ahead and tell his parents. She'd gone up to Leysdown the week before to see if he was there. She'd planned telling him that he could now pick her up from the house – her grandmother had decreed that as they were getting married, she had no objection.

But he hadn't been there. There were many reasons why he wasn't there that particular weekend. That's what she told herself. He'll be here next week, she told herself, and kept telling herself that all week.

One reason above all others that he wasn't there lurked in her mind: he'd told his parents and they had forbidden him to see her again. It was the stuff of nightmares and wouldn't go away. She had no way of contacting him. All she could hope was that he'd be there the following week.

He'll be there, she assured herself. Tomorrow he'd come down from London with the rest of the gang.

Once she'd finished, she folded the baby clothes and put them in a pile beside the machine.

She was immersed in thought when suddenly the flame on the oil lamp flickered. Taken unawares, she sucked in her breath and looked over her shoulder.

Just a draught, she told herself. Gran was back.

She got up and went to fill the kettle. Her grandmother would appreciate a cup of tea.

'Do you want a digestive with your cup of tea,' she called out?

There was no reply.

The door between the kitchen and the passage leading to the front door made a creaking sound as it opened. Everything in the cottage creaked, especially at night – the doors, the windows, the roof trusses; but mostly the floorboards. And nothing fitted very well; certainly not the doors and windows, everything warped with age.

'Marcie.'

At the sound of his voice, she almost dropped the kettle.

A smiling Alan Taylor was standing in the middle of the kitchen.

His eyes dropped to her belly.

'I thought as much when I saw you the other day. You're in the family way.'

She didn't answer. The hand that held the kettle was shaking badly. She made a great effort to place it on the draining board before she dropped it.

What was he doing here?

'I guessed you were here,' he said, his smile broadening, his eyes shining. 'I saw your gran go out so thought I might pop in. We've got a lot to talk about, you and me, Marcie Brooks. We've got plans to make, especially now.'

Inside she was alarmed. Outside she frowned. 'I don't know what you mean. What plans?'

'Marcie, baby,' he said, stretching out his arms as though expecting her to run into them. 'You know what plans I'm talking about, Marcie. Plans for you, me and the baby. We'll go away from here. We'll be a family.'

Marcie was horrified. Her face must have shown it.

Alan looked quite put out. 'What are you looking at me like that for? It's my baby. Right?'

There it was – confirmed; the thing she'd been dreading.

She'd avoided him since that fateful night when she'd passed out at his place. A part of her hadn't wanted to believe that he'd done what he'd done. She'd convinced herself that it couldn't be true, that the evidence was too flimsy. But here it was. He was standing here practically admitting that he'd raped her. The thought of it made her sick – and much more besides.

Raised hopes about her and Johnnie getting married and living happily ever after were dashed by his confession. What should she do?

It was difficult to confront the problem with her emotions in such disarray, yet confront them she must. He had to be told. He had to understand.

'No!' she said, shaking her head frantically. 'No. I'm marrying Johnnie. I WANT to marry Johnnie! It's his baby.' She folded a protective arm across her belly. 'It's OUR baby. Mine and Johnnie's. Now get out. Get out of here. You disgust me! You really disgust me!'

There was a bitter taste on her tongue. Her last words were laced with hate.

Alan's eyes glittered like a slot machine sorting out the numbers when it's deciding whether you've won or not. But in Alan's case there was only one winner – there must always be only one winner – himself.

He shook his head. 'You sound just like your mother. She didn't know which side her bread was buttered either, turning me down in favour of a two-bit crook like your dad.'

Marcie felt her legs go weak. This man had actually tried to seduce her mother? Her thoughts reeling, she reached back with both hands, gripping the draining board for support.

'Get out! I hate you.'

He stood regarding her for a moment, and then he shook his head slowly, reached out a hand and touched her face.

'No you don't,' he said. 'You're young. You don't know what's best for you. Not yet. But you'll come round to it. You have to.'

She trembled. How could she have possibly considered him a substitute father?

'No!' She shook her head vehemently and clung to the draining board even more tightly. 'You can't make me.'

His grin was wide and, it seemed to her, full of teeth – or perhaps it was just a trick of the light. His face was a dull yellow thanks to the muted glow of the oil lamp.

'Oh yes I can.'

He didn't shout. He didn't reach out and grab her or any of the melodramatic things she'd seen at the pictures. His tone was low and chilled her to the bone.

'Think how upset your family will be. Your dad will probably give you a good hiding. Am I right, or what?'

'No. He'll give YOU a good hiding! I'll tell my dad the truth – that you raped me.'

He laughed. 'I'll tell him that you were a right little Lolita. You've heard of her, I bet. Couldn't get enough of older men. Threw herself at them, she did, just like you did me. That's what I'd tell your dad, though not only him. I'd spread the gossip around. And then of course your family's name would stink more than it already does. Your dad's an old lag; your stepmother's the village bike – everybody's had a ride. Think how the kids would be treated then.'

She didn't know where the courage came from, but Marcie was suddenly overwhelmed with the determination to stand up to him. She would not be intimidated. She would not allow her family to be the target for every gossip-hungry individual around.

'Then I'm going to the police. I'm going to tell them what you did.'

He raised his eyebrows. 'And what about the boyfriend? Will he want to marry you when he hears the kid might not be his? Well, will he?'

He turned sideways on, smiling like the winner he always strove to be.

'I'll give you overnight and tomorrow to think about it, then I'll be round for you Saturday morning.'

'What about Stephanie? What about Rita?'

He shrugged. 'They're both big enough to look after themselves. They've been scrounging off me for years. Now they can get off their fat asses and make their own way in the big bad world.'

People turned to salt in the Bible, but after he'd left Marcie felt as though she'd turned to ice. She couldn't move. Even when he caressed her cheek she didn't move. It was only after some minutes that she realised he was gone and that her grandmother was home and seemed very agitated.

'What is wrong?' Her face was stiff with alarm.

Marcie shook herself out of her trance.

'Nothing!'

It was obvious from the look on her grandmother's face that she didn't believe her. There was no knowing what the old dear had seen in the tea leaves round at Edith Davies's house. But she couldn't admit that Alan had been here. The man she'd thought so warm and friendly had issued her with a dreadful ultimatum. In her young mind there was only one thing she could do about it. She had to get away from Alan Taylor. She had to leave Sheppey for her family's sake, for Johnnie's sake, for her own sake, and for the baby's sake.

'Gran? I'm going away with Johnnie. His parents have offered us rooms. They've got a big house in London. I'm not saying I won't come back. I will. Of course I will.'

The look on her grandmother's face was unexpectedly forthright. 'I know,' she said quietly.

'You do?'

Although she told herself that she shouldn't be surprised, her grandmother's calm response took her totally by surprise.

'I saw it coming,' said Rosa Brooks.

'In the tea leaves?'

Rosa patted her chest. 'In my heart.'

Marcie's breath caught in her throat. Oh God, she didn't want to leave. But she must; for the sake of her family, she must.

Her voice trembled when she spoke. 'Will you say goodbye to everybody for me? Tell Dad I'll send him the consent forms. Will that be alright? And I'll write to you, Gran. I promise I'll write to you.'

Rosa Brooks had a reputation for being curt, even cold. Rarely did she reveal her emotions or wear her heart on her sleeve as some would have it. Tonight her eyes sparkled.

'Write to me with your new address and I will take care of everything,' said her grandmother.

The loving smile that crossed her grandmother's lips was for her and her alone. Things will be fine,

Marcie told herself. You're doing the right thing and things are *bound* to be fine!

On Friday night she was waiting at the bus stop when Johnnie came by. She was so relieved to see him that she didn't question why he hadn't come to see her the previous week. He pulled over and waited for her to get on, then suddenly caught sight of the old suitcase she was carrying.

'What's that?'

'I've left home. My gran wouldn't let me stay there once she found out about the baby.' It was a lie but she didn't want to mention Alan Taylor and for Johnnie to question whether the baby was his.

'What about your dad? Will he sign the consent forms?'

'We'll write to him from your place. Writing is best when you need someone to think calmly,' she said, taking leaf out of her grandmother's book.

She could see the look in his eyes, though his silk scarf still covered half his face and his voice was muffled. He hesitated in answering, eyeing her as though he were thinking things over. Her heart lurched in her chest.

'I have to warn you. I haven't told them about the baby. But we'll be welcome. I'm sure we'll be welcome.'

She wasn't sure he sounded very confident. A few

days ago everything had been going to plan. Now everything seemed to be unravelling.

Johnnie drove carefully all the way to London in consideration of Marcie's condition.

She couldn't help feeling apprehensive. He'd told her very little about his parents. She felt nervous about meeting them, afraid she wouldn't meet their standards, and afraid they wouldn't meet hers.

Chapter Thirty-seven

Johnnie parked the bike in a gravel driveway while Marcie stood with her mouth open looking up at the house he lived in.

'I've got a confession to make,' he said after he'd taken off his helmet and his white silk scarf. 'My name's not Johnnie Hawke. Well, it is Johnnie, but it's Haskins: John Edward Haskins. I thought Hawke sounded more impressive.'

Marcie nodded mutely. She had a feeling that she was going to find a lot more surprises in Johnnie's life.

To begin with, she had never suspected that Johnnie's family were well off and never ever had Johnnie confessed that his father was a vicar! Maurice Haskins's hair was collar length and coal black. Unlike his son his eyes were dark and he had a large nose. Marcie couldn't help thinking that he suited the name Hawke more than Haskins.

'He's right trendy for a man of the cloth,' Johnnie told her, looking amused by her surprise. 'Mum's OK too.'

'Call me Jane,' said Johnnie's mother. She had a refined but friendly face and pale-blonde hair held back by a black velvet Alice band. A box-pleated skirt matched a pale-blue twin set. Pearl earrings matched a double string around her neck and she wore sensible shoes. Her smile was quick and ready as though well rehearsed.

'I'll get the box room ready for you.'

Marcie thanked her. The feeling that she was imposing on them wouldn't go away.

'Up here,' said Jane Haskins, taking charge of the battered brown case.

Marcie glanced nervously at Johnnie. He'd taken off his leather jacket and boots at the front door. A row of tartan slippers sat on the lower shelf of an old-fashioned hall stand. She'd almost laughed out loud to see him slip his feet into a pair.

The room was up at the top of the house. The vicarage was three storey plus cellars, and was built in a mock-Tudor fashion. To Marcie's eyes it was the most impressive house she'd ever been in.

'This is lovely,' said Marcie once her suitcase was lying on the bed. 'Dead posh. Poshest house I've ever been in. The view's lovely too.'

It wasn't exactly true. Dormer windows and tree-lined avenues gave way to red roofs and chimney pots. The air smelled different around here – smutty and dusty – and she found herself missing the smell of the sea.

Jane Haskins spoke first. 'It's Johnnie's I take it.'

Marcie nodded dumbly. Of course it was. Weren't they going to believe her?

Johnnie's mother seemed to sense her nervousness. 'Never mind. We'll talk about it later.' She sounded kind, but perhaps showing kindness was just part of the stock in trade of a vicar's wife. It was almost imperceptible, but Marcie noticed the tightness of Jane Haskins's smile.

The door closed. The tension and travelling had worn her out so she slumped down on the bed, too tired to even take her coat off.

Her eyes alighted on a small wooden crucifix hanging on the wall above her head, the only adornment in the whole room. She said a little prayer. 'Please God. Make them like me.'

Her eyes closed and she slept. In her dreams an odd observation came to her: Johnnie looked nothing like either of his parents.

Downstairs a nonchalant Johnnie was placing a record on the radiogram: Duane Eddy singing 'Come on Everybody'. It was the first record he'd ever bought. He'd told Marcie once that 'Twist and Shout' by the Beatles was his favourite. The truth was he couldn't stand them – their hair, their dress sense or their simple, sentimental songs.

Just as he'd expected, both parents came into the room and turned the atmosphere oppressive. The room already felt clammy and darkened quickly as the clouds gathered and the rain began to fall.

His mother's eyes stayed fixed on his face as she lowered herself into a chintz-covered armchair. His father stood unblinking in front of the fireplace as though he were about to impart a sermon.

To some extent that's exactly what he is going to do, Johnnie thought. I'm the sinner who's strayed from the path. He stayed in cool dude mode and waited for the storm to break.

'John, my son, perhaps I was naïve to think that your life would run along tramlines, but I truly think I believed that. I even once entertained the hope that you might follow in my footsteps and enter the Church. However, I did not expect you to bring a young woman here in such an advanced condition.'

'She's pregnant,' snapped Johnnie, eyes lowered, hands shoved in pockets. Why couldn't his father ever get straight to the point? Why couldn't he use the right words, or even the less welcome phrases? 'Or to put it another way, Dad, she's up the duff or got a bun in the oven, and I did it!'

Johnnie's smile was purposely disrespectful. His parents had bred that in him, though they wouldn't see it that way. Wishing to appear modern, they'd chosen to explain things to him rather than use any enforcement whatsoever. Half the time he hadn't understood what they were on about. Whatever had made them believe that a nine-year-old could under-stand the subtleties of an adult relationship?

His father took a deep breath and shot a worried look at his wife. 'The point is, John, what are you going to do about it?'

Throwing one leg over the chair arm, he slung himself into the chair matching the one his mother was sitting in. 'Marry her, I suppose.'

Again a look flashed between his parents. He guessed what was coming. Who said charity begins at home?

His father opened the proceedings. 'And what about your studies? You've been working so hard at them these last few weeks. Indeed, you've hardly left the house. Do you still wish to attend Oxford?'

Johnnie shrugged. 'Not now.'

He didn't confess that he'd been chewing things over for a few weeks, deciding which meant the most to him. He'd decided on Marcie.

'Where is she from?' his father pressed.

'Sheerness on the Isle of Sheppey.'

He made a tutting sound. 'Just as I suspected. The wrong side of the tracks for you, my boy. You cannot possibly contemplate marrying her. Just think of it. All that education wasted and for what? A lapse of judgement on a one-night stand should not stand in the way of a university education.'

Johnnie looked up at him from beneath a thick fall of hair. 'Marcie was not a one-night stand.'

'All the same, John—'

What are you saying, Father?' Johnnie snapped. 'That she's working class and we're not? If you want your parishioners to think you're modern, Father, then you're going to have to shelve that attitude. I thought that everybody was supposed to be equal in this day and age. Is that right?'

He saw his father's jaw clench and knew that not for the first time the urge to lash out at his son's disrespect had almost overpowered him.

His mother joined the fray. 'You cannot marry that girl, John!'

Now it was his turn to be firm. He was almost as tall as his father when he got to his feet. He looked straight into his eyes.

'I'm going to marry Marcie. I WANT to marry Marcie! I'm going to the café. Tell Marcie I'll be back later.'

He stormed out of the room.

Maurice and Jane Haskins were the epitome of controlled emotions. The Reverend Maurice Edward Haskins remained standing at the mantelpiece, pipe clenched between his teeth, his dark eyes appearing to be staring into infinity. His wife, Jane Alicia Haskins, sat primly in her armchair, knuckles tightly clenched.

'Well,' she said at last. 'That's all the thanks we get for looking after him all these years.'

'He's not a puppy, Jane. We didn't buy him from a pet shop.'

'It wasn't that different. A little gratefulness wouldn't go amiss.'

Her husband sighed. 'He doesn't know he's adopted, Jane, so why should he be grateful?'

Marcie didn't hear his bike rumble into life and roar off in the direction of the North Circular. The past few months had drained her. She slept in the best bed she'd slept in for a long time.

It was the sound of the front doorbell that finally awoke her. The glow of sodium streetlights streamed through the window, turning the grey walls yellow.

Her heart raced as she pushed herself up onto her elbows. Surely her father hadn't found her that quickly?

Dragging herself to the edge of the bed, she sat gripping the dusky pink counterpane. The voices from downstairs were muffled. It couldn't possibly be her father. He'd be trumpeting by now if he thought he'd found her.

All the same there was something worrying about the tone of the visitors' voices and that of the vicar and his wife.

Her shoes had come off and it wasn't easy getting them back on. Her feet were swollen. Barefooted she went over to the window and looked at her watch. One-thirty. Crikey! Had she been asleep that long?

She looked beyond the laurel hedge to the street and saw a police car. It occurred to her that perhaps her father had enlisted their help in finding her. On the other hand he tended to shy away from the law.

Then another thought hit her, a thought so terrible that she felt her throat closing in and her chest tightening.

Throwing her shoes to the floor, she hurried as best she could along the top landing, down the stairs, along the second landing and the last flight of stairs.

Johnnie's parents were sitting in the room they'd been in earlier when Johnnie had told them about the baby. They looked ashen and pale and didn't look up when she entered the room. There were also two policemen, both standing, both looking very serious.

One of the policeman's eyes flickered over her swollen belly.

A claw of fear tightened around her heart. 'What's happened? Where's Johnnie?'

They didn't ask her who she was. They just told her that he'd been speeding along the North Circular Road towards the Mile End Café. He'd lost control on a bend.

'A tanker had spilled oil on the road earlier that day. I'm afraid he skidded into the path of an oncoming bus.'

Chapter Thirty-eight

The funeral was quite an event – Johnnie's friends heard about it and came along en masse on their motorbikes, their leather jackets shiny black in a downpour of rain.

The Reverend and Mrs Haskins shared a large black umbrella. The service was being conducted by a bishop, a friend of the family.

Mrs Haskins had hardly spoken since the accident and when she did it was in sharp, minimal staccato. Johnnie's father seemed more self-contained, his expression stoical as though maintaining a front for the benefit of the relatives, even though he was the closest of the relatives.

Marcie found it difficult to understand how self-contained they were. She sensed they were grieving, but hadn't seen them cry. There was just an anguished look in their eyes, as though they were reliving Johnnie's life somewhere deep in their minds.

She consoled herself with the fact that they were of a different class and born into a different age than she. They were grieving in their own way, a way she didn't quite understand.

Alone beneath a black umbrella loaned to her by Johnnie's parents, Marcie followed the proceedings as if in a dream – this couldn't really be happening. Whoever heard of a funeral where the graveside was lined with so many young faces mourning the loss of one of their own?

She'd not written to her family, even to tell them what had happened. Somehow putting pen to paper made things more real than they actually were – if she didn't write the details down, then they might not be true and Johnnie would come swinging through the door, his white silk scarf hiding the lower half of his face.

Her family didn't have Johnnie's address so wouldn't come looking for her and there was no point asking any of his friends – Johnnie had been careful not to disclose the fact that he lived in a vicarage and that his father was a vicar. He'd even changed his name to something less ordinary: Johnnie Hawke, not Haskins.

She'd made further attempts to write, but on each occasion she was overcome with a sudden bout of shivering. She was numb, too shocked by what had happened, and in despair at her circumstances.

Weeks passed before she finally began to get a grip on things. Even Jane Haskins returned to being her normal self before Marcie did and she got the impression she was not wanted there.

They urged her to write to her family. She

explained that her mother was dead, that her father had remarried and that there was nobody else to go back to, except her grandmother.

'I think they've disowned me,' she lied.

It hadn't been her intention to lie, but something about their attitude angered her. Her grief for Johnnie was still so raw – like an open wound. She couldn't understand how his parents could be moving on so quickly, and yet ignoring the one link to Johnnie that remained. For God's sake, they had only just lost their only son. Didn't they want any part of their grand-child? Despite all their imperfections, her own family wouldn't have acted like this. Their constant nagging only made her more determined to stay – simply to annoy them.

Seemingly resigned to the fact that she wasn't yet ready to move out, Jane Haskins made sure by having coffee with her every morning and tea every after-noon. On each occasion she began doling out advice, sympathising with Marcie for her predicament, and making suggestions about what she should do next.

'There's no point in ruining your life. Think of the future. Think of what is best for you and the child. Where will you live if you keep it? A cheap room somewhere with a childminder to look after it when you go out to work? National Assistance? You won't get much from them, I can tell you.'

The same advice was given over and over again.

Marcie was not immune to her advice. What she was saying made sense. As an unmarried mother she could offer little to this child. One question kept raising its head, and it was all to do with Jane and Maurice Haskins. One day she asked it.

'This child is your grandchild. Why don't you give it a home yourselves?'

Jane had very thin lips and wore a muted tone of pale pink. When her jaw tightened it was as if her lips had been sucked into her mouth.

Thoughtfully, she placed her cup and saucer back onto the silver tea tray.

Marcie sensed an announcement was about to be made. It turned out she was right.

'Besides the fact that we are too old to cope with an infant, I think you should know that Johnnie was not our own flesh and blood. He was adopted.' Jane waved a hand at their comfortable surroundings. 'He was brought up in comfort. He had everything a boy would want. This is what your child could have if you opt for adoption with a childless couple who are young enough and fit enough to cope with a baby. It would be a very Christian thing to do. The child would be happy and so would the new parents. It makes sense. You know it makes sense.'

A time followed when she felt more alone than she ever had in her life. The big rooms of the vicarage echoed with secretive whispers. She knew without being told that Johnnie's parents were discussing her future.

She spent most of her time thinking about what Jane had said. This lump was her baby, but in all honesty what did she have to offer it? Not nearly so much as Johnnie had had, that was for sure.

The welcome when first arriving here with Johnnie had been restrained; it had been obvious from their tight smiles and muted kindness that they were disappointed with their son's choice. A lifetime of preaching against sin – especially of the carnal kind – was difficult to discard even when faced with the prospect of an illegitimate grandchild.

She caught the Reverend and his wife exchanging looks just after interrupting their conversation when she'd come on them by chance in the kitchen, the drawing room or the library.

They'd clam up once she entered, but the day came when they finally laid it on the line.

The coffee and teatime advice had continued. She wasn't actually being browbeaten, but they were presenting her with a very strong case for adoption. The world was her oyster if she were free of encumbrances.

'Don't let your heart rule your head.'

'Think of the child.'

And all the time she lost herself in the splendid

rooms of the vicarage. Her child too could have something like this.

Another coffee time, and her decision was made.

'I think I've decided to have it adopted,' said Marcie.

Jane Haskins breathed a sigh of relief, leaned across and covered her hand with her own.

'Very wise, my dear. I'm sure you won't regret it.' She got to her feet. 'We'll make arrangements. Everything will be taken care of. You don't need to worry about a thing.

It was some weeks later when they asked her to come into the drawing room. A pale winter sun was doing its best to brighten the day. The window faced south. Dust motes danced on the shaft of light piercing the plain net curtains.

The room was comfortable but plain. A pea-green rug sat in front of the black slate fireplace. If it had been earlier on in her pregnancy Marcie might have thrown up, but as it was she was well past that stage. The end was in sight.

'We've made the arrangements,' said Jane Haskins who was sitting in her usual place, her hands clasped in her lap. 'Maurice will fill you in on the details.'

Stiffly, as though she were wearing a crown, she turned her head to her husband for support.

Johnnie's father paced the room until he was

standing in front of the window, the light behind him and his hands folded behind his back. Marcie had gone to church on a few occasions and had seen him standing like this in the pulpit.

'You're going away,' he said. 'Pilemarsh Abbey is in the country, so there'll be nobody you know there. Everything will be paid for and everything will be taken care of. The establishment is well organised for girls who . . .' He paused. It occurred to her that he was swallowing some remnant of a sermon full of fire, brimstone and damnation.

Girls who are no good and end up in hell.

He didn't go so far as to say something like that, but the unspoken words hung in the air between them.

'You're telling me that I'm being sent to a home for unmarried mothers.'

'They'll look after you and do what has to be done. The child will be well looked after,' said Maurice Haskins. 'I'm sure they'll find a very good home for it.'

Chapter Thirty-nine

The fat little bus snorted its way along the country road, the sound of its grating gears reverberating between high walls and hawthorn hedges.

Not everything was countryside because there was a town nearby. There was a factory making windows, obtrusive in the middle of fields. Storms of fallen leaves raced before the wind, a tumbling mix of red, yellow and brown.

Marcie sat silently staring out of the window, her gaze fixed on the passing scene. She was thinking how different things would have been if Johnnie hadn't been killed. She missed him dreadfully but with every passing day their brief time together seemed more and more like a dream. She sometimes wondered whether the news of his death had reached the little house in Endeavour Terrace. Presumably not, seeing as no one had been in touch. She'd considered writing to tell them of her decision, but the longer she put it off the harder it became.

Johnnie's parents had wished her a stiff goodbye. They were generous enough, giving her an envelope containing ten crisp five-pound notes.

'To set yourself up once the baby has been adopted.'

Refusing the money was considered and rapidly discarded. Only a fool would refuse it.

She moved her gaze from the window to her belly. Bigger and bigger it had grown. The doctor at the clinic in London advised her she would have a big baby.

'Might even be twins,' he said, 'but I doubt it. I can only feel one head in there and I don't like taking an X-ray at this late stage.'

She patted her bump. Strange how you get used to things, she thought. Even Sheppey seemed like a lifetime away. At times it felt as though she were floating in a great sea of trouble.

Pangs of regret accompanied her on the journey.

I should have written.

As for Alan – I shouldn't have liked him so much.

It's my fault in a way.

I shouldn't have gone to his house that night.

I shouldn't have accepted a lift in his car.

The family will be ashamed of me.

The prospect of being alone with strangers until the baby was born alarmed her.

There were three other people on the bus, one with a suitcase sitting on the seat beside her.

The other passengers were a man and a woman. As they got off Marcie watched them walk by. The woman was wearing a red and black checked mohair coat and ankle boots – the old-fashioned kind trimmed with fur and a zip up the front.

The bus trundled on. A small motorcycle overtook it. She heard the driver swear and exchange a few more well-chosen words with the conductor.

'Bloody maniacs. Ought to be banned, the bloody lot of them!'

No! She wanted to shout. No! They are not.

She thought of Johnnie and the pride he'd had in his bike. Her heart ached for the sound of his voice, the casual off-handedness hiding his natural sincerity.

Her attention was brought back to the present. Blinking back the tears, she clenched her jaw so hard it hurt. She had to think of the future. The child would be better off being adopted just like Jane Haskins said.

When the scenery became boring and the nervous churning of her stomach too much to bear, Marcie eyed the only other remaining passenger. She was sitting at the front of the bus, smoke from a cigarette circling her head. The chignon at the nape of her neck shone a healthy pale gold. Pearl earrings glinted from her lobes each time she turned her head to look at the view or light another cigarette; she'd smoked a whole packet on the journey, Marcie noticed.

They had to be going to the same place. Please God that it's so, prayed Marcie. She hated the thought of being the only new arrival there.

Hidden by overhanging branches, the bus stop was not apparent until the bus slithered on wet leaves and eventually came to a halt.

Colder now as apprehension kicked in, she purposely fixed her gaze on the other side of the road to Pilemarsh Abbey, the place she was destined for.

Gaps in the trees disclosed acres of ploughed field on the other side of the road. The wind blew the grass on the verge. The trees were tinged with the first leaves of spring, a lovely apple-green colour.

It took quite an effort, but she eventually turned her head for the first sight of her destination.

A wall of grey stone ran along her side where the bus had stopped.

There was no point in hesitation. This had to be done.

The gap was narrow. Her small suitcase and her expansive belly contrived to prevent her from easing out.

Just as she'd hoped, the other passenger was getting off too. 'Need a hand?'

Marcie's eyes travelled upward to a coat loosely belted over a stomach that was as big as her own.

She quickly judged the girl to be around her own age, but totally different in looks and colouring. Whereas Marcie had naturally blonde hair, blue eyes and a heart-shaped face, the one she looked up at had wide-set blue eyes, high cheekbones and a straight nose above full, sensuous lips. Her hair was unmistakeably platinum blonde and straight from a bottle.

Marcie could be regarded as pretty, the blonde with the pearl earrings had a handsome face, the sort seen on Greek statues at the British Museum. She also wore very nice clothes, not so much expensive as wisely chosen to appear that way.

Awestruck in a way she hadn't been since her schooldays when the gymslip-clad Head Girl had allocated her the job of milk monitor, she managed to blurt a swift, 'Thank you.'

The tall blonde beamed as she grasped the worn hide handles and took the lead, moving sideways down the aisle. Marcie struggled to her feet. The feeling of being cast adrift, like a broken boat from a world-class liner, was less intense than expected.

The conductor eyed them in a surly manner and offered no assistance. Once their heels were digging into the soft grass verge, he sniffed and pointed to a sign and a gateway a few yards along the road. Like the bus stop it was half hidden by branches.

'That's the place for fallen women,' he said, his tone as contemptuous as the look he gave them. 'It's like a bloody great rowing boat in that place – oars on both sides!'

Appalled at his meaning, Marcie blushed to the tips of her hair. Luckily she wasn't easily roused to temper; things had to be pretty dire before she lashed out.

The platinum blonde was less restrained. Setting down her case, she stuck her fists on her hips and jerked her head high, her eyes blazing.

'Whores! Is that what you mean, you dirty old sod? Now that's where you're wrong. Didn't you know? This place is being turned into a convent!' She jerked her thumb at Marcie. 'She's got the job of Mother Superior, and I'm the bloody Virgin Mary 'cause I like seeing men go down on their knees before me! Now sod off! Go on. Shove off and punch a few tickets, you bald-headed old coot!'

The bus conductor snorted and threw one last insult. 'Tart!'

The blonde picked up a fallen stick and took a run at him. Despite her girth, she ran fast and looked strong enough to land a blow. 'And who makes us tarts, eh? Men! That's who! Prince Bloody Charming until there's a bun in the oven!'

Firing puffs of black smoke from its noisy exhaust, the bus pulled away, the gears grating against the worn cogs, as the dying pistons rapidly coated the engine with choking layers of carbon.

The world around it responded to its passing, last year's dead leaves swirling like dancing dervishes, finally settling in crisp brown heaps at the roadside.

The blonde glowered after it, her cheeks pink from the morning chill. 'Men!'

Marcie wasn't fooled by the jutting firmness of the

girl's chin. There was also moistness in her eyes. Still, she had to admire her defiant stance, the way she stood with her fists clenched and head held high.

Finally they stood alone.

'I'm Sally,' said the blonde, swiftly turning round and taking Marcie unawares with a firm handshake.

'I'm Marcie.'

Heaving her elegant shoulders Sally turned her classic features to the sign and the entrance to Pilemarsh Abbey. Her breasts, heavily expectant with baby milk, heaved her coat lapels apart when she sighed. 'Well. Let's get it over with.'

Pouncing on her suitcase and gripping it with a firm hand, she began to walk.

Eyeing the sign and the grey stonework with heavy misgiving, Marcie followed, though slowly, taking in every little detail, the curling paint at the corners of the sign, the way the leaves of the poplar trees rattled like tiny bits of metal, and the height of the walls – mostly the height of the walls. They were huge and meant to keep people in.

Sally got to the gate first, stopped and waited for her to catch up.

'Sorry,' said Marcie, puffing and rubbing at the hollow of her back.

'What for?'

'I'm a bit slow and my back aches.'

The classic features softened. 'Nervous?'

Marcie admitted that she was. 'My stomach's doing somersaults.'

Sally laughed. 'Of course it is. There's a baby in there aching to get out and live.'

'I've never had a baby before.'

Sally's laughter died away. A spark of fear lurked in the clear-blue eyes.

'Neither have I. So it's a first time for both of us.'

Turning she scrutinised the gate as though she were looking for something in particular, perhaps for a way in that would be of advantage, unobserved by the authorities vested in the place. 'No,' she said at last. 'Can't find it anywhere.'

Bemused, Marcie eyed her with puzzlement. 'Can't find what?'

'The sign – the one that says "Abandon hope all ye that enter here".'

Marcie couldn't help but laugh and found herself feeling immediately better. The nervousness was put on hold – at least for the moment.

There was a twinkle in Sally's eyes. 'That's what it's supposed to say above the entrance to Hell, and we can't be going there, surely.'

Marcie pulled a rueful expression. 'I hope not.'

Sally turned a graver expression back to the entrance and gave a disdainful snort. 'Come on. Let's see what sort of place this is.'

Chapter Forty

A woman wearing the sombre uniform of a Salvation Army captain smiled and took her suitcase. 'Please come this way, Miss Brooks. Welcome to Pilemarsh Abbey.'

Marcie's eyes swept from the building and over the dark uniform of the small woman with rounded hips and belly, and apple-red cheeks.

'It's an odd name.'

The woman looked surprised. 'Odd?'

She saw the pale eyes flicker as though searching for some logical response to a question she didn't entirely understand.

'It doesn't look like an abbey. It looks like a house.'

'Ah!' she finally said in a condescending manner. 'You're a Catholic, aren't you my child, and thus may have been expecting an abbey or convent-type of hospital. I'm afraid it's just a name given it by some past owner, though for the life of me, I can't think why.'

Marcie tipped back her head, her gaze skimming over the Gothic-style arches above each window. 'Perhaps the name had something to do with hopes of going to Heaven.' Her own words surprised her, but not as much as they surprised the woman.

The round face convulsed with confusion. 'I'm sure . . . I don't know,' she blustered.

Marcie's attention was taken with another girl who had arrived by car. She was brown and pretty with velvet eyes and a graceful figure.

The car was a shiny black Rover that someone must have taken an age to polish.

A woman stuck her head out of the car's rear window and addressed the Captain.

'Do you have a telephone?'

The Captain nodded against the stiff bow of her bonnet as she smiled.

'Yes. Indeed we do.'

'Good.' The woman's dark eyes turned to the girl. Judging by their looks, Marcie was looking at a mother and her daughter.

'They have a telephone.'

'So I hear,' said the daughter.

'Good. I'll be in touch, darling.'

'Give it a few weeks. It should all be over by then. I'll let you know if it happens before then, but please don't visit me. I don't want that.'

The mother nodded. 'I understand. Now take care, darling.'

Mother and daughter kissed. Even though their lips barely brushed each other's cheeks, Marcie could sense the great affection between them. Seeing that made her feel incredibly bereft; she wondered how her mother would have acted in such a situation. She liked to think she'd be just like that, or perhaps even better – imploring me to keep the child, promising to stand by me regardless, she thought.

The weak sunlight flashed on the girl's earrings.

'Goodbye! Goodbye!' The mother of the girl called goodbye until she was too far away to do anything but wave a gloved hand.

The girl turned to the Captain. 'Right. I'm ready now.'

The Captain had very red cheeks and an amiable disposition. Her expression exploded with puce-coloured joviality. 'Jolly good. Jolly good. Do come this way. You'll be sharing a room between the three of you. You'll have a lot in common. All three of you are at the same stage of expectancy . . .'

The red-veined cheeks, her facial skin as pitted and dented as that of an orange, and her joyous expression were as much a part of her character as the thick spectacles sitting on her nose. She chattered all the way to the front door.

The girl who had arrived by car adopted an aura of calm detachment. Marcie exchanged a brief look with Sally and mouthed the word 'posh'.

Prams were ranged along the path running the

length of the building. Some of the babies were crying, their little fists punching at the air.

The little band slowed as they passed as each occupant, who in turn joined the cacophony of sound.

'They're waiting for their feeds,' her escort explained.

A bell sounded from within the building. It reminded Marcie of infants' school, but instead of children a bevy of young women tumbled out of the door, peeling off to either side and taking charge of a pram.

'The mothers,' explained her companion, her face and body seeming to swell with pride, as though she were some sort of queen bee and these were her workers merely responding to orders. 'They've come to collect their babies for their evening feed. Babies are fed every three hours for twenty minutes' duration.'

The eyes of each new arrival followed the mothers swooping down on children they would soon give away.

Marcie guessed that these mothers had been lurking just inside the door, ready to spring forward at the first strike of the bell. Only a few were less than enthusiastic, eyeing the infants as though they constituted a severe intrusion on the life they'd planned for themselves. Did they really consider their babies in that way, she wondered, or was their defensive attitude a cover for deeply held pain?

'Now then,' said the Captain, her stout bosom

thrust proudly forward. 'The home is divided between those awaiting the arrival of their babies, and those who have already delivered prior to adoption.'

Adoption!

The word jangled in her brain. Up until now it hadn't figured too prominently. The Reverend Haskins and his wife had chosen their words carefully – almost discreetly.

'The child will be placed in a nice family home.'

In the aftermath of Johnnie's death she'd allowed herself to be swept along by outside forces, his parents in particular. She hadn't protested or even considered that there might be an alternative. The modern age still frowned on girls who got pregnant without a wedding ring on their finger, so there was no way she could possibly keep her baby.

Their room was just about big enough to take three single beds. Sally had bagged the one by the window. Marcie threw her suitcase onto the one immediately behind the door.

Allegra, the girl wearing Carnaby Street clothes and genuine Courreges boots, placed her luggage on the third bed.

'Then I suppose this is mine.'

Her voice smacked of Chelsea and the West End of London.

'I suppose it is,' said Sally.

Marcie couldn't help but remark on the bags. 'They're smart.'

'Pigskin,' said Allegra as she pulled off gloves that matched the luggage both in colour and material. She looked sniffily around the room. 'This room must have once been the broom cupboard.'

'And you're used to something better, I suppose,' snapped Sally with scathing sarcasm.

'Actually I am.'

'Well aren't you the lucky one, your ladyship – though lady is hardly the right word, is it. Opened your legs and dropped your drawers same as we did.'

Marcie felt the need to intervene. 'Look. There's no point in going on like this. We'll be sharing this room for a little while. It's best that we all get on together.'

Both girls were older than her. They looked surprised that she sounded so authoritative.

While Sally and Allegra turned their backs on each other and began unpacking, Marcie bided her time.

After removing her shoes, she slumped down on the bed and wondered how long it would be before she was not just Marcie Brooks but Marcie Brooks and child. But that wasn't all she was thinking. Annie came to mind, crying for her feed just like the newborns lying in their coach-built prams. Unlike the newborns Annie was fed whenever she was hungry and certainly not to a timetable.

Chapter Forty-one

One day on and things didn't seem too bad. Anyway, you have to adjust, Marcie told herself. You have to face this, get it over and get on with your life. The two girls she shared the room with had much the same attitude – except that Sally couldn't help digging at Allegra.

'She's such a bloody toff,' spat Sally at their first mealtime when Allegra was still queuing for food.

'You mean she's not the sort you see serving behind a counter in Woolworths,' a bemused Marcie responded. Mentioning Woolworths reminded her of Babs. Strangely enough she found herself missing her even though they hadn't really got on.

'She still needs bringing down a notch,' Sally was saying.

'Live and let live,' said Marcie, but she doubted her room-mate could do that. There was bound to be friction between the two from day one – and there was.

As Sally polished her nails, Allegra took a satin and lace nightie from one of her pigskin bags. Unlike her room-mates she had not transferred her garments into the utility vintage chest of drawers. After selecting what she wanted the bags were pushed back under her bed.

Marcie was flicking through a woman's magazine that Allegra had loaned her. Women in the most wonderful fashions imaginable smiled out at her. Their skirts were incredibly short, their legs long and encased in multi-coloured tights. They were posing at odd angles, accentuating their slender legs and the geometric designs they were wearing. Even their straight, glossy hairstyles had an angular look about them.

Marcie was enthralled. 'I've never read a magazine like this. It's wonderful.'

She turned over another page.

'Have you ever had your hair done at a really top-notch hairdresser?' she asked Allegra.

'Sassoon. The very best,' Allegra replied.

'Your hair does look nice.'

'Thank you.'

'This underwear,' said Marcie, dropping her gaze back to the magazine. 'Do they really make such wonderful stuff in Paris?'

'Where else?'

'Oh, I don't know,' Sally interrupted, a cigarette stuck in the corner of her mouth. 'Surprising what you can get in the Old Kent Road or Petticoat Lane.' She was painting her fingernails a delicate shade of pink.

Marcie sighed. 'And these models. They're so beautiful. I've never seen . . .'

She was about to say she'd never seen such flawless-looking women and that they had to be foreign because they were so slim and chic – nothing like British women – but she stopped in mid-sentence when she saw that Allegra had taken a huge Kashmir shawl from her luggage and wrapped it around herself.

'This place is so chilly – typically British,' in her usual refined manner.

Marcie's jaw dropped. It was as though one of the models themselves had stepped out of the magazine – except for the fact that Allegra was so obviously pregnant.

'Well that explains a lot,' said Sally looking her up and down.

Allegra frowned. 'What do you mean by that?'

'You're obviously foreign otherwise you wouldn't feel the chill. Touched with the tar brush are you?'

Allegra clenched her jaw and a faint flush came to her cheeks.

'You're very rude.'

'We all are,' said Sally, her face wreathed in clouds of cigarette smoke. 'We played rude games with boys we shouldn't have played with.'

'That's not what I meant,' snapped Allegra.

Their arguing was giving Marcie a headache. She was sensible enough to know that there had to be harmony if they were to share this room even for a short time.

'Stop it both of you! We're all in the same boat. And Sally – my grandmother's Maltese so don't start giving anyone any grief about being foreign. Let's just cut out the bickering and give each other a bit of support. It'll make life easier for all of us. Yes?'

The other two looked at her in surprise. It was becoming obvious that she might be the youngest but she was more focused than they were on what really mattered.

Allegra stated that she was off to the lavatory at the end of the landing.

'Stuck-up cow,' muttered Sally.

Marcie eyed Sally's hard frown. She'd been relieved and even a bit awestruck when they'd first met, but the glorious goddess had feet of clay. She felt obliged to share her feelings.

'She's beautiful. Even though she's got as big a belly as we have, she's still beautiful.'

Sally grumbled a reluctant agreement. 'Stupid though,' she added with ill-disguised envy. 'Fancy getting herself knocked up and sent here.'

'Yes. Stupid,' said Marcie, throwing Sally a knowing look. 'Just like us.'

Their eyes met. There was no denying that they were of the same opinion. Although as roundly pregnant as they were, Allegra was beautiful. Her eyes were a greenish-grey, odd in such a dusky skin, and her hair was glossy and black. Her clothes were out of this world.

'Did you see the stuff she's got? Clothes like hers cost a packet,' Sally said suddenly.

Marcie agreed and hid her smile. Sally did not dislike Allegra; she was jealous of her.

She left the magazine lying open on the bed and looked out of the window. An oak tree with a very stout trunk held her gaze. A wrought-iron seat circled its base. She found herself wondering at the skill needed to make such a thing. A stupid thought really. What did it matter?

Sally slid off the bed. 'How about we take a look at what she's got in there?'

There was a hint of schoolgirl wickedness in Sally's eyes.

'You can't go prying!'

Sally shrugged. 'I won't take anything. But I'm curious. I bet I'm right. She's got such lovely things. Her family must be worth a fortune. Did you see the car she came in? Chauffeur driven. No bumping along on a bloody bus like us. Doesn't it make you wonder though? I mean, why is she here? Why didn't her parents pay for her to get rid of it?'

'Perhaps she's Catholic,' said Marcie. Just like me, she wanted to add. But she didn't. Sally was right. It did seem a bit strange that Allegra was here at all.

'You can nosy if you like, but count me out,' she said.

Sally sniffed, got back onto the bed and dabbed the last morsel of varnish onto her little finger. 'Wouldn't hurt to ask if she's got anything spare, though, would it?'

The object of their conversation chose that moment to re-enter the room. She glanced at them over her shoulder as she reached with long, graceful arms into one of the pigskin suitcases. After some careful delving she extricated a green silk kimono-style dressing gown.

Sally opened her mouth to make a comment, but someone knocked at the door, then pushed it open. A head appeared.

'You're wanted downstairs in the surgery for exam-ination. Bring your dressing gowns.' The woman's gaze dropped to Allegra's dressing gown. 'You might as well go first seeing as you've got yours ready. Follow me.'

Allegra's astonishing eyes were like twin moons as she glanced over her shoulder.

Marcie glimpsed the look in her eyes: a resigned compliance mixed with apprehension.

The dressing gown rustled as she folded it over her arm. Sally eyed it enviously before Allegra swept out of the room.

'Marilyn Monroe was wearing one just like it in a film I saw,' she whispered to Marcie.

Marcie didn't answer. Her gaze had shifted back to the oak tree. She wished she was home, the house noisy with the shouts of her half-brothers, the smell of thick stew filling the tiny kitchen.

Chapter Forty-two

It was Saturday morning and as usual Rosa Brooks was sitting at the kitchen table contemplating the job in hand. The framed photographs had been taken down from the mantelpiece and were lined up in front of her along with the silver polish and two dusters.

She eyed each of them one by one – the sepia print of her parents, stiffly posed as though to move or smile might bring rebuke from the Almighty Himself. Her gaze went to her husband, young and handsome in his naval uniform, her son and present daughter-in-law on their wedding day, and her grandchildren. The sight of them pained her. She had not managed to hold the family together and she wished she had someone to confide in. There was only one other person she had truly ever confided in.

Her eyes went back to her husband's photo. A part of her had died with him. Did she really talk with him or was she deluding herself?

Since living in an empty house of late, she'd asked herself that question on a number of occasions. Did she really have a gift for seeing and hearing what others did not, or was it merely the fancy of an old and increasingly lonely woman?

She feared the latter most of all. The house echoed without her family to rattle its old walls and she wouldn't be the first old woman to be considered mad because she continually talked to herself.

Her son, Antonio, had been transferred from the London hospital to the one in Dales Road close to the Abbey. She'd visited him almost every day, trying to convince him to move back in with her.

'Babs won't come back to me if I do,' he'd told her. 'But don't worry. I'll be over to cut the lawns and do any odd jobs you want, don't you worry your head about that.'

She hadn't been worrying her head about the lawns at all. She got up from the table and looked out to where her cockerels used to live. Her son had filled it with tools and things he assured her were of use to him.

She eyed the shed with misgivings. Getting rid of the chickens and tearing it down had been a whim that had come to her in the middle of the night. She'd presumed it was Cyril telling her to get rid of them. Now she wasn't quite so sure.

Brooding on thoughts of the past, she went to a locked drawer in the old bureau she kept under the stairs. Layers of tissue paper protected small family mementos such as a baptismal bonnet, baby's bootees, a pressed flower from Mary's wedding bouquet, and a photograph of Mary and her son on their wedding day.

Her first inclination had been to tear it up when she learned that Mary had run away with another man. But something, perhaps Cyril's voice, had bid her stay her hand, even though she'd stressed how angry she was that her son had had to sue for desertion and become divorced. They were Catholics for goodness' sake!

Not too sure of what the truth was, she'd relegated the grainy photograph to the drawer.

Her old fingers traced Mary's lovely features that so resembled those of her granddaughter, Marcie.

'Where are you now?' she whispered.

She wasn't just talking about Mary. Marcie too had run away.

Her reverie was interrupted by a loud knocking at the back door. In her hurry to answer it, she placed everything back into the drawer but left it unlocked.

Garth was standing there with his mouth open. He looked expectant but also nervous, not unusual for a poor soul used to being rejected. A roll of creamy creased paper was tucked beneath his arm.

'What is it, Garth?'

Pleased that he hadn't been turned away, his face burst into instant animation.

'I've brought you some of my drawings – new drawings,' he corrected himself.

Rosa opened the door wide. 'Come on in. Sit down.'

She made tea as he made himself comfortable, glad to have someone visit even if it was only Garth.

She set the tea in front of him along with a plateful of digestive biscuits.

'So what have you got to show me?'

His latest portfolio of pictures was still rolled up on the table. The family photographs in their silver frames had caught his attention.

'Who's that?'

He was pointing to the photograph of her parents.

'My parents.'

'Who's that?'

This time he was pointing to one of her grandsons.

'Archie,' she said after a close squint to make sure she had the right one. 'I think he was just nine months in that photo.'

Garth went through the whole series of photographs with the exception of her husband.

Rosa began to get impatient. 'What have you been drawing, Garth?'

Beaming with delight, Garth unrolled the sheath of paper.

Rosa noticed the smell of ox liver and saw the smear of blood on one corner.

'Marcie and the man,' said Garth.

Rosa looked at the drawing. Marcie appeared to be walking along the pavement and a pale-green car appeared to be following her.

Garth's other drawings – the one of her own chicken coup and the one of Marcie alone in the house – had unnerved her. This drawing unnerved her even more.

'Do you know this man?' she asked Garth.

Garth nodded vigorously. Biscuit crumbs fell from his shirt collar and onto his moth-eaten pullover.

'The man who took us to the pictures. It wasn't a cowboy,' he added disappointedly.

Rosa felt a cold chill overcome her. She didn't really need to know who this man was. She was also beginning to piece things together regarding the night when Mary, her son's first wife, had run away.

There'd been an argument. Alan Taylor had come round and persuaded her son to be calm.

She hadn't been party to all that was said and done. Less than five years old, Marcie had been ill in bed with suspected scarlet fever. That fact alone had made her turn her face against Mary. How could a mother run off when her daughter was so sick?

She sighed. 'Garth. Have another cup of tea. Would you like more biscuits?'

Garth said that he would.

As he gobbled down her whole stock of digestives, he went through sheet after sheet of drawings.

Rosa wasn't really seeing them – she was seeing instead the events of that night in a clearer perspective. Why now, she asked herself?

She vowed that once Antonio was out of hospital

she would tackle him about the happenings of that night. In the meantime she forced her attention back to Garth and his vividly coloured artwork.

'And this is Marcie coming home.'

Rosa made no comment. Her eyes were brimming with tears. Garth, this dearly imperfect soul, was telling her that her granddaughter would be coming home. She believed that too.

'Are you staying to help with the polishing, Garth? I am also having mutton stew for lunch. Would you like to stay and help me with that too?'

A fresh trail of saliva poured from the side of Garth's sagging mouth. There was no need for a verbal response. He began polishing, his tongue lolling from the corner of his mouth, aiding his concentration.

Picking up Cyril's photograph, Rosa frowned as a sudden thought came to her. 'Garth, you did not ask me who this was?'

Garth's face was a picture of concentration. His eyes slid briefly sidelong before going back to his polishing.

'Him. The man who comes with you when you visit my mum.'

Rosa sat stunned.

She finally found her voice.

'Is he here? Now?'

'No. He's with Marcie.'

Chapter Forty-three

Pilemarsh Abbey bore more than a passing resemblance to a workhouse or prison. Gothic carvings snaked around doorways, dark panelling cloaked the walls and there was no electricity on the upper floor. Ugly suits of armour hammered into shape by nineteenth-century industrialists rather than medieval blacksmiths stood in alcoves or stairwells, giving the place a malignant, brooding atmosphere. The windows were their eyes on the world outside the sombre walls, rattling when the wind whistled through the gaps.

It was Marcie's turn to be examined. The heavy oak staircase led down to the brown pool of lino that was the reception hall. Immediately opposite, an arrow on a black and white sign pointed to the surgery, matron's office and doctor's office. To the right, fixed to a double doorway beside an oil painting of a woman wearing an old-fashioned riding habit, was another sign saying 'Delivery Rooms'.

She shivered at the prospect of what was to come. She so wanted it over, for the months to whiz past and resume her normal life – whatever that meant.

She swept off to the left, found the right door and entered.

The surgery's walls were painted in the most putrid shade of eau de nil; enamel-framed screens were folded loosely in one corner and a metal-framed trolley squeaked when a nurse wheeled it close to the examination couch. Staff, surroundings and furniture all smelled of carbolic.

She was ordered to take off her clothes behind the screen and to put on her dressing gown.

'Lay down, please.'

She heaved herself onto the accommodation couch.

The doctor had a baby face and pale hair. The merest hint of a moustache shadowed his top lip and she fancied he'd purposely deepened his voice in a bid to be taken more seriously.

His hands trembled slightly as he approached her. Eyeing him sidelong, she tried to deduce what his problem was.

Drink?

Stress?

She couldn't believe that examining the bellies of young girls could lead to the latter, though there might be a case to answer for the former.

She shivered, and not just because her dressing gown was rolled up and a sheet placed across her stomach was pulled down.

'Have you given Nurse a water sample?'

The doctor was addressing the nurse as he said it
. . . *as though I've lost my voice.*

The nurse, her headgear as stiff and broad as a
starched tablecloth, answered that she had and that
the sugar test was negative.

The doctor made a humphing sound – something
halfway between approval and 'What have we here?'

The hands that pressed around the perimeter of
her swollen belly were cold as ice. She grimaced. He
hadn't attempted to warm them beforehand, and
neither had he apologised.

His voice slid an octave higher as he looked into
her face. 'A few days and it will be all over. A fortnight after that you can leave here and forget it ever
happened.'

Forget it? How could she forget it?

But you will, she told herself. You have to.

Turning her face to the wall she squeezed her eyes
shut and prayed it was all a dream. When she opened
them again, nothing had changed. What had she
expected?

At last the prodding finished.

'Be sure to see the receptionist on the way out,'
said the doctor, his pink cheeks glowing in his round,
chubby face as he smiled. 'She will pass you a set of
rules and information.'

It was the first time a smile had lifted his baby boy

features before he resumed scribbling copious notes. The smile was tight and not really for her, merely the satisfaction of a man with too many patients and not enough time to deal with them all properly.

Sally was sitting outside the door.

'So what is it? A baby or just fresh-baked bread making you a bit bloated?' said Sally.

'He's got cold hands,' said Marcie hugging her dressing gown more tightly around her.

'Hope he warms them up a bit for me.' She added a wink.

As directed, Marcie made her way to reception.

'Sit here,' said the big woman with iron-grey hair. Like her co-workers she was dressed in a Salvation Army uniform which seemed two sizes too small.

She was shuffling papers with the easy dexterity of someone used to collating information in strict alphabetical order. She drew a single sheet from out of the melee of manila folders and crisp paper. 'This is the Pilemarsh regime. Study it, memorise it if possible, and ask questions now if you wish.'

She passed it across the busy desk, which was a mass of labelled folders, wire trays and receipts speared on metal spikes.

Marcie began reading the long list just in case she might have a question.

'Well, hurry along,' said the woman. 'I haven't got all day.'

'I thought I had to read this in case I have questions,' said Marcie.

The woman's thin purple lips tightened into grim accusation. 'Do not take that tone with me! It is your fault you are here, not ours. Rules are rules.'

The rules and associated timetable were discussed in their first-floor room halfway down the corridor.

Allegra's fine voice was the first to reflect their shared feelings. 'This is outrageous.'

Sally was more scathing. 'Looks as though everyone here is a chief – there's no bloody Indians!'

Marcie shared their dismay. 'I can't believe it. According to this we've got to do all the cleaning, washing and ironing.'

A deep frown dented Allegra's dark brows. 'I've never done housework. We have servants.'

The other two went quiet and just stared at her.

She glared back. 'Well? Can I help it?'

Marcie was the first to recover. What was the point of getting at each other? They had quite enough to contend with.

'They obviously like to keep costs down.'

Sally glowered at her newly painted fingernails and sighed. 'And they were just getting nice.'

'I've got some cream,' said Allegra. She reached into her pigskin vanity case and passed Sally a pink jar with a gold-coloured top.

Sally shook her head. 'Thanks all the same. I think I've got something better than that.'

Allegra shrugged and put it back in her bag. 'Just trying to be friendly.'

'Fine. Just as long as you're not being charitable.'

Marcie found Sally's attitude unnecessarily scathing. 'I would have liked some of that cream,' she said lightly. Infighting seemed such a waste of time. They were here only temporarily and might just as well make the most of it. Keeping the peace was becoming a habit.

'You can have some of what I've got. Here you are. Vaseline,' said Sally. 'It cost only pennies and is just is as good as anything.'

Marcie wanted to say that Allegra's cream was expensive and bound to be better, but Sally would be hurt. 'I'll try a bit of both. I've brought none myself and I wouldn't want to leave either of you two with nothing.'

She thought of Johnnie as she rubbed the cream into her hands. He'd said that motorbike oil kept his hands nice and soft. Nonsense, of course, but still it made her smile.

'A penny for them,' said Sally.

Marcie looked up. 'What?'

'You were smiling to yourself,' said Allegra. 'Were you thinking of him? The one who had his wicked way with you?'

Marcie blanked out the episode with Alan Taylor before answering. 'He died in a road accident. He was riding his motorcycle on the North Circular.'

She didn't add that his parents had made him angry. She didn't know the full details of course – they hadn't said so in so many words – but she knew they hadn't wanted him to marry her. There were just a few overheard words. '*You can do so much better than her.*'

Her two room-mates both said that they were sorry to hear that.

'My bloke kept telling me he was going to marry me as soon as his ship came in. When it did I was five months gone and he'd signed on as crew on a freighter going to New Zealand.'

'Not nice,' said Marcie. 'I bet you were livid.'

Sally nodded. 'So was his wife. The bloody sod never let on he was married. But that's men for you. Have their fun and head for the hills – or in my case for the sea.'

Allegra was folding things up and putting them away in one of her pieces of luggage.

Both Sally and Marcie exchanged a look. It was obvious Allegra would offer nothing of her personal history unless she was asked.

'Come on, princess. Tell us how you got knocked up,' said Sally in her brash Cockney manner.

Allegra visibly paled. 'I don't wish to talk about it.'

Marcie was willing to let it go at that, but Sally was like a dog with a juicy bone; she insisted on hanging on.

'Come on, Allegra. Your parents have got a few bob; they could have paid for you to get rid of it. And before you say that it's illegal, bollocks! I've heard it's possible. Christ, I would have done the same myself if I'd had the ready cash.'

Allegra looked as though she'd been stung. The pretty lace underwear she'd been folding – underwear that would only fit her once she'd delivered – was squeezed between her hands.

'We're Catholics. We don't believe in that.'

'So why didn't he marry you?' asked Sally. 'Come on. Tell us.'

It was obvious from Allegra's face that something was hurting her very deeply. It was also obvious that her seemingly cool attitude to having her child adopted was only a façade.

'I think that's her business,' said Marcie.

'Oh, come on—' Sally began.

'Leave it,' snapped Marcie.

There must have been something in Marcie's expression that pulled Sally up sharply. She seemed in two minds about resuming before she looked into Marcie's eyes. Whatever was there warned her off.

Chapter Forty-five

The dining hall at Pilemarsh Abbey was one of the few general rooms in the building that didn't have panelled walls.

'Look at it,' muttered Sally. 'They even Bible bash when you're eating.'

Marcie tried not to look at the religious texts Sally referred to. Like strings of Christmas tinsel, they were festooned around the walls three deep, the shiny brown writing catching what light came through the pigeonhole windows 20 feet above their heads.

'They're hoping to reform us,' said Allegra as she slowly spooned the contents of her dessert dish into her mouth. 'What is this?' she asked suddenly, referring to her spoon.

'Semolina,' said Marcie. 'Don't you like it?'

Sally was eyeing Allegra over her second cup of tea. 'Not used to it, your ladyship?'

'No. Not really,' Allegra replied, appearing unaffected by Sally's attitude. 'But I'm hungry and not likely to get anything else. I'll cope.'

Sally pursed her lips and looked daggers.

Marcie was impressed by Allegra's apparent calm.

She also felt strangely privileged to be a bridge between these two totally different, but strangely alike young women. They were both proud and although they didn't know it, both were from more upmarket backgrounds than she was.

They'd exchanged details of where they were from, but Marcie had been loath to go into any great detail about her family. She'd told them that her mother was dead, that her father had married again and that she had half-brothers and sisters.

She did not tell them about her father's prison record or the event with Alan Taylor. She wanted to cling on to the most likely probability that Johnnie *was* the child's father. It was the one thing that would help get her through this.

Marcie threw in her own observation on life and food at this place.

'We all have to manage with what we have, and we all have to get along together. After all, look what we've got in common.'

Sally and Allegra exchanged cryptic glances before steadying their gaze on Marcie.

'You mean we all have big bellies,' said Sally with a half smile.

'Yes.'

'And wish it had never happened,' added Allegra, dropping her spoon into her dish.

'Yes.'

'Did he love you?' It was Sally addressing Marcie.

Marcie pretended that the mouthful of food prevented her from answering. But she nodded.

Sally had another go at asking Allegra how she'd got pregnant.

'Look,' Marcie began. 'Just let it drop—'

'It's OK,' said Allegra

She dropped her eyes and studied her long, slim fingers as though she were trying to sum up the courage to go on.

'I was raped. I was walking late at night. Silly really. A man attacked me.' Sally took another sip of her tea and said, 'Oh!'

Marcie looked around the room at the sixty or so young women, some still pregnant – most of those who had given birth looked pensive as though still considering their options.

Her attention went back to her food.

Sally asked her how come she'd got pregnant.

'I used the pill, but it didn't work.'

'I'm going to get some of those,' said Sally. She turned to Allegra. 'How about you?'

Allegra shook her head. 'No. I'm going to get married and have a lot of children.'

'But you'll always remember this one,' said Marcie blurted without thinking.

The others made no comment. They all knew she was speaking the truth.

Marcie was sound asleep when she felt someone shake her arm. Blinking herself awake, she saw Sally was bending over her.

'I need a wee and the chamber pot's full.'

'Empty it,' Marcie whispered hoarsely.

She rolled away, tucking her chin beneath the bed sheet.

Sally stayed put. At last she said, 'I'm frightened of the dark.'

'I told you before, there's a light on the landing.'

'I'll get into trouble if I turn it on.'

Marcie sighed and opened her eyes. 'All right. I'll come with you.' She swung her legs out of bed. 'But YOU have to carry the potty,' she whispered.

The brown lino floor was cold to their bare feet so they both tiptoed along the landing to the sluice and the deep sink situated at the end of the corridor.

A frosted window let in enough light so they could see what they were doing. The effluent was poured away, the tap turned and a gush of cold water flushed it clean.

'I can't see why we can't all have our own potty,' Marcie observed. 'One isn't enough for all of us.'

'Do you think we should ask for another?' said Sally.

'You mean you want me to ask for one.'

'You're so much braver than the rest of us.'

It struck Marcie that Sally's brash exterior hid a marshmallow interior.

'Allegra should take her turn to empty the po.'

Marcie pointed out that she never used it.

'That's ridiculous. She can't avoid using it.'

Marcie shook her head. 'It amazes me that she manages to hold herself so long, but she does.'

'Probably has a servant to empty it for her at home,' grumbled Sally.

She took her cigarettes and matches out from her bra.

She held out the packet. 'Want one?'

'I don't usually . . .' Marcie began, then took one. She didn't usually hang around in places like this. Come to that, she didn't usually find herself pregnant.

In the quiet space of this other world, their only real respite from the regimentation and religion of Pilemarsh House, they smoked and for a moment were silent.

It was Marcie who spoke first.

'You shouldn't be so hard on Allegra just because she's rich.'

Sally seemed to think about it for a few minutes. 'I have to hit out at someone, otherwise I think I'd cut my wrists.'

'What?'

Marcie was horrified. 'You wouldn't really. Surely not.'

Sally shrugged. 'I get depressed at times.'

It was hard to believe that someone like Sally could ever feel that way.

'She has everything I want: money, beautiful things. What do I have? Nothing.'

'You're beautiful.'

'Come on! Stop pulling my leg.'

'I'm not. I mean it.'

'But I'm not rich, not like she is.'

'But you will be. One day.'

Sally eyed her quizzically. 'How do you know that?'

Marcie shrugged. 'I don't know how I know. I just do.'

'Oh! I see! You're a witch.' She peered over her shoulder. 'So where's the black cat and the broomstick?'

Marcie hugged herself. She hadn't meant it to sound as it did. 'There's no need to laugh at me.'

Sally frowned. 'I'm not laughing.'

Marcie's hair fell around her face. Pregnancy had not diminished its lustre and she hadn't put on as much weight as some of the girls.

'You might do when I tell you.'

'Tell me what?'

'My grandmother is able to see things – you know – in the future. She reads tea leaves and stuff.'

'That's fantastic.'

'I don't know about that. I suppose I'm kind of used to it. She always said I had the gift too if I'd just believe in myself a bit more. She may be right. Sometimes I just get a sense of things—'

'I'm impressed. That's really fab.'

Marcie looked surprised. 'You mean that?'

'You bet I am!' Her expression changed. 'And what about our room-mate? What sort of future is mapped out for her?'

Eyes downcast, Marcie shook her head. She couldn't sense anything about Allegra. 'Who knows?'

'Never mind about her. Just keep telling me that one day I'm going to be rich and you'll be my friend for life.'

Sally threw her cigarette end into the sink then proceeded to pull up her nightdress and heave her backside over the sink.

'Might as well while I'm here. Save filling up the chamber pot.'

'Allegra is very beautiful – like Carmen Miranda,' blurted Marcie. 'My grandmother watches old films with her in. She dances around with a pile of fruit on her head.'

'Carmen . . . ?' Sally looked at her in amazement for a moment before she burst out laughing. 'Carmen bloody Miranda!' She continued to hoot with laughter. 'Carmen . . . de . . . dee . . . de . . . dee . . . da . . .' she sang, grabbed the pot from Marcie's hands and wiggled her hips in time to her song.

Because Marcie started giggling too, and with the sluice room filling up with the tune and the laughter, they failed to hear the quick marching footsteps.

'Who's talking out there?'

Sally thrust the pot back into Marcie's hands. She almost dropped it, slopping the last of the washing mixture so that it splashed up the wall.

'It's the old battleaxe,' Sally murmured.

The woman they referred to was the same one who had distributed the rules and timetable as though she were Moses himself, and the Ten Commandments had just been committed to quarto size paper.

They were becoming used to the fact that she was the main enforcer for the strict regime that was meant to return them to the straight and narrow. Captain Wilma Turnbull was so dedicated to the cause of redirecting the lives of the inmates that she was rarely off the premises. Straight backed, bewigged and poker faced, the running of the establishment occupied the centre of her life.

'Probably convinced that the place can't run without her,' Allegra had said.

Marcie had dredged deep for an obvious truth. 'There are a lot of people in the graveyard who thought the same about their places of work.'

Dark, long and contorted by an awkward angle, Miss

Turnbull's shadow fell over them from along the passage. She walked stiffly, her hands clasped behind her back, her feet encased in sensible, flat black shoes, placed perfectly with each step, heel to toe, heel to toe. It looked as though she were measuring something that fell in a perfectly straight line alongside her gaunt shadow. Obviously she had dozed off in the chair in the nursing office because her wig was slightly lopsided.

Sally noticed and hid a smirk behind her hand.

It was rumoured that Miss Turnbull was completely bald beneath her wig and not just grey.

'Have you not read the rules?'

Sally answered. 'Yes, Miss Turnbull. We were just—'

'How many girls does it take to empty that!' Her fingernail made a clinking sound as it connected with the vitreous china.

Marcie had had enough. 'Not as many as it takes to fill it! Do you think we can have a pot each, Miss Turnbull? The amount of water we're passing nowadays is enough to send over Niagara Falls. And that's what our single pot is going to be: Niagara Falls – all the pee pouring over the rim.'

Miss Turnbull looked fit to bust a gut, her wig seeming to quiver on her head.

Sally stifled a giggle.

Miss Turnbull threw her a disparaging look, her mouth as straight and wide as a letterbox. Her shoulders quaked.

'Get back to your room. And remember. No talking outside your room. Girls who have recently had babies are trying to get some sleep.'

Staggering with laugher, Marcie and Sally scurried back along the corridor.

'Back to our virgin beds,' said Sally loudly enough for Miss Turnbull to hear.

Marcie fell asleep with a smile on her face.

In the morning she pushed herself up on her slim hands and pushed back the covers. She winced as she dragged her legs over the side of the bed, tucking her nightdress below her belly so she could more easily inspect her ankles. She sighed at the sight of them. 'Looking over my belly is like trying to peer over the top of a mountain. I vow that I will never allow myself to get fat again – certainly not on a permanent basis.'

Allegra slipped out of her own bed and cast a worried frown. 'Are you alright?'

Marcie nodded. The sight of the hem of her nightdress skimming her slim ankles was incredibly reassuring. 'Just a twinge.' She wriggled her toes. 'My ankles are still slim.'

'Is that good?'

'I think so.' She turned to Sally for a second opinion. 'Sally, do you think—'

One swift glance at their room-mate's bed and she stopped in mid sentence. 'Where's Sally?'

They exchanged an apprehensive look, noting her nightdress slung down on the coverlet.

'She left in a hurry,' said Allegra. 'And very early. I didn't hear her go.'

'She should have put her nightdress away. Miss Turnbull won't like that,' said Marcie eyeing the rumpled nightdress with a look bordering on terror.

Allegra pursed her lips and reached for her towel.

Marcie busied herself tidying Sally's bed. She folded the nightdress and put it under the pillow.

'You should leave it for her to do,' Allegra pointed out.

'Oh no! What if Miss Turnbull comes in while she's not here? She'll be in terrible trouble.'

Marcie's adherence to rules made Allegra smile. 'Rule number twelve, nightdress must be folded neatly and put away. Eight lashes or solitary confinement for a week?'

'Just the confinement,' said Marcie with a weak smile.

Allegra laughed.

Marcie's smile widened to a broad beam.

'So where is she?' Slipping her slim arms into the silky softness of the silk kimono, Allegra went to the window. Despite her girth she walked on tiptoe, reluctant to feel the cold lino the length of her foot. Palms flat, she braced herself against the windowsill and looked out, her breath misting the window panes and mixing with the condensation already there.

'There she is.' She pointed.

A figure in a full-length red coat stood out like a sore thumb – a ladybird among a gathering of dung-coloured beetles.

'She's not really doing anything wrong. Just taking a morning walk.'

Allegra raised her beautifully arched eyebrows.

'The staff won't think that. We've all done wrong. That's how they and the world sees us.'

Chapter Forty-six

Once her son Antonio was safely out of hospital, Rosa Brooks deigned to visit him and his family at their new house. She'd visited him in the hospital regularly enough, but refused to visit the new house while he was not in it.

Once she did she was quite surprised. It was bright and had a homely feel. Never, ever would she admit it to Babs, but her daughter-in-law had done a pretty good job furnishing the place.

A smart Axminster carpet covered most of the living-room floor. The remaining floorboards were covered in linoleum slotted around the edge. There was none beneath the carpet itself.

She'd also got herself a G-Plan sideboard and dining set. Rosa made a stab at how much she'd spent: quite a lot. Presumably Antonio had provided the ready cash. She didn't ask exactly how her son acquired his money – it was enough that he provided for his family. Where it came from was of little relevance. The family came first.

He'd relinquished his job with Alan Taylor.

'You two are not as close as you once were. There is a reason for this?'

Tony Brooks couldn't meet his mother's eyes. She was his own mother yet she scared him, mostly because she knew him so well.

'I'll get a job somewhere. I've got friends.'

He didn't want to admit anything about how and why they'd fallen out. Neither did he want to drop Alan in it. There were too many skeletons in the cupboard and if he wasn't careful one or two might fall out.

He was desperate to know whether his mother had heard from Marcie.

She shook her head when he asked her. 'I do not know where she is. I only wish I did.'

Her gaze drifted to the boys playing in the back garden. There was no reason, as far as she was concerned, for Marcie to run away. Her father had agreed to let her marry Johnnie and she herself had voiced no objection, so why had she gone the way she had? 'They say history repeats itself,' she said without thinking.

She caught sight of her son's face and instantly regretted it. 'I did not mean that she has met the same fate as her mother—'

Her words seemed to catch in her throat like the spines of thistles.

Tony rubbed at his eyes with the fingers and thumb

of one hand. 'Please, God, no,' he whispered. 'Please, God, no.'

Rosa sat for a while in the dark that night. At first she didn't hear the knock at the door, she was so lost in thought.

Whoever was knocking was very determined.

Rosa got up from her chair. 'Alright, alright, I am coming,' she said.

Garth had taken to calling on her more frequently these days and it wasn't in her to tell him not to keep bothering her. His face lit up at the sight of her.

'I can't stop,' he said as she opened the door wide enough for him to enter. 'I've got a shilling to get myself some chips. But I did you a picture. I thought you might like it.'

She thanked him, took the picture and watched him lollop off down the garden path.

Placing the rolled-up piece of paper on the table, she lit the gas and put the kettle on. Something stopped her from unfurling the crumpled paper on which Garth drew his pictures. She'd lost faith in her gift of late, so even though she felt that her husband, Cyril, was here urging her to look at the picture, she determined not to. It wasn't until about three in the morning that the urge was so strong it stirred her to full wakefulness.

Without recourse to dressing gown or slippers, she went down the narrow staircase to the ground floor.

The room was in total darkness. She turned on a light, went through to the kitchen and turned that one on too.

The piece of paper had probably been used to wrap half a pound of sausages and was a bit crumpled.

Once she could see what he'd drawn, her eyes filled with tears. This was not what she'd expected. This was not at all what she'd expected.

It was still dark when Marcie awoke. She heard the clock down in the ground floor hallway strike two, and yet she knew that wasn't what had woken her.

Pain rolled from her breasts to her loins, her belly pulsing with each muscular contraction. On raising herself up on her hands, she felt the wetness of her bedding. She was frightened. Oh God, she was frightened.

'Sally? Sally?'

The hump that was Sally moved slightly and murmured a response.

Marcie raised her voice. 'I've started. Help me.'

Everything moved swiftly from then on.

Her wrists were strapped to the trolley. 'For safety,' they told her. 'To stop you falling off.'

She didn't care that it smacked of torture and murmured prayers on the way to the delivery room. When was the last time she'd done that?

The main part of the old building echoed to new

sounds, shouted orders, quick marching and the continuous opening and closing of doors.

Nurses in stiff headdresses flapped around her. She saw the doctor's pale young face peering down at her.

The pain went on and on.

'She can't bring it,' somebody said.

'Her blood pressure . . .'

'I'm going to have to cut along the perineum. Pethidine. We need Pethidine.'

Marcie rolled her head from side to side. She was sweating and hot and in terrible pain. She had reached that moment when she didn't care what they did or what happened.

'This will help the pain,' someone murmured against her ear.

She felt a needle being plunged into her thigh. Then there was nothing, not until she heard a faint cry sounding so, so very far away.

Everything was white when she came round. The walls, the ceiling, the furnishings; even the air itself seemed to be fuzzy. It was as though a thick gauze veil hung before her eyes.

Like a morning mist the whiteness slowly dissipated. The walls turned to sickly green. A nurse she had not seen before smiled down at her. She had deep-brown eyes brimming with kindness.

'Just rest,' she said. Her voice was as kind as her eyes.

Marcie closed her eyes. She was weary and aching, and yet there was only one thought at the front of her mind.

'Where's my baby?'

'Just rest.'

A terrible panic grabbed hold of her. She managed to get herself up on her elbows.

'Where's my baby? Is it dead? Was it born?'

Using both hands, the kindly nurse pressed her back onto her pillow.

'You gave birth to a little girl.'

'A girl!' Her voice was full of wonder.

The nurse was saying something. She caught what it was.

'Now you mustn't worry yourself about anything. Just rest and in less than a fortnight your problems will be over and you'll be able to go home.'

Nothing could have prepared Marcie for how she was feeling. Nothing counted except one thing above all others. 'I want my baby!'

'You can have your baby, but not if you take on so. Once you've calmed down and taken stock of the situation, you can feed her. But you have to be calm. It does no good to be overenthusiastic about the child.'

What an odd thing to say, Marcie thought to herself. I must not be overenthusiastic – and then it hit her. The nurse was telling her that she must not get too attached to the child. Her little girl was being put up for adoption. They probably had parents already picked out for her. The adoptive parents would see the little bundle of flesh take her first steps, say her first words. They'd be there on her first day at school. They'd love her and she would love them for doing so. It was likely that she'd never know she was adopted or who her real parents were.

A whole day later, once she had calmed down and thought very carefully how she should approach this, she was allowed to see her baby. Not allowed to get out of bed, the baby was brought to her. On her right wrist she wore a pink band. The band simply said 'Baby Brooks'.

'Joanna,' she said softly as she took the tiny hand in hers. 'Your name's Joanna.'

The name had come to her out of the blue; Joanna was as close as she could get to Johnnie. Her lost love deserved a part of him to live on.

Two days later she was allowed back into the room she shared with Sally and Allegra. Joanna went too.

Both Sally and Allegra had given birth to boys.

'I never believed it could be so painful,' said Marcie as she stroked the side of her baby's head. 'I never thought you would ever come, Joanna,' she said to the baby.

Sally rebuked her. 'You shouldn't give her a name.'

'Why?'

'She's not yours to name. You're going to give her away.'

Allegra looked up from repacking and smoothing her beautiful clothes. She was already thinking of life away from this place. 'Sally is right, Marcie. It will only make it harder.'

Marcie felt as though her heart had swollen to twice its normal size. There was no arguing with what they were saying, but never had she felt so full of love.

'Her name's Joanna.'

Chapter Forty-seven

Rita Taylor was stretched out on the sofa eating chocolates, eyes glued on the television. All around her drawers and cupboards hung open. Items of clothing had been flung over the back of the sofa; more items were scattered over the floor. This included chunks of orange, red and blue glass – modern chunky vases bought by her father at extortionate prices. Some of the glass was in pieces having been smashed against a wall.

Rita didn't move when she heard the front door slam.

'I'm home!'

Her father's cheery disposition evaporated on seeing the state of the room.

'What the fuck . . . ! What's this?'

'*Coronation Street.*'

'I don't mean that! I mean this!'

Alan Taylor was standing in the middle of something resembling a war zone.

Rita shifted herself and chose another chocolate. 'She's gone.'

'Then good riddance to the old tart. But why my

Whitefriars! What the fuck did she do that for?' His voice broke with emotion as he stared down at the chunks of heavy glass. They looked like coloured ice in a sea of blue and orange Wilton carpet.

'Because she couldn't find a mirror to break and leave you with seven years bad luck,' said Rita once she'd swallowed most of the chocolate she was eating. Not once did her attention stray from Elsie Tanner who was presently coming on strong to Len Fairclough.

Alan picked up the biggest chunks of glass. He regarded the jagged edges and the multi-coloured shards scattered all around. There was no chance they could be mended. They were finished – just like him and Stephanie.

'After all I did for her . . .' he muttered.

'Never mind. At least you won't have to worry about a divorce,' remarked Rita.

He scratched his head and nodded. That much was true. It wasn't common knowledge but he'd never married Stephanie despite her pleading. Still, it definitely had its advantages. Not having been married in the first place also meant he didn't have to pay maintenance.

'I suppose she ran off with another bloke.'

Rita filled him in on the details. 'Someone she met at the club years ago.'

'Really?'

He couldn't help sounding shocked. What surprised him the most was that he hadn't had a clue that she was leaving. The bitch!

'Well, I suppose it's good riddance then.' He leaned over the back of the sofa and gave his daughter's shoulder a squeeze. 'You're beyond the age of needing a mother anyway.'

'Too right.'

'I take it this is a good programme,' he said, nodding at the screen.

'Great.'

'You're not going out tonight?'

Rita loved this new drama series and her father's interruptions were beginning to get on her nerves. 'Look, Dad. I'm having second thoughts about being a mod. I have to think things through.'

Alan grinned. 'You mean the bloke you currently fancy is a long-haired git wearing a leather jacket and riding a motorbike. Right?'

The credits were rolling. *Coronation Street* had finished, Elsie was considering her options with Ken and her son was in some kind of trouble – as usual. Rita would watch what happened next week. Her eyes were shining with excitement when she turned round to face her father.

'I'm back with Pete. It was off with him and now it's on again. We met up again the other week and, well, one thing led to another. And guess what he told me? His mate, Johnnie, the bloke Marcie was sweet on, has been killed. So where's Marcie? Her family said she'd gone off to live with him and his parents until they got married. But guess what?'

'You keep me guessing a lot,' said her father. This was the first news he'd had about Marcie for ages. But he was patient. He left his daughter to tell him at her own pace.

'Pete and the boys went to the funeral. And guess what?'

'Not another guess!'

'His dad was a vicar!'

'Is that so?'

'St Luke's, Pimlico. That's where Pete told me he lived, though he'd always played it down. Johnnie didn't like people knowing that his dad was a vicar.'

Rita carried on talking about Pete and how wonderful it was to make up and how they'd talked about getting engaged, and married, and having their own house . . .

Alan wasn't listening. In his head, he was making further enquiries, diving into his car and heading for London, more specifically, St Luke's, Pimlico.

Chapter Forty-eight

Rosa Brooks had made the mistake of buying a sketch pad and a box of poster paints for Garth. Since then he'd made a habit of setting himself up on her kitchen table. While she cooked and cleaned, he drew and painted to his heart's desire.

'Some of my pictures are stories,' he told her, 'and some are for real.'

He did her one of vegetables growing in the garden. The detail was quite explicit – the vegetables were growing in the exact same place as where the shed now sat.

She pointed that out to him.

'Yes, but this is how they would have looked like if we had planted them.'

Rosa frowned. 'We?'

Garth nodded. 'Tony was digging there, it was raining and dark and I had nowhere else to go.'

Rosa nodded gravely. Garth's mother was famous for turning him out when the occasion demanded. There was no room for a backward son at one of Edith Davies's liquor parties.

'I helped him,' he said, as he gravely outlined his hand with a blue-tipped paintbrush.

'He asked you to help him,' Rosa stated.

Garth shook his head. The tip of his tongue protruded from the corner of his mouth.

'He didn't seem to see me. And then the other man came.'

'Other man?'

'The one who came to the pictures with me and Marcie.'

Rosa knew he meant Alan Taylor. Garth was a sweet soul but it wasn't wise to accept all he said as gospel truth. She had to confront her son. She had to know what he'd been doing that night and why Alan Taylor had turned up.

'I hid,' said Garth.

'The other man did not see you?'

Garth shook his head.

And my own son was too drunk to realise that someone had been helping him dig.

The next question was the most difficult to ask.

'Was my son burying something in the hole you were digging?'

'A sack.'

'A sack?' Her old heart doubled its beat. *Holy Mother of God, give me more time. I promise I won't protest when the time comes. But not now. Please not now!*

'A sack of something.'

*

Marcie had disobeyed the rule that baby must lie outside the main entrance in her pram in all winds and weathers. She'd been promised to a bank manager and his wife. They were unable to have any more children and required a companion for their three-year-old boy.

'As though Joanna is a puppy,' she'd said contemptuously.

The papers were being drawn up. It had been pointed out to her that she was under age and thus an adult would have to sign for her. Miss Turnbull offered her services.

Marcie had fled the oppressing brown décor of the old dragon's office and gone out into the fresh air. On the way she grabbed Joanna from her pram and ran with her to the seat beneath the tree.

Again and again she had wished for a miracle, waking in the middle of the night, fear lying like a damp blanket against her skin. Miracles were the only option she had left.

The summer was cool, but she didn't care. Well wrapped up, mother and baby remained sitting on the wrought-iron seat beneath the oak tree. She was running her fingertips over Joanna's soft cranium when she sensed a shift in the state of things.

For a brief moment the sun warmed her face, then was gone again.

'Hello, Marcie.'

For a split second she could barely breathe. She looked up and there he was. Alan Taylor!

The colour drained from her face. 'What are you doing here?'

Nothing had changed. She saw the same old cockiness as he sat down beside her.

He reached out and touched the baby's fingers.

'Boy or girl?'

'Girl.'

The sound of her own voice seemed far away.

Joanna's tiny hand had slipped out of her mitten. Very gently, Alan pushed it back in again. Joanna reacted, her hand curling around Alan's thumb.

He looked up at her suddenly.

'I suppose you're wondering how I found you.'

Dumbstruck, she only managed to nod her head and say, 'Yes.'

'Our Rita's become a rocker again. She's back with that Pete. He told her that Johnnie had got killed on his bike and that the service had been at his old man's church. So I went to the vicarage. Told him I was your dad and was worried about you.'

Alan's fair hair was slicked well back from his face. 'And before you ask, no I didn't tell your dad that I was coming here. I wanted to come alone.' He looked down at the baby. 'I wanted to see my kid.'

'She's not yours!' she snapped, cuddling Joanna more tightly.

He eyed her searchingly. 'You don't know that for sure.'

The way he looked at her brought back her horror on discovering what he'd done. He saw that look and blushed like a girl.

'I'm sorry. I was well out of order. But I'd been drinking . . .' He rubbed at his eyes and all over his face. 'I was crazy for you.'

'Just as you were for my mother?'

The remark took him by surprise. Alan Taylor always had an answer for everything, but on this occasion he looked lost for words. At last he seemed to snap awake. He shook his head.

'She told me to get lost. But instead, she was the one who got lost.'

Marcie was instantly alert to whatever information he was about to give. 'Where did she go?'

He shook his head again. 'Sorry, love. I don't know. Truly I don't.'

'Did she go off with somebody?'

He seemed to think about this for a moment, his eyes narrowing as he passed the palm of his hand over his chin.

To Marcie it seemed like an hour before he answered, though it was only minutes.

'I can't see it myself. There had to be something, but . . . hey . . . what do I know?'

Then came the most terrible question of all, the

one that had been haunting her so vigorously of late.

'Did my father kill her? Is she buried beneath the shed?'

His look was penetrating. His jaw moved from side to side as though he were chewing something.

'Look. There's something else I want to talk to you about. Steph's buggered off. I can give you and the kid a home. Me and Steph were never married so I'm free to do what I like. Marry me and we're a family. What do you say?'

Her jaw dropped. This was the man who had got her drunk and then raped her. Before she could answer, he voiced the main advantage, the one she could not easily ignore.

'Joanna wouldn't have to go for adoption.'

'She doesn't have to! I could raise her by myself.' All the advice she'd received had told her such a thing wouldn't be wise, but deep down a small niggle kept telling her otherwise.

His eyes fixed on hers as he shook his head slowly. 'You'd be an unmarried mother. Nobody would want to give you a job. Nobody would want to rent you a flat.'

'I could go home – back to Sheerness.'

'And embarrass your family? I don't know your gran that well, but I do know she's old school. You get married before you sleep together and not the other way round. And as for your dad—'

'How is he?'

'He's fine.'

Sensing he was on a winning streak, Alan carried on with a list of reasons why she should marry him.

'The gossips would still have field day,' she pointed out.

'But not for long. Girls who get into trouble are forgiven once they've got a ring on their finger and a husband at their side. Think about it.'

She did think about it and realised he was right. Girls who got into trouble and gave birth to bastards were never allowed to forget the fact. If they married, even after the event, the past was put behind them.

Marcie looked down into her baby's sweet face. Joanna yawned and clenched her fists – as though she wants to take on the world, Marcie thought. Getting involved with the man who had attacked her was the last thing she wanted to do. The whole thought of Alan touching her again made her feel ill. And yet, even in the few days she had known her baby daughter, she knew there wasn't a thing she wouldn't do in order to keep her safe – and close. Was she willing to sacrifice her own happiness for the sake of Joanna? Of course she was.

The thing is I want to be there when she does take on the world, she thought. I want to see her take her first steps and go out on her first date. 'I want to watch her growing up,' she said at last, voicing her feelings.

Alan spread his hands and shrugged. 'There you are then.'

A sudden thought came to her. 'They're signing the papers today; or rather Miss Turnbull is signing on my behalf.'

Alan got to his feet. 'Is she now? They like their paperwork, don't they. I had to give them your dad's name and my address before they even let me in the door. Well, we'd better go and sort things out then, hadn't we.'

Miss Turnbull was not amused. She met them just inside the front door. Alan wasted no time telling her exactly what was going to happen. He turned to Marcie. 'Give me the baby and get your things.'

Miss Turnbull's face turned from slightly pink to deep puce as Marcie handed Joanna over to Alan and dashed for the stairs.

Up in the small room she'd shared with Sally and Allegra, she threw everything into her old battered case. Before dashing back downstairs she paused to consider more fully what she was doing. Alan had taken advantage of her when she'd been at her most vulnerable. She wouldn't be doing what she was doing at all except for one thing – or rather one person. Joanna

She dashed back downstairs.

'But everything is arranged!'

Miss Turnbull sounded as though she were fit to burst. Her angry voice had set Joanna crying.

'Then UNARRANGE them,' Alan said.

He handed the baby back to Marcie.

'Look,' said Miss Turnbull, waving the adoption papers in front of his face. 'These have been long and laboriously filled in, and they're in triplicate. Think carefully about what you're doing.'

'I know damn well that paper can be ripped to bits if need be.'

Miss Turnbull's tight little mouth turned tighter. 'The child was born a bastard!'

Before Miss Turnbull could say another word, he snatched the papers from her hand, ripped them into pieces and threw them up into the air.

'Sod your forms! Sod your arrangements, and sod you!' He turned to Marcie. 'Come on. Let's go home.'

Sally and Allegra had got wind that something was up and were waiting for her by the front door.

'We heard the good news,' said Sally.

'One more goodbye,' said Allegra giving her a kiss. 'You're very lucky to have a dad like yours.'

Marcie didn't bother to correct her. Neither did Alan.

'Everything to your liking, madam?' asked Alan.

He kept whistling and humming. She sensed his spirits were soaring. Why hadn't she seen how he felt about her?

It doesn't matter now, she said to herself. You're doing this for Joanna.

She had no other option but to marry Alan. Hadn't her father said he would throw her out if she ever brought such trouble home? He'd only come round when he thought she was going to marry Johnnie. Only by marrying someone else would she be respectable. All the same, it would be nice to have some time at home before the wedding.

On the journey home he told her in more detail about Steph leaving, reiterating that they'd never got round to getting hitched. They also discussed the options available to them regarding getting married and where they should live. Marcie found this the most difficult to contemplate, yet Alan enthused about the options.

'You could move into the bungalow, or we could buy something you like better. The choice is yours.'

Yes. The choice was hers, but one she was hesitant to make.

Moving in with Alan straight away was an option he preferred but she wasn't quite so sure about. After all they weren't married. She finally came to a conclusion.

'I'll stay with my grandmother at first until we're married.'

He laughed at that. 'Keeping up appearances, are we?'

'Why not?'

'That's fine by me. It'll take a couple of weeks to

sort matters out. And we'll have a party – a bloody wedding reception. You just see if we don't.'

Another more pressing question lay heavy in her mind. Again she broached the subject he'd been loath to answer earlier.

'Is my mother buried beneath the shed?'

She fancied the car swerved a little – not much but just enough to make her realise that the question unnerved him.

'No. Of course not.'

Chapter Forty-nine

Rosa Brooks eyed her son. He was sitting in his armchair and chewing his thumb.

'Stop doing that. You did that as a little boy when I accused you of doing something wrong.'

He looked up at her uncomprehending. 'What?'

'You are chewing your thumb. You always did that when you were a little boy.'

Exasperated by her presence, he folded his hands in his lap and fixed his eyes on a cracked tile in the beige-coloured grate which was plain but modern. It shouldn't be cracked, he reasoned.

Rosa sipped at her tea. Babs wasn't in but at least Antonio knew how to make a cup of tea.

'You buried something in my garden. Do not deny it. I know what I know.'

She saw that her words had taken him unawares. He stared round eyed at this woman who everybody believed could see things they could not. Nobody could have told her, so how could she know?

Suddenly he covered his face with his hands, shook his head and shouted, 'I don't know! I don't know! I don't bloody know!'

He said it with such great vehemence that she truly believed him. Anyway, she had not brought her son up to lie.

Sighing, Rosa put down her cup and got to her feet. 'I am sorry, Antonio, as I do not wish to do this, but feel I have no choice. Though Shalt Not Kill, says the Bible. I have to make sure that such a great sin has not been done beneath my roof!'

'Mother! You can't!'

She eyed him contemplatively. Never had she questioned his methods of making money, and never would she have shopped him to the police. But this was different.

'I have to.'

Antonio Brooks was well known to the police, so it didn't take them long to send a digging team along to the cottage.

Rosa Brooks stood watching, her sense of doing right for once outweighing her love for her son. A detective asked her where Antonio was.

'We'd like to ask him some questions.'

'At home?'

'No. He wasn't there.'

'He will be back. He'll never leave Sheppey. This is his home.'

Seeing he was unlikely to get any information, the detective returned to where a large pile of earth grew ever larger.

The smell of turned earth permeated the air. Rosa Brooks refused to leave the house but stood defiant at the back door as the hole grew bigger and bigger.

The police had questioned when the chicken house had been erected. Rosa had shrugged and said it was years ago.

The police asked questions of the neighbours. Mrs Ellis, who now had a completed nuclear fallout shelter in her garden, had enlightened them.

'The old chicken house used to be over in the corner. The new one was put up in the early fifties round about the same time as the first Mrs Brooks disappeared.'

The two women of separate generations stood slightly apart, both coldly isolated in their respective worlds.

Two hours or more passed before she saw one of the police officers making his way towards the house. The sight of him filled her with dread. He looked down at the path as he walked. Rosa knew what that meant. He was considering most carefully what he had to say, and yet he didn't need to say anything. She already knew, or thought she did. The puzzling thing about it was that Cyril hadn't mentioned any restless spirit around here, and neither had she sensed the presence of one.

Rosa had been through difficult times before – the war was bad enough, though the Isle of Sheppey hadn't endured any bombing, the enemy preferring to fly past and bomb London. But this was different. This terrible moment was not about tragedy afflicting strangers; this was her family and in particular her son.

She braced herself for the terrible truth. It was she who spoke first.

'Is it her? Is it my daughter-in-law?'

He shook his head. 'No, love. It's a dog. A big dog. Did you ever have a dog?'

She shook her head. No. She'd never had a dog, and what was it doing there in the first place?

The green Jaguar slid into its parking place in the gravel-filled drive. Alan had half expected Rita to be stood there waiting for him but Tony Brooks was standing there instead, hands in pockets, his dark eyes glittering beneath frowning eyebrows.

Alan helped Marcie out of the car before going to him.

'This is a surprise, Tony old mate . . .'

Tony looked right past him to his daughter. 'Is that my grandchild?'

Marcie hugged her daughter. 'Yes. It is.'

'And the kid on the bike was the father?'

Again she said that this was so and added, 'He died.'

'Look, I was going to tell you,' Alan began to say.

It happened so suddenly. Her dad lashed out. Alan went flying, flat out on the gravel, his head crashing onto a rosebush.

Tony Brooks addressed his daughter. 'You didn't have to run away. I was going to sign for you. You knew that. So why did you run off like that?'

'There were reasons,' she blurted out.

She looked down at Alan. He was still sprawled in the dirt but coming to and already rubbing his chin.

Marcie bit her lip. The sight of a man who had once seemed so big and strong now looking small and nervous filled her with sadness. She forced herself to concentrate on the best way to handle him.

'I wanted to tell you I was coming home, but there wasn't time. Joanna was about to be adopted. Alan found me and tore up the adoption papers.' It was never going to be easy saying the next bit, but she had to.

'Alan wants to marry me and give Joanna a name and a home.'

'Does he now! Well there's generosity for you. And why would he want to do that, I wonder . . . ?'

Leaning down, he grabbed Alan's arm, dragging him to his feet.

Alan was panting. A scratch from cheekbone to jaw was weeping blood. His hair was awry, his clothes dirty.

For the first time ever, Marcie saw Alan Taylor's face drained of confidence.

'I didn't touch her,' Alan babbled.

Her father flashed a dangerous-looking smile. 'You wouldn't dare.'

She didn't contradict him.

Tony Brooks was now holding his old mate by his shirt collar.

'You've been playing me for a mug all these years, Alan. You told me I murdered my own wife and buried her. Now it turns out there's only a bloody dog buried there – an Alsatian according to the coppers. Now tell me, what the fuck was that all about?'

Marcie stared wild eyed at the two men. 'What?'

Her father explained quickly what had been discovered beneath the hen house. He sounded embarrassed. 'What sort of bloody fool am I?'

'You thought you'd killed her?' Marcie questioned incredulously.

Her father spread his hands helplessly. 'I didn't know. I knew I'd been drinking. I feared the worst.' He turned to Alan. 'He made me believe the worst. Now I want to know the truth.'

Alan hedged. 'It's complicated—'

'Try me. I might be a bit thick, but try me.'

Alan looked nervously around. 'Can we go inside? The neighbours will be watching—'

'And I need to change and feed the baby,' Marcie added.

They went into the house. Marcie listened as the two most prominent men in her life sorted out their differences.

Alan began to explain. 'I just needed you on board.'

466 • *Mia Dolan*

'To take the rap for the job.'

'That's it. But I paid you for it.'

'So let's get this straight – it's a guard dog, right? And I killed it.'

Alan nodded. 'Yep, but you felt bad about it. You brought the bloody thing back with you. You buried it in the garden but were so pissed you didn't remember doing it. I just kept you guessing so you wouldn't step out of line and drop me in it. That's the truth. The honest to goodness truth.'

'So where's Mary? Where's my wife?'

Alan shrugged. 'I don't know, mate. I really don't. If I knew I'd tell you, though I'm not too sure that she really went off with someone else.' He gave a little nervous chuckle. 'You know me. I'll try it on with any bird. But your Mary? No way. She wasn't like that.'

Marcie tucked her bosom back inside her blouse when she felt Alan's eyes on her.

'You alright, love?' said Alan.

She wanted to say she was not his love. Not yet at any rate.

Her father now turned his attention to her.

'So what now?'

His thick fingers were folded in front of him. Alan asked him if he'd like a whisky. He declined – a first as far as both Alan and Marcie were concerned.

'Alan's offered to give the baby a name,' repeated Marcie.

Her father blinked and turned to Alan.

'She's just a kid.'

'And deserves a better start in life,' snapped Alan.

Marcie could see that the old dynamics were returning between these two. They were both dishonest, though perhaps in different ways.

'I'm going round to live with Gran until things are sorted,' said Marcie, getting to her feet.

'I'll get the car out,' said Alan.

Her father pushed him back down into the chair. 'She's my daughter. I'm taking her round home. Give me your car keys.'

As her father loaded her belongings back into the car, Marcie decided there was something that needed to be said. 'Alan, I'm grateful for what you've done, but you have to know that I don't love you. I'm not saying I won't marry you but I don't think I could ever love you, not after what you did to me. And my dad. Do you understand that?'

He nodded silently then watched her get into the car and be driven away.

Chapter Fifty

'Gran's,' she blurted out once they were in the car. 'I don't want to go to your house. I want to go home to Gran.'

Her father didn't push her to go home with him to Babs and the others. He didn't press her to do anything and neither did he ask her how things had been since he'd last seen her.

She voiced the thought that had bugged her all the way from Alan's place to Endeavour Terrace.

'What's Gran going to say?'

He shrugged. 'I don't know. You know how she is. A bit old-fashioned. But I'll stick by you, girl. You know that, don't you?'

Yes. Somehow she knew he was telling the truth. She'd seen his eyes light up at the sight of Joanna. The big strong man had turned into a marshmallow, but her grandmother might be more hostile. Her grandmother believed in marriage. She thought for a moment and came to a decision.

'I want to go in the back way.'

'OK. I'll bring your case.'

'No. Stay here.'

He got out his side, opened the door for her and the baby and helped her out.

'Leave my suitcase on the front step.'

'I thought I'd wait just in case—'

'Go. Please.'

It felt strange to give him orders and to see him obey so quickly.

He nodded silently then watched her leave him, heading for the entrance to the back lane.

The lane was unchanged except that the nettles and tall grass smelled of summer.

She paused at the gate. The recognisable figure dressed in black was sitting outside the back door, knitting needles click-clacking as always. Everything seemed the same and yet it was not.

Marcie's breath caught in her throat. Her grandmother seemed to have shrunk since she'd last seen her. Never had her face looked so pale and her frame so small. Her clothes were still black and even from a distance it was possible to see that there was more grey in her jet-black hair.

The reason was obvious: so much had happened in the past year or so; everyone had gone; her grandmother was alone with nothing more than memories.

Marcie felt her loneliness. Feeling it, actually *feeling* it, surprised her. She hadn't realised such a thing was possible.

Dry paint flaked onto her hand as she pushed the gate open. It squeaked on its rusty hinges. The gate, the cottage and the woman sitting outside the back door were suffering from neglect. But that didn't mean she'd be welcome here. It didn't mean that at all. She'd left home without any notice. What was more she had left as a frightened little girl and returned as a woman and a mother.

At the sound of the gate, her grandmother looked up. The needles stopped clicking.

Marcie found herself getting more nervous but forced herself to put one foot in front of another. Halfway up the garden path she stopped.

'Gran?'

She waited, standing between the sunset and her grandmother.

Rosa Brooks shaded her eyes with one hand. Her chest heaved as she caught her breath, her smile as warm as the sun.

'You are home.'

She said it with wonder. The last rays of sunset bathed her upturned face with a rosy glow.

'Home,' Marcie repeated.

Her grandmother nodded in that wise owl way of hers. 'Your grandfather told me you would come home.'

Her words were the key that opened the flood-gates. Marcie burst into tears and fell to her knees, her head and the child falling onto her grandmother's lap.

'Please forgive me,' she sobbed against the worn black skirt.

Hands wrinkled with age and rough with work took the child from her arms.

'What is her name?'

'Joanna.'

'I like that.'

'Can I stay here?'

Her grandmother looked at her as though it were the strangest question in the world.

'Of course you can. This is your home.'

'And Joanna?'

Already her grandmother was rearranging the child's shawl, inspecting the tiny fingers, stroking the silky soft cheek.

'Of course. This is her home too. Your grandfather would expect it.'

The smell of a freshly cooked pie drifted out from the kitchen; the smell of home and family.

'I told Dad to leave my suitcase outside the front door. Alan Taylor brought me home.'

'But he is not the father of this child.'

'No. He's dead.'

'I know. I saw it in a picture.'

Marcie didn't query where she'd seen the picture. All that mattered was that she was home. So far she hadn't mentioned Alan's offer to marry her and her grandmother did not press her about her plans for the future.

'You're home. That's all that matters.' Her grandmother's smile lit up her whole face. Never had Marcie felt so loved and so wanted. It also occurred to her that she never wanted to leave this place. Yet surely marrying Alan Taylor was the right thing to do? For Joanna's sake?

He called round the next day complete with a big bunch of flowers. Despite her declaration that she did not love him, he clearly still presumed that she would marry him. Her grandmother let him in, offered him tea – which he declined – but did not leave the room.

'An unwed girl must be chaperoned,' she explained firmly.

The look on Alan's face was something to behold.

Marcie hid her smile.

Alan continued to come round at every opportunity except when he knew her father might be there. Two weeks after her return his visit coincided with that of her father.

The door opened. There stood Alan looking bright and breezy.

Tony Brooks glared at him.

For a moment Marcie could feel the friction between them fizzing through the air like electricity.

Alan's smile was hesitant, but he stood his ground. 'Tony! How are you, my old mate?'

Marcie could see that her father was no longer in awe of Alan. She assured herself that they wouldn't come to blows.

Her father remained surly.

'What is it, Alan?'

'A letter came for Marcie.'

Marcie's father frowned. 'Why would a letter go to your place?'

Alan shrugged and looked uncomfortable. 'I don't know. I haven't read it.'

'It's alright, Dad.'

She took the letter from Alan's outstretched hand. The envelope was crisp and white, the paper it was manufactured from obviously expensive. Normally any letter would be opened immediately, but this one was a surprise. The postmark said London.

Marcie became aware of the silence. Looking around she saw that everyone was watching her.

'Go upstairs and read it, Marcie.'

It was her grandmother who'd spoken. In the previous weeks she'd often shown how caring she was. They'd talked about her future. Her grandmother had pointed out the pitfalls of marrying or not marrying. There was so much to consider. Marcie had reiterated that she didn't want her daughter to grow up under a cloud. Surely it was best to be married?

Her grandmother had sighed. 'That decision is up to you.'

'Do I get invited in for a cup of tea?' Alan was asking.

Marcie didn't wait to hear his answer. The letter intrigued her, but not until she was upstairs sitting on the edge of her bed did she open it and read.

Dear Marcie,

We didn't have much time to say goodbye because you left so quickly. Sally reckoned your father looked a dish. I said that didn't really matter as long as you had someone to love you. Even so, we both think you very brave to be keeping your baby and wish we'd had the courage to do the same.

My mother's coming to fetch me shortly and I'm going to ask her to give Sally a lift to London. She knows someone in Battersea. It's not too much of a detour from Chelsea.

I've put my address at the bottom of this letter. Do try and write.

Sally's also put an address where she can be reached, though reckons she won't be there very much. Fancy free yet again, she reckons men will be falling at her feet and drinking champagne out of her shoes! The blonde bombshell is back, she says, and swears she never was cut out to be a mother. It appears you are the lucky one. You've

*got your baby and a family to support you. That
really is all that matters.*

*Despite me knowing that for me it was the right
thing to give up my son, there is a wound deep
inside me that I don't think will ever heal. I think
Sally feels much the same. I know she cries more
than she admits to.*

I am envious of you. We both are.

God bless and take care. AND DO WRITE!

The letter was signed by both Allegra and Sally. Pilemarsh had insisted that Alan leave a contact address
as her supposed next of kin, and her room-mates had
felt moved enough to write.

Their words shone through her tears. She was
envied! The idea made her sit up straight and exhale
a deep breath. Suddenly the future no longer seemed
as bleak as she'd imagined. It felt as though a door
had been opened in her mind. Why did she have to
marry Alan Taylor? Why did she have to marry
anyone at all? She could raise her daughter herself –
with her grandmother's help. It wouldn't be easy, but
Rosa Brooks had raised her son's children without
much help from either him or Babs. Marcie could do
the same. She could find a job and support Joanna
while her gran looked after her during the day. It
didn't matter what the job was, anything would do.
Or maybe she could use her talents as a dressmaker

and work at home so she could look after Joanna herself. A strange warm feeling washed over her along with so many ideas about what she could be and where she was going.

One thing was true above all else: no matter what she decided there would always be someone to catch her if she should fall. She had her gran, her dad, friends even. And, above all, she had her daughter. She would not have to live with the deep regret of having given her child away. She had Joanna and she also had hope for the future which they would face together.

Ebury Press Fiction Footnotes

Turn the page for an exclusive
interview with Mia Dolan ...

EBURY
PRESS

What was the inspiration for Rock A Bye Baby?

I think it's always best to write about what you know so *Rock a Bye Baby* has been inspired by my own life and the people I knew when I was growing up. I personally enjoy stories of ordinary people surviving all that life can throw at them – and that's *Rock a Bye Baby* in a nutshell!

Your novel is wonderfully realistic in its portrayal of a young working class girl growing up in the 1960s, but have you shared the same experiences as any of your characters?

Well, I was brought up and I still live on the isle of Sheppey so a lot of Marcie's teenage experiences are similar to my own. Like her, I also had a child at seventeen and I was unmarried at the time.

Marcie's grandmother is Maltese, is there anything that drew you to that country?

In fact my grandmother was also Maltese. She met my English grandfather in Malta just before the

Second World War. She came to England with him at the start of their married life.

Marcie's grandmother, like you, is psychic and it seems Marcie has inherited some of her grandmother's skills, albeit in a lesser way. Do you think everyone has an innate psychic ability?

I do believe that everyone has a sixth sense, some more than others. To me, it's the same as any skill – like being able to sing, or dance or paint. Everyone can do these things to some extent but some are more gifted than others. I also believe that psychic gifts can run in families in the same way as a gift for singing can.

Who are your favourite authors?

I am an avid reader – I read at least two books a week. These range from chick lit and romantic comedies, to crime and science fiction/fantasy. Given this, I'm afraid my list of favourite authors is rather too long to list here!

Which classic novel have you always meant to read and never got round to it?

I have always meant to read *War and Peace* by Tolstoy. I've been told that it's a great read and – because I read so fast and hate it when I reach the end of a good book – the sheer size of it makes it appealing!

What are your top five books of all time?

It Shouldn't Happen to a Vet (James Herriot)
Lord of the Rings
The Da Vinci Code
Bridget Jones's Diary
Reaper Man (Terry Pratchett)

What book are you currently reading?

The Nation (Terry Pratchett). I'm a huge Terry Pratchett fan!

Which fictional character would you most like to have met?

Dr Dolittle (I would love to be able to get him to ask my huge puppy why he feels the need to sit on my lap!)

Who, in your opinion, is the greatest writer of all time?

That's too difficult! I'm one of those people who finds it easy to get completely consumed by a great book. Given this, I'm always changing my mind about who I think is the best writer. If I'm lost in a good story then I tend to think that author is the best I've ever read . . . until I move on to the next page-turner!

Other than your work as a psychic and as a writer, what other jobs or professions have you undertaken or considered?

I have worked in many strange and not so wonderful places and have had a number of 'normal' jobs over the years. I've worked in a joke shop where my biggest problem was kids letting of stink bombs. Like Marcie, I've also sold candy floss to tourists in Leysdown.

I have been working as a professional psychic since I was 26 years of age so most of my working life has been in this field. However, I always say that my biggest skill is helping people feel better at the worst times of their lives, regardless of the psychic element.

Marcie's story continues in Anyone Who Had a Heart, **is there anything you can tell us about the next book . . . ?**

I can tell you that it's already underway! I don't want to give away anything here but suffice it to say there will be some great twists and turns that I don't think the reader will see coming. Or at least I hope not . . .

Marcie's story continues in . . .

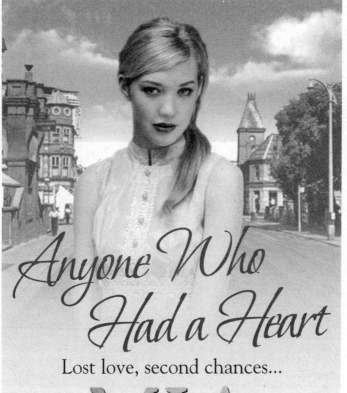

Anyone Who Had a Heart

Lost love, second chances...

MIA DOLAN

The *Sunday Times* bestselling author of *The Gift*

Available in October

MIA DOLAN

Wishing and Hoping

Even a small town girl can have big dreams...

Coming in February 2010